RUSHING IN

A SMALL TOWN ROMANCE

BAILEY BROTHERS
BOOK 4

CLAIRE KINGSLEY

Always Have LLC

Published by Always Have, LLC

ISBN: 9798571832274

Edited by Eliza Ames

Cover by Lori Jackson

Cover Model: Lucas Loyola

Cover Photography by Wander Aguiar

www.clairekingsleybooks.com

❀ Created with Vellum

For the shy, the quiet, and the scared. Bravery isn't the absence of fear. It's feeling fear and doing it anyway.

You are brave.

ABOUT THIS BOOK

She's the one girl he can't have.

With his dimpled grin and devilish charm, firefighter Gavin Bailey is hot as a five-alarm fire and twice as dangerous. The youngest of five brothers, he's the daredevil of the family. Until the unexpected strikes and he finds himself sidelined.

Skylar Stanley's life didn't just fall apart. It exploded. Spectacularly. Dropped by her publisher and her agent, and dumped by her boyfriend, she suddenly has no place to live and a career circling the drain. She comes home to the quirky, feuding small town she hasn't lived in since Kindergarten to pick up the pieces. And hopefully find her mojo.

Gavin would happily help Skylar get her groove back—in and out of the bedroom—except for one big problem. Her dad is Gavin's boss, mentor, and the closest thing he's ever had to a father.

As much as Gavin loves racing headlong into danger, Skylar is a risk of a different kind. One that he's determined to avoid.

But the line between friends and lovers gets awfully

blurry, and Gavin just might find the one thing that truly scares him.

Losing her.

Author's note: The wild child of the Bailey clan meets his match in a shy writer who's braver than she thinks. A sexy, feel-good story with pranks and shenanigans, Bailey-style brotherly love, a rescue kitten, plus delightfully dirty fantasies come true and a happily ever after that will make your heart burst with sunshine and rainbows.

The Bailey Brothers series is meant to be read in order. Start with book one, **Protecting You.**

PROLOGUE
SKYLAR

*This prologue also appears as the epilogue at the end of
Unraveling Him: Bailey Brothers Book 3.*

"*S*kylar, we need to talk."

It wasn't just that phrase—naturally so loaded with meaning—that made my stomach twist into a knot of dread. It was Cullen's tone. Flat. Emotionless.

"Sounds serious," I said, trying to keep the mood light in case I was overreacting. Maybe we needed to talk about where to make dinner reservations, or a similarly innocuous subject.

Cullen stood in the kitchen of our apartment, all California-boy handsome with his ice-blue eyes, tan skin, and natural highlights in his thick, dark blond hair. Trade his button-down and slacks for a pair of board shorts and a muscle shirt, and he would have fit right in on a beach somewhere.

Which got me thinking... a California surfer boy discovers a body while he's on a deserted beach at sunrise—

"Skylar," Cullen snapped. "See? You're not even listening to me."

"I'm sorry, I just had an idea. What did you say?"

"It's over."

His words hit me like the jab of a needle straight into my chest, the shock of them rendering me briefly speechless. I stared at him while he took his phone out of his pocket and the corner of his mouth twitched in the hint of a smile.

"What did you say?"

He pocketed his phone, his eyes flicking up to meet mine. That almost-smile on his lips melted into pinched annoyance. "You're going to make me repeat myself again? Let me guess, you were brainstorming more book ideas that you're never going to write."

Ouch. Talk about hitting below the belt. "No. I just don't understand what you're saying right now."

"Why are you making this hard?"

"How am I making this hard? You throw the words *it's over* at me, completely out of nowhere, and I'm supposed to just carry on with my day?"

"Well, no, obviously not."

"Then what do you think I'm going to say? Of course I'm going to ask you what you mean."

"Fine," he said, like my asking for clarification was the most annoying request ever. "I'm not happy. I haven't been for a long time. So this is it. I'm done."

"Since when are you not happy?"

"I just said I haven't been for a long time."

I stared at him, bewildered. Cullen wasn't what you'd call a happy person—never had been. He was serious and stoic. Focused and responsible. Happy wasn't his vibe. But the idea that he'd been unhappy *with me* was such a foreign concept, I didn't know how to make sense of it.

There had been no warning. None at all. I'd thought he was fine.

I thought *we* were fine.

That wasn't even the half of it. I thought we might be forever.

The buzz of the refrigerator suddenly roared in my ears, like a thousand mosquitos flying around my head. I tried to hold still—tried not to twitch. He'd tell me I was being dramatic and unreasonable. *Calm down, Skylar, the fridge isn't loud.*

The vibration crawled up my spine. I couldn't stand still anymore. Not right here. Stopping myself from sticking my fingers in my ears, I wandered into the living room.

"This is just... really sudden," I said.

"That's not my fault."

"Excuse me?" I whirled on him. "You're breaking up with me and it's not your fault?"

He let out a heavy sigh. "No, it's not my fault that this is taking you by surprise. You should have seen this coming."

"How could I have seen this coming? We had sex *last night*. You didn't seem unhappy when you had your dick in me."

"Jesus, Skylar, don't be vulgar."

"Why didn't you ever say anything? Why didn't you tell me you weren't happy?"

"It's not like you've been fully invested in this relationship. You moved out for months."

"I moved in with my mom so I could take care of her after her surgery. What does that have to do with anything?"

"You said it would be a few weeks, and months later, you were still living there."

I gaped at him. "I moved back. And she's my *mom*, Cullen. She needed my help."

He shrugged, like her relationship to me wasn't a factor. "We grew apart a long time ago. You're just too busy living in fantasyland to realize it."

I swallowed hard. Was he right? I was distracted a lot. Had I been so lost in my own head that I'd missed the signs? Had I neglected him so much that he'd fallen out of love with me?

He pulled out his phone again and typed something.

"What are you doing?"

He finished, then slipped his phone back in his pocket. "Nothing."

"Will you stop having a conversation with someone else while you're throwing my life in the garbage?"

"Don't be so dramatic."

"I'm not being dramatic. Are you dumping me as a client too?"

"That's best for everyone involved."

I couldn't think clearly. Too many emotions whipped around inside me, like a tornado flinging debris across the landscape of my heart. Cullen Bell wasn't just my boyfriend of three years and the man I currently lived with. He was my literary agent. My link to the editors at the big publishing houses.

Including the publisher who'd dropped me last year.

And the others who might pick me up.

Not that I'd written anything new in months.

Oh my god.

"So that's it? You're done with me?"

He opened his mouth to answer, but his phone buzzed in his pocket and he pulled it out again.

A sick realization spread through me, like dark smoke

filling a room. The back of my throat burned and the knot of dread in the pit of my stomach grew.

"Who is she?"

His blue eyes lifted, his expression devoid of any emotion. "Don't."

"Are you cheating on me?"

"Skylar, don't make this worse."

"Answer the question."

"I'm trying to make this easier on you. You don't need to go there."

"By acting like this is my fault?" I crossed my arms. "Who is she?"

He glanced away.

"If you're leaving me for another woman, the least you can do is tell me who she is so I—"

"Pepper Sinclair."

I clicked my mouth shut. Maybe he was right. I should have seen this coming.

Pepper Sinclair was perfect. A New York Times best-selling author of inspirational women's fiction. She was stunningly beautiful with flawless skin, perfect bone structure, a gorgeous smile, thick hair, and the type of boobs that most women had to pay a lot of money for.

Her social media following numbered in the millions, men and women hanging on her every word, clamoring for glimpses into her perfectly tailored, manicured, pristine life.

Everyone loved her.

Including, apparently, my boyfriend. Who was also her agent.

"Wait, Pepper's married."

"Not that it's any of your business, but she's getting a divorce."

Maybe not so perfect after all.

Not that it mattered. She was still stealing my boyfriend.

I looked away, my eyes stinging with tears. Cullen had taken her on as a client last year, after they'd met at a writer's conference in Denver. I'd been there, too, dutifully attending the meetings Cullen had set up with editors, trying to salvage my quickly spiraling career.

And I'd seen them together at the hotel bar.

They hadn't been touching—nothing overt. But the way he'd looked at her...

Weeks later, after mulling it over for way too long, I'd asked him about it. He'd gotten mad. Accused me of not trusting him.

"How long?" I heard myself ask.

"Does it matter?"

"Yes. How long?"

"Why are you making this harder on yourself?"

"Because I need to know the truth."

He let out an irritated breath. "Denver."

My lip trembled. I caught it between my teeth so I wouldn't cry. I was *not* letting him see me cry. He'd just tell me I was being overly sensitive anyway.

I took a slow breath through my nose. "You've been cheating on me with Pepper Sinclair since last year?"

"You're making it sound worse than it is. In Denver, we..."

He trailed off, looking away again. But there was no shame or regret in his posture or expression. He just wanted to finish this conversation so he could move on with his day.

"In Denver, you what?"

"Why are you—"

"I'm not making this hard, Cullen. That's on you. I didn't make you have an affair with a married woman who's also your client. You did that."

"Fine, you want to make me say it? In Denver, we didn't sleep together, but... other things transpired. Since then I've been seeing her when I go to New York. I didn't tell you because I didn't want you getting all depressed. Things were bad enough after your series got dropped. I figured I'd give you some time to at least get writing again. But that's obviously not going to happen, and I can't keep waiting around for you to decide you're over your writer's block."

It was hard to get any words out, my voice almost a whisper. "All that time?"

"What do you expect? You're always distracted, always thinking of some plot or another, but you haven't written anything in who knows how long. You spend all your time watching serial killer documentaries and looking up poisonous household chemicals or the best ways to hide a body. It's disturbing."

"I write suspense novels. It's research."

"It's like living with the creepy goth girl who sat in the back of class and threatened people with voodoo dolls, only wrapped in a beautiful package. You look so normal."

If I'd ever wondered what it would feel like to have my very existence completely rejected, apparently this was it.

"Look, you need to move out," he said. "Pepper's telling her husband today and she's bringing her stuff here after."

"You're moving her in?"

"Well, yeah, she's leaving her husband. She can't exactly stay there."

"You're leaving me. Why don't you move out?"

He looked at me like I'd just suggested he start eating meat again. "It's my apartment."

The refrigerator's buzz ceased, leaving behind an emptiness in the air. It was his apartment. He'd lived here first. In fact, everything in it was his. It had been fully furnished, the kitchen and bathrooms fully stocked, when I'd moved in. Almost nothing was mine.

I was simply a guest who'd been here for an extended sleepover.

A guest who'd overstayed her welcome.

Calmly, I turned and walked to the bedroom. Took my suitcase out of the closet and started packing.

So calm. Deadly calm.

The beginning to a domestic suspense novel flitted through my head. A jilted wife, forced to move out of the home she loved due to her husband's infidelity. Her husband is found dead the next morning. She's the prime suspect, and—

"What are you doing?"

I glanced over my shoulder at the man I'd once thought I might marry. My voice sounded strangely flat. "You just broke up with me, so I'm packing."

"You were staring at the wall."

Turning to face him, I crossed my arms. "You know what, Cullen? Fuck you. You were never trying to make this easier on me, or give me time to start writing again, or keep me from getting depressed. You wanted to avoid telling me that you're a cheating piece of shit. Because deep down, you know you were wrong. You know you betrayed me. And one of these days, you're going to wake up and realize it. You're going to realize what you lost. And when you do, I'll be long gone. So get out and let me pack."

He held up his hands in a gesture of surrender and backed away. "Fine."

I went back to folding my clothes and placing them neatly in my suitcase. They weren't all going to fit, and I didn't have another bag.

I decided to take Cullen's.

Because fuck him.

But when I pulled his suitcase out of the closet—it matched mine—I couldn't hold back the tears.

Strands of long hair stuck to my wet cheeks as sobs bubbled up from my chest. I splayed my hand over my heart, suddenly understanding the term *heartbroken* with perfect clarity.

I'd thought I loved him. I'd thought he loved me.

Apparently I'd been wrong. Horribly wrong.

I needed to call my mom. I'd have to go to her place. I wasn't the sort of girl who had many friends; I was too shy. And my best friend Ginny didn't live nearby. Fortunately, I knew Mom wouldn't mind.

Except I scrolled past my frequently used contacts— which was all of three people, Mom, Cullen, and Ginny— and stopped at a different number.

Dad.

Norman Stanley. Fire Chief, Tilikum Fire Department.

I didn't know why I had the urge to call him. He wasn't the parent I normally went to in a crisis. In fact, I didn't even see my dad all that often.

But somehow the pieces of my cracked and bleeding heart yearned for the comfort of my father's voice.

If he'd even answer. He was probably on duty. It seemed like that was all he ever did—work.

Still, I decided to give it a try. I brought up his number and hit send.

He answered on the first ring. "Hey, Skylar."

A flood of renewed tears ran down my cheeks and I could barely croak out a single word.

"Daddy."

1

GAVIN

A trickle of sweat slid down my spine and the hot air around me was thick with smoke.

"How we looking up there, Gav?" Chief's voice crackled on my radio.

I keyed the remote mic on my radio to reply. "A lot of smoke. Dirk might want to pull his crew out for a bit once we get this fireline cleared. They're looking a little rough."

As if on cue, the guy about ten feet down from me coughed.

"Copy that. Just get that debris cleared so you can get out of there."

"Will do, Chief."

Clouds of smoke billowed from the trees, casting a dingy haze over the landscape. I could taste it in the air, the acrid bitterness sitting on my tongue. A few inches from my feet, the ground sloped down—precarious, but not too steep to hike—until it dropped off abruptly into the valley below. A dry creek bed meandered across the bottom.

Beyond that, the burn raged, the forest glowing red.

It looked like hell down there.

Levi's chainsaw roared next to me as he sliced through a trunk that clung to the rocky ground. He kicked the small tree, tipping it downslope so it could fall. The branches scraped across the ground as it slid, stirring up dust.

I adjusted the sixty-pound pack on my back, re-gripped my Pulaski—a tool with an ax on one side and a horizontal adze blade on the other—and attacked the stump that was left.

Chief had once told me that wildland firefighting was long hours of monotonous, backbreaking work punctuated by brief moments of sheer terror. In my experience so far, he was not wrong.

Except for the terror. I'd been right up against the edge of an out-of-control burn last season, and it hadn't scared me. Got my blood pumping, though.

But mostly, we cleared a lot of debris.

A wildland firefighting crew worked alongside us. They'd been out here for the last few weeks, working to contain the forest fire that had eaten up tens of thousands of acres as it came down from the North Cascades, ripping through the dry mountain forests. Municipal fire departments like ours didn't always work these kinds of fires. Brush fires, sure. But widespread forest fires weren't usually our area.

Unless they were really big, or too close to town.

This one was both.

Levi straightened his back and wiped grime and sweat from his forehead with the back of his wrist. "Fuck, it's hot."

"No shit."

Our faces were smeared with soot and dirt, mingling with sweat from the hundred-plus degree heat. The September sun mercilessly baked the mountains, cooking everything like one of Gram's pies. It had been a hot, dry summer without a drop of rain for the last two months. Even now that it was almost fall, there was still no sign of precipitation.

Without another word of complaint, Levi and I both got back to work. We had a job to do. Bitching about it wasn't going to make it better.

Besides, I didn't care that it was hard. That my muscles ached, my hands were raw, the smoky air seared my lungs, and the heat did its best to suck every ounce of energy from my body. I lived for this shit. Needed it.

Gram inexplicably called me Otter—which was the least manly animal name ever—but really, I was a shark. Not because I was a bloodthirsty, vicious predator. I was actually a pretty nice guy. But sharks had to keep moving or they'd die.

That was me. A shark, always moving.

I'd tried to get Gram to change my nickname—I thought I had a damn good argument—but she'd just laughed at me.

But out here, digging a fireline so the burn would run out of combustible material if it decided to chase up the side of the valley, I was moving.

Besides, I hadn't joined the fire department so I could spend my days rescuing kittens out of trees.

Levi and I dug the stump out of the ground and sent it down the slope. The guys around us dug and sawed and cleared. We had to get down to the mineral soil, where there was nothing left to burn. The top of a cliff wasn't the ideal place for a fireline—usually a two- to four-foot trench—and right now, the fire wasn't moving this direction. But there was a house not fifty yards behind us, so we couldn't take the chance of the burn turning. If it did, it could get ugly fast.

Dirk, the wildland crew captain, walked by. His face was

as dirty as mine no doubt was, grime caking into the lines around his eyes. He gave us a nod, his gaze sweeping over the ground, tracking our progress.

He wanted off this ridge as much as we did.

A breath of air brushed past my face, making my nose twitch. I stopped, lowering my Pulaski again. Inhaled deeply. It still smelled like smoke—no more than it had a few minutes ago—but something was different.

I could feel it.

"Fire's gonna turn," I said.

Levi glanced back at me. "You think?"

I scanned the forest below us, glowing red with heat, spitting clouds of smoke into the sky. Nothing looked different. Not yet. But I had a feeling.

"Yeah." I sniffed again. "Smells wrong."

Levi nodded. "Radio Chief. I'll go tell Dirk."

Under any other circumstances, Levi wouldn't have listened to me. I knew it, he knew it. I was the little brother. The screw-up. The wild one. If we'd been sitting at home, or in a bar, or driving down the road, he'd have blown me off. But when it came to a crisis situation, if danger was involved, my instincts were... well, they were fucking weird is what they were. I was almost always right.

I radioed Chief.

"Go ahead."

"Chief, just a heads up, I think the fire's going to turn."

"Understood." Chief knew it, too. "Do you think it's time to move out?"

I glanced back at the house. Wayne and Mary Risley's house. They'd lived there for thirty years. We couldn't let it burn. "Not yet. We can finish up here."

"Okay. Helitack crew will be there soon with a bucket drop."

A fresh wave of smoke blew over us and the guy next to me coughed again. "Maybe tell them to hurry up with that."

"I will. Don't do anything crazy, Gav. That's an order."

My mouth hooked in a grin. "Course not, Chief."

I never did anything crazy. Not by my standards, anyway. Other people seemed to disagree, but as far as I was concerned, the things I did were completely sane.

Going against my instincts—now *that* would have been crazy.

Levi came back. "Dirk radioed the Incident Commander. Helitack crew should be here soon."

"Yeah, Chief told me."

"We should—shit!"

I whipped around to see what he was looking at.

Down the line, a group was working on a snag—a dead tree clinging precariously to the edge. The sawyer had lost his balance and dropped his damn chainsaw. The guy downslope from him shuffled his feet, trying to get out of the way of the deadly blade.

He slipped.

The chainsaw clattered against the rocks, spitting dirt into the air. It missed the guy below, sliding past him. It roared its way down the slope and dropped off the edge.

I was already running. Because the guy on the slope was going to fall.

My feet ate up the ground between me and the sawyer at the top. He stood, dumbstruck, his hands open at his sides.

"Gavin, wait," Levi called behind me.

The guy on the slope bent at the waist and grabbed at the scrubby ground, his fingers digging for purchase. His feet scraped against the dirt, like something below had reached up and clutched his ankles. A fire demon lashing out with red hot rage, pulling its next victim to his demise.

Fuck that.

Turning sideways, I scrambled down the slope toward him, keeping my feet angled for maximum grip. Rocks tumbled down the hill, jarred loose by my boots. There was almost nothing to grab onto, save some thin roots and a few dry shrubs clinging to the rocky ground, but I'd been rock climbing for years. I'd be fine.

"Hang on, buddy," I shouted.

He turned his feet outward, slowing his descent almost to a stop. His hands braced against the ground and he looked up at me, his eyes wide with fear.

I let gravity do the work, pulling me down, and the friction from my boots kept me from sliding out of control. My heart beat hard in my chest and the heat of the day, the smoke, the fatigue in my arms were gone. Nothing. Unimportant. Adrenaline washed it all away, like icy cold river water.

I was going to get this guy out. Safe. I knew it.

So I wasn't scared.

He was, though, and that was not good. Rescuing someone in a panic was always dangerous.

I slowed down when I got close to him and found a rock to wedge my foot against. "Hey, brother. Don't move, okay? What's your name?"

"Robby."

"How long have you been on the wildland crew?" I asked, just to get him talking while I pulled a coil of nylon rope out of my pack.

"First season."

"No shit?" Smoke billowed around us, stinging my eyes. "You're going to have a badass story to tell when you go home. Chased down the slope by a runaway fucking chainsaw."

His mouth started to hook in a grin but his eyes widened, and before I could take another breath—let alone reach him—his feet slipped.

Primal fear contorted his features as he fell backward.

I heard him hit the bottom. "Fuck."

People shouted at me from the top. Probably telling me to climb back up. No one wanted Robby to die—whether they knew his name or not—but I was just one guy without proper rescue equipment, clinging to a too-steep slope with a raging forest fire below pumping smoke into the air.

"Robby!" I called.

"Here," he answered, his voice distorted with pain. He was alive, but injured.

"Are you bleeding?"

A pause. "Uh, no. But I think my leg's broken."

Shit. That meant Robby wasn't climbing out on his own.

We needed a rescue team. Now.

"He's down there," I called to Levi at the top. "Possible broken leg."

"Get up here, Gav," Levi called back.

And I was going to. I really was. A rescue team would come and they'd get Robby out. They'd do a better job than I would anyway, with the right equipment and—

A flicker of warmth against my cheek made me turn toward the burn.

It was coming. It was going to jump that dry creek bed and crash through the valley like a tsunami of flame, eating everything in its path.

Including Robby.

I met Levi's eyes. He opened his mouth, probably to yell at me to come up. But Robby didn't have time.

My decision made, I took hold of one end of the rope

and launched the other toward Levi. He caught it, still yelling something at me.

But I was focused on one thing and one thing only. Getting Robby out.

I shifted my feet to slide down to the edge, where the slope dropped off. I let go of the rope, leaving it to dangle over the side, then slipped off my pack and let it drop.

Then I pushed myself away from the slope and jumped.

It was high enough that I knew it was going to hurt when I landed, so it was no surprise that it did. I kept loose and rolled as soon as I hit, but that didn't stop pain from shooting through my shoulder and back.

I ignored it. Paused for half a second to make sure no sharper jolts of pain manifested—none did—and got to my feet.

Smoke was thicker down here, trapped against the valley wall. The head of the fire wasn't far and I could feel the heat of it beating at me.

"Gavin, check in. Now!" Levi's voice roared through my radio.

"I'm good. Secure the rope. I'm gonna get him up."

Robby was on his back about ten feet away, reaching down to hold his thigh.

"I got you, man," I said, picking up my pack and jogging to him. "You're going to be fine."

In an ideal situation, I'd have properly secured his leg before even thinking about moving him. But we didn't have time for ideal.

"Robby, I'm not going to lie, this is going to suck ass. But it's better than being crispy fried."

Through the dirt on his face, he was pale, sweat gleaming on his forehead. But he nodded. "Yeah, okay. What do we do?"

I pulled a second rope out of my pack and tied it around him, fashioning a makeshift harness. "I apologize in advance to your balls, but they'll thank me later when they're still attached to a live body."

Through his pain and fear, he chuckled. Good. He was tough enough to laugh. He'd make it.

I looked over at the burn. The trees were glowing red masts jutting into the air, the hot embers like a thousand mocking eyes. Deadly hot smoke billowed upward, polluting the pristine sky with gray. A wave of heat washed over us, making Robby flinch and raise his hand to shield his face.

It was coming.

The dry creek bed had plenty of debris. The burn wouldn't stop until it chased up the cliff and hit our fireline. Until it ran out of fuel.

Not today, Satan. We were getting out of here.

"Can you stand?" I asked.

"I'll try."

I helped him to his feet and draped his arm over my shoulders. He used me as a crutch, hobbling as I kept him upright. We quickly made our way to the cliff wall where my rope still hung down. I gave it a tug and radioed Levi.

"I've got Robby harnessed. He has a busted leg, so you guys have to do most of the work to haul him up."

"Jesus, Gav. Copy that."

"He's going to give me so much shit for this later," I said while I secured the rope to Robby's harness. "Of course, when he watches that fire run up this fucking cliff, he'll know I was right."

"Thanks, man," Robby said, his voice shaking.

I put my hand on his shoulder and met his eyes. "You

can do this. You hear me? Embrace the suck and get your ass to the top."

He nodded. "Got it."

"Levi, bring him up."

The rope went taut. Robby used his hands and good leg to climb up the cliff face while they pulled from above.

Damn, that had to hurt.

But dying would be worse, so...

I backed up so I could watch Robby through the smoke. As soon as they got him secured up top, they could throw the rope down to me. Climbing this would be easy. I did shit like this all the time.

Not usually with a raging forest fire at my back, but hey, I loved new experiences.

The fire whispered behind me, the voice promising death. It would burn me to ash, reduce me to nothing. Wipe me from the face of the earth.

It was getting hotter, wasn't it?

Slowly, I looked back over my shoulder, then radioed Levi.

"Bro, when did you say that helitack crew would get here?"

"They're less than ten minutes out."

Well that sucked. Because that was more time than I had to spare.

2

GAVIN

"Gavin, get out of there," Levi said through the radio.

My eyes darted around, looking for an escape route. "No shit, bro. I'm working on it. Anyone else got a rope up there?"

"Maybe. Hold tight."

Rope wasn't standard gear for us or for wildland crews. It was a *me*-thing to carry rope—and a fucking good thing for Robby. But it was taking too long to get him to the top. I didn't have time to wait down here.

This was a seriously shitty place to be. If I went left or right, along the wall, I'd get cooked before I found an escape route. That meant there was nowhere to go but up.

A nice metaphor. It wasn't going to get any worse.

I could live with that.

Time to climb.

Finding grips in the rock, I started to scale. I just had to make it to the edge, where it went from sheer cliff to steep hill. Once I got that far, I'd be able to scramble up, more or less on my feet. Or maybe by then Robby would be at the top and they could toss me the rope.

In the meantime, all those rock-climbing hours were sure coming in handy.

"Gavin, check in," Chief said. "They're moving everyone off the fireline."

Wedging my boots into the rock, I made sure I could let go with one hand, then answered. "I'm climbing up. Did they get Robby out yet?"

A gust of wind, hot enough to sear my arm hair, buffeted me.

That wasn't good.

"He's fine. But Gav, we've got all the makings of a firestorm right where you are."

I reached up, feeling around for another handhold. Dug my fingers in, pressing them as if I could indent the rock itself to give me just a little more purchase, and pushed upward with my feet.

Inches. I was moving inches.

And I was out of time.

I was going to get cooked against this rock like a virgin sacrifice to an ancient fire-breathing dragon.

Yeah, there was no way I was going out like that.

Reaching for my radio one last time, I called Chief. "Jumping back down. Deploying fire shelter. Come get me when it's over, Chief."

I didn't have time to wait for his reply. For the second time today, I jumped off the side of a cliff.

I rolled into the fall. The last thing I needed to do was break a leg trying to stick the landing. I launched to my feet and ran to where I'd left my pack.

Another blast of hot air hit me and for a second, I thought it might be too late. Voices talked to me over the radio, but I didn't have time to stop and answer. In about thirty seconds, fire was going to engulf the valley, eating up everything in its path. If we'd done enough at the top, it would stop there. The crew and the houses beyond would be safe.

As for me, that was a little less certain.

I ripped the fire shelter out of my pack and grabbed the handles. Turned my back on the fire and shook it out. The fabric shelter was a bit like a six-foot long silver Twinkie. I guess that made me the cream filling. Probably a bad metaphor, and I didn't know why I was thinking about junk food right now.

The hot wind made deploying the shelter a huge pain in the ass. But I'd practiced this dozens of times with leaf blowers aimed at me to simulate these conditions.

Time seemed to slow. The twenty seconds it took me to deploy the shelter and take cover felt like minutes. I stepped into the footwell, put my body through the rectangular hole in the shelter's floor, and covered myself. Then I hit the dirt, face down, with the shelter around me. I pinned it to the relatively cool ground with my elbows, knees, and the toes of my boots. Its main job, besides keeping the fire from burning me alive, was to trap breathable air. There was about to be a severe lack of oxygen down here. I needed a good supply of air if I was going to live through this.

For a second, everything went silent. Nothing but the sound of my breath echoing inside the shelter.

Then the roar.

Holy shit, it was so fucking loud. Gritting my teeth, I held the shelter down with my hands, elbows, knees, and feet. Hot wind buffeted me, like a tornado was ripping through the valley. I wondered if I'd be able to stay on the ground. The heat was intense, even through the protective layers of the shelter.

Bits of debris hit me and a nearby tree—or something—burst into flame with an ear-splitting boom. It sounded like the fucking apocalypse out there.

I didn't know how long the burnover would last. Could be fifteen minutes. Could be longer. I decided to be ready for the worst and hope for the best. That a rescue team would be down here before I'd even peeked outside to see if it was safe yet.

The flames roared over me, hellish and loud. I could just hear Chief's voice over my radio. Telling me to stay calm. Stay put. Don't move. Breathe.

I listened to him, my only link to the world of the living, while the inferno raged mere inches from my skin. Glad I wasn't completely alone.

This sucked, but at least I was going to live.

I was pretty sure, anyway.

Contrary to what my brothers liked to say, I didn't have a death wish. I just liked to have fun. Hell, I had the opposite of a death wish. I wanted to live big. I knew all too well how easily life could be taken away. I wasn't going to waste mine.

Fuck that.

Sweat dripped off my nose, landing in the dirt. The air was starting to feel stale and close. It was hot as fuck in here. I felt like a baked potato. Probably looked like one, too.

Would the oxygen last long enough?

It fucking better.

The wind kicked up again, blasting over me in hot waves. The noise drowned out whatever the voices in the radio were trying to tell me. I thought I caught the word bucket. Hopefully that meant the helitack crew was overhead with a bucket drop. They'd douse the area with fire suppressant, which would mean getting to me sooner.

More debris rained down on me. I shifted my legs to keep the shelter pinned down tight. My throat was dry and scratchy, but there wasn't anything I could do about that. I just coughed into the dirt and hoped nothing big landed on me.

Gradually, the hellish noise receded. The air outside seemed to still, or at least stop whipping over me like a fucking tornado. I knew it was too soon to check conditions, but damn, I wanted to. It was hard to keep from jumping up to look around. But if I moved too soon, I'd get a lungful of hot ash and die in seconds.

I'd come this far, I wasn't going to die now. Not when all I needed was a little patience.

Next time one of my brothers called me impulsive, I was totally pulling out this story.

Thinking of my brothers made me think of Gram. I hoped she didn't know what was happening. I'd tell her later, and watch while she shook her head and breathed out a sigh of relief that, once again, her youngest cub had defied the odds.

Not that she'd be surprised. I always did.

The roar of the inferno didn't return. Either it was burning itself out or the bucket drop had worked to dampen the intensity here. It was probably safe to break the seal on the shelter and peek out at ground level, but I decided to wait a little longer, just in case.

"Gav, check in when you can." Chief's voice was monotone, all business. Professional. But I knew him. I could hear the worry he was trying to hide.

Time was hard to judge with my heart pounding and my limbs tingling from all the adrenaline coursing through my system. So I counted backward from three hundred. Five minutes, give or take, and I'd check my surroundings.

I got to two hundred, no new sounds.

One-fifty. No debris.

One-twenty. The air seemed still.

One hundred. Nothing new.

Down to sixty and I was pretty sure a second wall of flame wasn't coming. But I made myself count all the way to one anyway.

I felt like I'd been encased in concrete, my careful movements sending cracks snaking across the surface. I was going to feel this tomorrow. Shifting a little, I pulled the edge of the shelter out from under me and looked.

Everything was black and red.

The air was still thick with ash and smoke, and glowing embers peppered the landscape. It was hot, but not deadly hot. Just I-don't-want-to-be-down-here-too-long hot. The air I'd trapped in my shelter now seemed fresh and clean compared to the thick post-burn atmosphere. But I could breathe.

I got to my feet and let the fire shelter fall. It looked like the end of the fucking world. Trees blackened, debris everywhere. I turned around and saw that the side of the hill was scorched clean.

I grabbed my radio. "Chief, it's Gavin. You wanna get me out of here now?"

"Holy shit, Gav," he said, a rare burst of emotion coming through in his tone. "They're coming for you. Are you injured?"

"Don't think so. Did everyone get out in time?"

"Yeah, everyone's fine, including the kid you saved. They're transporting him to the hospital. Crews are on their way to the command post."

I closed my eyes for a second and let out a breath. Fuck yes. "Awesome."

A helicopter whirred overhead. Thank fuck I didn't have to climb out of this hell hole.

"I see the chopper. Get some beer on ice for me. I could really use a cold one."

"You and me both, son. Don't jump out of the helicopter on your way back."

I cracked a smile. "No intention of that, Chief."

The helicopter hovered above, the wind kicking up ash and dust. I pulled my bandana up to keep the worst of it out of my lungs and shielded my face with my arm. The crew lowered a rescue line and it was the best thing I'd seen all day.

They took me to the landing pad near the command post. Eric, one of TFD's paramedics, was there to meet me. Obviously I could walk under my own power, but he insisted on bringing me to the aid station to get checked out. I complied.

No injuries. My skin felt a little tender, but the mild burns didn't require any treatment. Mostly I was just dirty, tired, and dehydrated. Eric made me down a bottle of pink shit—an electrolyte drink—before he'd let me go, then gave me strict instructions on my hydration protocol for the next twenty-four hours.

I assured him I'd be a good boy and drink my liquids. I didn't tell him a lot of that was going to be beer as soon as I got back to town.

Levi stalked over to the aid station, looking like he was ready to do what the fire hadn't—kill me.

"Holy shit, you scared the fuck out of me." He grabbed me and hauled me into a bear hug.

I hugged him, slapping his back a few times. "I'm fine, bro."

"That was stupid." He pulled away to look at me. "Really fucking stupid."

"What part was stupid? The part where I saved a guy's life?"

His brow creased and he shook his head. "You almost died today. Doesn't that mean anything to you?"

"No, I lived today." I took another swig of the pink shit. "And so did Robby."

"You keep taking chances like that and one of these days your gamble won't fucking pay off. Nobody wins every time."

I grinned at him. "I do."

That only made him angrier. "You were reckless, Gav. You can't be reckless in this job."

I stepped closer. "That kid would have died if I hadn't gone down there. We both know that. I had my PPE. The fire shelter did its job."

His jaw hitched.

"Come on." I slung an arm around his shoulder. "I need to go check in with Chief."

An hour later, and after a similar lecture from Chief, Levi and I headed back to town for a mandatory forty-eight-hour rest period. I didn't want it—one night with a few beers and a shower, and I'd be good to go tomorrow. But regulations were regulations, and as everyone kept pointing out, a fire shelter deployment was a big deal.

I texted Logan on the way to the station, sending him a covert selfie of me and Levi. We were on different shifts, so he'd be heading out to the fire front in the morning.

We got to the station and I decided I wanted that beer now. And yeah, I kinda wanted to go hang out and brag about my near miss. The grime left on my face would just make the story more exciting.

"Bro, we can shower later," I said. "Let's go get a beer. Come on, I almost died today."

Levi glared at me.

My phone binged with a text from Logan. He and some of the guys were already at the Caboose.

"I'm walking over to the Caboose. You can do what you want."

"Whatever," Levi said. "I'm taking a fucking shower."

"Suit yourself, bro. I'll buy you a beer when you get there."

The Caboose was only a few blocks from the station. Still a little high on adrenaline, I walked to the restaurant and bar that had been our prime hangout for years. Logan and a few more guys were in the parking lot.

"There's the baked brotato," Logan called.

He and the other guys gave me a round of applause. I paused at the curb to bow before crossing the street.

"Just a day at the office," I called, grinning as I stepped off the sidewalk. "You guys—"

BAM!

I hit the pavement, blinding pain shooting through me, and my head swam with confusion. The weirdest thought went through my mind.

Did I just survive a forest fire only to get hit by a fucking car?

3

SKYLAR

*O*h my god.

I wasn't breathing. Air rushed into my lungs in a gasp and I pried my hands off the steering wheel.

I'd just hit someone.

With my car.

Move, Skylar. Call 911. Do something.

I flew out and rushed to where he lay on the pavement a few feet from my front bumper. He lifted his head and blinked at me. And then he did the strangest thing.

He smiled.

The corners of his mouth turned upward, and through the dirt on his face, I could see a very cute set of dimples.

Why was I thinking about how cute his dimples were? I'd just hit this man.

"Hey," he said.

I crouched next to him. "Oh my god, I'm so sorry. Are you okay? Of course you're not okay. I'll call 911."

Our gazes met, and for a second, I was frozen. His soft brown eyes held mine captive and warmth filled me. Butterflies in my stomach suddenly took flight, flapping their tiny wings. Unable to stop myself, I reached out and gently smoothed his hair back from his forehead.

God, he was gorgeous.

He opened his mouth as if to say something else, but several men ran over from the adjacent parking lot, breaking the spell.

"Holy shit, Gavin."

"Are you okay?"

"Can you move?"

I stood and fumbled for my phone, but one of them put a hand on my arm.

"It's okay, I'm already on with dispatch." He had a phone to his ear. "We're TFD."

TFD. Tilikum Fire Department. These guys were firefighters? That was lucky.

"Hang in there, broller coaster," one of the guys said. He was kneeling next to the victim. My victim. "You're all right."

"I tried to stop," I said, although no one was paying attention to me. But it was true. I'd come around the corner and he'd walked right out in front of me. He hadn't even looked.

It wasn't long before an ambulance arrived, lights flashing. Soon after, a police cruiser. The paramedics loaded Gavin onto a gurney. At least I hadn't killed him. Not instantly, at least. My mind cataloged everything I knew about internal injuries. Why were they being so slow? He could be bleeding out right before our eyes and—

"Miss?"

I gasped. Someone was trying to talk to me. "What?"

A man in his fifties wearing a sheriff's department uniform placed a gentle hand on my shoulder. "Let's get out of the street, okay?"

"I didn't mean to hit him. He walked out right in front of me. I tried to stop. I hit the brakes—"

"I know." His voice was calm and soothing. "He's going to be okay."

"But they should really check for internal bleeding. He could have ruptured his spleen. Or worse, his liver. You can live without a spleen. Liver, not so much. And the bleeding could kill him if left unchecked."

"They're taking good care of him." He guided me onto the sidewalk. "What's your name?"

"Skylar Stanley."

He raised his eyebrows. "Are you related to Norman Stanley?"

"Yeah. He's my dad."

"Okay. I'll call him."

Great. I get into town and the first thing I do is run over someone. Way to make your daddy proud, Skylar.

They closed the ambulance doors. I started to ask if I should go with him, but snapped my mouth closed. That didn't make any sense. The paramedics were taking care of him; he didn't need me.

But I was still oddly disappointed to see him go.

There was clearly something wrong with me. Had I hit my head on the steering wheel? Maybe I needed medical attention.

The small crowd disappeared, and the cop—he introduced himself as Jack Cordero—moved my car so it was parked on the side of the road. Then he checked my license and registration and asked me a lot of questions about what had happened. I answered as best I could, trying to be a grown-up and not burst into tears.

It was hard.

But I didn't want to be one of those weepy girls who'd

make a scene in an attempt to get out of trouble. It had been an accident—he knew it, and so did I—but still.

Although maybe hitting a pedestrian on my first day in town was just par for the course at this point. My entire life was in shambles. Why not make it a little worse?

In the last six months I'd been dropped by my publisher, then cheated on and dumped by my boyfriend. As a consequence, I'd lost my literary agent—because that was what happened when you dated your agent and he cheated on you and subsequently dumped you. I'd lost my apartment—it had been his, not mine—and decided to move back to the town I hadn't lived in since I was in kindergarten.

Because, you know, moving in with your dad when you were in your mid-twenties because you basically had nowhere else to go and your career was in the toilet was every girl's dream.

Eventually, Dad pulled up in his Tilikum Fire Department truck. Just the sight of his face, with all that parental sympathy in his eyes, sent a few tears trailing down my cheeks. I quickly swiped them away.

"Skylar, are you okay?" he asked.

"I'm fine."

"She wasn't going very fast," Jack Cordero said. "Turned the corner right as Gavin started to cross the street."

"She hit Gav?" Dad asked, his eyes widening.

Jack nodded, and it was so weird, but he almost didn't seem surprised. Like his expression said, *of course she hit Gavin, who else would it have been*?

"Do you need anything else from her, or is she free to go?" Dad asked.

"We're good here."

They shook hands.

"Thanks, Jack. Appreciate it."

"Anytime."

Dad turned to me and let out a long breath. He looked tired and worn, like he hadn't slept in a while. "Let's go home."

Home. Such a strange concept. I didn't feel like I had one anymore.

"Okay."

Before I got in my car, I glanced over my shoulder, looking in the direction the ambulance had gone. Wondering if Gavin was okay.

4

SKYLAR

$\mathcal{I}$ parked next to my dad's truck and gazed up at his old two-story house. I'd lived here when I was little, but I didn't remember much of that time. Only bits and pieces.

It was odd that he'd kept it. When he and Mom had divorced twenty years ago, Mom had packed me up and taken me with her to her hometown of Spokane, several hours away. Dad had stayed here, living all by himself in this big four-bedroom house. Even though I rarely came to Tilikum to visit—he usually drove to Spokane to visit me— he hadn't downsized.

I'd never thought much about that, but now that I was in front of his too-big-for-just-one-man house, I had to wonder why he still lived here. Maybe moving would have been too much trouble. He probably lived at the firehouse more than here, anyway. Maybe he just didn't care.

It was in good repair, the yard neat. A concrete path led from the driveway to the door and the curtains in the front window were closed. Inside was an empty front room—no furniture at all, just a big rug in the center of the maple hardwood floor—and a similarly empty dining room.

His living space was all at the back of the house. A kitchen with a breakfast nook and a family room with a couch, recliner, and TV. The only attempt at decoration was some framed photos of me. Mostly older ones, from when I was little, although he had my high school graduation picture on the wall. Everything was clean, but sparse. Of course, he lived here alone. How much of a mess could one man make?

"I suppose you remember your way around." He set his keys on the kitchen counter. "Your old room has a bed in it, but if you like one of the others better, I can move it."

"I'm sure it's fine."

"Do you need help unloading your car?"

I sank into a chair at the small white breakfast table. "Probably, although I don't have much stuff. Can we deal with it later, though? It's been a long day."

"Yeah. For me, too."

"Dad, I swear I didn't see the guy in the street. It was an accident."

"I know."

"Is he going to be okay?"

He took the chair across from me. "Yeah, I talked to one of his brothers on the way over here. He's fine. Just a broken leg. He'll sleep in his own bed tonight."

"He looked awful."

"Well, he'd just come in from the front line of the wild-fire up north."

My eyes widened. That was even worse. "Are you kidding?"

"Nope. He saved a guy's life today, then almost lost his. I

have a feeling he was going for a celebratory beer when he stepped out in front of you."

"So he's one of your firefighters and basically a hero." And the most gorgeous man I'd ever seen, but I was absolutely *not* thinking about that. "I almost killed him. Clearly I'm going to be the most popular girl in town."

"Don't worry. You know how it is. Everyone will talk for a while, but it'll die down. Sooner or later, something new will come along and give them something else to talk about."

I tucked my straight brown hair behind my ear. Actually, I didn't know what it was like. I barely remembered living in Tilikum. But I decided not to point that out. "Should I go see him at the hospital?"

He shook his head. "No, you don't need to do that. Like I said, they won't keep him overnight."

I glanced away, feeling an odd dip of disappointment. Why was I so preoccupied with seeing him again? "I still can't believe I did that."

"Accidents happen. Even Gavin knows that. Truth be told, I'm surprised it took this long for him to get hit by a car."

"What?"

He hesitated for a moment. "Gavin Bailey hasn't exactly grasped the concept of his own mortality yet."

Gavin was a Bailey?

"So you don't just know him because he's a firefighter. He's *that* Gavin."

"Yeah, you remember Gavin Bailey, don't you?"

I didn't. Not personally. Only the things Dad had said about him, as well as his brothers, over the years. It seemed like he always had stories to tell about the Bailey brothers.

"I haven't actually seen any of the Baileys in a long time,"

I said. "But I guess this will make for an interesting ice breaker."

Dad cracked a smile. "I suppose so." He paused again, like he was thinking about something. "Speaking of ice breakers, I know you just got here, but your mom said you might need some help getting to know people."

"You talked to Mom about me already?"

"We're your parents," he said with shrug, as if that explained everything.

Not that Mom was wrong. I'd always been shy, and I had a hard time meeting new people. It made me nervous.

"I'll be fine, Dad. And I already met Gavin Bailey." *And maybe I really should go see him at the hospital.*

"I think she probably meant you might need help making a friend or two."

"And by that you mean a *girlfriend* or two, not a fire-fighter I hit with my car."

He chuckled. "By that I mean not a playboy firefighter with a very charming smile."

God, his smile *had* been charming. Hypnotic, even.

"You don't have to worry about that. Guys like Gavin Bailey aren't interested in girls like me."

He looked skeptical. "You're a pretty girl, Skylar. Guys like Gavin Bailey are always interested in pretty girls."

I tucked my hair behind my ear, not sure how to reply to my dad's compliment. "Well, he and I didn't exactly get off to a great start. And I'll be fine. I'll admit, meeting people is not my best skill. But Mom's only worried because she's such a social butterfly, she doesn't understand my introvert ways."

"Hmm." He rubbed his chin. "I realize you're an adult who can take care of herself. But I'm still your dad. I worry."

"Thanks, Dad. I'll be okay. I just need to get my feet under me."

He nodded slowly, but I could tell he wasn't convinced. "You've been through a lot recently. A breakup is never easy."

I glanced away. That wound was still open—raw and fresh. "It's hard, but I'll get over it. And I know I could have gone to live with Mom, but I don't know. I just needed to get out of town for a while. Get my head together."

When Cullen had come clean about his affair with one of his other clients—a married woman, no less—he'd informed me I needed to move out immediately. Asshole. For reasons I still didn't understand, the first person I'd called was Dad. His barely masked anger when I'd tearfully vented to him on the phone had made me feel a bit better. And he'd offered to let me come stay with him if I needed a place to go.

I hadn't gone that day. I'd spent the last week at my mom's, just a few miles from the apartment I'd shared with Cullen.

I'd been an anxious wreck. It had been hard to make myself leave the house for fear I'd run into Cullen. Spokane was a city—albeit a small one—so the chances of randomly seeing him out and about were low. And Cullen only lived there part time. He kept a studio apartment in New York City—ostensibly to be closer to his publishing industry contacts, but now I knew he'd used it for other, more cheaty reasons.

In any case, the city I'd grown up in had suddenly felt like a pressure cooker of terror. So I'd taken Dad up on his offer.

"Do you need me to take care of anything for you?" His eyes narrowed and his voice hinted at some protective-father danger.

"No, Dad. I just want to start over."

He nodded in understanding. "Okay. You take your time getting settled. I need to go pop in to the station for a couple of hours. I was out at the incident command post for the wildfire all day and now I've got some work to do for my regular job. Do you need anything before I go?"

It was probably my fault that Dad had to go back to work. My car accident had interrupted his day. "No, I'm fine. I'll just bring in my clothes and stuff. Then probably watch some mindless TV."

"Sounds like a good plan. I'll get dinner on my way home, how about that?"

"That'd be great. Thanks, Dad."

He stood and placed a light kiss on the top of my head before leaving.

Closing my eyes, I let out a long breath. It was beautifully quiet, the absence of noise doing wonders to soothe my raw nerves.

Although I was off to a rocky start, maybe coming to Tilikum had been the right move. Maybe small-town living would help me get my mojo back.

Maybe I'd actually be able to write again.

That would certainly help my floundering career, although I no longer had an agent. And I wasn't exactly swimming in my own industry contacts. I didn't like that part of the job. I just wanted to write books, not network with people.

Of course, the writing books part wasn't exactly happening either. For months I'd been struggling with the worst case of writer's block I'd ever had.

I checked my phone and saw a text from my best friend Ginny. She'd been checking up on me regularly since my life had imploded last week.

Ginny: *Hey, sweetie. Did you make it to your dad's?*

Me: *I'm here. But this should probably be a phone call conversation.*

Ginny: *Oh god. What happened now? Don't text back, I'm calling.*

A second later, my phone rang.

"What happened?" Ginny asked as soon as I said hello. "You never want to talk on the phone."

"I know, but I don't want to type it all out."

"Did Cullen come crawling back already?"

"No. Definitely not. I'm sure he's happily making room for Pepper Sinclair's designer wardrobe and makeup collection." I paused to take a fortifying breath. "I ran over someone."

"What?" she shrieked.

Wincing, I moved the phone away from my ear. "Okay, maybe that's not exactly accurate, since I don't think my tires touched him. But I definitely hit a pedestrian."

"Oh my god. Is he okay?"

"I guess he's fine. My dad said he has a broken leg, but he'll go home from the hospital tonight. I hope they checked for internal bleeding. Do you know how much force it takes to rupture a spleen? I still think maybe I should go down there."

"I don't know how much force it takes to rupture a spleen, but I'm sure you do. Let's maybe not go down that grisly tangent; we can assume your fire chief father knows what he's talking about and that the hospital staff are taking care of him. How did you hit a pedestrian?"

"I turned a corner and he walked right out in front of me."

"Well, that sounds like his fault."

"Ginny."

"I'm just saying. We learn to look both ways when we're like four. Wait, he isn't a little kid, is he?"

"No, thank God. His name's Gavin Bailey. He's a fire-fighter who works for my dad."

"Ooh, hot firefighter? Tell me more."

"I didn't say he was hot."

"Is he, though?"

I hesitated, but what was the point in lying? "He's very hot. And probably as dangerous as a five-alarm fire. Or however many alarms big fires can be. But I don't want to talk about that part."

"Why not? This could be the beginning of a beautiful love story."

I rolled my eyes. "That's a big, fat no."

"Come on, you're a writer, don't you think that would make a cute story? Think of how adorable it would be to tell your grandkids you met when you hit him with your car."

"That's not the kind of story I write. If it were one of my books, I'd probably manipulate him into letting me move in with him so I could play out some weird obsessive fantasy stemming from acute childhood trauma and I'd wind up murdering him. Or wait, maybe I'd be the innocent party and he'd be the crazed murderer, and I'd almost get myself killed when I stumbled upon something he didn't want anyone to find in the course of trying to be nice and help take care of him."

"Oh my god, are you writing again?"

I wanted to lie to her and say yes. But I didn't. "Not really."

"Those are both really good ideas."

"Yeah, and the second I try to write either of them, my brain will shrivel up and forget how to spell the word *the*, let alone how to craft an entire novel."

"You've written twelve novels, Skylar. A dozen. Your brain still knows how. You just have to figure out what's blocking you."

"Thanks, Doctor Ginny."

"Can we go back to the hot firefighter?"

"Let's not."

She sighed. "Fine. Maybe just plan on staying home for a while until this cloud of bad luck passes. Sounds like it's become dangerous to innocent bystanders."

"You're telling me."

"Are you okay?"

"Yeah, mostly. My life sucks, but it has to get better from here, right?"

"That's my girl. Of course it does. I think going to live with your dad is going to be the best decision you've made in a long time."

I didn't share her confident optimism, but it was still nice to hear. "Thanks."

"Do you want some good news to make you feel better?"

"Yes, please."

"I'm coming to visit you."

My back straightened. "What? When?"

"I'll be there next week. I talked to my boss already and I'm going to do a piece on Tilikum."

Ginny was a travel writer, but she didn't just write about tourist attractions, accommodations, and restaurants. She dug into the cities and towns she visited, learning about their history. Her pieces were full of local stories and folklore, as well as where to shop and dine.

"Really? You're right, that is great news."

"Isn't it? As soon as you said you were going to stay with your dad, I started working the angle with my boss. Not that it was a hard sell. A small town in the mountains has plenty of appeal. And from what I've seen online, it's adorable."

"It is a cute town. Lots of history, so you'll have plenty to write about. Just wait until you hear about the town feud."

"Please tell me you're not kidding and there really is a town feud."

"I'm not kidding. The Bailey family and the Haven family have been feuding for generations."

"Why?"

"I actually have no idea. I just know they orchestrate pranks on each other, back and forth. And there are places you can't go if you're on one side or the other. Well, you could, I guess. No one would actually stop you. But people don't. They have two of almost everything: two banks, two barber shops, two breakfast diners, two flower shops, two pizza places. It goes on and on."

"Oh my god, this is fascinating. I'm in love already."

"Do you have a place to stay or do you want me to ask Dad about staying here? He has room."

"No, I already found a rental. But thank you."

"Of course."

"So even though I'm coming soon, I'm still going to call and check on you. Just so you know."

"Yeah, I know. Thanks, Ginny."

"You bet, sweetie. I'll talk to you soon."

"Bye."

I set my phone down and tilted my head, my vision going hazy. My mind went to what Ginny had said about me hitting Gavin making a good story.

The first time we met, I hit him with my car...

A woman visiting a small town filled with secrets accidentally hits someone on her first day there. Although it's an accident, she feels guilty for his injuries and takes it upon herself to visit him in his convalescence. Interestingly, as soon as the man is laid up in the hospital, the string of terrifying murders that plagued the town abruptly cease. Did she mow down the killer? Or is the killer the doctor who treats him, using the man's unfortunate accident as a way to frame an innocent for his crimes?

Sucking in a breath, I jolted back to reality. That wasn't a bad story idea.

My fingers tingled and words swirled in my head. A warm spark of creativity flashed to life.

Feeling a sudden burst of panic, I ran outside to my car. *Must get laptop. Must type before it's gone.* I grabbed my laptop bag out of the passenger seat and flew back into the house.

I took my laptop to the kitchen table. I sat, then pulled it out and logged in. Opened a fresh document.

Don't be scared, Skylar. Just type and the words will come.

Except, they didn't. I wrote a sentence. Deleted it. Wrote another. Deleted it. I tried just writing a synopsis, but even that was too much.

I couldn't do it, and I had no idea why.

5

GAVIN

*T*he grass in Lumberjack Park was wet from the rain that had finally come to the mountains. Two solid days of it, like the sky had saved up all the moisture and dumped it on us in one continuous deluge. The wildfire wasn't completely extinguished; hot spots could last underneath piles of ash for weeks. But it had done a lot to calm it down so it no longer threatened Tilikum.

That was good news. But walking in wet grass on crutches was a royal pain in the ass.

They squelched in the muck, getting stuck in the particularly squishy places. It had been about a week since the accident, so my armpits were toughening up. But I could have lived without the constant need to pry the rubber ends out of the wet soil.

Of course, I didn't really need to be here, either. I could have stayed home.

My brothers and a handful of other Bailey relatives ran formations, practicing for the upcoming flag football season. Tilikum took its traditions seriously, and the annual flag football league was no exception. There had been a

Bailey team since the beginning. The Havens had a team, too, the assholes. So did the Montgomerys, the Pines, and the Saxons. There was also the town team, for anyone who wanted to play who wasn't related to one of the family teams. It had been that way for decades.

And I'd played every year since I was sixteen.

I fucking loved flag football. I loved sports in general, but football had that gladiatorial thing going for it. You couldn't tackle anyone, which was kind of shitty, but chasing a guy down intent on subduing him—even if it was just by pulling a flag attached by Velcro—was pretty awesome.

And this year I couldn't play.

Stupid broken leg.

They had Asher at quarterback, which was a good call. He had a crazy good arm. Evan and Logan were playing wide receiver, and Levi was lined up behind Asher as running back. We had some cousins on the line—big guys —along with a dude named Paul who'd married into the family. My cousin Gena was out there, too. She was a kick ass receiver.

Half the team was on the other side, playing defense for the scrimmage, and Jack had taken over for my great-uncle Wendell as coach. Jack wasn't a Bailey, but Grace was now, and Jack was her stepdad, so we'd decided it counted.

I leaned on my crutches and watched Asher execute a play. He attempted a pass to Evan, but it was incomplete.

"You gotta get open if you're going to run that one," I called.

Evan glared at me. He probably growled, but he was too far away for me to hear him.

I'd come for the first practice of the season tonight because... well, because I was bored as fuck. I was on leave from work, so I had all kinds of free time. But I couldn't do any of the cool shit I usually did. I was starting to realize that all my hobbies required two legs. Rock climbing, ice climbing, hiking, swimming in the river, jumping in the river, swimming in the lake, jumping in the lake, mountain biking, baseball, dirt bike riding, martial arts... and of course, flag football. Two-leg activities. And I only had one.

Could have been a lot worse, of course. I was going to heal. I just had to find something to do in the meantime.

Bored was not good for me. I tended to get into trouble when I was bored.

Jack's wife, Naomi, walked onto the field with her son, Elijah. Naomi was Grace's mom, which made her my brother's mother-in-law. I wasn't sure if that meant we were related now, but it was close enough. I'd grown up next door to her, so she was family either way.

I waved to her and Elijah. He was getting tall—hitting that first pubescent growth spurt. They waved back. Jack called for a water break, then walked over to kiss his wife and give Elijah a big hug.

They were such a cool family.

I moved over to a bench and eased myself down. Logan came over with a water bottle and sat next to me. His flannel shirt and lime green swim trunks were splattered with mud, as were his white tube socks and shoes.

"Hey, brofa."

"Brofa?"

"Bro on a sofa." He took a swig of water. "I know it's a bench, but close enough. Are you pouting already?"

Logan had been out at the wildfire all week. Even once it had started raining, the crews had stayed to do spot checks and cleanup. I hadn't seen him since the day of the accident.

"I'm not pouting."

"Could have fooled me. Come on, it's a broken leg. You're lucky it wasn't worse."

"Lucky would have been not getting hit by a car."

"Fair point. Guess you used up all your luck out at the burn."

He was probably right. Maybe I'd given some of my luck to Robby. That was a worthy sacrifice.

"What am I going to do for another five weeks? I can't just sit around."

"I thought it was seven more weeks in the cast."

"Whatever. I'm a quick healer."

"What'd you do the last time you broke something?"

"Last time they put me in one of those boots so I didn't have crutches. I was on light duty at work so at least I had something to do."

"See? Pouting."

Fine, maybe I was pouting.

"Was that really Chief's daughter who hit you?" he asked.

A vision ran through my mind. Me, lying on the pavement, looking up at a face. The most beautiful face I'd ever seen. For a second, I'd honestly wondered if I was dead. Light had framed her dark hair like a halo, and when she'd touched me, the pain had disappeared.

"Yeah, it was her."

"You realize you're going to have to give him shit about that, right?"

My mouth twitched in a grin. "Oh yeah."

"Good. I was starting to think you were getting depressed or something."

"I'm not depressed, I'm bored and my leg itches." I paused for a moment. "She grew up hot."

"Who?"

"Chief's daughter."

Because fuck, she really had. Unless I'd hit my head and that ethereal memory of her was a pain-induced fabrication. Long dark hair. Big brown eyes. Probably looked bananas in a bikini.

Or naked, but that was taking things a little too far, considering who she was.

He elbowed me. "Dude. Don't."

"Don't what?"

"Don't start that shit. Not with her."

"I'm not starting anything."

"You just said she grew up hot."

"It's just an observation. You saw her. She did grow up hot."

"Yeah, I did, and you're right, but you know you can't chase her."

"Who said I was going to chase her?"

He shook his head. "I know you love danger in all its forms, but use your brain. This one isn't worth the risk."

He was right. Even though she was the most beautiful girl I'd ever laid eyes on, Skylar Stanley was completely forbidden—to me and my brothers at least.

Not that Asher and Evan counted anymore. Asher was married, and he and Grace were pregnant with their first baby. Evan had gotten engaged to his girlfriend Fiona a couple of months ago. Baileys were dropping like flies, and I had no intention of being the next one.

And Chief's daughter? I wasn't stupid. Even I knew how big of a mistake it would be to go after Skylar Stanley.

Which, okay, made it really tempting.

But I wasn't going to succumb to that. There were plenty of girls in the world. I wouldn't risk my career, or my relationship with Chief, over one of them.

"I know. Even I'm not that crazy."

Jack called for the team to huddle up.

Logan got up and cast me a sidelong glance. "We'll see."

Before I could argue with him, he ran onto the field.

They executed a few more plays. Asher looked good out there. The team hadn't been the same without him when he'd been in prison—which had been such bullshit anyway. Of course, nothing had been the same without him. It was good to have him home.

I hung out on the bench and gazed at the wet ground. My mind wandered to pretty brown eyes. The feel of her fingers gently sliding through my hair.

The football flew past my face, almost hitting me in the head.

"Watch out, Gav!"

Shit.

I really needed to stop doing that. As much as I didn't want to admit when my brother was right, he had a point about Skylar.

So why did I keep thinking about her?

This wasn't normal for me. Sure, I liked women. A lot. And if a girl caught my eye, I didn't hesitate to go after her. But I'd never been this preoccupied with a girl before.

Especially a girl I'd already decided I wasn't going to chase.

I wasn't an idiot. Serious relationships weren't my thing. Going after Skylar, tempting as it was, would be a huge mistake. Because what would happen when it ended? Chief would be pissed at me. Worse, he'd be disappointed in me. Even if she was the one to end it, he was her dad. He'd be on her side. I'd take the blame.

That was a mess I didn't want to clean up. No matter how tempting she was.

A few fat drops fell from the sky and I decided that was my cue to leave. I squelched through the wet grass to my truck. Luckily I'd broken my left leg, and my truck was an automatic, so I could still drive.

I didn't feel like going home, so I headed into town and parked outside Grace's coffee shop, the Steaming Mug.

Crutch, step, crutch, step, I made my way to the door. Now I had to open it. Damn it, everything was hard with a broken leg.

I looked through the glass to see if someone could open it for me, and my eyes landed on a girl at a table.

Oh shit. It was her. Skylar Stanley. My boss's daughter.

My boss's *hot* daughter.

Her hotness hadn't been a pain-induced hallucination. She was every bit as gorgeous as I remembered.

But it wasn't just the way she looked that had me captivated. There was something about her. About the way she stared off into the distance, her eyes unfocused. It made me want to know what was going on in that head of hers.

What are you thinking about, Sky?

This was a bad idea. She had all the makings of a Gavin lure. And I couldn't take the bait.

But before I could go anywhere, she caught sight of me. She flew out of her seat so fast, she almost knocked over her chair, and rushed to open the door.

6

SKYLAR

*T*ry a change of scenery, I'd thought. The coffee shop downtown looked cute. Maybe it would help and I could get some work done.

This wasn't helping. It was so much worse.

I stared at the man on crutches, standing just outside the door. It was him. Right here, practically in the same room with me. Gavin Bailey.

I didn't know if I was ready for this encounter.

Except, oh my god, he couldn't open the door.

That was totally my fault, so I jumped out of my chair and darted to open it for him.

"Thanks." He moved past me to come inside, then he stopped and his eyes met mine.

Uh-oh.

Never in my life had an *uh-oh* been so fraught with meaning.

Uh-oh because he was looking at me and I was looking at him. It felt like a zap of electricity arced between us—a flash of energy reaching from deep in my chest, right into his.

And uh-oh because his mouth curled into a subtle smile, puckering his dimples. It made me want to step closer and run my fingers through his hair again.

What was even happening?

My tongue felt thick and awkward. A half-formed, inarticulate jumble of words swirled through my head and the soft music in the background suddenly rang too loud in my ears. It was like I could hear each individual string of the acoustic guitar thwacking against the wood.

Still, I somehow managed to form a coherent sentence. "Do you want to sit down?"

He gazed at me like I'd just said something incredibly interesting and blinked a few times before answering. "Yeah, I'd love to."

I pulled out a chair for him and realized too late that it was at my table, and I didn't know if he wanted to sit with me, or just sit down. But he lowered himself into the chair and leaned his crutches against the table.

"I guess we didn't actually meet the other day," he said as I took my seat. "I'm Gavin."

Name. Don't tell him he's hot. Just tell him your name. "I'm Skylar. Um, Skylar Stanley."

My voice was so little and timid. I hated sounding like that, but the obvious shyness in my tone only made my instinct to hide stronger.

"Nice to officially meet you." He flashed a smile, the full force of those dimples and white teeth shining directly on me. It was like looking at the sun.

God, he was gorgeous.

"I'm so sorry about hitting you. I can't believe I broke your leg. Does it hurt a lot?"

"No, it's not bad."

"I swear, I looked. I wasn't texting or anything. I looked and turned the corner and then bam, there you were."

He reached over and laid his hand on top of mine. The sudden contact felt like another bolt of electricity. A blush hit my cheeks and the warmth of his skin on mine was somehow soothing and arousing at the same time.

His eyes flicked from my face, down to our hands, then back again. He opened his mouth like he was going to say something, but closed it again and quickly took his hand away.

"I'm really fine," he said, and I saw him flex his hand under the table. "I'm the dumbass who walked into the road."

"I guess that's why adults teach kids to look both ways before crossing the street." I pinched my lips closed. I'd meant that as a joke, but maybe it had just sounded rude. "Sorry, sometimes I'm bad at verbal conversations."

Especially when I'm struck stupid by a hot firefighter.

Which had literally never happened to me before.

"Well, at least you're a good driver." He winked, the corners of his lips lifting.

I laughed, feeling a little of my anxiety dissipate.

"So..." He rubbed his hands up and down his thighs. "Aside from running into clueless pedestrians, what are you doing back in Tilikum?"

He had no idea what a loaded question that was. But I wasn't about to give my life story to someone I'd just met. "I just needed a change of scenery."

"Good choice. We have great scenery."

The way he stared directly at me when he said that, I wasn't sure if it was meant to be flirtatious—like I was great scenery—or if he was talking about the objectively beautiful scenery outside.

I tucked my hair behind my ear, trying not to let my brain get too sidetracked. "Yeah, it's really beautiful here."

"You're a writer or something like that, right?"

"I am. How'd you know?"

"Your dad is my boss, and he talks about you. What kind of stuff do you write?"

His ability to effortlessly keep the conversation going was such a relief. I never seemed to know what to say next, but answering questions was easy. "I write suspense novels, usually about serial killers, although one of my biggest sellers is technically a thriller."

"What's the difference?"

"Between thriller and suspense?"

"Yeah."

"There's not necessarily a standard definition, but most agents and editors consider a novel a thriller if the protagonist is in danger from the outset and the reader has basically the same information as he or she does. A suspense usually means the reader knows things the protagonist doesn't. So the reader waits with suspense to see if the protagonist discovers the danger in time." I shut my mouth again. "Sorry, that was probably more information than you wanted."

"Not at all." He leaned forward and rested his forearm on the table. "That's awesome. I don't think I could sit still long enough to write a page, let alone a whole book."

I shrugged. "I've been having a hard time lately, too."

A pretty blond woman dressed in a pink blouse and cropped pants came over to our table. "Hey, Gav. How's the leg?"

"Mostly just itches. Have you met Skylar?" He turned to me. "This is my sister-in-law, Grace. She's my brother Asher's wife."

Grace gave me a warm smile. "Hey, I heard you were in town. It's nice to see you again. I think we were probably in elementary school the last time I saw you."

"Probably."

"I was just with your hubs," Gavin said. "He was looking good at quarterback. How are you feeling?"

"I feel amazing, actually." She rested a hand on her stomach and turned back to me. "He's asking because I'm pregnant."

"Congratulations."

"Thank you." She smiled again and there was so much joy in her eyes, it made my heart flutter a little. "I feel really good. No morning sickness or anything. I'm a little tired, but I can't complain. So far being pregnant agrees with me."

"You're a brave woman," Gavin said. "Baking the first Bailey cub of the next generation."

"Logan has a pool going to guess the gender," she said. "Want in?"

Gavin tilted his head, as if he'd be able to tell whether Grace was carrying a boy or a girl by looking at her. She wasn't even showing yet.

"Boy," he said, his voice full of confidence.

"That's what Gram said, too."

"Of course she did. Because it's a boy."

"You're probably right. Baileys produce a lot more boys than girls."

"I guess our boy swimmers are the aggressive ones."

Grace laughed. "Something like that. Anyway, do you want anything? I can have Jenna bring it over so you don't have to get up."

"That would be awesome." His gaze swung to me. "As long as Skylar doesn't mind."

He was making me feel a little jittery, but not in a bad way. "No, I don't mind."

"Your usual?" Grace asked.

"Yes, please and thank you," he said, flashing her another grin.

"One salted caramel mocha with whip coming up."

He leaned closer and whispered, as if he were telling me a secret. "I kind of have a sweet tooth."

"Did you know that the researchers who discovered the artificial sweetener sucralose were actually attempting to create an insecticide?" I asked.

"I didn't know that."

"Apparently one of the researchers was asked to test the substance, but he thought he'd been instructed to *taste* it. Fortunately for him, it wasn't toxic. And it tasted like sugar." I pressed my lips closed. "Sorry, I don't know why you'd need to know that. I did some research on potentially toxic household substances once and fell down a rabbit hole."

"I thought you were going to say someone dared him to taste the bug poison."

"That wouldn't have been a very smart dare to take. Although getting the words *taste* and *test* wrong when you're trying to make insecticide seems like a pretty big mistake."

He smiled at me again with a look in his eyes like he wasn't sure what to think.

Which was understandable, considering I was babbling about insecticide and artificial sweeteners.

The barista brought Gavin's coffee to the table. He thanked her, then brought the mug to his mouth. When he set it down, a little bit of foam was still on his upper lip. I watched his tongue dart out to lick it off.

He leans close and his tongue brushes the tip of mine, a tanta-

lizing taste that sends a shiver down my back. Our lips press together, my eyes fluttering closed, and—

I blinked the vision away. Where had that come from? I shifted in my seat, hoping he hadn't noticed that I'd been briefly overtaken by a kissing fantasy.

Except his eyes were on my mouth. Was he staring at my lips because I'd been staring at his? He didn't look away, and my gaze dipped again. What would that mouth feel like on mine? On my skin, trailing down my neck, or finding the hot bundle of nerves between my—

He cleared his throat and I practically jumped out of my chair.

"Sorry," we both blurted out at the same time.

I pressed my lips closed, and his hooked in a little smile. He glanced away, like he was confused about something, and took a drink of his coffee.

It felt like I needed something to do with my hands, so I picked up my almost-empty cup. I was used to being flustered when I met someone new, but this was different. Something about Gavin Bailey made my heart flutter and a cascade of tingles rush through my body.

Hopefully I wouldn't start babbling morbid facts about gunshot wounds or decomposing bodies. Sometimes I did that when I was nervous.

Gavin's phone dinged and he took it out of his pocket. His face fell. "Damn. My brother Logan needs a ride home."

Our eyes met again and that arc of electricity was back, sparks flying in the air around us. I desperately wanted him to stay, and for a second, I was almost overcome by the urge to lean over and kiss him.

Sucking in a quick breath, I tore my eyes away. "Well, it was nice to meet you. Officially."

"Yeah, you too." He stood and got his crutches under his arms.

I got up and followed him to the door, then opened it for him. He walked through and glanced back at me.

"Thanks. I'll see you around?"

"Yeah, I'm sure you will."

His eyes flicked up and down and he nodded, a little smile stealing over his features. "Bye, Skylar."

"Bye."

I stood there in a daze while the door fell closed behind him. What had just happened? Sure, he was attractive. Jaw-droppingly gorgeous, to be exact. But that didn't account for the way I floated back to my table, my hand still tingling from where he'd touched me.

Now was not the time for me to get hung up on a guy, no matter what he looked like. I'd just been dumped, for good-ness sake. And I needed to get my career back on track. Figure out how to start writing again.

I sat down and opened my laptop, determined to focus. But no matter how hard I tried, I couldn't get Gavin Bailey out of my mind.

7

GAVIN

*W*hat the fuck was that?

My head swam as I hobbled out of the coffee shop, leaving Skylar behind. Tempting was one thing, but I'd sat there staring—daydreaming about making out with her.

Okay, fine, I'd been daydreaming about more than just making out.

But why had I acted like an inexperienced kid? I was never like that around girls. Something about Skylar had emptied my brain. I'd touched her hand out of nowhere, stared at her mouth, and had I even said anything interesting? Probably not.

This was very not like me. Usually I was charming as fuck.

Of course, I didn't need to be charming with her. I didn't want to go over that argument with myself again, so I just struggled into my truck and went back to the park to pick up my brother.

~

THE NEXT DAY, I was no closer to figuring out why I'd been so weird with Skylar. I couldn't stop thinking about her, either. About her captivating eyes and full lips. The way her soft skin had felt when I'd touched her hand.

Touched her hand? I was getting a fucking boner remembering the way her hand felt. What was that about?

Cara—Grace's bestie—had texted me earlier, asking if I'd come over, so I drove over to her place and parked outside her hillside house. I didn't know what she had going on, but it was better than trying to talk myself out of going over to Chief's house to see if I could covertly touch Skylar's hand again.

Seriously? What was wrong with me?

Cara's house was hella nice. She had money. Lots of money. I didn't know why—I'd never asked—but it was obvious that she did. Even in college she'd driven an expensive car. And remodeling this place had to have cost a fortune. She liked to throw parties, so I'd been here plenty of times.

I liked Cara, and she was crazy hot. She had that wild redhead thing going on. Cara was dangerous, and normally that kind of thing was like crack to me. But as much as I liked flirting with her, I was just messing around. I'd never really seen her as a girl I could get dirty with.

Not that I thought she'd invited me over to get dirty. She hadn't made it clear what she wanted. But with a girl like Cara—who didn't really date guys so much as decide that she'd allow one to give her orgasms for a while—you never knew what she was going to do.

But at this point, I was too curious not to go in. I knocked on her door.

A second later, my phone buzzed.

Cara: *Come in. My hands are dirty.*

Hands were dirty with what?

I opened the door, crutched my way inside, and pushed the door closed behind me.

"I'm in the kitchen," she called.

My crutches clicked on the wood floor. Most of the downstairs was wide open with big windows showcasing the view of the river. It looked like a magazine spread or a showroom. Almost too perfect—hardly looked like anyone lived here.

Except for the kitchen.

The big island was cluttered with ingredients, bowls, cups, random utensils, and a lot of flour. She had a martini with two olives and her phone was on a stand, paused on what looked like a cooking video.

Cara stood with her hands held up at boob height, wincing like she'd just gutted an animal and was covered in blood, rather than a messy combination of flour, sugar, butter, and probably something else, given how drippy it was.

"This asshole said to mix by hand, but mine doesn't look anything like his."

I step-crutched my way into the kitchen. "What are you doing?"

"Baking."

"Are you sure?" I glanced into the soupy mess in her bowl. "What are you trying to bake?"

"Cookies."

"That doesn't look like cookie dough."

"I know," she groaned. "These are supposed to be foolproof, but apparently Chef fucking Hartley hasn't met me."

"Who's Chef Hartley?"

She nodded to her phone. "Guy in the video."

"Well that's your problem. You don't learn to bake cookies from a fancy chef on the internet."

"Who are you supposed to learn from, then?"

"Native grandmas. Or non-Native grandmas, but you can't convince me that Native grandmas don't have something special when it comes to cooking. There's a reason Gram's pies win at the Mountain Man festival every year and I'm sure it's genetic."

"Well, I don't have a grandma, Native or otherwise."

"No, but you have the next best thing."

"What's that?"

"Me."

"You know how to bake cookies." Her voice dripped with skepticism.

"Fuck yeah, I know how to bake cookies." I moved to stand next to her and started pushing stuff around to clear a space on the counter. "I learned from the best. Dump that out. We'll start over. By the way, how'd you text me if your hands are covered in that disaster you thought was cookie dough?"

"I voice texted." She dumped the bowl and rinsed it out.

"Cool. Okay, do you have chocolate chips?"

"Yeah, four or five different kinds. I wasn't sure what to get, so I bought some of everything."

I glanced at all the shit she'd left on the counter. "I can see that."

She dried out the bowl with a clean towel and set it on the counter. "When I texted you to come over, I figured we'd just fumble around the kitchen and then have to dare each other to eat what we made. Not that you'd know what you were doing."

I laughed. "I spent a lot of time in the kitchen with

Gram. Probably because I was the youngest. She always put me to work."

"Of course she did."

"Why the sudden interest in learning to bake?"

"I'm just bored. Thought I'd find a new hobby."

"Does that have anything to do with your bestie having a baby?"

She picked up her drink and took a sip. "Obviously. Everyone knows I'm overly attached to Grace."

"You guys do have a weird relationship."

"I know."

Poor kid was lonely.

I used her phone to find a recipe that looked close to the one I remembered and walked her through it. Chocolate chip cookies weren't hard, but if you didn't know anything—which Cara clearly did not—there were plenty of ways to go wrong. I showed her how to measure everything properly and to follow the recipe directions, not just dump everything in a bowl at once. Then we dropped the dough in little balls on a cookie sheet and put them in the oven.

"You're going to have to take these home with you," she said, dropping another row of cookies on the second baking sheet.

"Why?"

"Because otherwise I'll eat them all. I can't be trusted."

"No problem. I'll take them to the firehouse. They'll last about five minutes." I went around the island and hoisted myself onto a stool, then leaned my crutches against the counter. "Just keep doing what you're doing until you run out of dough. I need to sit for a minute."

"Does your leg hurt?"

"Yeah, and my other leg gets tired from doing all the work."

"I should send Sven to see you."

"Who's Sven?"

"My massage therapist. His hands are magical. I don't know how I ever lived without him." She picked up her martini and took a sip. "I made Grace let me schedule her regular prenatal massages. He does in-home appointments so I'll just text you."

"Thanks. That sounds awesome."

"You're welcome," she said brightly.

When the first batch came out of the oven, we let them cool for a few minutes, then taste tested. They were perfect —a little crisp around the edges with chewy middles and gooey chocolate chips.

"Holy shit, Gav, you weren't kidding." Cara licked chocolate off her finger. "You really can bake cookies."

"Told you."

"I must admit, I'm impressed. Turns out you have a side to you I never knew about."

When the cookies were all finished, she packed most of them into a couple of plastic containers and put them in a bag for me. I figured I'd head straight for the firehouse and share the goods while they were still warm. Chocolate chip cookies were best that way.

I drove down there and got out, struggling a little with the bag. Maybe I needed a backpack or something. I went inside and slowly made my way up the stairs. The kitchen was empty, but the cookies wouldn't last long once word got around that they were here. I opened one of the containers and left them on the counter.

Chief came in with an empty coffee mug. He was looking a little rough—tired with a stoop to his shoulders. "Those look good. Did Gram make them?"

"Nope, Cara and I did."

He raised his eyebrows while he poured some hours-old coffee into his mug. "Should I try one or just leave them for the guys?"

"You should definitely have one. They're good."

He reached for one but hesitated.

"It's not a prank," I said with a laugh. "On my honor. They're good."

"Mind if I ask why you and Cara were baking chocolate chip cookies?" He grabbed one and sniffed it.

I shrugged. "We were bored."

"Good reason, I suppose." He took a bite and his skepticism melted like one of the chocolate chips. "Okay, you're right. These are good."

"Told you."

He took his cookie and coffee to one of the small round tables and sat. Grateful to be getting off my feet—or foot—for a while, I sat across from him.

"You feeling okay, Chief?"

"I'm all right."

"You sure? Is your back bothering you again?"

His brow furrowed. "How did you know my back was bothering me?"

"It's kind of obvious when you stand up, hold your back, and wince."

"I'm not very good at hiding it, am I?"

"Not really."

"You have a lot of your Gram in you," he said. "You notice things."

I shrugged. "I guess."

"You have a lot of your dad in you, too."

Clearing my throat, I glanced away. I didn't really like talking about my parents. They were a shitty topic for me, best avoided. I decided to change the subject.

"How's Skylar doing?"

"She's getting settled." He took a sip of coffee. "But she's a bit shy. Has a hard time meeting people."

I thought about mentioning that I'd seen her at the coffee shop yesterday, but I had a feeling I'd accidentally say something weird. Like how I'd touched her hand and it had felt like my entire life had flashed before my eyes.

A life with her.

Fuck. I needed to get my head together, so I went for a little humor instead. "Yeah, she had to run me over to meet me."

He gave me a wry look, but I could see the hint of a smile. "Anyway. I suppose it's not easy being new in town, but I'm a little worried about her."

"Why?"

"She spends a lot of time alone."

The thought of Skylar being lonely tugged at me. Shy girl. New in town. There wasn't anything I could do about that, but I hated the idea of her being all alone.

Except... maybe there *was* something I could do about that.

Chief finished off the cookie and I stared at the wall, suddenly at war with myself. Because I had an idea.

A bad idea.

But so tempting.

Maybe even irresistible.

"Chief, I think I can solve both our problems."

"Both? What's your problem?"

"I'm bored off my ass. I can't even be on light duty for a while. I need something to do. I only know like three cookie recipes, so that's going to get old fast."

"And my problem is?"

"You're worried about your daughter."

"I'm not making the leap. How can you solve both problems?"

My lips curled in a smile. Yep, I could totally do this. "I'll be Skylar's first friend in Tilikum."

I could totally see Chief trying to keep his face neutral. "Hmm."

"I know what you're thinking—"

"I'm pretty sure you don't."

"Just friends, Chief."

He eyed me over his coffee mug.

"I'm not suggesting I date your daughter. You said she's shy and doesn't really know anyone in town yet. I'm the opposite of shy and I know pretty much everybody. We can hang out, I can show her all the cool stuff there is to do. Introduce her around. I can help her get used to Tilikum life."

"Why do I feel like I'd be inviting the wolf into my pasture?"

I grinned. "Evan's the wolf. I'm just an otter."

With a soft laugh, he shook his head. "Don't get me wrong. I've known you your whole life. I know what you're made of, and it's the same stuff your dad was made of. Which is also why it makes me a little nervous."

"How much trouble can I really get into? I only have one leg."

He raised his eyebrows. "You and I both know if you're presented with a cookie jar, you're going to steal a cookie."

I put my hands up in a gesture of surrender. "I'm not going to steal this cookie. Besides, I know how to make my own cookies."

His brow furrowed.

"That kind of sounded like a masturbation joke and I totally didn't mean it that way."

He rolled his eyes.

"But I don't have any issues with that, so you know, if the cookie jar started to look really tempting, I could always take care of things myself. Make my own cookies, so to speak."

"Jesus, Gav."

"I'm just saying. It's like a release valve."

"Okay, I get it. Look, Skylar's a grown woman. She can be friends with who she likes. You don't need my permission."

"Awesome."

"But Gavin." He met my eyes.

Wow. I'd never taken the full force of a protective father stare before. It gave me a quick hit of adrenaline. "Yeah?"

"She's been through some stuff recently. Be careful with her."

"I will. She'll be totally safe with me. In fact, she'll be safer with me than she would be on her own because I'll be able to help her steer clear of any guys who you'd want to keep her away from. Not that I'm assuming she'd date those guys if left on her own. She's probably too smart for that."

"Even smart girls can get caught up with the wrong man."

"One of the many reasons she needs me."

He nodded slowly, and I could tell he was getting into this idea.

I sure was. Okay, yes, I was attracted to her, and usually when I was attracted to a girl, I pursued her relentlessly. But I could hang out with Skylar and help her acclimate to Tilikum without crossing that line. I wasn't a total animal. I had some self-control.

I could resist the cookies in this cookie jar.

It was simple. I'd be friends with Skylar, and that was all.

Now I just had to talk her into it.

8

SKYLAR

*T*he water pouring out of the faucet in the kitchen sink caught my eye. Absently, I rinsed off the plate in my hand, pondering the clear liquid flowing from the tap.

A waterfall. No, a dam—maybe one built by beavers. Sticks and debris everywhere. Maintenance workers wade into the murky water to clear some of the mess and find it's not just river detritus causing the blockage. It's a body.

I made a mental note to research the effects of prolonged submersion in water on a corpse.

Again.

My Google search history was rather morbid. Job hazard.

But... where was the story?

The homicide detective trying to make a name for herself gets caught in a web of lies and danger as she digs into the murder? Internal cover-ups and conspiracy? Or is it a family member of the victim, intent on proving it wasn't suicide, who stumbles on a secret society, and the penalty for revealing its existence is death?

A knock at the front door jolted me from my thoughts. I took a quick breath and turned off the water. Leaving the plate in the sink, I went to answer the door.

If the knock had startled me, the person standing outside almost made me jump out of my skin.

Gavin Bailey.

My heart suddenly beat too fast and a flush hit my cheeks. Great, I was blushing for no reason. I opened my mouth to say... something, I didn't really know what, although *hi* would probably have been a decent start. Only I got all tangled in my thoughts, still half-thinking about a body caught in a beaver dam and how it had gotten there.

"I don't know," I blurted out.

The corner of Gavin's mouth hooked in a smile. "You don't know *what*?"

Oh god, how embarrassing. "Nothing. I'm sorry. I was thinking about something else and I guess my brain wasn't finished thinking it."

"What were you thinking about?"

"A body caught in a beaver dam."

"How'd it get there?"

"That's what I don't know. But that's not even the most important question."

"It's not?"

"No."

"Then what is the important question?"

"Where's the story?"

"That is an important question." He shifted his weight on his crutches. "Can I come in?"

"Oh, yes. Sorry again."

"No problem. I've just been on my feet a lot today."

I stepped aside so he could come in and it was impossible not to notice the way his muscles flexed as he walked. The crutches necessitated use of his upper body strength, something he clearly had in spades. He wasn't huge and bulky, but he was athletic. That was a good word for it. And toned. So very, very toned.

And now my face was getting warmer.

I couldn't stop thinking about what Ginny had said about Gavin being a hot firefighter. Because Gavin Bailey was the *definition* of hot firefighter. He was January and December and all the months in between in every hot firefighter calendar ever made.

If you were into that sort of thing, of course.

Which I wasn't.

Okay, that was a total lie.

Gavin had thick dark hair, sharp cheekbones, a strong jaw, and soft brown eyes that did all sorts of terrible things to my insides when he looked at me. And his body. God. I followed him into the kitchen, tilting my head to watch his ass as he walked. The way he filled out his jeans was nothing short of remarkable.

"Sky?"

I gasped, realizing that not only had I walked into the kitchen without noticing where I was or what I was doing, but he'd sat down at the table, leaving his crutches leaning against it while I'd been lost in thought.

"Sorry. I was just… thinking again."

"About bodies found in a beaver dam?"

No, but that's a better answer than the way your ass looks in your jeans. "Yeah."

"Is that for the book you're writing? I guess that's a dumb question. Of course it is. You're not a detective or FBI agent who'd be investigating a real body found in a beaver dam."

"No. Just a writer. And not really. I was just doing the dishes and it got me thinking."

"You do that a lot, don't you?"

"What?"

"Think."

I blinked at him. "Doesn't everybody?"

"No."

Laughing softly, I sat at the table with him. "I suppose it was my turn for a dumb question. Of course not everybody thinks a lot."

"Nope. I have some friends who never think about anything. Or at least it seems like they don't."

"Then what do they do all the time?" I asked, although I hadn't really meant to ask it aloud.

He tapped the table with his index finger. "They *do* stuff, I guess. Work, eat, hang out with their buddies or girl-friends, drink beer, sleep."

"Sounds kind of nice. Simpler."

"Simpler than what?"

I took a deep breath to clear my head. "Simpler than thinking too much. Which I'm pretty good at doing."

"Overthinker, huh? Good to know."

"Why is that good to know?"

He shrugged. "Just is."

I narrowed my eyes at him. "What are you doing here? My dad's at work."

"Oh, I know. I was just there."

"So why are you here?"

He grinned at me, flashing those dangerous dimples. "I brought cookies."

"That's... nice but strange."

"Why strange?" He set a plastic container on the table.

"Do you always bring random girls cookies?"

He paused, like he was thinking about it. "No. But you're not a random girl either. Anyway, I made cookies earlier and I figured I'd bring you some."

"You made these?"

"Yep. My friend Cara was bored and invited me over to bake with her."

His friend Cara? What did that mean? And why did the thought of him baking cookies with someone named Cara make my spine prickle like I'd been poked with a needle?

"Oh."

One corner of his mouth lifted in a half-smile. "Not that kind of friend." He took a cookie out of the container and set it in front of me. "Try one."

I glanced between him and the cookie.

"Are you always so suspicious? Here." He took the cookie, broke it in half, shoved some in his mouth, and set the other half back in front of me.

I picked it up and took a bite. My teeth sank into a perfect combination of chewy and crumbly. The chocolate chips were still a little warm and melty.

"Wow. This is really good."

He licked the corner of his mouth and I was too mesmerized by the sight of his tongue on his lip to realize he was, consciously or unconsciously, signaling that I had chocolate on my face. Until he reached over and swiped it with his thumb.

His sudden touch surprised me so much I gasped.

Then he put his thumb in his mouth and sucked off the chocolate.

It was moments like this that made me question the power of the brain body connection—or at least question which direction it ran. Was my brain in charge of my body, or the other way around? Because right now, my body was telling my brain things that were very bad.

So very, very bad.

Flee, Skylar. Run like the wind. Save yourself.

I stood abruptly and grabbed a paper towel off the roll. "Do you need one?"

"Sure."

I didn't know why I was so flustered. I told myself—firmly—to get it together, and handed him a paper towel.

"Thanks."

For a second, I contemplated whether I should sit down again. A part of me wished he'd go. He made me jumpy and that smile of his was a deadly weapon.

But another part of me—a big part, if I was being honest—did want to sit down. Wanted to hear him talk and gaze at him in all his hot firefighter glory.

A firefighter. I'd never written about a firefighter before. His nemesis could be a serial arsonist and when a string of seemingly unrelated fires turn deadly—

I gasped. Again. Not because Gavin had interrupted my thoughts. He was just sitting there, casually watching me. Patient. Like he wasn't annoyed that my attention had just wandered for who knew how long.

"Sorry." I sat down.

"That's okay. Still thinking about bodies in beaver dams, or was that something new?"

I smiled and tucked my hair behind my ear. "Something new. I was thinking about how you're a firefighter." I left out *hot* deliberately. "And how I've never written about a fire-fighter before."

"But where's the story?"

"Well... maybe there's an arsonist. And the firefighter

wants to help catch him. Or her, although I think arsonists are statistically more likely to be male."

"What if the firefighter is the arsonist?"

"That could be an interesting twist. Although it changes the dynamic of the story. Does the reader know he's the arsonist? Or is that slowly revealed throughout the course of the book?"

"What if the firefighter arsonist is friends with a detective who's on the case? And the detective has to face the reality that he's investigating his friend."

"Arson and betrayal. That's definitely compelling."

"Too dark?"

"I write about serial killers. Too dark isn't really an issue."

"Fair enough. Well, if you need to do any research on firefighters, I'm your guy. Although I guess you could just talk to your dad."

"Speaking of my dad, did he send you here?"

"Nope." His lips popped on the P. "But I did tell him I was coming. He's totally on board."

"On board with what?"

"With me being your first friend in Tilikum."

"That's why you brought me a cookie?"

"Cookies are a great way to make friends."

I laughed. "True."

"Here's the thing. You're new in town and you could use someone to show you around. Introduce you to people, help you navigate the ins and outs of life in Tilikum."

"Could I?"

"Definitely. And I'm the perfect guy for the job."

"And why is that?"

"Who else has tons of time on his hands, knows pretty much everyone, and is also super fun to hang out with?"

"I don't know. I'm new in town."

"Exactly."

"So... you want to be friends because you're bored?"

His brow furrowed. Nothing sexy about that expression. Nope. Not at all.

Liar.

"What makes you think I'm bored?"

"Aren't you? I assume you're on leave until your leg heals."

"Yeah. And, you're right, I am bored. Although not right now. I haven't been bored since I got here. And that's not the reason I want to be friends."

"Why do you want to be friends?"

"Because you're interesting and cool to hang out with. And, okay, I do need something to do and showing you around Tilikum sounds fun."

This made me nervous. Gavin Bailey made me nervous. He was trouble. I could feel it.

"I'm sure you're really nice. But no matter what my dad told you, I'm fine. I don't need someone to take me under their wing and show me around town. I can find my way on my own."

"But that won't be nearly as much fun."

That half smile and those dimples hinted at all kinds of fun.

Trouble. This one was trouble, Skylar. Dad even said so.

"My friend Ginny is coming to town soon. She'll be staying for a while."

"So?"

"So then I'll have a friend in town."

"She'll be even newer than you are. That's just the blind leading the blind."

I laughed. "It's not like this is high school and I'm going

to forget how to find my locker or where to go for third period math."

"No, it's worse. It's adulthood."

"Are you one of those people who loved high school?"

He scowled. "God, no. I hated high school."

"Really? You weren't the popular football captain or something?"

"No, I was. But I still hated it."

I didn't know why I found that so fascinating. But I did. "I doubt it will surprise you that I was the mousy shy girl who never talked."

"That does surprise me, actually."

"I was. We wouldn't have been friends."

"That's okay."

"Why?"

"Because we're friends now."

"Are we?"

"Yeah." He smiled, like something he was thinking amused him. "Don't think, just answer fast. Do you want to be my friend?"

"Yes." I blinked in surprise.

He pointed at me. "See? Told you."

I laughed. "How do I know this isn't all a ploy to get in my pants?"

"Man, I really want to be offended by that, but it's a fair question. I'm good at ploys to get in a girl's pants. But that's not what I'm doing. I even promised your dad."

Promised my dad? That was interesting. Promised him what? That he wouldn't try to get in my pants? That he had no intention of dating me? It made sense, in a way. Dad was Gavin's boss. He'd want to tread carefully where his boss's daughter was concerned.

And maybe that was easy because he wasn't interested in me anyway.

But something about that promise, well intentioned though it might have been, poked a latent sense of rebellion deep inside me.

I nervously tucked my hair behind my ear again, shaking off the little rush of heat trying to surge through my veins. "Well that's good. Because my pants are fully buttoned right now."

"Come on, Sky. Just humor me. Let's hang out tomorrow."

"Hang out and do what?"

"I'll come up with something awesome. Don't worry about that."

"I worry about everything."

"You don't have to worry about this." He paused and caught his lower lip with his teeth for a second. "Besides, it's the least you can do. You did hit me with your car."

I crumpled the paper towel in my fist and tossed it at him. "That's not fair."

Laughing, he batted it away. "I'm teasing. How about this. Please hang out with me tomorrow?"

Oh my god. As if anyone could tell that man no when he looked at them like that.

Which was precisely the problem.

Gavin Bailey was trouble.

Irresistible trouble.

"Okay. I'll hang out with you tomorrow."

He smiled again. Cute brown eyes, white teeth, dimples. God he was adorable.

So.

Much.

Trouble.

"Awesome. It'll be the Adventures of Gav and Sky."

Adventures? That word gave me a ping of anxiety. What if he wanted to do something scary?

But as we made plans to get together the next day, all I could really think about was how much I liked it when he called me Sky.

9

SKYLAR

a jittery buzz of nervous energy thrummed through me as I sat waiting for Gavin at the Steaming Mug coffee shop. I glanced down at my clothes. Had I worn the right outfit? The September air was chilly, the leaves starting to turn orange, yellow, and red. I'd chosen a pale blue sweater, jeans, and a pair of not practical, but very cute heels.

They were low heels, nothing crazy. Blue with little white polka-dots. I hadn't worn them in... I didn't know how long. I didn't have occasion to wear heels all that often. Since I found myself with the need to venture outside the relative safety of my dad's house, I'd decided it was the perfect opportunity to treat myself to cute shoes.

And I'd hoped the chance to wear them would distract me from my anxiety over today's... whatever this was.

It wasn't working very well.

The barista worked behind the counter, steaming milk for someone's order. The soft hiss of steam prickled down my back, making all the little stabilizer muscles in my neck and shoulders tighten. Logically, I knew the sound wasn't loud. No one else in the shop seemed bothered by it. But it made me long for my noise-canceling headphones.

I fidgeted with a napkin, twisting it back and forth. I knew I didn't have a good reason to be so anxious. Gavin was just going to show me around town, not take me skydiving or something equally terrifying. My state of distress didn't make sense.

But I felt it anyway.

It made an uncomfortable pressure bloom between my legs. My cheeks warmed and I tried not to squirm in my seat. I hated it when this happened. Sometimes my hyper-sensitivity triggered an inexplicable sense of arousal. It was like my body went on high alert and everything—and I mean everything—responded. It was so embarrassing to feel suddenly turned on by nothing.

Taking a deep breath, I did my best to ignore the feeling. I glanced at the napkin in my hands, twisted into a narrow strip. Like a rope.

Rope... A series of murders occur across a large area, all with one thing in common. Strangulation. The victims have no apparent connection to each other. How is the killer choosing them? Who will be next? What clues are left behind that might point the investigators in the right direction? Is it a vigilante? Does it dredge up unresolved issues from childhood trauma for the investigator on the case? How does—

The door opened, jarring me from my thoughts. It was someone on a mobility scooter, the kind you'd find in a grocery store, with a roomy wire basket in front.

Wait, Gavin was driving.

Oh my god. Had he hurt himself again and now he couldn't walk?

I sprang from my chair. "Gavin, what happened?"

His scooter burst forward, then he jerked to a stop just shy of hitting a table.

He grinned at me. "Hey, Sky."

"Did you hurt your other leg? Where are your crutches?"

"No, I'm fine. I left them at Nature's Basket."

"Why would you leave your crutches at the grocery store?"

"Because I borrowed this." He gestured to the scooter. "I figure if I'm going to show you around town, it'll be easier if I don't have to walk on crutches the whole time."

"I don't think those are meant to be borrowed off premises."

"I left a note. I'm sure it's fine. Are you ready?"

"Um..."

"You can bring your coffee."

"That's okay, I'm finished, but—"

He put the scooter in reverse, and it started beeping. I glanced around the shop. A few people were watching him with irritated expressions. I winced, wondering if I should apologize.

"Hey Sky, can you get the door?"

"Oh, yeah."

I held the door open while he struggled to turn the scooter around. There wasn't much room between the tables. After a few starts and stops, he just backed up through the opening, beeping the entire way.

"This thing is harder to drive than I thought it would be."

I laughed. "Sorry. I'm not laughing at you."

"You're totally laughing at me, but that's okay." He backed up a few inches, straightened the wheels, and moved forward again. "I think I'm getting it now. Do you want to ride with me?"

I had a sudden vision of straddling Gavin's lap on the scooter. Sliding my leg over one side and settling on top of him. Feeling the pressure of the bulge in his pants pressing between my legs.

"No. No, I'll walk," I said quickly.

"Okay. Let me know if you change your mind. Your shoes are cute, but if your feet get tired, you can totally hop on."

Hop on Gavin Bailey? God, why did that make me think of sex? That wasn't what he meant, and I was sure he wasn't thinking about sex. A little burst of tingles between my legs almost made me clench my thighs together.

I nervously tucked my hair behind my ear. "Thanks. I'm sure I'll be fine."

"Okay. Tilikum town tour commencing." He gestured to the coffee shop behind me. "That's the Steaming Mug, of course. Grace runs it."

"It's nice. Good coffee."

"Yeah, and it's a great place to meet girls." He winked, those dimples of his puckering in his cheeks.

"Good to know."

He grinned and pulled ahead, so I took a few quick steps to follow.

"Across the street is Bigfoot Diner. They're open for breakfast and lunch. Best pancakes in town." He pointed to another restaurant a block over. "That's the Copper Kettle Diner. We don't go there."

"Let me guess. That's a Haven restaurant?"

"Yup. So it's a no-go when you're on the Bailey side."

"And hanging out with you puts me on the Bailey side, I suppose."

"The Stanleys have always been on the Bailey side. But yeah, hanging out with me does it too. Especially since we're being seen together in public." He lifted his hand and waved to two men standing outside the Copper Kettle. "Hey, Theo. Garrett."

Both men scowled at him.

"Nice ride," one of them said, his sarcasm clear as day.

"Thanks. Did you enjoy your donuts?"

"Fuck off, Gavin," the other one said.

I took an involuntary step backward, although neither of them seemed interested in coming over here. They turned their backs on us and went into the diner.

"What was that about?"

Gavin gave an amused chuckle. "That was Garrett and Theo Haven. We sent them donuts filled with mayonnaise the other day. It's the second time we've done it, but judging by the looks on their faces, they forgot to check before eating them."

"Gross."

"It's a classic."

We made our way up the sidewalk and Gavin pointed out businesses and places of interest. Like I'd told Ginny, there were two of most things. Some were near each other, like the two diners. Others had streets or blocks separating them, like the two beauty salons. There wasn't any rhyme or reason to it. No dividing line that kept the two sides of the feud separate. Just places some people frequented, or didn't frequent, according to their loyalty.

Gavin seemed to know just about everybody. He charmed his way through town with his easygoing smile. Waved to people across the street. Said hello to those who were close enough. We stopped for a moment so Doris Tilburn—a woman who looked to be in her sixties and owner of the Angel Cakes Bakery—could sign his cast.

A group of squirrels scattered outside Happy Paws, the

pet supply store, when we approached. Gavin peeked in and waved to someone inside.

"You really do know everyone, don't you?" I asked.

"More or less." He jerked forward as he brought the scooter to a stop. "You sure you don't want a ride?"

I'd have to sit on his lap, which was oddly tempting.

I settle onto his lap and drape my arms around his shoulders. He hooks an arm around my waist and his hand slides up to cup my breast while our mouths meet for a deep kiss—

Oh god, I was doing it again.

"You okay?" Gavin asked.

"Yes, fine. Sorry. This sweater is just a little warm. I thought it would be colder outside. Are you warm?"

He shrugged. "I'm comfortable."

"It's probably just me."

He smiled, and for a half a second, I almost did climb in his lap.

"Shall we continue?" he asked.

"Yes. Lead the way."

We kept walking and the large pinup girl statue outside the Dame and Dapper Barber Shop caught my eye. She was dressed in a skimpy red dress and fishnet stockings, and she had a large handlebar mustache and pointy beard.

"What's that?" I asked, pointing to her.

"Oh, that's Lola. Haven't you ever seen Lola?"

"I've seen her, although I didn't know she had a name. But why does she have facial hair?"

"Yeah, I wouldn't know anything about that."

The way he said that made me think he knew everything about it.

A man in a white apron stood in the Dame and Dapper doorway. Crossing his arms, he leveled a glare at Gavin.

"Hey, Bruce," Gavin said. "I like Lola's new look."

He narrowed his eyes and shook his head, muttering something under his breath.

Gavin chuckled as we moved past.

A little farther down the street, we came to the Zany Zebra, a burger and ice cream place painted with white and black zebra stripes. For the first time since I'd gotten into town, a strong childhood memory came back to me.

"I think Dad used to take me for ice cream there," I said. "It was back when he had an old convertible. We used to go for long drives and I think we'd come through town and get ice cream."

"That's awesome," Gavin said. "They have great ice cream. We can get some if you want."

"No, I'm good. But thanks."

We kept going and Gavin stopped again, right across from the Caboose.

"And here's where an unsuspecting firefighter, fresh off the front lines of a wildfire, was tragically injured."

"Because he stepped into the street without looking both ways."

He grinned. "Touché. Although my story's funnier."

"What's funny about being hit by a car and breaking your leg?"

"What isn't funny about it? I survived a fire shelter deployment only to get hit by a car. It's hilarious."

I laughed softly. "I guess that's one way to look at it."

"Are you hungry?"

"I am, actually."

He gestured to the Caboose. "Should we go grab some food?"

"Yeah, that sounds good."

He grinned again and that smile was not helping ease the tingling between my legs.

The scooter beeped as he backed up and maneuvered it so he could cross the street. "I think I'm getting better at this. Okay, you see me looking both ways this time, right?" He looked right, then left, then right again.

"Yes, I think we're clear."

"Can't be too careful. There are some crazy drivers around here." He glanced at me. "Although I guess I'm safe, since you're here with me and not behind the wheel."

I laughed again and it occurred to me I hadn't laughed this much in... I didn't know how long. After several years dating a man who almost never smiled, let alone laughed, the contrast was striking.

"Very funny," I said wryly.

"I'm just messing with you." He winked at me again. "Let's go.

10

GAVIN

_G_etting to a table in the Caboose wasn't easy. Maybe I should have gone back for my crutches first. I left the scooter in a parking spot and managed to lean on things and hop my way inside, then to a booth. I'd figure out how to get back outside when the time came. No big deal.

Skylar sat across from me and smoothed down her hair. It was hard not to stare at her. She had delicate features— high cheekbones, cute nose, a sweet mouth. The Stanleys had Native blood in their family, like we did, and it showed in Skylar, especially in her deep brown eyes, olive skin, and straight dark hair.

She was really fucking pretty.

Smelled good too. Every time she got close, I caught her scent. It was sensual and warm. Made me feel a bit like I'd taken a long swallow of whiskey.

But that was the kind of thinking that was going to get me in trouble.

It wasn't just that I'd told Chief I'd stick to being friends —that I wouldn't sneak a cookie from the cookie jar. Skylar had her defenses up, big time. I had a feeling she'd been hurt, and maybe that was why she was here in town. As fun as it would have been to see what it took to get past those defenses, I was strangely reluctant to go there.

Which was very weird and unlike me. Normally I couldn't resist a challenge. But it was like my danger instinct was telling me to chill out with her.

Still, I liked her. Which was why this *be her friend* thing was the best idea I'd had in a while. Even if my dick wanted different things.

"If you like onion rings, they're really good here," I said.

"I do like onion rings."

The server came over and we placed our orders— cheeseburgers with a side of onion rings for both of us.

"What made you want to become a writer?" I asked after the server left.

"I've been writing stories since I was a kid. It's just something I love to do. Although I guess when I was a kid, I wasn't writing about serial killers."

"Your parents might have worried if you were."

She smiled. She was so pretty when she did that. "Yeah, they would have. What about you? Did you always want to be a firefighter?"

"Oh yeah, since I was little. I debated between this and the Coast Guard, but being a firefighter meant I could stay in Tilikum, so firefighter it is. What made you start writing about serial killers?"

"I guess it started as a way to cope with my fears. I'm a pretty anxious person, but writing lets me create worlds where I can face scary things in a safe way."

"Why? What are you afraid of?"

She shrugged. "Everything?"

"Come on, you're not really afraid of everything."

"No, I guess not. I'm not even afraid of specific things, necessarily. I just get anxious a lot."

"So you're not afraid of something like heights?"

"No, I'm terrified of heights."

"That's a specific thing."

"True. But being afraid of heights doesn't impact my life very much. It's easy to avoid."

"Then what are you scared of that's hard to avoid?"

"Why are you so interested in my fears?"

I shrugged. "Because I'm interested in you."

Her dark eyes held mine for a moment. Made my heart beat a little harder. She was so intense. Like there was a lot more going on in her head than she let other people see.

"People make me nervous, especially if I don't know them. I never know what to say and I worry about what they're thinking and whether I look stupid or they think I'm crazy or weird. I get anxious when I go somewhere new. I worry about getting lost or something unexpected happening and being unprepared or not knowing what to do. I don't like feeling uncertain." She glanced away again. "What are you afraid of?"

"Nothing."

Her eyebrows drew together. "Everyone's afraid of something."

"Maybe I am and I just haven't found it yet. But so far, nope. I don't get scared."

"Ever?"

"I don't think so."

"You're a firefighter. Haven't you ever been in a situation that scared you?"

"No. I've been in dangerous situations plenty of times, but I wasn't afraid. I get amped up on adrenaline a lot, but I don't think that's the same as fear. It doesn't make me want to run away. It makes me want to dive in head first."

"Into a fire?"

I smiled. "Not if I can help it. But if I have to, I will."

"Without fear."

"Yeah. When shit hits the fan, my instincts are sharp. Things get very clear. It's almost like I know what's going to happen, so I know I don't have to worry."

"You didn't know you were going to get hit by a car." Her mouth twitched in a smile.

"No, that one caught me by surprise. I can't claim I never get myself into trouble, or never get hurt. I've probably broken more bones than all my brothers combined."

"Well, fear does serve a purpose. It keeps us out of danger."

"Sometimes. And sometimes it just gets in the way."

"I'm afraid I'll never write another book." She clapped her hand over her mouth, eyes widening. Taking a deep breath, she lowered her hand. "I don't know why I just told you that."

"Why are you afraid you won't write another book?"

"Because I haven't written much of anything in months. Nothing usable. I keep going from idea to idea, starting new things and never getting anywhere with them."

"Why?"

"That's the problem, I don't know. I've never been so blocked before. Writing was always challenging work, it wasn't like it was effortless and suddenly it got hard and I can't handle it. But I sit down to write and there's just... nothing."

"Is that why you moved out here? To see if it would help you write?"

She hesitated for a moment. "Mostly, yes. But I'm afraid that maybe this is permanent."

"It's definitely not permanent."

"How do you know?"

"Because it doesn't make sense that it would be. You don't just forget how to write books when you've already done it... how many times?"

"Twelve."

"You've written twelve entire novels?"

She smiled again, and man, I really liked making her do that.

"Yes. But my last book didn't sell as well as the publisher wanted, so they dropped me. I don't even have anyone to publish another book if I actually manage to write one."

"Is that why you're blocked? Because your publisher dropped you?"

"You'd think so, but no. It started before that happened."

"That sucks."

"I know, that would at least be an answer."

Our food came and the conversation turned to other things while we ate. I asked her about growing up in Spokane and where she'd gone to college. And I told her some stories about working with her dad. She was so easy to talk to, it felt like we'd known each other forever.

After we finished, I hopped my way outside, back to the mobility scooter. This thing sure had come in handy. It was kind of a pain to drive, but it was better than walking all over town on one leg.

I tried to turn it on, but nothing happened.

"Uh oh."

"What's wrong?"

"I think the battery died."

Well this was inconvenient. We were all the way across

town from Nature's Basket. I couldn't walk very far without my crutches, and I'd left those there.

"Do you want me to walk to my car and come get you? Or go get your crutches? Or go get help?"

"I don't want to make you do that. I can call someone to pick us up."

Evan had a truck. He could run into town, pick us up, and help me get the scooter back to the grocery store. I pulled up Evan's number and hit send.

"What do you want, Gav?"

"Hey, how's it going?"

"I'm working."

"Cool, then you probably need a break."

"No."

"You sure about that? You work a lot."

He didn't reply.

"Look, I just need a ride."

"No."

"Come on, bro. The scooter I took from Nature's Basket ran out of batteries and—"

"Do you have an actual problem, or a Gavin problem?"

"An actual Gavin problem."

"I have to get back to work."

"But Evan—"

He ended the call.

"Such a dick," I muttered.

Logan was on duty, so he was no help. I didn't know what Asher was doing today. Probably coaching. But Levi was off. I didn't really want to call Levi. He'd give me a harder time than Evan. But I was kind of out of options, so angry twin it was.

"Yeah?" he answered.

"Hey, bro. I have an issue."

"What?"

"So you know how I'm hanging out with Skylar and showing her around town?"

"No…"

"Yes you do, I told you. Anyway, I borrowed one of the scooter cart things from Nature's Basket and it kind of ran out of batteries and I'm on the other side of town and can't get it back to return it. And I really need to return it. I left a note saying I would."

"Jesus, Gav."

"Can you come get us?"

"Why the hell did you take a scooter from Nature's Basket?"

"Because I have a broken leg."

He was quiet for a long moment. "Where are you?"

"Caboose."

"Fine."

"Don't hang up yet."

"Why?"

"You should probably bring a ramp. To get the scooter in the back of your SUV."

"Why do you always do shit like this?"

"Like what?"

He groaned. "Skylar is stuck with you?"

"Yeah."

"Fine. But I'm only coming down there because of her."

"Whatever works, bro."

He ended the call and I slid my phone back in my pocket. "Problem solved. Levi's on the way."

We hung out in the Caboose parking lot waiting for Levi. It didn't take long for him to get here. He parked next to me and shot me a glare when he got out of his blue SUV.

I introduced Skylar to Levi and he said a polite hello. I

knew the only reason he wasn't giving me more shit was because she was here. He opened the back and pulled out a piece of plywood to use as a ramp.

Levi ran inside and got Hank, the Caboose owner, to come help him push the scooter into the back of his SUV. They got it loaded up—it fit, but only just—and I thanked him. Skylar stood off to the side, looking adorably nervous.

A woman pushing a stroller down the sidewalk slowed as she passed. I glanced at her, but looked away. It was Annika Haven, and I was highly conditioned to ignore her, and any other female Haven. I liked a challenge, and okay, sometimes I set my sights on a girl mostly because I couldn't have her—case in point, every teacher I'd ever crushed on. But going against the feud? That was different. Even I didn't like danger that much.

Besides, Annika had a kid. That was way too much adulting for me.

I caught Levi watching her. Not that I blamed him. Even though she was a Haven, Annika was hot.

I was loyal, not blind.

But I was still going to give him shit about staring at her. I was the youngest. Giving my big brothers shit was my place in the world.

I leaned close and lowered my voice. "Bro, I know she's a total MILF, but you should probably stop eye fucking her out in the open."

He whipped around to face me, rage burning hot in his eyes. It occurred to me that maybe I shouldn't push him too hard, considering I couldn't fight back if he decided to tackle me.

"Shut your mouth, Gav." The warning in his tone was unmistakable.

I liked giving him shit, but not too much shit. After all, he had come down here to help me out.

"Just messing with you." I clapped him on the shoulder. "Thanks again for coming. I'm pretty sure Skylar is strong enough to push the scooter back to the store, but that would have been hard on my ego." I winked at her.

"Whatever. You owe me."

"I totally do."

Levi drove us over to Nature's Basket. The manager, Ed Michaelson, came out and helped us get it out of the SUV. He'd gotten my note.

He rolled his eyes at me, but I was pretty sure we were cool.

After Levi left, I gave Skylar a ride back to the Steaming Mug where she'd left her car. I probably could have just let her out and gone home, but it was hard to tear myself away from her. So I got out and walked with her to where she'd parked, about a block from the coffee shop.

"Thanks for hanging out with me today," I said.

"You're welcome. Thanks for the tour."

"Anytime."

She smiled back and for a second, I got caught in her dark eyes.

Fuck, she was beautiful.

That *no* I was holding onto really wanted to switch sides and become a *yes*.

Go for it, Gav. Chase her. See if you can catch this one. It'll be fun.

It would be fun.

My eyes dropped to her mouth. I bet kissing her would feel amazing. And the way she was looking at me, with her chin tilted up, she'd probably let me.

But I couldn't ignore the buzzing in the back of my

brain, telling me to back off. It was like standing at the top of the slope looking down at the wildfire, and knowing it was going to turn.

So I pulled my gaze from her lips, tempting as they were.

"Have a good night," I said. "I'll text you?"

"Yeah. That would be great."

Walking away from her was harder than it should have been. If she'd been any other girl, I wouldn't have left her there. I'd have gone for it.

But she was Skylar Stanley, so that wasn't going to happen.

11

SKYLAR

My fingers rested on the keyboard, unmoving. I traced the familiar ridges on the F and J keys with the tips of my index fingers while I gazed out the window.

Lips. Full, soft lips. What would it be like to be kissed by those lips? Would he be rough, or gentle? Or maybe a delicious mix of both?

What would it feel like to be kissed by someone who really *wanted* to kiss me?

Sucking in a quick breath, I blinked at the screen. I'd written those words. God, what was wrong with me? I quickly backspaced to get rid of the errant sentence. I was supposed to be writing about a serial killer, not a woman pondering the nature of a man's kiss.

But after hanging out with Gavin yesterday, I was having a hard time thinking about anything else.

My mind kept drifting to the way he'd looked at my mouth when we were saying goodbye. That subtle dip of his attention had sent a cascade of tingles across my skin. Just thinking about it now gave me a twinge of pressure between my legs. And it wasn't the embarrassing hypersensitivity-induced arousal that tended to hit me at inopportune times. This was different.

Had he been thinking about kissing me? What would I have done if he had? If his mouth had followed his gaze and dropped to connect with mine. Would I have kissed him back?

I would have. Eagerly. And I didn't know how to feel about that.

Wanting to be kissed by a guy I barely knew was not normal Skylar behavior. I was firmly a take-it-slow and play-it-safe kind of person. I didn't open up to people easily, emotionally or physically. When I'd first started dating Cullen, I'd thought he was a good fit for me primarily because he was so patient. He hadn't pressured me to get physical with him right away. It had felt as if he were giving me time and space to get to know him first—time that I'd needed.

But how well had I really known him? It was clear now that I hadn't known him at all.

And here I was, daydreaming about kissing Gavin Bailey, a man I'd practically just met.

Stranger still, I wasn't just daydreaming about kissing him. I'd spent my morning daydreaming about doing a lot of things with Gavin, and kissing was merely the beginning.

That wasn't normal Skylar behavior either.

The desk Dad had set up for me in my bedroom looked out over the front yard. His house was on a quiet side street, not far from downtown Tilikum—and the firehouse, of course. This was a nice spot for writing. Peaceful. Not too many distractions, although the neighbor's little dog chasing the squirrels that ran across the fence was amusing.

Chasing. Running up the stairs with Gavin at my heels, his hands playfully grabbing for me. He slams the bedroom door behind us and immediately rips off my clothes—and his. Our mouths tangle as we fall onto the bed. His muscles flex as he crawls on top of me and—

A knock at the front door jolted me back to reality. I blew out a breath and picked up a notebook to quickly fan my face.

I went down the stairs with a little thrill of anticipation making my tummy flutter. I wasn't expecting Gavin, but what if he'd decided to drop by? That thought made me both excited and nervous.

Before I could get myself too worked up, I answered the door. It wasn't Gavin, but the little flare of disappointment was immediately tamped down by the smiling face on Dad's doorstep. Ginny.

She threw her arms around me and wrapped me in a tight hug. "Oh my god, I missed you so much."

I hugged her back. "I missed you too."

After a squeeze, she let go. Her brown hair was in a cute bun and she wore a light blue trench coat. "Are you okay? You seem surprised to see me."

"I was just... doing a little writing and I guess I lost track of where I was. I forgot you were getting into town today." I stepped aside and gestured for her to come in.

"You were writing?" She came in and I shut the door behind her. "Is that good news, or are you just going to delete it later?"

"I guess *writing* might be an exaggeration. I was staring out the window a lot." *And fantasizing about getting naked with a firefighter.* I led her back to the kitchen. "Do you want some tea?"

"Tea sounds great." She took her coat off and hung it on the back of a chair, then sat.

I eyed the plastic container of cookies Gavin had left. "Cookie?"

"Yum. Yes, please."

I put the tea kettle on and got us each a cookie on a little plate.

"Did you make these?"

"No. Um, remember Gavin Bailey, the guy I hit with my car?"

"The hot firefighter?"

I glanced away. "Yes, well, he made them."

"He brought you cookies?"

"Yes."

"Let me get this straight. You run over a hot firefighter and then he bakes you cookies?" She broke off a piece of cookie and popped it in her mouth. "Oh my god, that's good."

"I didn't run him over."

"I know. I'm being mildly dramatic like you were when you told me about your little accident. How is he, by the way?"

Distractingly sexy. "His leg is broken, so obviously that's impacting his life. He's on leave until he's out of his cast. The crutches are uncomfortable, but his leg itself isn't bothering him too much."

She raised her eyebrows. "That was a very detailed answer."

"Was it?"

"I thought you'd just say he's fine or something." She broke off another bite of cookie. "So he brought you cookies, and..."

"And, nothing. Well, we hung out a little bit yesterday. He was just showing me around town."

"Skylar Stanley, you went on a date with him and you didn't tell me?"

"No, no, no. It wasn't a date. I'm not dating."

"Why not?"

I blinked at her. "Is that a serious question? I'm fresh off a very shitty breakup and let's not talk about my career. I'm not exactly in a good place right now."

"Did he know it wasn't a date?"

"Of course he knew. He specifically said he wants to be friends."

"Hmm."

"Trust me. There's nothing going on with me and Gavin. How was the drive out here?"

"I hear you changing the subject, but I'll allow it. The drive was fine. Beautiful, actually."

"How long do you think you'll be in town?"

"A few weeks at least, but my schedule is pretty open, so I'm flexible. How's your mom?"

"She's fine, although she's been weirdly busy lately. Seems distracted when we talk on the phone." The tea kettle whistled and just as I got up, someone knocked on the front door.

"I'll do that, you go get the door," Ginny said.

"Thanks."

I left her to make the tea and answered the door. As soon as I opened it, my stomach did a belly flop. It was Gavin.

"Hey, Sky."

The sight of him hit me like a lightning strike. "Hey. Come in."

He grinned at me, dimples and all. "Thanks."

His gait was a rhythmic click, thud, click, thud. Crutches, shoe, crutches, shoe. Every step made my heart flutter in my chest.

Ginny put the mugs of tea on the table, her eyebrows raised.

"Oh sorry," Gavin said. "I didn't realize you had someone over. I'm Gavin Bailey."

"Ginny Vandervelden."

"I can come back later if you—"

"No," Ginny said brightly, cutting him off. "You're fine. Come on in."

He grinned at her and a strange sense of panic flared in my chest. Not only was Ginny beautiful, she was outgoing and friendly in ways I was not. She was also available in ways I wasn't—single, and more importantly, open to dating. What if Gavin liked her? Not just liked her, but *liked* her.

Why was that thought so awful? Gavin and I were just friends. And barely that, we'd practically just met.

He leaned his crutches against the wall, then hopped to the table on his good leg and pulled out a chair. His arms flexed as he lowered himself into it. "Did you just get into town?"

Ginny took her seat. "I did. It's cute. I can't wait to explore."

I braced myself for Gavin to offer to show her the town, like he'd done for me. Which was fine. Wasn't it? Why wouldn't it be?

Because then you weren't special.

"It's not too big, so it's pretty easy to find your way around," Gavin said. "But if you need any recommendations, let me know."

My eyes flicked from Gavin to Ginny. No tour? No offer to be her friend and steal a mobility scooter from the grocery store so he could show her around?

"Thanks," Ginny said. "I just might take you up on that."

I realized I was still standing next to the table like a

weirdo, not offering him any refreshments even though Ginny and I had ours. "I made tea. Do you want some? Or a cookie? I have a few left."

"I'll always say yes to a cookie."

I got him a cookie out of the container, then took a seat and slid my tea over to my spot. I glanced at him, wishing I could think of something to say. But all I could seem to think about was his mouth and what it would feel like to kiss him.

His gaze moved to my lips, just for a second, but it was enough to make my heart flutter again.

"Sky, how's the book coming?" he asked. "Are you still blocked?"

Blocked. Distracted by you. Maybe both. "Yeah, still struggling."

"Man, that's rough. I'm sure you'll figure it out, though."

"Thanks. Do you know when you get to go back to work?"

"When I get the cast off. Hopefully the doctor will put me in one of those boot things. Then I'll at least be able to walk and I can be on light duty."

"You must be looking forward to it."

"Yeah, I am." His eyes held mine again and for a second, I forgot anyone else was here. "So, I came over to see if you wanted to go for a walk down by the river, but since you're busy, maybe we could do that another time?"

My gaze flicked to Ginny—she wiggled her eyebrows at me—then back to Gavin. "That sounds great."

"Okay. I should quit bugging you. You two probably want to hang out." He got to his feet and leaned on his crutches. "Nice to meet you, Ginny."

"You too."

"See you, Sky. I'll text you."

He walked down the hallway and I followed so I could open the door for him. He gave me another smile as he walked out the door.

I went back to the kitchen feeling a little dazed.

Ginny's eyes were huge. "Oh my god. Oh. My. God. You admitted he was hot, but I was not prepared for that."

"He is, isn't he?" I sank down onto my chair.

"And he's super into you."

"What? No he's not."

"Are you blind? Yes, he is."

"He could just as easily be into you."

She laughed. "Oh honey. He's not. Trust me. He wasn't rude or anything, but you were the only one in the room."

"I guess."

"And he calls you Sky? How cute is that? Even the asshole-who-shall-no-longer-be-named didn't call you Sky."

I did like it when he called me Sky. It seemed like an obvious nickname, but everyone in my life had always called me Skylar. The way Sky sounded on Gavin's lips...

His lips on my neck. And his tongue. He licks my skin like I'm dessert and he wants to spoil every meal—

Ginny tilted her head. "Hey, sweetie. You still here?"

I blinked, coming back to myself. "Sorry."

"More dead bodies appearing in that head of yours?"

"No. I mean, yes."

"You're such a liar."

"I know."

"He's hot as sin. There's nothing wrong with imagining what it would be like to have him put out your fire."

I laughed. "I wasn't—"

She cut me off with a look.

"Fine, I was. But I have to get that out of my head."

"Why?" She put up a hand. "I know, you just got out of a

long-term relationship and everybody says rebounds are bad. Just for the record, I disagree with that, as long as you're not trying to replace an ex with just any warm body. If you happen to meet someone shortly after a breakup, and you have actual chemistry, it doesn't mean you have to blow them off because you haven't gone through some arbitrary period of mourning."

"I'm just not sure if I'm ready."

"That's fair too. There's also nothing wrong with having a little fun with a hot firefighter. It doesn't have to be serious."

I laughed again. "You're implying that having a little fun with Gavin is even an option. I have no reason to believe he sees me like that."

"That's because you're in denial." She took a casual sip of tea.

"No, I'm not."

"That's exactly what a person in denial would say."

"Okay fine, I'll be honest. I'm attracted to him. And I don't mean I think he's nice-looking and a coffee date would be pleasant. I mean every time I'm around him, and even when I'm not, I can't stop thinking about all the dirty things I want him to do to me." My cheeks flushed hot. "I can't believe I just said that out loud. Even to you."

"You can always admit those things to me. What are best friends for?"

"Yeah. You know me, I embarrass too easily."

"Skylar. Stop apologizing for being who you are. You're reserved and you like quiet places and you blush at the mere mention of dick. I love all those things about you."

"Thanks." I paused for a moment. "Gavin scares me."

"I bet he does." She took a sip of her tea. "Do you want my advice?"

"Absolutely."

"Don't stress about it. Just let things unfold and see what happens. Maybe you guys will stay friends. But he also dropped by just to see you, so I still say he's into you."

I wrapped my hands around the warm mug. I had a lot of feelings about all this, but maybe Ginny was right. I had enough going on in my life, I didn't need to stress about how I felt about Gavin Bailey—or how he felt about me.

As for what to do about the increasingly dirty daydreams? That was another story.

12

GAVIN

*M*y stomach was so full it was making me sleepy. I stretched out my broken leg, leaned back in my chair, and crossed my arms. The conversation at Gram's big farmhouse table drifted past me. I was too drowsy to pay close attention to what everyone was talking about.

It was Tuesday, which meant Bailey family dinner. And a too-full-to-function Gavin. But Gram had made pork chops and potatoes, so who could blame me for stuffing my face? Her cooking was the best.

Asher and Grace sat across from me, and Fiona and Evan were on my left. Levi and Logan were both off duty tonight, so they were here too. And Gram sat in her usual spot.

If any more of us brought someone home, Gram was going to need a bigger table.

Not that it was likely. Logan didn't exactly date girls you brought home to meet your family. And Levi didn't date at all, as far as I knew. Or if he did, he kept quiet about it.

What was Skylar doing tonight?

That was a weird thought to have out of nowhere.

I peeked at my phone just in case she'd texted me. She hadn't, which was oddly disappointing, since I wasn't expecting her to. But I hadn't seen her today and I was kind of bummed about that.

Actually, I was *a lot* bummed about that.

But her friend was in town, so she was busy.

And okay, I was kind of pouting because I'd been hoping to do something with her today.

"So are we going to talk about it, or just pretend it isn't today?" Asher asked.

His question got my attention, because like everyone else in this room—with the possible exception of Fiona, unless Evan had told her—I knew exactly what he was talking about.

It was our mom's birthday.

"Mom's birthday," Levi said, echoing my thought.

The table quieted, like it always did when we acknowledged our parents. I kept my eyes on my empty plate, bracing myself for the inevitable. For everyone to start talking about them.

I hated it when they did that.

"How old would she have been this year?" Logan asked.

"Fifty-four," Gram said.

"Do you guys remember when Dad threw her a big birthday party?" Asher asked.

"Vaguely," Evan said.

I didn't. I'd probably been a baby.

"I just remember bits and pieces of it," Asher said. "I think Dad put trick candles on her cake."

"He did," Gram said with a soft smile. "By the time she realized they were going to keep lighting after she blew them out, she was laughing too hard to try."

"I remember how much they smiled," Grace said. "They always seemed so happy."

"They were," Gram said. "Their love was big. For each other and for their boys."

I shifted uncomfortably in my seat, hoping they'd change the subject.

"The thing I remember most is her reading to us," Logan said. "It's not a clear memory, but it seems like she did that a lot."

Levi nodded. "I remember that, too. I think she did."

"On the couch before bed," Evan said. "And we'd fight over who got to sit next to her. Except Gavin. He sat on her lap."

"Oh yeah," Logan said, his mouth twitching with a smile.

I didn't say anything. Because I didn't remember any of it.

I didn't remember them.

When they'd died, Asher had been nine, Evan around eight. The twins had been six. All old enough to form lasting memories of our parents, even if they were only vague ones. Even Grace remembered them. But I'd been four—too young to keep any of those memories.

I knew what they'd looked like, but only because I'd seen pictures. I knew stories about them, but only the things I'd been told. None of it lived in my head. I couldn't conjure a single image of my mother or my father. Not even one.

And I hated that I was the only one who couldn't.

Still, I didn't want to be an asshole about it. So whenever this happened, and everyone seemed to need to talk about them, I just kept my mouth shut until it was over.

Tonight, though, the subject made me fidget. My leg itched inside my cast and my ass hurt from the way I'd been sitting. I shifted in my chair again.

Asher kissed the back of Grace's hand. Fiona leaned against Evan's shoulder. Logan glanced at Levi and he nodded, as if Logan had said something out loud—but he hadn't. Silent acknowledgments of shared grief, and shared comfort.

I didn't have anything to add and my mood was quickly turning shitty. Which meant it was time for me to go.

"We'll take care of your plate, Otter," Gram said.

She was such a mind reader.

"Thanks." I pushed myself to my feet and hopped to where I'd leaned my crutches against the wall. "I'll see you guys later."

"You heading home?" Levi asked.

"Yeah. Eventually."

"You okay, brocamole?" Logan asked.

"Other than my leg itching, yeah." I went over to Gram and leaned down to give her a kiss on the cheek. "Thanks for dinner. I'm stuffed."

"Have a good night, Otter," she said. "Be careful out there."

"I'm always careful."

Logan snorted.

I'd have flipped him off, but there was no way to do that without Gram seeing. "Later."

I went out to my truck and climbed in. My body thrummed with restlessness. Dissatisfaction. I was no stranger to this feeling, but normally when I got this edgy I was able to do something about it—do something with the excess energy coursing through me.

I'd jump in the river or off a waterfall. Go rock climbing, or ice climbing in the winter. Maybe grab Logan or some friends and see what kind of trouble we could get into in town. Have a few beers, maybe pick up some girls.

None of that was working for me right now, either because I physically couldn't—stupid broken leg—or because it just didn't sound like any fun.

I really was in a shitty mood if going into town, getting a few beers, and picking up girls didn't sound like fun.

My whole body ached with the desire to move. To climb and sweat and balance on the edge of... anything. I was the shark again, swimming too slowly to stay alive.

Drowning.

I couldn't climb anything right now, but I could still get around—sort of. I drove out to where the old railroad tracks crossed through town. They were long abandoned—no more trains chugged through Tilikum like they had in the old days. Which made it a good place for a flat hike.

It was dark, and there was a chance I might come across a wild animal. Not exactly ideal conditions, but maybe that was why I'd come out here. I needed to do something, and if I couldn't do any of my usual things, an after dusk walk down the train tracks by myself scratched at least some of that itch.

Gravel crunched as I walked alongside the track, the only noise in the dark stillness. It was getting colder, especially at night, and the chill air tickled my nose.

Movement on the other side of the tracks caught my eye. There was something over there, near the trees. Small, though. It didn't seem big enough to be a raccoon, but maybe it was a baby. Which wouldn't exactly be good news. Mama raccoons were vicious when they were protecting their young.

It was possible I knew that from experience.

I got out my phone to use as a flashlight, shining the beam of light into the trees.

A squirrel sat at the base of a tree, its gray tail standing up like a bushy little flagpole. That was weird. I didn't think squirrels were nocturnal.

It came closer, then stopped on the track. I didn't know why it would be out after dark, but it probably associated humans with food.

"I don't have anything, dude."

It darted ahead, following the track, then stopped and looked back at me.

I felt like I was about to be pranked. Why else would a squirrel be out at night, acting like it wanted me to follow?

Because it was really acting like it wanted me to follow.

Had Fiona trained this one? She'd trained the squirrels out at Evan's house to go through an obstacle course. That had come in handy when we'd loosed Tilikum's squirrel population on the Timberbeast Tavern—the Havens' hangout—after they'd pulled off an admittedly spectacular prank involving goats, peanut butter, and bird seed.

But no one had told me to come down here, so how could they have set up a squirrel prank aimed at me?

Still, this was weird.

But obviously I was going to follow it.

As soon as I started moving again, it ran along the rail, disappearing into the darkness ahead.

"This is fast as I go, buddy."

When I caught up, he'd gotten off the track and waited about six feet away, on the far side. Careful not to trip over the rail or wood beams, I crossed the tracks.

He darted away and ran up a tree.

Shaking my head, I laughed at myself. A random squirrel was running around in the dark and I'd thought he was leading me somewhere.

In my defense, Tilikum squirrels weren't normal. He could have been leading me somewhere.

A tiny noise caught my attention, so faint I wasn't sure I'd actually heard anything. I held my breath. There it was again.

I moved closer to the trees. Whatever it was, it was low to the ground. I shined the light around, looking. Because it almost sounded like—

A pair of eyes glowed bright when my light moved past. Cat eyes.

Kitten eyes, to be exact.

It was curled up in a small hollow at the base of a tree, but it wasn't much of a shelter. It mewed at me—a tiny sound that tugged at something in my chest.

I swept the light around, looking for any sign of the mother cat or the rest of the litter. But the kitten was alone.

"Hey, little one." I leaned my crutches against the tree and crouched down. "Are you all by yourself out here?"

The kitten crept out of the hole to sniff my outstretched fingers. Its fur was dirty. I didn't know a lot about cats, but I knew if this kitten had a mom, it would be cleaner than this.

I scooped it up and peeked under the tail. Pretty sure it was a girl.

Jesus, she weighed nothing. Just a scrap of fur in my hand.

Her little mews sounded like she was crying now, so I tucked her against my chest and gently rubbed the top of her head with my thumb.

"Shh. You're okay."

Obviously I was taking her with me.

I couldn't carry her and walk with my crutches, so I slipped her into my front coat pocket. It was high on my chest and just big enough that her skinny little body fit inside with her head poking out. Hoping she wouldn't jump out, I grabbed my crutches and started back toward my truck.

Maybe the squirrel had been leading me somewhere after all.

"You need a mommy, don't you little snuggle nugget? Well, now you have one."

The kitten settled into my pocket, her tiny mews quieting. Did Skylar like cats? Not that she needed to like cats for me to have one, but it made me wonder. I kind of wanted to go straight to her house to show her.

Okay, I *really* wanted to go straight to her house to show her.

Mostly because now that I was thinking about her again, I wanted to see her. And that strange preoccupation made me hesitate. Besides, it was late. We'd hang out again sometime—hopefully soon—and I could introduce her to my new baby.

For now, I'd get this little squeaker home.

13

GAVIN

The kitten's tiny claws pinched my skin as she climbed up my shirt. I gave her a hand, helping her settle on my shoulder. She liked it up there, and she was so small I barely noticed her, except for the slight tickle of fur against my neck.

She'd spent the night curled up in bed with me, happily purring. I'd taken her to the vet first thing this morning. Dr. Lennox had said she was lucky I'd found her. She was barely old enough to be away from her mom. They'd cleaned her up—turned out she was black and white—and given me special food for her. Other than being tiny and hungry, she seemed to be in good health. She just needed to put a little weight on and she should be okay.

Levi walked in and stopped in his tracks. "What's that?"

"What's what?" I asked around a bite of cereal.

"Is that an animal?"

"She's a kitten. I found her by the train tracks."

"You brought a stray cat home?"

"What was I supposed to do? Leave her out there?"

He eyed her, his brow furrowing. "No. But you don't think you're keeping her, do you?"

"Of course I'm keeping her. She needs a mommy."

"A *mommy*?"

I just took another bite of cereal.

"I don't think we're supposed to have pets in this house."

"Who has a pet?" Logan came out of his room looking rumpled, like he'd just woken up.

"Gavin brought home a stray cat."

Logan stopped and looked around. "Seriously? Where?"

"She's sleeping," I said. "Don't wake her up, you guys, she's been through a lot."

"What are you going to do with it?" Logan asked, peering at the kitten on my shoulder.

"That's a weird question," I said. "I'm going to take care of her. I'm her cat mom."

"I think you mean cat dad."

I rolled my eyes. "No, I mean cat mom. According to Google, it's primarily the female cat who cares for her kittens. The cat dad might help her out, but it's just as likely that he won't. My little squeaker here doesn't need a cat dad, she needs a cat mom."

"Dude, having a pet is a big responsibility," Levi said. "She needs a litter box and veterinary care and—"

"Way ahead of you. Took her to the vet this morning and picked up a litter box on the way home. But thanks for the tip."

"I'm just saying—"

"You're just saying you don't think I can handle taking care of a kitten."

"That is what it sounded like," Logan said.

"Do you think he can take care of a kitten?" Levi asked, gesturing to me.

Logan shrugged. "Probably not."

"See?"

I glared at them both. "You guys realize I'm no longer ten, right?"

"You've just never had to take care of anything besides yourself," Levi said.

"And let's be real, your track record there is questionable," Logan added, gesturing to my leg.

"Whatever, Chip and Dale. I've got this."

Levi glanced at Logan. "Apparently we have a cat now."

"Are we allergic to cats?" Logan asked.

"I'm not," Levi said.

"Well if you're not, I'm not."

I shook my head and shoveled more cereal into my mouth. The kitten rubbed her head against my neck and I reached up to give her a little pet with my index finger.

"Gram said her furnace was making a weird noise, so I'm heading over there to check it out," Levi said.

Logan dropped into a chair and raked his fingers through his messy hair. "Need help?"

"No, I've got it."

"Cool. I told Chief I'd come in and help with a training exercise," Logan said.

I grunted, mildly jealous. Chief usually had me come in to help with training exercises. Stupid broken leg.

"What are you doing today?" Logan asked. "Other than being a cat mom?"

"I don't know. I have an appointment with Sven, but that's it."

"Who's Sven?"

"Cara's massage therapist."

"Wait, what?"

I poked at my cereal with my spoon. "I'm getting a massage by a guy with magic hands. Cara set it up for me."

"Who said he has magic hands? Cara?"

"Yeah. I guess he does Grace, too. He's supposed to be really good."

"What the fuck? Does Asher know about this?"

"That his wife got a massage?"

"No, that a fucking guy named Sven was touching her."

"I don't know. Probably. It's a massage, bro, those are a thing."

Scowling, he glanced away.

The corner of my mouth twitched in a grin. "Are you jealous?"

"Jealous that you're getting a massage? If I want a massage, I can go get one. I don't need some dude named Sven."

"No, are you jealous that Sven gives Cara massages?"

"Why the fuck would I be jealous of that? He's taking his life into his own hands, but that's his problem, not mine."

I laughed. "Come on, bro. We both know she's not actually evil."

"No, she is actually evil."

The kitten stretched out a paw, so I reached up to make sure she didn't tumble off my shoulder. "I think she's just misunderstood."

He snort-laughed.

I knew I was risking life and limb by poking at him about this, but I couldn't resist. Besides, I had a broken leg and I was holding a kitten. There was no way he'd tackle me right now.

"Okay, but real talk, you'd totally bang her."

"Fuck no, I wouldn't."

"Wait, have you already?"

"No."

I actually believed him, but this was too much fun. "Yes you have. That's why you guys hate each other so much. You fucked once and got under each other's skin."

"No we fucking did not."

"You sure about that? You hate her a lot for a guy who hasn't been in her pants."

"What the fuck does that have to do with anything?" His face reddened. "I can't stand her because the very sight of her pisses me off, not because I fucked her once."

"Okay, sure."

"It's true."

"Yeah, I believe you."

His nostrils flared and if I hadn't been holding the kitten and had a broken leg, he would have wrestled me to the ground by now for sure. "Fuck off, Gav."

"So touchy. You know, you could do a lot worse than Cara."

"No, she's the literal worst." He stood abruptly, pushing his chair back. "I need a shower."

"If Sven does a good job, do you want his number? You seem stressed, I bet a massage would be good for you."

"Shut the fuck up."

I snickered as he walked down the hall toward the bathroom.

"You're lucky your leg is broken, asshole," he called over his shoulder.

"I know." I petted the kitten again. "I'm lucky I have you, too, aren't I?"

The rest of the day stretched out in front of me, alarmingly empty. I needed to go to Happy Paws and get some cat toys, and I had that appointment with Sven. But other than that, I didn't have much going on.

Maybe Skylar was free. I texted her to find out.

Me: *Hey Sky. What are you up to today?*

Skylar: *I'm writing. Or trying to.*

Damn. If she was working, I should leave her alone. That was no fun.

Me: *If you want to do something later, let me know.*

Skylar: *Okay.*

Her non-committal answer tempted me like a playground dare. I had the urge to text her back—relentlessly, if necessary—until she agreed to hang out with me.

But that was a *Gavin on the prowl* move. Not a *Gavin's just her friend* move.

Although would it be so bad if I applied my usual tactics to a friendship? Or would that take me into *chasing her* territory?

This was so weird. I had friends who were girls, so I knew guy/girl friendships were doable. I'd been friends with Grace my entire life. I was friends with Cara and Fiona. There were other girls I hung out with sometimes who were just friends—girls I hadn't dated and didn't intend to. And okay, maybe I flirted with them a lot, but that was just for fun—or in the case of Fiona, to get a rise out of my brother. When it came to those girls, I didn't have arguments with myself over how much I was going to text them.

The kitten shifted on my shoulder and mewed, a tiny little squeak. I scooped her into my hand and held her against my chest.

"Don't worry. I'll be a good cat mom. The squirrel thought so. He led me right to you."

She mewed again.

"What's all the squeaking about?" I gently stroked her head. "Maybe that's just who you are, huh? A little squeaker? Actually, that's not a bad name—Squeaker. How about Princess Squeaker? That's more majestic, and you're definitely my tiny princess."

Her squeak told me she approved.

I finished my breakfast, then got Squeaker settled in my room. It was nice having an actual bedroom. I'd crashed on the couch at our old house for like a year. And now my brothers couldn't claim I didn't live here.

Assholes.

They were *my* assholes, but still.

My massage wasn't until later today, so I decided to head into town and get some more kitten supplies. I had the basics, but my Princess Squeaker was no basic bitch. She needed some good shit for an awesome kitty life.

Missy Lovejoy down at Happy Paws helped me find everything I needed for Princess Squeaker, including a pink rhinestone collar, a little cat bed, a scratching post, and some toys. I thanked her for her help and took everything out to my truck.

I glanced across the street at the Steaming Mug. And right in the window was Skylar.

She had her laptop open, but I could tell at a glance she wasn't looking at it. Her face was tilted toward the window, her eyes unfocused. What was she thinking about? Finding dead bodies in a beaver dam? Or something else this time?

I watched her for a long moment, fascinated. Her lips moved slightly. Not as much as if she were talking to herself, but enough that I could tell there were words running through her mind.

Those lips. Her tongue wetting them as I slide inside her, slow but deep, savoring the first thrust. She moans in my ear and—

My crutch slipped off the curb and I almost pitched forward into the street. I used the other crutch to regain my balance before I could fall flat on my face.

Shit. That would have sucked.

I took a deep breath to shake off the Skylar sex fantasy, looked both ways—I was not getting hit by a fucking car again—and crossed the street to the Steaming Mug.

Her expression didn't change as I wrangled the door open. Whatever she was seeing, it wasn't here. Her eyes moved to her screen and she typed something. Then her eyebrows drew in and she shook her head.

I went over to her table, but she didn't look up.

"Hey, Sky."

Gasping, she jerked in her seat, her eyes flying up to meet mine.

"Sorry. I didn't mean to startle you."

"That's okay." She took a deep breath. "I was just..."

"Thinking?"

"Yeah."

I pulled out the other chair and lowered myself into it. "I know you're busy, so I won't stay long. I just saw you through the window and thought I'd come say hi."

She smiled. "Hi."

The urge to reach over and touch her was almost irresistible. I wanted to trace my fingertips along her arm, feel her smooth skin.

But after that sex fantasy had just about made me step into oncoming traffic—figuratively speaking, there hadn't been any actual traffic—I kept my hand to myself.

"Are you working on your book?" I asked.

"Trying to. I decided I need to pick a premise and stick with it, even when my other ideas start to seem like they're so much better. But I'm still struggling to get the story off the ground. I feel so distracted."

"By what?"

"Um..." She met my eyes and I had a flash of her face

mid-orgasm, while I held her hair and made her look at me while she came.

Jesus, Gav. What the fuck?

"I'm distracted by a lot of things, I guess," she said.

"Yeah, I kind of know the feeling." Although I doubted her problem was having uncontrollable sex fantasies about me.

My phone buzzed, then immediately buzzed again, so I took it out of my pocket to check. It was my brothers in our group chat.

Levi: *Gram's furnace is probably going to need replacing soon. It's old AF.*

Logan: *Shit.*

Asher: *I'll get some quotes so we know how much it's going to cost.*

Levi: *Do you think she can afford it?*

Asher: *I don't know.*

Evan: *We'll figure it out if she can't.*

Asher: *Do any of you know how stable she is financially?*

I sure didn't. Gram had never discussed money with me —not hers, at least. I'd just always assumed she and Grandad had saved enough for her to live comfortably. Plus, she owned her house and all the surrounding acreage. That had to be worth a lot.

Levi: *I don't have any details. We should probably talk to her about that.*

Me: *You know she'll just tell us it's none of our business.*

Asher: *There's nothing wrong with making sure.*

Me: *I'm not arguing, I just know what she'll say.*

Logan: *I bet she's fine. Grandad probably stashed money all over the place.*

That made me smile. He probably had stashed money all over the place. That seemed like a Grandad thing to do.

Me: *Check behind his Cherry Coke fridge out in the shop.*

Skylar was quietly typing, her eyes intent on her screen. I didn't want to interrupt her, so I just hung out for a while. You'd have thought I would have been bored—if I'd been anywhere else I would have been. But I wasn't. There was something about just sitting at a table in a coffee shop with Skylar that was weirdly soothing. The click of her fingers on the keys lulled me into relaxation. I almost felt drowsy.

It was nice.

Eventually, she blinked, gasping like she'd forgotten to take her last breath. "I'm so sorry."

"For what? You're fine. Although I should probably get going. I'm getting a massage."

"That sounds nice."

"Yeah, apparently this guy is really good. I'm all jacked up from walking weird." I got up and tucked my crutches under my arms. "Bye, Sky. I'll text you later."

She nodded and gave me that cute shy smile of hers, and suddenly I really didn't want to leave. But she was trying to work, and I'd probably been distracting her. And I did want that massage. My back felt all knotted up.

So I left. And it was the weirdest thing, but not ten seconds after I walked out the door, I already missed her.

14

SKYLAR

$\mathcal{M}$y feet ate up the small amount of space in my bedroom. Back and forth, over and over. I was too anxious to sit, my heart beating wildly in my chest.

I was probably overreacting. That was one of my superpowers. But my mind was fevered, my fingers itching to know if it had been a coincidence.

I'd written an entire chapter in the coffee shop, all with Gavin sitting at my table.

My fingers had flown across the keyboard, the words coming easily. The scene had taken shape in my mind, the main character's motivations, thoughts, feelings, and actions all crystal clear. I'd been able to see the dark forest, feel the debris crunching beneath my feet. It had all been there, ready for my brain to turn into words, sentences, paragraphs.

Even more amazing, the result wasn't awful.

Sure, it would need work, especially as the story progressed. Revisions were part of the process. But this didn't need to be relegated to my alarmingly large collection of cut text files. I didn't have the heart to delete things outright, but my folder of discarded half-written chapters had turned into a graveyard of abandoned ideas.

Rest in peace, stories that could have been.

But this? This wasn't garbage. I could feel it.

The problem was that once Gavin had left, the words had dried up.

It was utterly inexplicable. He'd come into the coffee shop, made a little conversation, and then sat quietly at my table while my mind had gone crazy. While the words had poured out of me as easily as if someone had turned on a faucet, ideas flowing like water. When I'd come to, it had been like waking from a too-long nap. My mind had been so focused, so captivated, I'd barely remembered where I was.

Then he'd gone, and it had stopped.

I'd tried to get it back—tried everything. But the words wouldn't come.

It was entirely possible that I was just done for the day. I'd used up my creative well and tomorrow I'd be right back at it. After all, Gavin Bailey's presence couldn't possibly contain that kind of magic—that kind of power. This had to be my overactive imagination making connections that didn't really exist.

But I had to know for sure. So I'd texted him and asked him to come over.

A knock at the door roused me from my tangled musings and I raced downstairs.

Gavin's dimpled grin when I answered the door almost rendered me speechless. "Hey, Sky."

"Hi," I managed to get out. *Pull yourself together, Skylar, he's not that good-looking.*

Okay, yes he was.

"What's up?" he asked.

"I need your help with an experiment."

His eyes swept up and down, and he caught his lower lip between his teeth. Suddenly I was thinking about a very different kind of experiment. Heat rushed to my core and my inner thigh muscles twitched.

Focus, Skylar.

"What do you need me to do?" he asked.

Other than give me a much-needed orgasm? "Come in. Upstairs. Wait, can you do stairs?"

"Yeah, I've got it."

I let him in and closed the door behind him, then led him up to my room.

He hesitated just inside the doorway, leaning on his crutches as he glanced around.

Gavin Bailey was in my bedroom.

It made me wonder how different things would have been if I'd grown up here. If my parents hadn't divorced and I'd spent my childhood around the Bailey brothers, instead of hearing about them second hand. Would Gavin and I have been friends? Would a teenage me have invited a teenage him up to my bedroom?

Probably not. He would have looked right past me at that age.

"You can sit on the bed if you want," I said. "This is probably going to sound weird."

"Not gonna lie, I'm curious as hell right now." He laid his crutches on the floor and hoisted himself onto the bed.

"When we were at the coffee shop earlier today, I wrote an entire chapter."

"That's awesome, Sky. Good for you."

"Thanks. Specifically, I wrote it all when you were there. Before you came in, I'd barely written anything. And after you left, it was like... I don't know, it was just gone."

He picked up the pillow next to him and put it behind

his upper back, then settled against it. "So you're saying you could write when I was there and couldn't after I left."

"Yes. Apparently. Maybe it's a coincidence, but now I really need to know. I haven't written that much in one sitting in months."

"You want me to sit here while you write to see if it happens again?"

"Yes."

He clasped his hands over his middle. "Okay."

"That's it? You don't mind?"

The corner of his mouth turned up in a grin. "Nope."

How was he so adorable?

But I hadn't invited him over so I could contemplate his attractiveness.

"Do you want something to do while I work, or will you be fine just like that?"

"I'm pretty comfortable. I got that massage and I feel awesome." He shifted against the pillows and glanced around the room again. "Are those your books?"

I had a small stack of them on a shelf next to the closet. "Yeah."

"Can I read one?"

Normally I would have cringed in horror at the idea of someone reading one of my books in the same room as me. But for some reason, Gavin reading my work didn't send me into a tailspin of anxiety.

"Sure. Any preference as to which one?"

"Surprise me."

I grabbed one about an FBI profiler working to solve a series of murders that turn out to be the same killer who got away from him a decade earlier. It had a lot of twists and turns, and some rather graphic crime scene descriptions.

But all my books were at least a little morbid, so there was no sense in trying to hide that from him.

Cullen had disapproved. Encouraged me to tone it down. Especially in this book.

Shaking off that unpleasant thought, I handed the book to Gavin.

"This is fucking awesome." He ran his hands across the title, down to my name printed in large letters at the bottom.

"Thanks. I hope you like it."

"I'm sure I will." He opened it and flipped to the first chapter. "Okay writer monkey, get to work."

Leaving him to it, I sat down at my desk. Flipped open my laptop, took a deep breath, and laid my fingers on the keyboard.

At first, nothing happened. I was hyper aware of Gavin on the bed behind me. He turned the page, the sound of the crisp paper making the hair on my arms stand on end, and I wasn't thinking about the story. I was thinking about him.

This had happened at the coffee shop. When he'd first sat down with me, I'd been completely distracted, daydreams running rampant through my mind. So this time, I let the fantasy play out.

I crawl on top of him. Brace myself against the headboard while he unzips his pants. He's commando, no underwear to get in the way. I'm in a dress so all he has to do is slide my panties to the side and—

He turned another page. I sucked in a quick breath, feeling my cheeks heat up and the throbbing between my legs intensify.

He moves my panties to the side, aligns the tip of his cock with my opening, and I slide down onto him. His fingers dig into my hips as he moves me up and down.

God, it would feel good.

I blinked, my attention turning back to the words I'd written earlier. I forced myself to stop thinking about sex with Gavin, and re-read the last few paragraphs.

And then, as if by magic, I started to write.

The distracting arousal hadn't gone anywhere. I squirmed in my seat a few times, trying to get comfortable. But the physical sensations in my body faded. Because right now, my main character was about to miss an important clue. Something that was going to come back to haunt her later.

I wrote in a frenzied rush, my sense of time and space falling away. My body relaxed as my fingers clicked on the keyboard without stopping. No barriers. No inner voice jumping in to interrupt the flow of thoughts. I just wrote.

Reaching a natural break in the story, I once again became aware of reality. The glow of the laptop and the plastic keys beneath my fingertips. The chair. Gavin on the bed behind me. The lingering pressure of arousal from my earlier fantasy.

But there were words on my screen. It had worked.

For the moment, I didn't let myself ponder the ramifications of only being able to write when I was with Gavin. I'd figure that out—somehow. I just read the result, bracing myself for it to be a nonsensical jumble of useless prose. Or worse, a retelling of the sexual fantasy I'd indulged in before I'd started.

It was neither of those things. Instead, I'd written a very usable chapter that posed enough interesting questions to hopefully keep the reader turning the pages.

Satisfied and bewildered, I closed my laptop and turned around.

Gavin's eyes were glued to the pages of my book. By his

expression, I guessed the main character had probably just discovered the first murder scene. It was pretty grisly.

"It worked," I said.

He jerked, like I'd startled him. "What?"

"The experiment worked. I wrote another chapter."

With his finger holding his spot, he closed the book. "No shit?"

"I've written more today than I have in the last few months combined."

"That's awesome." He held up the book. "You're really good. This book is so intense. My heart's still pounding."

I smiled, his compliment filling me with warmth. "Thank you."

"I'm serious, I've never read anything like it. It felt like I was right there. Although you've got some messed up shit in that head of yours." His mouth hooked in a grin. "I like it."

"Thanks. My..." I paused and avoided saying that Cullen was my ex. "My agent thought I'd sell better if I toned things down."

"No way. The crime scene was graphic, but it wouldn't have been nearly as good if you'd skipped all the details."

"That's what I said. Ultimately, my editor agreed, although I had to argue with her about it too."

"I'm glad you stood up for yourself."

I smiled. "Thanks. Me too."

A flash of my earlier fantasy came to mind, as did the knowledge that we were alone in my bedroom. Dad was at work, and it felt inexplicably naughty to have Gavin stretched out on my bed like that.

My eyes flicked to his groin. I couldn't help myself. His jeans barely concealed the bulge in his pants, and I had to glance away quickly.

"I know you can't come over and sit around every day while I write, but—"

"Sure I can."

I laughed. "No you can't."

"Are you assuming I don't have time? Because honey, right now I've got more of that than I know what to do with. But if you're saying that because you don't want me to, that's another story."

"I just can't ask you to always be here when I need to write. That's not really a solution to my problem. Not long term, at least."

He shrugged. "Maybe you just need a jump start. How about I come over tomorrow and we see if it works again?"

"Really?"

"Yeah. But can I bring my kitten? I don't think she should be alone too long."

Oh my god, he needed to stop being so cute before I lost my mind and launched myself at him. "Of course. I didn't know you had a kitten."

"Yeah, Princess Squeaker. A squirrel led me to her and I rescued her."

"That's so cute."

Our eyes met again and suddenly my tummy was a whirlpool. Why did I react to him this way? It was like he made my hormones go crazy.

"I should probably get back to my kitten." He held up the book, his finger still marking where he'd left off. "Can I borrow this, though?"

"Really?"

"Don't hold out on me, Sky. I need to know what happens."

"Of course you can. You can keep it if you want. Let me

get you a bookmark." I found one in a box I had left over from a book signing and handed it to him.

"Thanks." He tucked the bookmark between the pages, then closed it again.

I picked up his crutches and held them while he swung his legs over the edge of the bed and stood. "I can carry the book down for you."

He went down first and I followed. I walked him out to his truck and waited while he put his crutches inside and hoisted himself into the front seat. Then I handed him the book.

"Thanks again for coming over."

He grinned. "My pleasure. Glad it worked. I'll see you tomorrow?"

"Yeah."

We held there for a second, eyes locked, and I had the most inexplicable urge to rush in and kiss him. I could practically feel his lips pressing against mine. His hands pulling me close, finding their way beneath my clothes.

He looked away first, breaking the spell.

I stepped back before I made things more awkward than they already were. God, what was I doing? There was something seriously wrong with me.

He shut the door and started the engine. I took slow steps backward. It was like I was having a hard time pulling myself away from him. He winked at me and backed up out of the driveway.

God, that wink. It sent a tingle down my spine and made me want to giggle like a shy little girl.

I went inside, feeling rather bewildered. I wasn't sure if it was the lingering effects of Gavin's wink and dimpled grin combination, or all the writing I'd done today. Maybe both.

But a lot of it was Gavin.

I couldn't remember the last time I'd eaten, so I went to the kitchen and poked around in the fridge. Before I'd settled on anything, there was a knock at the door.

My heart lurched and a heady mix of anxiety and excitement raced through my veins.

Was Gavin back? Had he forgotten something upstairs?

This schoolgirl-esque reaction was so silly, but the butterflies fluttering in my stomach didn't seem to care.

I went to answer the door, but it wasn't Gavin standing on the step.

It was my mom.

15

SKYLAR

*M*om smiled and held her arms out. She was typically put together in a pretty white blouse, light gray slacks, and black stilettos. "Hi, honey."

"What are you doing here?" I hugged her, smelling the familiar scent of her perfume.

"I thought I'd surprise you and see how you're doing."

"I'm definitely surprised. Do you want to come in?"

Her eyes darted around in a quick glance, like she was taking in the house. "I'd love to."

"Dad's at work," I said, stepping aside and shutting the door behind her.

She followed me to the kitchen. "That's probably for the best. Am I interrupting anything? Are you busy?"

"Not at all. It's so good to see you."

And it was. I'd always been close to my mom. It was strange to be far enough away that I couldn't just pop over to her place whenever I wanted.

She looked around and I wondered what she thought of the home she'd once shared with my dad. She must have a lot of memories, although I assumed it looked a lot different from when she'd lived here.

"It's good to see you too," she said and took a seat at the table. "I've been worried about you."

I sighed. Of course she was. That was what moms did. "I'm fine, Mom. Tea?"

"That would be lovely. So tell me how things have been since you moved."

I put some water on and the first thing that sprang to mind wasn't that I'd been writing or that Ginny was in town. It was Gavin.

I tried to push him out of my mind and focus.

"Things have been good. I'm pretty well settled here. There's plenty of room and Dad just kind of does his own thing while I do mine."

"That doesn't surprise me. Do you have a place to work?" Her voice was hesitant, and I knew what she was really asking—are you writing again?

I got two mugs out of the cupboard. "Yeah, I have a desk upstairs and there's a cute coffee shop in town. As for the question you didn't ask, yes, I've actually done some writing."

"Have you? That's great."

I decided not to mention the Gavin effect. Why was I able to write when he was around? It didn't make sense, but I needed time to unravel that one.

"Yeah, more than I have in a long time. I'm kind of afraid to jinx it, honestly."

"I think you were right about the change of scenery. How's Gavin?"

The tea bag packet flew out of my hand mid-rip. How did she know? "What?"

"Gavin Bailey. He's the one who stepped out in front of your car and broke his leg, isn't he?"

"Oh, yes." I grabbed the tea bag and took a breath to calm the fluttering in my stomach. "He's okay. I'm sure it's no fun to have a broken leg, but he'll be fine."

"Have you had the chance to talk to him since it happened?"

"Yeah, I have." I poured the hot water, debating whether to tell my mom I'd been hanging out with him. I didn't know why. Normally I told my mom everything. Well, not *everything*. Things like sex fantasies were outside the realm of our usual conversation.

Now I was just being silly. I could tell my mom I'd become friends with Gavin without mentioning that the mere sight of him ignited a flurry of arousing daydreams.

I brought our tea to the table. "Actually, I've hung out with Gavin a few times. He can't work until his leg heals, so he has time on his hands. He showed me around town. And then... well, he kind of came over today."

Mom raised her eyebrows as she pursed her lips around her mug. "Did he, now?"

"Mom. Stop."

She put her mug down and her lips twitched in a subtle smile. "I just think it's interesting that you made a friend so quickly. That's unusual for you."

"Gavin is... persistent. And I mean it when I say we're friends. Don't go getting any ideas."

"The look on your face is giving me ideas."

"What look?"

She smiled again. "The look that tells me I need to have a chat with your father about what kind of man Gavin Bailey turned out to be."

I rolled my eyes. "Mom."

"Okay, okay. I'll stop pressing you about it. I'm just relieved."

"About what?"

"The fact that the mention of another man is making you blush like that leads me to believe you're not wallowing in distress about your breakup with the dipshit."

I pressed my hands to my cheeks. "Am I blushing?"

"A little."

"We really are just friends. I'm not wallowing because of Cullen, but I don't think I'm ready to jump into anything either."

"Nothing wrong with that. So have you heard from the dipshit at all?"

I laughed softly. "No. Apparently he's too busy wrecking someone else's marriage."

"I'm sorry that happened to you, but I'm so glad you didn't marry him."

"So am I." I blew on my tea and took a sip. "Is it weird that I don't want him back, but it still hurts?"

"No. Anyone would be hurt by what he did to you. I can't even imagine what he was thinking. You're a beautiful, intelligent, creative, wonderful woman. He'll never do better than you."

"Thanks, Mom."

"Any luck finding a new agent?"

"No, but I haven't really tried. I will, but I think it would be better if I had a book ready to go before I start querying again."

Mom opened her mouth to reply, but the front door opened and we both turned to look.

Dad came in, dressed in his TFD shirt and dark pants, and paused in the entrance to the kitchen.

Oh boy.

"Caroline."

She smiled at him over the rim of her mug. "Norman."

I held my breath while they eyed each other for a long moment. Sometimes my parents were civil to each other. Other times, not so much. They were so different—opposites, really—it was hard to imagine that they'd ever been a couple.

"I thought that was your car outside," Dad said. "Hope you managed to keep under the speed limit in that thing."

"I'll drive like a grandma when I am one." She pointed at me. "But not too soon."

I laughed. "No danger of that."

Dad leaned against the door frame and crossed his arms. "What brings you to Tilikum?"

"Our daughter, obviously."

"Didn't think I could cope on my own?" Dad asked.

"I'm not questioning your parenting abilities," Mom said. "She's been through a rough breakup. I want to make sure she's all right. And before you say I could do that with a phone call, I realize that, but Skylar doesn't like to talk on the phone."

"Can't blame her there," Dad mumbled.

"The house looks like it's holding up well," Mom said, glancing around. "Although clearly it's been a long time since a woman lived here."

"Indeed it has."

Was that a dig at my dad for still being single? It was hard to tell. As far as I knew, neither of them had been in a real relationship since their divorce. Mom had been on dates, but never progressed to anything serious—no one had ever earned an introduction to her daughter, at least. If my dad dated, he kept quiet about it. Although I was under the impression that he didn't.

"Are you off for the night, or just making a pit stop before you head back to your firefighter slumber party?" Mom asked, her lips twitching in a smile.

"I'm off for the night. What about you? Taking a vacation day or two?"

"Not exactly." She casually sipped her tea. "I'm temporarily without employment."

"Are you serious?" I asked. "What happened?"

"It's a long story."

Dad cleared his throat. "We have time."

"Well, after my surgery last year, I couldn't go back to work right away. Apparently that was an unforgivable sin and I wasn't exactly welcomed back with open arms." She set down her mug and flashed her beautiful smile. "But you know me. I always land on my feet."

Dad eyed her with suspicion. "And how long are you thinking you'll be in town?"

"That's the silver lining, isn't it? I'm free to make my own schedule."

"That doesn't answer my question."

"I'm keeping it open-ended. I think our lovely daughter had the right idea about a change of scenery."

I blinked at her, my mouth slightly open, not sure what to say. It would be nice to have her close by, but it had been two decades since my parents had lived in the same town. How was this going to work?

"Plus this way you have both of us here to support you." She stood and looked over at Dad. "Would you mind helping me bring some of my things inside?"

He narrowed his eyes. "And why would we bring your things inside?"

"Because I'm staying here, of course," she said, as if it were the most obvious thing in the world. "Don't start with me, Norman, you and I can sleep under the same roof for a little while. It's not as if you don't have the space, this house is huge."

"Space isn't a problem, but—"

"If it's really an issue, I'll find a rental. But I thought this would be good for Skylar."

I met Dad's eyes and shrugged. Mom had always been a bit of a windstorm. She knew how to whip through and shake things up, leaving you wondering what had just happened.

Dad sighed. "I do have room and you're welcome to stay. But Caroline, what's really going on here?"

"I told you, I lost my job. And what can I say, Skylar inspired me. I think a fresh start is what we both need." Her phone chimed and she took it out of her purse. "What good timing. They're here."

"Who?" Dad asked.

"The movers," Mom said cheerfully and swept out of the kitchen toward the front door, her pretty black stilettos clicking on the hardwood.

"Caroline," Dad called and followed her out.

Uh-oh.

I went out front and there was indeed a moving truck parked on the street.

"You're moving back to Tilikum?" Dad asked.

"Is that so shocking?"

"Yes, it actually is."

She crossed her arms and took a resigned breath. "I was out of work for longer than anticipated and my benefits were crap. I blew through my savings. Then I went back to a cut in hours and pay, so I got behind on my house payment. The bank is foreclosing and I had to move out."

"Well, shit," Dad said.

"I don't need a lecture on responsibility. I've been taking care of myself just fine. I'm just going through a challenging time."

"I'm not going to lecture you." With a sigh, he rested his hands on his hips and glanced at the house. "There are two empty bedrooms upstairs. Take your pick."

She flashed him a smile. "Thank you, Norman."

Mom was moving in? Oh dear god. I pulled out my phone. I was going to need some best friend backup for this.

Me: *Just a heads up, but my life just got slightly more complicated.*

Ginny: *Uh-oh. What happened now?*

Me: *My mom rolled into town. With a moving truck.*

Ginny: *No way. What?*

Me: *Yeah. She lost her job and had to move.*

Ginny: *And she's moving where? To Tilikum?*

Me: *Not just Tilikum. She's moving in HERE.*

Ginny: *Here as in your dad's house?*

Me: *Yes. Here as in my dad's house.*

Ginny: *Holy shit.*

Me: *I know. This is going to be complicated.*

Ginny: *Wow. Okay, keep me posted.*

Me: *I will.*

Mom greeted the movers and started directing them while Dad watched. I wondered what he was thinking. Probably wondering how on earth this had happened.

I went back inside to get out of their way, wondering if Tilikum was big enough for both of them.

16

GAVIN

*P*rincess Squeaker purred against the back of my neck. She was nestled in my hood—one of her favorite places to nap so far—while I drove to Skylar's house. The tiny vibration tickled. She'd eaten all her food this morning and was using her litter box like a champ. I was ready to call this kitten rescue a success.

I pulled up outside and eyed the house for a second. There was a red car out front that I didn't recognize. It didn't look like something Chief would drive, and Skylar's car was in the driveway.

Getting out of the truck with a broken leg and a kitten in my hood was slightly more complicated than without Squeaker. I didn't want her to tumble out of my hood—or claw the shit out of my neck, which was probably more likely if I lost my balance. But I managed.

I went up to the front door and knocked, a smile already stealing over my face. I was getting too excited for this. Skylar hadn't even opened the door, and I was already grinning.

Mellow out, Gav. Just friends. You've got this.

But Skylar didn't answer.

The woman who did was a knockout. Sure, she was probably old enough to be my mom, give or take, but I could appreciate beauty regardless of age. Her dark shoulder-length hair had a streak of silver in the front. Deep red lipstick and heels to match gave her a *don't fuck with me* vibe, as did her blouse and wide-legged slacks.

This had to be Skylar's mom—Chief's ex-wife—although I had no idea what she was doing here.

"Hi. Is Skylar here?"

Her eyes flicked down to my cast, then back to my face. "Gavin Bailey?"

"Yep."

"Look at you, all grown up. I don't know if you remember me; I'm Skylar's mom, Caroline."

I didn't remember her—not really—but the resemblance was clear. "Nice to meet you."

"Come on in." Smiling, she stepped aside. "You must have been a kindergartner the last time I saw you."

"Probably something like that."

She shut the door behind me and called up the stairs. "Skylar!"

The whole scene gave me high school flashbacks—picking up a girl for a date, hoping her parents wouldn't grill me too hard.

"I'm sure she'll be down in a minute," Caroline said.

I followed her into the kitchen and she gestured for me to take a seat at the table. The counters were a mess of pots, pans, dishes, and canned food, like someone had emptied all the cupboards.

"How long do you have to be in the cast?" she asked.

"A few more weeks," I said, lowering myself into a chair. "It wasn't a bad break."

"That's good." She shuffled a few things around on the counter. "How's Gram?"

"She's great. I don't think she's actually aging, so she's got that going for her."

"That doesn't surprise me. Does she still have her gardens?"

"Oh yeah. And chickens."

She smiled. "I always loved your gram. Such a wonderful woman."

"Yeah, she's the best."

"I hear you're a firefighter."

"Yes, ma'am."

"Oh for goodness sake, don't ma'am me. Call me Caroline."

I grinned at her. "Fair enough."

"How long have you worked for Norman?"

It was funny hearing her use Chief's first name. "I started out as a volunteer when I was eighteen, so about eight years."

"You must be very dedicated."

"It's the only thing I've ever wanted to do."

She opened a cupboard and started emptying the contents onto what little space was left on the counter. "Sounds like Norman. And your dad."

I glanced away at the mention of my father. She'd known him, of course. She and Chief had been my parents' best friends.

"Has Tilikum changed much from when you lived here?" I asked, hoping to change the subject.

"Not much. Things are... surprisingly familiar. Does everyone still hang out at the Caboose on weekends?"

"Yeah, most of the time."

"What about Norman? Is that where he spends his

time?"

"Once in a while, but you know Chief, he's not exactly the social type."

She started stacking canned food in an empty cupboard. "You don't know where he brings his dates, do you? I'm not trying to be nosy. It's just that Skylar wouldn't know, and since I'm in town for a little while, I wouldn't want to make things awkward for him."

I had to think about that one. "I have no idea. I can't remember ever seeing Chief with a date."

"No? Hmm."

"I think he mostly just works." I shrugged.

She shook her head. "The man needs to get out more."

"You know, I agree. What's the use in working hard if you don't play hard too?"

"Exactly." She paused to glance at me, the corners of her lips twitching in a subtle smile. "Not that I would wish a broken leg on you, but I think your little accident was fortuitous. If Skylar's going to have a fling to get over her dipshit ex, he ought to be someone who gets her out of her shell a little."

A fling to get over her ex? I cleared my throat and started to reply, but Skylar appeared in the doorway.

"Mom," she said, her voice alarmed.

"Oh hi, honey."

"Mom, please don't."

"Don't what? I was just chatting with Gavin. I haven't seen him since he was little."

Skylar closed her eyes for a second and let out a long breath. "What are you doing? Rearranging the kitchen?"

"That's exactly what I'm doing."

"Does Dad know?"

Caroline drew her eyebrows in. "No. Why?"

"Because it's his house," Skylar said with a soft laugh.

"He'll thank me later," Caroline said. "It's barely usable as is. I don't know how he manages to cook anything in here."

"Okay, well, have fun with that."

"Actually, I need to run to the market. I don't think he has a single spice that's not past its expiration date." She smiled at me. "Good to see you, Gavin."

"You too."

Caroline swept out of the kitchen, grabbing her purse on her way out the front door.

"Sorry," Skylar said. "My mom can be... a lot."

"She was fine. Is she staying here with you and your dad?"

"Yes." Her eyebrows knitted together like she was still confused by that reality. "It's... very weird."

"Do they get along?"

"Yes, and no. It's never seemed like they hate each other or anything, but they definitely know how to get under each other's skin. So them living in the same house, even temporarily, is a little scary."

"I bet they'll be fine."

"I hope so."

"I didn't know you were getting over an ex. Is that recent?"

She nodded. "Yeah, that's a lot of why I moved here. It was... messy."

I had no idea who this guy was, but I wanted to punch him in the face. "That sucks. But I already know you're better off without him."

"How do you know that?"

"If he let you go, he's an idiot. And you shouldn't be with an idiot."

She met my eyes and for a second, I was caught. There was hurt in those pretty brown eyes, but also something else.

Heat.

I was suddenly in dangerous territory. It would have been stupid to say I wasn't attracted to her. I'd fantasized about her too many times to kid myself. But her mom was wrong. I wasn't going to be the fling that helped her get over her dipshit ex. So even though the way she looked at me gave me very solid *kiss me* vibes, I wasn't taking the bait.

Yet.

No, there was no *yet*. I wasn't taking the bait at all.

But damn it, I wanted to.

Squeaker moved in my hood, crawling from behind my neck onto my shoulder.

"Oh my goodness, your kitten," Skylar said, clutching her hands to her chest. "She's so cute."

I reached up and plucked her off my shoulder. "I almost forgot she was back there. She likes to sleep in my hood."

"Can I pet her?"

"Of course."

I held Squeaker while Skylar gently stroked her.

"She's so soft."

"Yeah, she is." I brought her closer to my face and kissed her head. She squeaked.

"I see where she gets her name. Didn't you say you rescued her?"

"I found her out by the old railroad tracks the other night."

"Are you serious? Do you think someone abandoned her?"

"It looks like it. But she has a mommy now, so she'll be

fine." I lightly kissed her again. "Isn't that right, Princess Squeaker? So, time to get to work?"

"Do you mind coming upstairs again? Or I can bring my laptop down here."

"Upstairs is great, actually. That way I can stretch out my leg." I deposited Squeaker back in my hood and got up.

Skylar handed me my crutches. "Thank you again for coming over. I tried to write this morning, but I didn't get very far."

"Never fear, Gavin Bailey to the rescue."

She smiled and it did something weird to my insides.

We went up to her room and I got comfortable on her bed. I took Squeaker out of my hood and set her on my chest. She curled up, her little purr-motor going.

Like yesterday, Skylar sat at the little desk in front of the window, her back to me. I'd brought her book, so I opened it to where I'd left off last night and started reading.

Sort of.

The book was damn good—she was seriously talented. But my eyes kept darting up to look over the top of the pages.

At Skylar.

I pulled my eyes back to the page and focused on what I was reading. For a while, Skylar wrote and I read, temporarily lost in her words. In the plight of the FBI agent trying desperately to uncover the identity of the killer before he struck again.

I finished another chapter and turned the page, but my eyes moved up again.

Skylar's hair hung down in a sheet around her shoulders. I could imagine all that silky hair fanned out over my pillow while she looked up at me, her lips parting in a soft moan.

I'd sink my cock into her, driving in deep. Cup one of her tits and suck on her nipple. Thrust in, then glide out through her wetness. In and out, hips jerking, heat and pressure building.

Fuck, I bet she'd feel good.

I took a deep breath and forced my eyes back to the page. Her fingers clicked on her keyboard, the rhythmic sound oddly soothing. She was definitely writing something. Maybe having me here was working again. I had no clue why me sitting here would help her write. But even though this should have been boring, it wasn't, and it had nothing to do with having a broken leg and not being able to do much anyway. I simply liked being here.

The room smelled like her, and lying on her bed—even knowing nothing sexual was going to happen between us—felt a little dangerous. A little risky.

Maybe that was because she lived with her dad—my boss—and he could come home at any time. I didn't think he was at work today, so I had no way of knowing when he'd return.

But the real risk wasn't that her dad might catch us making out in her room. It was the undeniable temptation of her. Holding myself back was the challenge.

I was basically reverse chasing her. And that held a weird kind of thrill.

How much temptation could I take and still resist? It was an interesting question.

So the next time my eyes lifted and my thoughts strayed to things I shouldn't be thinking, I indulged. Went deeper. Imagined her on her knees, my dick in her mouth. Her sweet brown eyes lifting to meet mine, shining with a wicked gleam. I imagined what it would be like to turn to putty in her hands—and mouth—while she sucked me off, making me come so hard I could barely stand.

I licked my lips, imagining her taste. Burying my face between her legs and eating her sweet pussy until she begged me to stop. Until her back arched and she clutched the sheets, moaning my name as she came in my mouth.

Blinking, I took a deep breath to clear my head. Unfortunately, that did nothing for the aching erection in my pants. Damn. I was going to have to take care of that when I got home.

Maybe I needed to whack off before hanging out with Skylar. Make a habit of it. Coming in hot with a loaded weapon was probably not the smartest move, given the circumstances.

I went back to the book for a little while and it was a testament to her writing that it held my attention, given how hard my dick was trying to distract me. But pretty soon the FBI agent was in serious danger and I couldn't stop reading.

"Hey." Skylar's soft voice jolted me back to reality.

I lowered the book. "Did it work?"

"Yeah. Like you said, Gavin to the rescue."

"It's what I do."

Princess Squeaker got up, stretched, and crawled down onto the bed. I sat up and swung my legs over the side.

I didn't particularly want to go, but I had a feeling if I stayed much longer, I'd screw up. Temptation would win. Sitting with her, here in her bedroom, was already making it hard to remember why holding back was so important. Why I couldn't sneak a taste.

"So, tomorrow?" I asked.

"You don't mind?"

Hell no, I didn't mind. For one thing, she was cool and I liked her. For another, this felt like a dare. How close could I get to the edge without falling. But I'd also promised to introduce her around, and our little Tilikum town tour had only been the beginning.

"I don't mind at all. But what are you doing next Friday night?"

Her lips parted in surprise. "I don't know. But—"

I grinned. "Don't worry, I'm not asking you out. But it's my brother Asher's birthday and they're having a party at my gram's house. It's the perfect chance for you to get to know more people."

She fiddled with a strand of hair. "It's not that I don't appreciate the offer, but crowds of people I don't know make me nervous."

"Will your friend still be in town?"

"Ginny? Yeah."

"Cool. You can bring her too. Worst case scenario, you hate it and you go home. Best case, you have fun and make some new friends." I flashed her another grin. "Besides, you'll have me."

She took a deep breath. "Okay. I'll come."

"Great."

Princess Squeaker batted at a little piece of dust drifting in the air. She chased it across the bed, coming close to the edge.

"I'll get her." Skylar stood and moved to scoop her up into her hands. "Silly kitten. You don't want to fall off the bed."

I stood, leaning on my crutches. "You can just stick her in my hood. She'll be fine there."

Skylar brought her around to my side of the bed and stepped close. I leaned down and she reached around to open my hood, then deposited Squeaker inside.

Still standing just inches from me, she adjusted the

fabric so Squeaker was secure. Her arms were around my neck, her face so close. I took a deep breath, inhaling her. God, she smelled good.

Just a taste. What would that hurt?

I licked my lips and the movement seemed to catch her attention. She froze, her eyes resting on my mouth. Slowly, her thick lashes lifted, bringing her gaze to mine.

If I'd ever been faced with a girl who really wanted to be kissed, it was now.

Her chin lifted slightly. My heart beat harder, thumping in my chest. Only a second passed, but it felt like time had slowed. I could already taste her. Feel her soft lips pressing against mine.

A knock on her bedroom door jolted me back to reality. Skylar gasped and took a step away.

"Hey, Skylar?" Chief said through the door. "Can I come in?"

She moved closer to her desk. "Yeah, what's up?"

Chief opened the door. His eyes landed on me, but he didn't look surprised to see me. He'd probably seen my truck out front. "What happened to the kitchen?"

"That was Mom. She's reorganizing?"

Chief groaned. "Of course she is. Hey, Gav. How's the leg?"

"Getting better"

"Good." His eyes darted between me and Skylar, and I really wondered what he was thinking. "I guess I'll go wait for Caroline."

"She's just trying to help, Dad."

He grumbled something that sounded like *infernal woman* and shut the door.

Skylar sighed.

I thought about asking if she needed an excuse to get out

of the house. She could come over to my place. My brothers were on duty until Saturday morning.

But after how close I'd just come to kissing her, I decided not to. Forcing myself to resist temptation was one thing, but I wasn't a total masochist.

Plus, Chief's brief appearance had been like jumping in the freezing cold river.

Resisting her wasn't just a game I was playing to amuse myself while I was laid up. I had reasons. Good ones.

And those reasons weren't going to change.

17

GAVIN

*T*he air in Gram's backyard was chilly, but propane heaters pumped out warmth, as did the bonfire Levi and Logan had built. Grace had strung lights around the porch and tied helium balloons to the railings at the bottom of the porch stairs. Despite Asher's insistence that we didn't need to make a big deal out of his birthday, she'd insisted on throwing him a party.

Personally, I was a big believer in birthday parties. In parties of all kinds, really. Life needed to be celebrated. Plus, any excuse for cake was a good thing.

Family and friends congregated in the kitchen, or in the warm spots outside. It was a beautiful night, aside from the early October cold. Sparks rose from the fire when Logan tossed another piece of wood on the growing blaze. Grace, Gram, and Fiona had set out enough food for twice as many people as were actually here, which was how we rolled when it came to these things. Gram liked to say she never wanted anyone to leave her house hungry, and always kept that promise.

I balanced on my crutches near one of the heaters, a

beer in my hand. It had been almost three weeks since I'd broken my leg, and I was starting to get edgy.

Okay, maybe not *starting* to get edgy. I'd been that way from day one. But it was definitely getting worse.

Under normal circumstances, I would have been doing back flips over the bonfire, or I'd have gone climbing this morning, or... something. Anything but what I actually did, which was mostly nothing. I'd played with Princess Squeaker, which was fun in its own way. But the energy building inside me needed an outlet, and I had several weeks left before I'd be free of the damn cast.

It was driving me up the wall.

As if to add insult to injury, my leg started to itch.

Skylar had texted me earlier to say she and her friend were coming, but they'd be a little late. I'd seen her several times in the last week. Mostly I just hung out while she wrote. I'd been reading her books and they were really fucking good. She had a twisted mind inside that pretty head of hers. I liked it.

I took a sip of my beer, keeping an eye on the back door for her. Maybe this party would get more fun once she got here.

Gram sat on the porch in her rocking chair wrapped in a thick sweater. Someone had fixed her a plate of food, and she watched the growing party with a contented smile. Fiona and Evan sat next to her, and Fiona might as well have been on Evan's lap, they were so close. They were getting married soon and it sounded like they'd decided to have it here.

Asher came out of the house and down the porch steps. He walked up behind Grace, kissed her neck, and slipped an arm around her waist so he could rest his hand on her belly.

A Bailey baby. That was some crazy shit. Of course, if

Asher hadn't gone to prison, they probably would have had kids years ago.

The restlessness I felt reminded me of when Asher had first been sent away. I'd been just a kid. September had rolled around again and I'd had to go back to school. Sit there in a classroom as if my oldest brother hadn't been forcibly ripped from our lives. Like everything was normal.

It hadn't gone well.

But I just hadn't seen the point in being there.

Looking back, I was pretty sure I'd only graduated because a few of my teachers had felt sorry for me and figured it would be better to just pass me and get me out of there. That, and Levi. He'd started picking me up himself and driving me to school to make sure I'd actually go.

Thank fuck that was over.

Cara wandered over to stand next to me with a wine tumbler in her hand. "Do you know how to bake muffins?"

"Yeah. Why? Did your YouTube chef fail you again?"

"Catastrophically. The first batch tasted like cardboard. The second were so hard I thought about searching for Harvey Johnston to see if he'd let me use his fucking pickax to break them open."

I laughed. "That bad, huh?"

"At this point, I should probably throw in the towel and find a different hobby. But I bought so much kitchen stuff, it would be nice to actually use it."

"You want me to come over and show you how to bake muffins?"

"I'll book you another massage with Sven."

"Done." I reached over and she shook my hand. "Why me, though? Grace can't be so busy that she wouldn't come over and bake with you."

"No, she would. But I want to bake muffins for her. The

other day she said she was craving them. And yes, I'm well aware that I could save myself the trouble and just go to Angel Cakes and order them."

"But you want to do something special for your bestie because you have an unnatural level of affection for her."

"You're surprisingly insightful."

"I get that a lot."

The back door opened and Skylar and her friend Ginny came out onto the porch. Skylar wore a black trench coat that belted at the waist. Ginny's coat was similar, only hers was blue and she wore it open.

Skylar's eyes darted around nervously, like a baby bird contemplating whether to take her first leap off a branch and try to fly. It made me want to take her hand and jump with her—show her she could do it.

"What do we have here?" Cara asked. "Do I spy with my little eye Chief Stanley's daughter?"

"Yeah, the one in black is Skylar. The other one is her friend Ginny."

"Uh-oh."

"What?"

"You like her."

I laughed. "Shut up, Cara."

"A crush on your boss's daughter. You really don't feel fear, do you?"

As if to punctuate Cara's point, Chief Stanley came out onto the porch behind Skylar.

I took a drink of my beer. "Skylar is hot, I won't deny that. But even I know where to draw the line. We're just friends."

"For now."

"Whatever. I'm a grownup. I can be friends with a hot girl. I'm friends with you."

"Yeah but you're not attracted to me."

"How do you know?"

"You know how to play cute very well, but you've never actually tried anything with me. If you wanted to get in my pants, you would have made an attempt by now."

"You're also surprisingly insightful."

She smiled. "I get that a lot. Now go hang out with your *friend*."

I handed her my empty beer bottle, just to be obnoxious, and crutched my way over to the porch. Skylar's nervous eye-wandering transformed into a smile.

Fuck, that smile.

"Hey, you made it," I said, making my way up the steps.

"Yeah, sorry we're late," she said.

"That's my fault," Ginny said. "I was working and got caught up in what I was doing."

"It's no problem. I'm just glad you came." I winked at Sky and the way it made her look a little shy and nervous again was fucking adorable. "Hey, Chief."

"Gavin," he said with a slight narrowing of his eyes.

"The food's all over there, and dessert is in the kitchen," I said. "Gram made cookies and I haven't stolen a single one."

Chief cracked a smile. "Okay, Gav. I'm going to go say hi to Asher and Grace."

I turned back to Skylar and Ginny. "You guys want a drink and then I can introduce you around? I'd get your drinks for you, but this crazy driver hit me and now I have to use these crutches to get around."

Skylar playfully smacked my arm. "Stop."

They grabbed drinks and I took them around, introducing them to people. Skylar had already met Grace, but I introduced the birthday boy. Fiona and Evan were at a table getting more food. Evan was his usual stoic self, giving them a hello and a chin tip. Fiona was friendlier, because of course she was, and happily chatted with both Skylar and Ginny for a while.

I introduced her to Cara, who gave me another knowing smile. Levi seemed to be trying to replace Evan as the grumpiest Bailey. He was polite, but didn't seem interested in talking for long. Logan was his twin's polar opposite, as usual, swooping in to shamelessly flirt with Ginny.

"I didn't say hi to your gram yet," Skylar said. "I should probably do that."

With Ginny laughing at Logan's jokes, I led Skylar up to the back porch. Gram still sat in her rocking chair, but her plate of food had been replaced with a cup of tea.

"Hi there, Otter," she said when we approached. "Is this Skylar Stanley, all grown up?"

I sighed at her use of my nickname. So not manly. "Yeah, Gram, this is Skylar."

"It's nice to meet you," Skylar said. "Or see you again, I suppose. Sorry, I feel like I should remember everyone."

"Don't you worry about it, little Sparrow," Gram said. "You were just a tot the last time you came over to play in my backyard. It's good to have you back."

"Thank you."

"Did I hear your mama's back in town too?"

"She is. She's staying with my dad, which is... interesting. But I'm glad she's close."

"Tell her to come on by and see me when she has time. I'd love to chat with her."

"I will."

"And let me know when your next book is coming out. I'm looking forward to it."

"Gram, you read Skylar's books?" I asked.

"Of course I do. I've read them all. The last one kept me up well past my bedtime."

Skylar leaned closer to me, her arm rubbing up against mine. "Wow. I never know what to say when someone I know tells me they read my books. So I guess... thank you."

"You're a real talent. You keep writing them, I'll keep reading them."

"I'm working on it," Skylar said.

We wandered back down the steps and stopped near one of the heaters. Ginny was still standing near the fire, talking to Logan. He grinned at her, and I could tell—from his body language to his facial expression—that he was really turning on the charm.

"Ginny looks like she's having fun with your brother," Skylar said.

"Yeah."

"What's he like?"

I thought for a second about how to answer that. "He's a good guy. But..."

"But what?"

"He's probably the kind of guy a girl should warn her friend about."

She laughed. "Aren't you that kind of guy too?"

"Me?" I put my hand on my chest. "Never."

"That's not what I heard."

"What did you hear about me?" I asked, genuinely curious.

She shrugged. "Something about being a playboy with a charming smile."

"I do have a very charming smile, that's completely true. I don't know about playboy, though."

"You sure about that?"

"Who called me a playboy? Was it your dad?"

"Maybe," she said innocently.

He wasn't entirely wrong. Chasing girls had been one of my favorite things since I was a kid. There had hardly been a female teacher or babysitter I hadn't crushed on. And post-puberty I'd taken my game to a whole new level.

I loved the challenge.

If I was being honest, it did kind of make me a playboy. Because I rarely dated anyone for long.

"I guess I come by that reputation honestly."

"Are you proud of it?"

I thought about that. "Not in the sense that I like to brag about my conquests or anything. I just like to have fun."

"And serious relationships aren't fun?"

"Nope. Who knows, I might settle down someday, but I'm too restless for that right now."

She was quiet for a moment. "You're right. Serious relationships aren't fun."

It kind of made me sad to hear her say that, but I wasn't sure why. I agreed with her, so what was the problem?

"Speaking of fun, question," I said. "Are you having fun tonight?"

She looked up at me, a smile dancing on her lips. "Yes, I'm having fun. Although..."

I waited a beat for her to continue, but she didn't. "Although, what?"

"I don't know if I want to tell you. It's embarrassing."

"Okay, now I really need to know."

She took a deep breath. "Sometimes when I'm anxious I feel... inexplicably aroused."

This just got interesting. "Aroused? Like sexually?"

"Yes. It happens at the worst times, and it isn't because there's anything arousing going on. I'm just hypersensitive to stimuli and it can make my body react in ways that don't make sense. Like a sudden sense of uncomfortable arousal."

"So you're saying being anxious makes you want sex?"

"Yes. I mean, not always. Not even very often, but sometimes."

"Does sex help? Like if you had sex, would you feel better?"

Her face whipped around, her eyes widening. "What?"

I laughed. God, she was cute. "I'm not saying let's go bang in my old bedroom upstairs, I'm just wondering if an orgasm makes you feel better."

She took another deep breath, like she was gathering her courage to admit the truth. "Yes. It helps."

One corner of my mouth hooked in a grin. "So if you don't have someone to give you an orgasm, do you do it yourself?"

She smacked my arm again. "Gavin."

"What? I'm just asking. You're the one who brought up sexual arousal." This whole conversation was making *me* uncomfortably aroused, but I was having too much fun teasing her to stop. "I'm just trying to be a good friend by listening and asking relevant questions."

"What do you think?"

"I think you do, but it's better when you get the real thing."

"I can't believe we're having this conversation."

"Sounds like when I was a teenager and I'd get a boner out of nowhere. It was like the thing had a mind of its own. I'd be reading a fucking comic book, and not even looking at boobs or anything. And bam, hard on."

"That's definitely similar."

"The worst was when I was around my brothers or a

bunch of friends. Getting a boner around a group of guys isn't ideal."

"That must have been awkward. And confusing?"

"A little. Mostly I just wondered how to keep it under control. Where's the worst place you've had it happen? A job interview? A funeral?"

She groaned. "I think the worst was at ThrillerFest. It's a big writer's conference and my publisher put me on a panel with a few other authors. We were supposed to answer questions about the publishing process. I was so nervous I thought I might puke, and then suddenly I felt..."

"Aroused?"

"Yes, but not just aroused. I felt desperate. I can't believe I'm telling you this. I didn't even tell Ginny this story. But I was up there on this little stage and I remember my face getting hot and my heart beating too fast. And other places felt... you know. There was a lot of pressure."

"So what did you do?"

"Nothing, really. I just lived with it until it went away. My ex was..." She trailed off and I waited again to see if she'd finish. This time she did. "My ex was at the conference too, but he wasn't interested in a quick trip back to our room when the panel was over. Said he was too busy."

"He turned down a quick fuck in a hotel room? Seriously, Sky, what kind of dumbass were you dating?"

She shrugged. "The boring kind, I guess."

"No shit."

Her tongue darted out to wet her lips. "So if you'd been there with me, you'd have taken me upstairs for a quickie?"

My danger instinct went absolutely crazy. Buzzers, alarms, and warning bells all went off in my brain at once. That was a loaded fucking question if I'd ever heard one.

Don't do it, Gav. Don't take the bait.

But I couldn't resist.

"Oh yeah. I would have taken you back to our hotel room and made sure you were satisfied." *Whoa, too close to the fire, Gav. Back up a little or you'll get burned.* "Assuming having sex was something we normally did anyway," I added quickly.

"Right, of course."

This conversation was about to come full circle. She'd brought it up because she was uncomfortably aroused *right now*. Was she hinting she could use my help in alleviating it?

As if my conscience needed the reminder, Chief came out onto the porch and sat next to Gram.

Well played, universe.

"Gram's pie isn't quite as good as sex, but it's close. Should we go get some?"

"I haven't eaten dinner yet."

"So? It's fun to eat dessert first."

"I guess I can't argue with that. Pie sounds great."

I took her inside and we helped ourselves to Gram's apple pie. After that, we mingled a little longer. Had some food, and I nursed a second beer. Skylar kept close to my side—so close her arm kept rubbing against mine. Even through our clothes, the contact was electrifying. More than once, I had to resist the urge to brush her hair back over her shoulder or tuck it behind her ear.

After a while, I had the distinct feeling that she was ready to go. She was just a little bit quieter, standing with her shoulder and arm subtly behind mine, so close she could have rested her cheek on my arm if she'd wanted to.

I leaned down and spoke softly. "Are you ready to get out of here?"

"It's not because I'm having a bad time. But yes."

"Did you drive yourself?"

"No, I came with Ginny."

Ginny had left the bonfire—and Logan—and taken up a spot next to Gram and Fiona. Gram was in storytelling mode, tipping back and forth in her rocking chair, speaking softly. Fiona and Ginny were watching her with rapt attention.

"I think my dad left already," she said. "But I can wait for Ginny. It's not a big deal."

"I can take you home."

"Are you sure? I don't want to take you away from your brother's party."

I could have told her the truth. That the only reason I'd stayed this long was because she was here. That I'd been restless and edgy until she'd arrived, and now I didn't want to be anywhere but wherever she was, even if it meant missing birthday cake.

But that was a little much, and treading way too close to that friendship line I was determined to maintain.

"I don't mind at all."

She looked up at me and a reflection of the firelight danced in her pretty brown eyes. "Thanks, Gavin."

Uh-oh. I was in so much trouble.

18

SKYLAR

A little thrill of excitement pulsed through my veins as I got into Gavin's truck. I didn't know why. He was only driving me home. Maybe it was the lingering effects of my weird anxiety-induced arousal. That, and the habit I'd developed of daydreaming about him. Spending the evening next to him, touching him, made those daydreams flash through my mind like a movie reel of erotic desires.

Never in my life had I been so physically attracted to someone. This went beyond my hypersensitivity, beyond a crush on a hot firefighter. Being near him made my body react in ways that felt foreign and frightening and exhilarating all at once.

Balancing on his good leg, Gavin slid his crutches behind the seat and hoisted himself in. He glanced at me, flashing a smile that puckered the dimples in his cheeks. "Ready?"

I pulled the seatbelt over my lap and clicked it into place. "Yep."

Ginny had offered to drive me home, but it had been

obvious she was having fun chatting with Gram and Fiona. I didn't want to make her go on my account. And when I'd mentioned that Gavin had offered me a ride, she'd hit me with a knowing smile.

She probably had the wrong idea. Gavin was only taking me home. It wasn't like he'd come inside and anything would happen. Heck, Dad had already left the party, so both my parents were home—which was still so strange I didn't know how to feel about it.

He turned the truck on and glanced at me again. "Are you tired?"

"A little. Why?"

"I was just thinking, it's not very late, and maybe instead of dropping you off, we could do something. With fewer people around, I mean. But if you're tired—"

"No," I said quickly. "I'm not too tired."

"Awesome. Maybe a movie?"

"Yeah, a movie sounds great."

"My place or yours?"

"Definitely yours, if you don't mind. My divorced parents are both home and it's... tense. And kind of awkward."

"Fair enough. My brothers are still at Asher's party and I'm sure they'll be out late. We'll have the place to ourselves for a while." He paused, clearing his throat. "You know, so we can pick whatever movie we want."

Another thrill of excitement—or was it nervousness?—jolted through me.

Gavin's house was only about a mile from Gram's, on a quiet residential street. A sign on the corner said Bailey Way, although it looked like a sticker over the real sign. Stars scattered across the night sky and the mountain peaks rose around us. Even at night, it was so pretty here.

We got out of the truck and Gavin gestured to the neighboring house. "Asher and Grace live there."

"And you live with Levi and Logan?"

"Yep."

"Is that why the street sign back there says Bailey Way?"

He laughed. "No, that's from a prank we pulled. It was about a year and a half ago, I guess? We put them all over town. The Havens removed them, but we kept replacing this one. They finally just left it."

I followed him inside and he flipped on the lights. The front room distinctly said *bachelor pad*. It had a worn couch and a couple of armchairs, a coffee table cluttered with video game controllers and a few beer bottles, and a big TV mounted on the wall.

Gavin leaned his crutches against the door so he could take off his coat. "Sorry. It's kind of messy. My brothers are basically wild animals."

"None of the mess is yours?" I nudged his arm, then shrugged off my coat.

"Of course not." He grinned. "They're not home, so I can throw them under the bus."

"Naturally."

"Princess Squeaker," Gavin called, getting his crutches back under his arms. "Mommy's home."

Gavin's kitten came out from the hallway, blinking sleepy eyes. She paused and arched her back in a long stretch.

"There's my tiny girl. Did you miss your mommy?"

I didn't ask why he was referring to himself as her mommy. That just seemed like something Gavin would do.

He called her over and she followed him to the couch. As soon as he sat down, she jumped up into his lap, purring loudly.

I sat on the couch next to him and tucked my legs up. "She sure loves you."

He petted her affectionately. "Yeah. So how do you feel about scary movies?"

"I don't know. They're not really my thing."

"Really? You write some scary ass shit."

"I know, but that's different."

"How?"

"Well..." I fiddled with a strand of my hair. "I guess because when I'm writing scary things, I know I'm in control. Writing helps me process my fears. When I was a little girl, I was terrified of being kidnapped by a bad guy. I used to have nightmares about being locked in a closet. I could picture it so clearly, everything from the way my heart would race, to the little sliver of light I'd see around the door. I could hear the footsteps of the bad guy coming closer. It was all so real. So when I got older, I wrote a book where something like that happens. The character isn't a little girl, she's a grown woman. But she's kidnapped and held in a closet, just like I used to be afraid of."

"Did it help? Are you still afraid of being kidnapped and held in a closet?"

"Nope, I'm not. I haven't had that nightmare since I wrote the book."

"Are all your books based on nightmares?"

"No, but I dig into my fears when I write. And I think it helps. I know I still get anxious about things, but writing suspenseful stories helps me temper some of my bigger, more outlandish fears."

"But no scary movies?"

I took a deep breath. "I haven't tried to watch one in a long time."

"I was just thinking it might be fun to watch something

similar to what you write. There's this one that has a similar vibe, although it's not nearly as good as your book. It's not a gory horror movie, but it's pretty intense."

"We can give it a try."

"Tell you what. If you hate it, we can turn it off and find something else."

"Deal."

Princess Squeaker seemed to have gotten her fill of snuggles from her cat mom. She crawled onto the arm of the couch and curled up to go to sleep.

Gavin grabbed a remote off the coffee table and got the movie started.

I could see why he'd suggested it. There were similarities to my books, particularly the one he'd been reading. But seeing it all on a screen was a different experience from writing. It was intense in a different way. The score added to the suspenseful atmosphere of the film, the music reverberating through me, making my hair stand on end.

Suddenly, my hypersensitivity-induced arousal was back. Heat bloomed in my core and a tingling sensation made me shift in my seat. The friction of my pants only made it worse. My heart beat faster and my cheeks warmed.

But maybe it wasn't my hypersensitivity that was causing it.

Gavin smelled amazing—somehow clean and masculine and rugged all at once. I treated myself to sneaky glances out of the corner of my eye, taking in his sharp cheekbones and strong jaw. His muscular arms and broad chest stretching the confines of his t-shirt.

Hot firefighter, indeed. And the kitten only made it worse.

Dad's subtle warning ran through my mind. A playboy firefighter with a charming smile. Gavin himself had admitted Dad was right about him. Obviously I didn't know Gavin's entire relationship history—nor did I want to—but I could fill in the pieces. He probably had a lot of flings, or at least avoided long-term attachments.

Which, right now, was kind of perfect.

I wasn't ready to jump into a relationship. But I liked Gavin, and I was undeniably attracted to him. I'd slept with him a dozen times in my mind already, something my overactive imagination had never done before. I'd never fantasized about Cullen, or the few guys I'd dated before him.

No one had ever made me feel this way.

Would it be so bad if things got a little bit physical between us? Assuming Gavin was interested in getting physical with me.

He'd looked at me like he'd wanted to kiss me the other day in my bedroom. If my dad hadn't come in, he might have done it. So it wasn't too much of a leap to consider the possibility that Gavin Bailey was attracted to me too.

I took a deep breath and squirmed again. *Movie, Skylar. Focus on the movie.* Gavin was right, it was intense. I found myself captivated, almost holding my breath, waiting to see what would happen next.

"Boo!" Gavin said out of the blue, grabbing my thigh and giving me a startling shake.

Shrieking, I jumped in my seat, clutching my hands to my chest. "Oh my god, you scared me."

He laughed. "Sorry, I couldn't help myself."

"Jerk," I said, playfully shoving his arm.

He grabbed my wrist, twisted toward me, and wrapped his hand around the other one. Suddenly we were face to face, his nose almost brushing against mine, my arms immobilized in his grasp. My heart beat harder, my breath caught in my throat, and my eyes dipped to his mouth.

Kiss me, Gavin. I want you to. I want it so bad.

I didn't know who closed the distance. Maybe we met in the middle. But in an instant, his mouth was on mine, his hands pinning my arms to the back of the couch. His lips were firm, insistent, and oh my god, so soft. I welcomed his kiss, parting my lips when I felt the slow sweep of his tongue.

His head tilted, his lips capturing more of mine, and the velvety softness of his tongue sent a shiver down my spine. Sparks exploded between my legs, the pressure growing more insistent by the second.

He stopped, suddenly pulling back, the abrupt separation sucking the breath from my lungs.

"Sorry," he said breathlessly.

"Don't be." Feeling bold—which was so unlike me—I leaned closer. Pressed my lips to his neck. "It's really okay."

He groaned, the vibration pulsing through my lips. I kissed his throat, feeling the scratch of his light stubble.

"Sky, I don't know if we should." His voice was husky.

I kissed his neck again. "You don't want to?"

Another groan. "No, I do. I just…"

I kept kissing him, reveling in this feeling of bravery. Maybe even recklessness. "You just what?"

"I don't know if this is the right thing."

"Why?"

Before he could answer, I pressed my lips to his. He still had my arms pinned to the couch and he wasn't pulling away. He wanted me. He just wasn't sure if he should.

He kissed me back, his lips pliant and warm. Our tongues brushed, sending a jolt of electricity pinging through me.

Gavin Bailey knew how to kiss. He didn't just purse his lips and make contact. He caressed my mouth with his. Slid his lips along mine, tasting me with his tongue. Then pressed with more force, sucking my lower lip into his mouth. I felt the quick scrape of his teeth, making me shudder.

More. I wanted all this and more.

But he pulled away again.

"Gavin, this is really okay. I'm saying yes."

"I know." He let go of my wrists and my heart sank straight to the pit of my stomach. "I just don't know if I should do this."

"I don't know if I should either. But I still want to." Vaguely wondering who I was and what had happened to mousy, shy Skylar, I continued, moving closer so I could whisper in his ear. "I want this, Gavin. But if you can't give it to me, I need you to take me home so I can take care of it myself."

A low groan rumbled in his throat and he manhandled me onto my back. I found myself beneath him, the weight of his body pressing between my legs.

"Is this what you want?" he growled, grinding into me.

"Yes."

He kissed me again, this time with ferocity, while he thrust his hips. His erection moved between my legs, giving me friction and pressure right where I needed it. I whimpered into his mouth, clutching his back.

"Right there?" he said near my ear, his hot breath tickling my neck. He thrust again. "You like that?"

I nodded, the sensations spiraling out of control.

"Is that what you need Sky?"

"Yes. Please."

He kept thrusting, rubbing me in a steady rhythm. Even through my clothes, it felt amazing. Heat and pressure built so fast, I gasped with the intensity of it, my eyes fluttering, cheeks flushing hot.

I ran my hands along his hard planes of muscle as his back flexed. He thrust harder and I gripped the fabric of his t-shirt. I wanted more—wanted to feel him sink inside me, his thickness filling me. But he was relentless, dry humping me like a man on a mission.

"More?"

All I could do was whimper. I was too far gone to form real words. My clit throbbed with hot tension, desperate for release. I rolled my hips against him, seeking more. Always more. His cock was rock solid, digging into me, promising blissful climax.

Any second now.

Just a little more.

He ground against me harder and a groan escaped his throat. My eyes rolled back as my body exploded into sparks. Pulses of pleasure rippled through me in waves, each thrust of his hips drawing out my orgasm to its pinnacle. I moaned, my inhibitions nowhere in sight, my body coming apart beneath him.

His rhythm slowed as my climax waned. I held onto him, breathing hard, the world coming back into focus.

For a moment, we lay there, his chest pressing against mine with his heavy breaths, his mouth near my ear. Letting my hands slide off his back, I shifted my hips.

"Don't. Move." His voice was strained.

I froze, scarcely daring to breathe. Was he close too? Was he afraid he'd come in his pants?

Oh my god, that was hot.

After hesitating another moment, he lifted himself off me, as if to get up. I reached for his groin, ready to grab his cock—happy to reciprocate that fantastic orgasm in any number of different ways.

But he quickly grabbed my wrist. "Don't."

Wait, what?

He rolled to a sitting position on the other side of the couch, leaving me with soaked panties and feeling very confused. I got up and smoothed down my hair while he rested his elbows on his knees and ran his hands up and down his face.

"You don't want... more?" My voice sounded small and timid, but my earlier rush of bravery was quickly wearing off.

"I'm okay."

"Because we can—"

"No." He took a deep breath and raked his fingers through his hair, then glanced at me. "Feel better?"

"Yeah, but—"

"Good."

"I didn't mean to leave you hanging."

"I'm fine."

He didn't seem fine. And neither was I. My orgasm buzz was deflating like a balloon. He was sitting on the far side of the couch, like he needed to put as much distance as possible between us without actually leaving the room. Maybe that was his attempt to save my feelings. If so, it wasn't working.

"Do you want to finish the movie?" he asked, not quite looking at me.

I gaped at him. He'd just given me an orgasm then recoiled away like he didn't want to touch me again. And now we were going to just sit here and pretend it hadn't happened?

"No. I think I'm going to go."

I stood and grabbed my purse so I could find my phone. My dad's house was probably walking distance, but I didn't know the streets well enough to navigate in the dark. Ginny would come get me, but I didn't want to bug her if she was still having fun. I'd just order an Uber. Were there Uber drivers in Tilikum? There had to be at least one or two. It was small, but not *that* small.

"Sky," Gavin said. "You don't have to go. Or at least let me drive you."

He started to get up but I held out a hand. "No. Don't, it's fine. You should probably rest your leg."

"But—"

"I just need to go," I said, cutting him off.

I didn't wait for a reply. Just walked out the door.

19

SKYLAR

I cast a suspicious glance at my phone, sitting on my desk. The notification light flashed, the tiny green dot making my stomach clench. Who had texted me? I wanted to look, and didn't want to look. Wanted it to be Gavin, and didn't want it to be Gavin.

We hadn't talked since I'd left his house last night. I still wasn't sure what had happened—other than he'd given me a breathtaking orgasm, then inexplicably wanted to go back to watching a movie, like nothing had happened.

I would have—

It didn't matter what I would have done. Gavin hadn't wanted it. Hadn't really wanted me.

I finished getting dressed, my mind a jumble of thoughts. Physically, I still felt great, which was such a strange contrast to the state of my brain.

Finally, I took a deep breath and picked up my phone.

It wasn't him.

Ginny: *Morning, sunshine. Want to meet for breakfast?*
Me: *I'd love to.*

Ginny: *How about that cute place downtown? Bigfoot Diner?*

Me: *Sounds good to me.*

Ginny: *Meet in about half an hour?*

Me: *See you then.*

This was good. Ginny would help me sort this out.

The sound of someone whistling greeted me when I left my bedroom. Was that Dad? Mom had been sleeping in the room across the hall, and her door was still shut. She'd never been much of a morning person, so I wasn't surprised she wasn't up and about yet. The whistling continued, followed by the metallic clang of a pot or pan. Was he cooking?

I went downstairs. The front rooms, which had been empty when I'd moved in, were now full of my mom's furniture. At first, they'd just stacked everything in a haphazard jumble. But Mom had said there was no reason we should all live in a house that looked like a storage facility, even if it was only temporary. She'd talked Dad into helping her arrange her couch, chairs, and coffee table, as well as her dining room furniture.

She hadn't gone so far as to put art on the walls or unpack all her decorative stuff. But there were a few things sitting out that hadn't been there a couple of days ago. A photo of me and Mom sat on an end table. And there were books and a few knick-knacks on a small bookshelf in the living room.

It didn't surprise me. Mom had always made sure her living space was not only tidy, but pretty as well.

I went back to the kitchen and found my dad, still whistling while he cooked breakfast. Bacon sizzled in a pan and there was a plate of pancakes on the counter. He cracked an egg into another pan.

"Morning," I said, half wondering who this man was and what he'd done with my father. I'd been living here for a month and I'd never seen him cook, beyond reheating things or warming up packaged food.

He glanced over his shoulder. "Morning. Hungry?"

"I was going to meet Ginny for breakfast soon, but I could eat here and just order coffee."

"Whatever works for you. It'll be ready in a few more minutes. There's coffee made if you want a cup now."

"Thanks." I poured myself a cup of coffee and sat down at the table. "What's the occasion? Or did you just feel like having a big breakfast?"

"Bacon sounded good." He paused to flip an egg. "I figured if I was going to make bacon, I might as well do breakfast right."

A vague memory flitted through my mind, wafting in on the smell of coffee, bacon, and maple syrup. A memory of this very kitchen, and me at this table. My legs swinging, too short to reach the floor, a plate of pancakes in front of me. Dad cooking breakfast for the three of us while Mom sat at the table with me, sipping coffee.

"You used to make us breakfast sometimes, didn't you?"

"He did," Mom said, appearing in the doorway. She wore a silky floral kimono that belted at the waist. Her face was fresh and makeup-free, her hair down, but even without all her usual styling, she looked beautiful. "For a while, it was our Saturday morning tradition."

"Yes, it was," Dad said without turning around.

Was it just me, or was he suddenly standing up straighter? Now that I really looked at him, I noticed his shirt was neatly tucked in. And had he gotten a haircut?

Mom got herself a cup of coffee and sat next to me. She flicked quick glances at Dad while she sipped.

This whole situation was so weird. I'd never been the kid who wanted to *Parent Trap* her parents back together. I'd always wondered how they'd ever gotten together in the first place. Growing up, it had felt like they got along for my sake, but a simmering tension had remained between them. Once in a while, that tension had snapped, and I'd watched whatever frustrations they still carried boil over.

Mom had been here for about a week and a half, and that tension hadn't gone anywhere. If anything, it seemed to grow by the day. So far, Dad had mostly grumbled about her presence, muttering to himself when he couldn't find things after her kitchen reorganization or shaking his head at the furniture decorating the other rooms. Mom had been her usual self, cheerfully doing what she wanted despite my dad's grumbling, all while casting him side-eye glances when he wasn't looking.

But how long before the pressure cooker burst and one or both of them snapped?

"I think I remember that," I said, hoping to keep the conversation on happy things. "I don't have a lot of memories of living here, but I do remember pancake breakfasts."

Dad brought over a plate with bacon, two eggs, and a stack of three small pancakes dripping with butter and syrup. He slid it in front of me with a grin. "Pancakes and bacon were your favorite. Hope they're good."

"It all looks amazing. Smells good too."

"Caroline?" he asked.

"Sure, why not? See, aren't you glad I fixed your kitchen? It's so much easier to cook in here."

Dad narrowed his eyes at her and went back to the stove without responding. I kind of wondered if that meant he agreed with her but didn't want to admit it.

"The Saturday breakfast tradition started before you

were born," Mom said. "We used to meet our friends at a diner on Saturday mornings. We all would have been out late the night before and we'd shuffle in, tired or maybe a little hungover. After coffee and a big breakfast, we'd perk up. But the diner went out of business and there wasn't another good breakfast place in town at the time."

"The Copper Kettle was open back then, but we didn't go there," Dad said.

"That's right," Mom said, her eyes unfocused. "Of course we didn't go there. That was the Haven diner. In any case, with our favorite breakfast place out of business, Norman started filling in the gap. Instead of shuffling into a diner downtown, he and I would just shuffle into our own kitchen. Then we had you, and it was easier to have our big Saturday breakfast at home anyway. We kept it up until you were three or four."

"Why did you stop?"

"Things change. Schedules get in the way." Mom's eyes flicked to Dad again.

"Firefighters work twenty-four-hour shifts," Dad said. "Sometimes that means not being home on Saturday mornings."

"Or in their beds on Friday nights," Mom said with a slight edge to her voice.

Dad shut a cupboard door—not quite a slam, but with more force than necessary. "Even if that's where they'd rather be."

"Would they?"

"It's just part of the job. There's not a guy on my crew who wouldn't rather be sleeping beside his wife."

"Well good for their wives," Mom snapped. "I'm sure they're very satisfied."

"I'm sure they are because they're patient enough to make up for the lost time later in the week."

"If later in the week ever comes and they're not left in bed alone wearing new black lace lingerie, waiting for their husband who isn't coming home because he's covering for someone on his crew. Again."

I stared at my plate, my fork dangling in my grasp. This conversation had turned very specific—and very mortifying—in the space of just four words. *New black lace lingerie.*

Oh god.

Dad dropped a plate of food in front of my mom. "When things like that happen, they have no idea their wives bought new lingerie or that they're at home wearing it. Believe me, they do not like missing out on that."

"Their wives don't like missing out on it either."

They both stopped and silence rushed into the room, like a wave breaking over the sand. Trying not to look at either of them, I picked at my breakfast. The buzz of the fridge made the back of my neck tingle uncomfortably. Should I change the subject? Stay quiet? Ask a question? Run while I could still get away?

Running seemed like my best option.

"Thank you so much for breakfast, Dad." I stood and took my plate to the counter. "I'll reheat some leftovers later. I'm full already."

Dad cleared his throat. "Okay, sure. Going to meet Ginny?"

"Yeah."

"Have fun, honey," Mom said.

"Thanks."

I hurried upstairs to grab my purse and phone. When I tip-toed back downstairs, the kitchen was relatively quiet.

They weren't arguing anymore, at least. I grabbed my coat, slipped outside, and left.

Ginny was in a window booth when I got to the Bigfoot Diner. I took off my coat and sat across from her.

"Hey," she said with a bright smile. "I ordered us both coffee, but I haven't ordered food yet."

"Thanks. I'll probably stick with coffee for now. My dad was cooking breakfast and I didn't want to hurt his feelings by not eating."

She shrugged. "No problem. I just wanted company."

"Yeah, I figured."

The waitress came by with a carafe of coffee and filled our mugs, and Ginny ordered breakfast.

"Speaking of your dad, how are things on the home front?" Ginny asked after the waitress left. "Did he cook breakfast for Caroline, too?"

"Yes, and somehow that led to them arguing about his old work schedule and…" I trailed off, not sure I wanted to dig into what they'd really been arguing about.

"And, what?" She blew on her coffee.

"The implication was the impact his schedule had on their sex life. There was mention of him missing out on her waiting in bed wearing new black lace lingerie. At that point, I started plotting my escape."

"Oh my god, that's both adorable and sad at the same time."

"And also very cringey to listen to your divorced parents have a thinly veiled argument about their former sex life at the breakfast table."

Ginny winced. "Yeah, that's not ideal. We can change the subject if you want."

"Thank you."

"So did Gavin take you straight home last night, or…"

I groaned, my shoulders slumping. "No."

"What happened?"

Taking a deep breath, I tucked my hair behind my ear. "We went to his house and started watching a movie. He startled me as a joke and then all of a sudden..."

She raised her eyebrows. "What? All of a sudden, what?"

"We were making out."

"Get it, girl. So what's the problem?"

Leaning closer, I lowered my voice. "The problem is, he dry humped me to a freaking orgasm, and then stopped."

"What do you mean, stopped? He just got up and that was that?"

"Yes."

"Seriously?"

"Yeah, he moved to the other side of the couch. I could tell he was keyed up, because, you know."

"His dick was hard," she said bluntly.

"Yes, and I was very clear that it was a yes from me and we could keep going. But he said no."

"Are you sure he didn't come in his pants and didn't want you to know?"

"Definitely not, although I think he was close."

Ginny's eyes were wide, and for a second, she just stared at me, her lips forming a little O. "So he gave you an orgasm and then didn't want to continue."

"Yes."

"I'm confused."

"Thank you," I said, my voice tinged with enthusiasm. "See? That's weird, right? It's not just me?"

"No, definitely not just you."

"He took some deep breaths and rubbed his hands up and down his face, and then he asked me if I wanted to keep watching the stupid movie."

"That's all just... very unexpected."

"I know."

"I thought Gavin was supposed to be the kind of guy who'd give you the orgasm and then happily take a blow job in return. Did you guys have a conversation about where things were going or something?"

"No, not at all."

"What about at the party?"

"No. I did tell him about my arousal thing, which now I'm regretting. Ginny, was it a *pity* dry-humping?"

"I can't imagine it was out of pity. Tell me one thing, though."

"What?"

"Was it good?"

I rolled my eyes, wishing I could lie to her and say it hadn't been very good anyway. But I couldn't. "It was amazing."

"I don't know if that makes it better or worse." She reached over and patted my hand sympathetically. "I'm guessing you haven't talked to him since."

"Your guess is correct. I left pretty abruptly. He offered to drive me home, but I was just so... confused and kind of embarrassed. And now I don't know what to do. Or what I want him to do."

"You like him."

"Yeah, I do. He still kind of scares me, but I like hanging out with him. And I know this makes no sense, but he's the only reason I've been writing lately."

"What do you mean?"

"You know how blocked I've been. Somehow when he's around, I'm not blocked. I have no explanation for it. He came into the coffee shop one day when I was trying to write and sat at my table for a little while. I wrote an entire chapter. A whole chapter, Ginny. Do you know how long it's been since I've done that?"

"Months?"

"Yes. After he left, nothing. It was like turning off a faucet. So later I invited him over to see if it would happen again."

"And it did?"

"Yep. He sat on my bed while I wrote and it worked. I wrote and wrote and wrote, just like I used to."

"That's so crazy."

"I know. I have no idea what's going on with that. But even without the writing thing, I don't want things to be all messed up between us."

"Do you think it's because he works for your dad? He doesn't want to get in trouble with his boss?"

"Maybe. He did say something a few weeks ago about promising my dad he wouldn't, but he wasn't exactly clear on what he wouldn't do."

"Well there you go. That's probably what's going on."

"So you're saying maybe there's a reason other than he's repulsed by me physically and he wishes he'd never touched me?"

She rolled her eyes. "Are all novel writers as dramatic as you?"

"I don't know. Probably."

"Anyone can see Gavin likes you. Whatever he has going on in his head, it's not that he's repulsed by you physically. I bet it's the *your-dad-is-his-boss* thing. He doesn't think he can date you."

I stirred some cream into my coffee, briefly pondering. "You know, the more I think about it, maybe he did the right thing last night. I don't know if I'm ready to be with someone new anyway."

"Hmm."

"What does that mean?"

"It means I think you're using Cullen as an excuse because you're scared."

"Of course I'm scared. I'm always scared."

"I mean scared of Gavin."

"I literally just said he scares me."

She regarded me with a motherly tilt of her head. "I mean you're scared of falling for him."

Glancing away, I let out a long breath.

"Do you want my advice?"

"Yes."

"If you want him, you need to tell him. And if you're not ready for a relationship, but you like hanging out as friends and you wouldn't mind adding a little lust-and-thrust into the mix, tell him that too. What's the worst that could happen?"

"He turns me down and it's so horribly awkward he never speaks to me again."

"Maybe I should have rephrased that. What's the worst that's *likely* to happen?"

"Same answer."

"All I'm saying is that if you don't go after what you want, you probably won't get it."

"Yeah..." I trailed off. I didn't want to admit she was right. Going after what I wanted had never been my number one skill. "But I don't think I'm using Cullen as an excuse for anything. I honestly don't think I'm ready for a relationship right now. In case you haven't noticed, my career is circling the drain. I need to focus on writing, and then finding a new agent, and landing a publishing deal. That's... a lot."

"You know, these days you don't necessarily need a

publisher. Authors publish their work independently all the time."

"I know that works for some people, but it seems so..."

"Scary?"

"Yes."

"Scarier than having to find a new agent and land a new publishing deal?"

"Why are you trying to push me out of my comfort zone?"

She smiled. "Because sometimes you need a nudge."

"How about this? I'll consider it and do a little research so I know more about it. Will that make you happy?"

"Yes."

"Can we talk about you now?" I continued before she could answer. "I saw you talking to Logan Bailey last night."

"Oh yeah. He was funny."

"Did you hang out with him more after I left?"

Her lips twitched in a smile. "A little."

I raised my eyebrows. "Did you go home alone last night or is there another reason for your sunny disposition this morning?"

She laughed softly. "No, I went home alone. We flirted a little and it was fun, but that was it."

"Okay. That's probably good."

"Why?"

"Gavin said I should warn you about Logan."

"Calling out his brother? Ouch."

"No, it was more like he was being honest with a friend. He said his brother is a good guy but probably the kind of guy you should warn your girlfriend about."

"I'm not even a tiny bit surprised."

"I also saw you talking to Gram and Fiona. Aren't they so nice?"

"I want Gram to adopt me. I seriously adore her." She put a finger to her lips. "Maybe I should make something happen with Logan just so I can have Gram for a grandma-in-law."

I laughed. "I don't know if Logan is the one to go after if marrying into the family is your goal."

"Good point. Besides, I'm too busy to think about getting married."

"Speaking of busy, how's your research going?"

Her eyes lit up. "Oh my god, so good. This town is a treasure trove of amazing stories. I've been to places with a lot of history plenty of times, but the way these people spin everything into a tall tale is absolutely fantastic. And don't even get me started on the feud. It's gold."

"Yeah? So you're finding a lot of stuff to write about?"

"Am I ever. I learned so much from Gram last night. You know what's crazy? No one knows how the feud started. I've talked to people on both sides, and the one thing they all agree on is that no one knows the real story."

"That's so weird."

"Isn't it? Honestly, I love it. I've met so many townspeople who have their own version, but all of them admit they don't really know. They've just made up their own theories. But then Fiona was telling me about some stuff Grace Bailey found. A woman named Eliza Bailey went missing, probably around the early 1920s or maybe a little bit before that. And there could be a connection to a man named John Haven, who also went missing. I'm not clear on whether they went missing at the same time, or if one of them might have been responsible for the other's disappearance or what. I need to dig into it and see what I can find."

"Maybe you'll uncover the origin of the feud."

"I'm kind of hoping I do. It's such a fun mystery."

"Keep me posted." My phone buzzed, the little noise rattling my ear drums.

Ginny met my eyes. "Maybe it's him. Check it."

I took a deep breath and pulled out my phone.

"It's him."

"He's reaching out. That means it's your move."

My move. I took another deep breath and read his text.

20

GAVIN

*T*he river meandered by, slow and lazy this time of year. It was cold out today, but I didn't care. If my leg hadn't been in a cast, I probably would have jumped in, just for the rush. There was something about dousing yourself in ice-cold water that felt awesome. Woke up the senses.

But I did have a cast, so I had to be content with sitting on a rock next to my truck, watching the river. It was one of my favorite places—which was probably why Gram had named me Otter when I was little. I'd always loved water.

I fiddled with my phone, impatiently waiting for Skylar's reply. My message had been simple and straightforward. *I'm really sorry about last night. Can we get together?*

Discontent made me edgy. I didn't like the way last night had ended. At all. I hadn't meant to upset her. I hadn't meant for any of it to happen. But man, when she'd whispered that threat of getting herself off if I wouldn't do it for her, I'd cracked.

The logic had made sense to my half-functioning, lust-filled brain. She'd needed an orgasm, so I'd given her one. Then I'd stopped. Kept from crossing that line.

But that had obviously hurt her feelings, because she'd bolted.

And now I felt like shit. She probably did too.

Finally—it hadn't really taken that long, but I was impatient as fuck right now—she replied.

Skylar: *What did you have in mind?*

Me: *First, do you need to get any writing done today? Because I can come over if you need me.*

Skylar: *I'm taking today off, but thank you.*

Me: *Okay, cool. Do you want to go to the drive-in with me tonight?*

Skylar: *There's a drive-in?*

Me: *Yeah, just outside town. I need to do some recon.*

Skylar: *Recon? For what?*

Me: *A prank.*

Skylar: *You're going to do a prank at the drive-in?*

Me: *Yep. Nick Haven owns it, so obviously we never go see movies there. But we have an idea for an epic prank. We just need to see what it'll take to pull it off. So I'm going to stake the place out. Are you in?*

Skylar: *Will we get in trouble?*

Me: *No.*

Skylar: *Even though it's Haven territory?*

Me: *We won't get caught. It'll be fine.*

It took her a long moment to answer. I could imagine her fiddling with a strand of hair, turning the idea over and over in her mind, trying to decide. I figured I'd give her another little nudge.

Me: *Come on, Sky. This is low-key Tilikum prank stuff. Perfect for a beginner. I promise nothing bad will happen.*

Skylar: *Okay. I'll come.*

Me: *Awesome. I'll pick you up at seven.*

Skylar: *See you then.*

Feeling exponentially better, I pocketed my phone, then tossed a pebble in the meandering river. Tonight was going to be fun.

Skylar answered the door already wearing her coat. She gave me a hesitant smile as she stepped out and shut the door behind her.

"Hey. Thanks for coming with me tonight."

"Thanks for inviting me."

Our eyes met and we just looked at each other for a few seconds. I wondered if I should say something else—bring up last night again. But if she wanted to talk about it, she probably would. Girls always brought up the subject when they needed to talk about their feelings or whatever. I waited, giving her a chance to say something if she needed to. She didn't, so I figured we were good.

Being near her again made my dick stand up and take notice. I covertly adjusted myself as soon as she turned to walk out to the street.

Man, the things this girl did to me.

We went out to my truck and headed for the drive-in. It was in a big clearing at the end of Icicle Road, out where an old Haven Timber Company sawmill had once been. I'd been out here a bunch of times, just to see if I could sneak in and watch a movie without getting caught. It wasn't too hard, and I always slipped ticket money into the concession stand window so it wouldn't be stealing.

But tonight, I didn't need to see if I could get in without being seen so I could watch a movie on Haven turf because of a dare or just to prove that I could. Tonight, I needed to go deeper.

"So what's the prank you guys are planning?" Skylar asked as we drove toward the edge of town.

"We want to hijack the movie and play one of our own."

"You mean like a bad movie or something?"

I grinned. "No, I mean our own movie. We'll shoot one, starring us."

She smiled. "That would be pretty funny."

"Right?" I was getting excited just thinking about it. "The trick is, we don't know for sure if they have a digital projector. Movies used to be sent out on those big film reels, but according to Levi, it's all going digital now. But the drive-in mostly shows old movies, so they don't necessarily need to upgrade. We heard a rumor that they just got a new digital projector, though. And if they did, it's game on."

"Wait." Her smile disappeared. "How can you tell if it's a digital projector?"

I shrugged. "I'm not sure. We'll probably have to break in to the projection booth."

"I don't know if we should do that."

"Don't worry. We'll only do it if we won't get caught."

"How could you possibly know that?"

"I have a sense about these things." I winked at her. "Trust me."

She twisted her hands in her lap. "This makes me very nervous. I was with Ginny when you texted and she kind of talked me into coming."

"High five, Ginny. You can stay outside if you want, but you don't have to worry. I won't let anything bad happen."

She glanced at me again, clearly not convinced.

"What's the worst that could happen to us?" I asked.

"We get arrested for trespassing and my divorced parents who are currently living together get in an enormous fight over who's going to come bail me out of jail and then I have to live with the fallout because the thing that made them snap was me?"

"That's... kind of specific. Are your parents fighting a lot?"

"Not exactly. They're mostly picking at each other and sometimes things get tense. But I keep wondering when they're going to blow up."

"How long do you think your mom will be living there?"

"I don't know. She hasn't said anything specific to me, but I assume she and my dad have talked about it. She's looking for a job, which makes me think she wants to stay in Tilikum."

"That's pretty cool. You could have both your parents close."

"Yeah, it would be. Although right now, I'm wondering if this town is big enough for both of them."

"Well they are living under the same roof. That's gotta be tense."

"So tense. I know I'm overly sensitive to... well, everything. But I feel like the entire house is charged with electricity. I'm surprised my hair isn't standing on end."

I opened my mouth to tell her she could always come hang out at my house if things were getting a little too real at home. But I figured I'd steer clear of that topic for now. Too soon.

I turned onto Icicle Road, but took another immediate right onto a narrow dirt road and pulled over. "We'll park here and walk through the trees. Someone might recognize my truck if I get too close, and the walk isn't bad."

She nibbled on her fingernail. "You're sure we won't get caught?"

I hesitated for a second, thinking about it, and slowly nodded. "I'm about ninety-percent sure."

"I guess those are pretty good odds."

"Really good."

"What would it take for you to not go? Like if you thought it was only fifty-fifty, would you still do it?"

"Fifty-fifty? Yeah, easy. Although maybe not with a broken leg. I'd want to be fully mobile in case I had to make a run for it."

"Make a run for it? That's not helping my anxiety."

I reached over and took her hand. "Sky, you've got this. We're just going to go take a look around. Besides, you did hit me with your car. You kinda owe me."

She smacked my arm. "That's so not fair."

"I know, I'm terrible," I said with a grin. "How about you think of this as book research."

"But I'm not writing about anyone breaking into a drive-in theater."

"Do you write about people breaking in to other places?"

"Well... yeah."

"Now you'll have firsthand experience."

Our eyes locked and a surge of heat swept through me. God, she was hot. The memory of her lips was still seared into my skin. That pretty little mouth had been on my neck, whispering in my ear. I'd only gotten a taste of her and fuck it had been good.

Too good.

Maybe too good to resist.

I wasn't sure whether I was going to win or lose this battle, or what winning or losing even meant. Because right now, the only thing I could think about was what Skylar sounded like when she was coming, and I wanted to make her do it again.

Bad idea, Gav. Don't steal another cookie.

"We should get moving," I said, finally. "We need to get in and out before the movie ends."

Skylar nodded, but I didn't miss the blush that hit her cheeks.

I loved a challenge, but holding myself back from her was turning out to be some masochistic shit.

A couple of slow breaths of cold night air helped clear my head. I put on a baseball cap and situated my crutches under my arms while Skylar got out and shut the door.

"Can I put you on flashlight duty?" I asked. "It's hard to do anything when I need my arms and legs just to walk."

"Yep, I've got it." She pulled out her phone and turned on the light, shining it in front of us. "Are you okay to walk through the woods in the dark with those things?"

"Sure, I'll be fine."

"You say that a lot."

"What? That I'll be fine?"

"Yeah."

That was an interesting observation. "You're probably right. But it's true."

"Okay, Gavin Bailey. I can't quite believe you talked me into this, but lead the way."

We crept through the woods, watching out for debris or other hazards that might make me fall flat on my face. When we got closer, we could see the glow of the movie screen, lighting up the clearing. The theater was at the end of the two-lane Icicle Road, a big turnaround providing the only way out. Cars were lined up in arc-shaped rows facing the screen and a building behind them housed the concession stand. Above that, the projector room.

I scoped things out as we got closer. There was a dilapidated chain-link fence surrounding the grounds, but I knew from experience there were at least three places where you could sneak in, the biggest one right in front of us.

"Okay, here's the plan," I said. "We're going to go through that hole in the fence and stroll in like we belong there."

"Aren't people going to recognize you?"

"If they get a good look at me, yeah. But everyone's paying attention to the movie." I fiddled with the brim of my hat. "And the hat helps a little."

"Are you sure?"

"Positive. I've done it before. The key to this kind of thing is to act like you belong. Then no one notices you."

She took a deep breath and blew it out through pursed lips. "I'm actually a little bit excited."

"See? This is fun."

"I don't know if I'm ready to go that far."

I nudged her with my elbow. "You're going to do great."

"What happens once we're in?"

"We have to play things by ear. I'm pretty sure the projector room guy comes down sometimes, so I'm hoping we get lucky. Otherwise I'll make something up and hope he doesn't realize who I am."

"This is a very loose plan, Gavin."

"I'm good at improvising. It's fine."

She took another deep breath. "Let's get this over with before I lose my nerve."

We made our way closer and ducked through the fence. I knew the risk of someone recognizing me was higher because of my crutches. I'd been seen walking around town with them. But there was nothing I could do about that now.

Besides, Levi and Logan had said they didn't think I could do it. I had to prove those dickheads wrong.

The smell of popcorn grew the closer we got to the concession stand. Skylar walked close to me, and from the corner of my eye, I could see her darting nervous glances at our surroundings. She was so fucking cute.

Most people were in their cars, watching the movie. A handful of customers lingered around the front of the concession stand with bags of popcorn, candy, and big cups of soda. We paused near the side of the building, far enough away that we were outside the circle of light surrounding it.

"What do we do now?" Skylar whispered, turning her face up toward me so I could hear her.

"We wait for an opportunity."

"What kind of opportunity?"

"I'll know it when I see it."

It only took a few minutes. The back door of the concession stand opened and a guy walked out holding a bag of popcorn, then shut the door behind him. A girl materialized from the shadow of the building. He kissed her, then handed her the popcorn. They left in the opposite direction. My instincts tingled.

"I'd bet anything that's the projector guy," I said, keeping my voice low. "This is our chance."

We hurried to the back of the building and luckily the door wasn't locked. I went in first, doing my best to keep the noise from my crutches to a minimum. The kids running the concession stand were in the front and luck was on our side once again—the stairs up to the projector room were right next to the back door.

Skylar came in after me and we went up with no one the wiser.

The projector room was smaller than I thought it would be. And darker. In the dim light, I could make out a desk with a computer, a bunch of cluttered shelves, and a big movie projector broadcasting tonight's film onto the huge screen.

Fuck yes. It was digital.

"Wow." Skylar turned a slow circle, taking in the room. "It's kind of creepy up here."

"It is, isn't it?"

"Is that what you were looking for?" She pointed to the projector.

"Exactly." I took out my phone and snapped a few pictures. "This is perfect."

She put her hand on her chest, a little smile gracing her lips. "My heart's beating so fast."

"I told you it would be fun."

"So this is what you do for fun?"

I glanced around at the cramped room. "Well, I've never broken into the projector room at a drive-in before, but yeah, basically."

She laughed softly and my eyes were instantly drawn to her lips. Those sweet, soft lips I'd tasted last night.

I knew what would make this night a lot more fun.

As if she could read my mind, she stepped closer. A look of resolve passed over her features, that little hint of fear dissolving from her eyes.

Our magnetism was too strong. I couldn't escape its pull.

Or maybe I didn't want to.

I leaned down, meeting her lips with mine. I knew I shouldn't—knew I was going to regret this later—but I couldn't resist. One taste of her and I was already addicted. I needed more.

With a low groan, I delved my tongue into her mouth. All the unsatisfied lust from last night ripped through me, making my cock strain against my jeans. She gripped my sweatshirt, lifting onto her tip toes, and I could feel her hunger. Her need.

Her hands moved lower and she brushed my cock

through my pants. I hissed in a breath, that light touch enough to make every muscle in my body tense in anticipation.

What was she going to do?

I sucked on her lip, letting it scrape against my teeth. She cupped me harder and I groaned into her mouth.

"Fuck, Sky. What are we doing?"

"What are the chances we'll get caught?" she breathed against my lips.

"Probably fifty-fifty."

"I'll take those odds."

She unfastened my pants, lowered the zipper, and sank down onto her knees.

"Holy shit."

Apparently I'd gone commando today—not so much a conscious decision as the result of needing to do laundry. Totally worked out in my favor. She looked up at me through her thick lashes and her tongue darted over her lips.

"Fuck," I growled.

I wanted to ask her if she was sure about this, but my brain was completely short circuiting at the sight of her on her knees in front of me, lowering one side of my jeans to expose more of my very hard cock. Plus, she looked pretty fucking sure.

I'd just trust her on this one.

The million-and-one reasons I shouldn't do this with her were nowhere in sight. She was about to suck my dick and there was a pretty good chance we could get caught. The combination was fucking crack to me. Impossible to resist.

Heat ran through my veins as she pulled my cock out of my pants. Parting her lips, she slid the tip inside. For the first time, I was glad I had these damn crutches. I wouldn't have been able to stay standing otherwise.

Her mouth was warm and wet. She took me in deeper, holding my stiff length at the base. Fuck, that felt good. She started to move faster and my eyes rolled back. I probably needed to be quiet so the kids working the concession stand below didn't hear anything, but it was hard to hold the groan in my throat.

Without warning, she plunged down on me, surrounding my cock with her wet mouth. My shoulders hit the wall behind me. Even with crutches I couldn't quite stay on my feet. But Skylar was fucking relentless, drawing me in and out of her mouth like a woman on a mission.

A mission to make me come.

She was going to succeed. Fast.

My orgasm built, the shock of her aggressiveness and the danger of getting caught making this the single hottest thing I'd ever done in my life. The pressure in my groin grew, tension surging through me. Skylar plunged down on me, over and over, my cock sliding in and out of her mouth.

Then she looked up at me again, those sweet brown eyes glinting with wickedness.

And I came fucking unglued.

I barely had time to give her a strangled warning. "I'm coming. Fuck."

She didn't stop. If anything, she doubled down. I watched as my glistening cock pulsed in her mouth, throbbing as I came down her throat.

My heart felt like it might beat right out of my chest. I took a few heaving breaths as I came down the other side.

She slid me out of her mouth and lightly swiped her thumb across the corner of her lips.

"Holy shit, Sky, that was the hottest fucking thing I've ever done. Or seen. Or anything."

Still leaning against the wall, I grabbed her hands to help her to her feet, ready to hug her or kiss her or maybe just rip her pants off and fuck her right here. She bit her lip, a hint of shyness returning to her expression as she stood.

"Did—"

Whatever she was about to say died on her lips and her eyes went wide.

I'd heard it too.

Someone was coming up the stairs.

21

SKYLAR

$\mathcal{M}$y eyes widened and my heart skipped. Someone was coming.

Oh my god, I'd just given Gavin Bailey a blow job in the projector room at a drive-in, and someone was coming up the stairs.

Gavin's dick was hanging out of his pants, still semi-hard, which was kind of blowing my mind. But this wasn't the time to contemplate how quickly he could be ready for round two after an orgasm. We were about to get caught.

"Your pants," I hissed, lunging at him to put his dick away.

"I got it." He tucked himself back in his jeans, then buttoned and zipped them.

"What do we do?"

"I'll think of something."

More steps outside.

"Is there a window?" I asked, feeling frantic.

He looked down at his cast. "Um."

"Right. Oh my god."

The door opened and a guy wearing a sweatshirt and jeans stopped dead in his tracks. "Who are you?"

Gavin tugged on the bill of his baseball cap. And then the weirdest thing happened. I started talking.

"I'm so sorry. My date was playing a little trick on me. He said the bathroom was up here and I was silly enough to fall for it. Maybe I shouldn't have had that second glass of wine with dinner."

"Oh." He looked me up and down like he was confused, which was completely understandable. It wasn't exactly a good cover story. "Well, you guys aren't supposed to be up here."

"Yeah, of course. Sorry about that." I pressed my lips closed before I kept going and awkwardly blurted out that this had been a great place for a spontaneous blow job.

Spontaneous blow job? Since when did I give spontaneous blow jobs?

Although, my god, it had been exhilarating.

Gavin gestured for me to go ahead and the guy moved out of our way. I quickly went down the stairs, practically holding my breath, wondering if he was going to recognize Gavin. But all I heard was the click of Gavin's crutches as he came down behind me.

I got outside and paused just long enough for Gavin to catch up. He kept our pace much slower than I wanted—I was ready to bolt for the hole in the fence.

"Stay with me," he said. "Remember, we belong here. We're going over there, no big deal."

My heart raced as we wandered away from the concession stand, like we didn't have a care in the world. When we got out of the circle of light, he picked up the pace. A minute later, we were scrambling through the hole in the fence, tasting sweet freedom on the other side.

I got out my phone to use as a light again and we found our way back to Gavin's truck. I wasn't going to feel safe until I was inside, so I rushed around to the passenger side and got in.

Gavin hoisted his crutches behind the seat and climbed inside, then shut the door.

"Oh my god," I said, holding my hands to my chest. "I can't believe we did that."

"I can't believe *you* did that."

He didn't mean breaking in to the projection room, and I knew it. I didn't blame him. I couldn't believe I'd done that either.

Then again, maybe I could.

Gavin Bailey scared me. But he also made me feel brave.

I shifted toward him. "I know that was a little bit crazy."

"I like you a little bit crazy."

The way he stared at me, his brown eyes smoldering, made the pressure between my legs grow. I was already keyed up from giving him that blow job. It had been reckless and scary and so freaking hot. I wanted more.

I wanted him. And I wanted him now.

He slammed his seat backward as far as it would go, then grabbed me, manhandling me onto his lap. My legs straddled him and why hadn't I worn a skirt tonight? Palming my ass, he pressed me closer, grinding against me, and oh my god he was hard again.

So.

Hard.

I was losing my mind—totally taking leave of my sanity —and I didn't care. Our mouths crashed together, our lips and tongues tangling with desperation.

He turned his attention to my coat, pawing at the belt tied around my waist. We paused just long enough to unfasten it and fumble with the buttons. A second later, he was ripping it off me and tossing it on the other seat.

Our mouths met again, silky wet kisses, the heat between us thick and palpable. The windows were probably fogging up, but I didn't care about that either. I just needed him to fuck me. Right now.

His hands slid up my back and he unfastened my bra with a quick flick of his fingers. Impressive. He pushed up my shirt, exposing my boobs to the chill air. I gasped as his mouth found one sensitive nipple. He cupped me in his hands as he licked one side, then the other.

Leaning my head back, I moaned. He sucked my nipple harder, sending shock waves of pleasure through my body. I rolled my hips, rubbing against his thick erection.

And I knew intimately how thick it was.

So.

Very.

Thick.

After a few more flicks of his tongue, he unfastened my pants. It wasn't easy to get out of them, but I wasn't letting that deter me. I pushed them over my hips and down my legs, then braced myself on the seat behind him and kicked them onto the floor. His didn't need to come all the way off. I just needed to free that delicious cock.

Feeling insane with lust, I unfastened his pants. His gorgeous cock was right there, hard and ready for me. He pushed his pants down his hips.

Damn it. My sense of responsibility wasn't completely lost in the haze of potent arousal. I was still on birth control, but we probably needed a condom.

Gavin was already on it. Breathing hard, he fished his wallet out of his pocket and pulled out a condom with an exhale that might have been relief. Feeling like I might very well die right here if he didn't fuck me soon, I waited while he rolled it on.

As soon as he was ready, I moved in closer again, shifting my legs to straddle his thighs. He held his cock at the base while I lined him up with my opening. Wetness was not an issue. I was wet and ready.

So.

Ready.

My eyes fluttered closed as I sank down on him. He stretched me open, giving me blissful pressure I'd never felt before. A sigh escaped my lips as his thickness filled me.

"Oh my god," I breathed.

"Oh, fuck," was his strangled reply.

I held on to the seat behind him and lifted up, tilting my hips. Then slid back down. Gavin groaned, his fingers digging into me.

Warmth spread through my core as I rode him, my inhibitions nowhere in sight. Never in my life had I had sex in a vehicle, let alone a vehicle parked in the woods just yards from a drive-in theater full of people.

Maybe that was why it was so freaking good.

He gripped my hips and guided me up and down his thickness. I moved faster, slamming down on him. He groaned again, a low sound that reverberated through my veins.

The drag of his cock made my inner muscles squeeze around him. Pressure grew and I whimpered and moaned as I chased the pinnacle, feeling delicious tension build.

Oh yes. He was so going to make me come.

This rhythm was perfect, so I kept going, holding the seat and squeezing my thighs to ride up and down his swollen cock. He jerked into me, thrusting up, driving deeper. His eyes were intense and the groove between his eyebrows was the sexiest thing I'd ever seen.

"Is that what you needed, Sky?" he growled. "You needed to get fucked?"

"Yes," I said, my voice breathless.

"I'll fuck you good." He slammed into me harder. "So fucking good."

Out of nowhere, a tinge of fear wormed its way through the haze of crazy sex. Was someone out there? Were we going to get caught?

I gripped the seat harder, my breath going ragged. Could I actually do this?

Now that I was thinking, I was too distracted. Suddenly I could feel the steering wheel behind me, the way my knee was slipping off the edge of the seat.

I wanted this. Wanted it so bad. But I didn't know if I could. Too many sensations warred for my attention. I couldn't focus.

Gavin reached up and gently gripped my chin, forcing me to look at him. "Right here."

"What?"

"Eyes right here while I'm fucking you." His gaze seemed to reach inside me. "I want to watch you come."

"But..."

"You feel that?" He thrust his hips up. "You feel my cock inside you?"

I nodded.

"You like that, don't you?" He thrust again.

"Yes."

"That's what I thought." He groaned again when I lifted up and slid back down. "Fuck, you feel so good. That's all there is right now, Sky. Just this."

With my eyes locked on his, I kept going, focusing on

nothing but the way he felt inside me. On his gaze holding me captive. On his hands, guiding me up and down. The outside world fell away, my fear disappearing.

"That's it, Sky," he growled. "You're so fucking hot. I'm going to come in you so hard."

I whimpered, riding him faster again, my climax building. The slow waves of pleasure became sharp bursts, each one bringing me closer to the peak.

Gavin grunted with his thrusts, still holding eye contact, that brow furrow sexy beyond measure. His forehead glistened with sweat and his jaw hitched.

"Fuck yes, Sky. That's it, baby."

A little shift of my hips drew him deeper and I threw my head back. In an instant, I was coming—spiraling out of control. I burst apart, waves crashing through me, leaving me breathless.

His cock throbbed inside me and he grunted hard. My orgasm wasn't finished, his reigniting mine. I cried out as the hot pulses of his cock exploded through me. My thighs clenched and my inner muscles squeezed.

Finally, we both stopped and I slumped forward, still bracing myself against the seat. He leaned his head back, his breath as labored as mine.

"Holy shit," he muttered.

Glancing around, reality started to come back to me. "Oh wow. I should get dressed."

I peeled myself off him and awkwardly rolled onto the passenger seat. With a dimpled grin, he handed me my pants. While I put myself back together, he discreetly removed the condom, tugged his jeans back up, and fastened them.

He ran his fingers through his hair, making it adorably messy. "Well that was... not what I was expecting tonight."

"Me neither."

And it was true, I hadn't been expecting it. Hoping, though. That was another matter.

I'd definitely been hoping.

He reached over and traced his thumb along my jaw. "Should we get out of here?"

"Yeah, we should."

He gazed at me for a second, and I wondered what he was thinking. But he just nudged my chin with his thumb and started the truck.

I let out a long breath, wondering who the heck I was, and what had happened to Skylar Stanley.

22

GAVIN

I parked on the street outside Skylar's house and walked up the path, past Chief's truck. Anticipation buzzed in my veins. She'd texted earlier to see if I'd come over for a writing session.

At least, that was what she *said*.

In reality, it probably wasn't code for a booty call. I'd been coming over to hang out with her while she wrote for the last week and a half or so. Whenever she asked me to come over so she could write, that was literally what she meant.

But that was before last night at the drive-in.

Still, I wasn't here expecting her to answer the door in her underwear or anything.

Especially because it looked like both her parents were home.

I hesitated before knocking. Things had seemed fine between us last night. The sex had been... well, it had been fucking amazing, there was no doubt about that. We'd both been amped with adrenaline after the drive-in. Adrenaline and a healthy dose of pent-up lust. Had it been a one-and-done, just a crazy thing we'd both needed to get out of our systems?

I wasn't sure.

Today I felt weirdly uncertain, a sense of unease tickling the back of my neck. I didn't have regrets, exactly. But last night probably shouldn't have happened. In fact, the last two nights probably shouldn't have happened. Yet, here I was, standing on her doorstep again.

I blew out a breath and knocked.

Chief answered the door and I had no idea why that surprised me so much—he lived here—but I almost jumped backward.

"Hey, Chief," I said quickly.

"Gav." He narrowed his eyes slightly and I swear to god, he knew.

Did he know?

Shit.

Don't look guilty.

How did a guy not look guilty? That wasn't an act I'd mastered. I'd never cared if I looked guilty before.

Shit. Again.

"Is that Gavin?" Caroline's voice came from inside. "Norman, don't lord over the doorway like that. Let the boy inside."

Chief rolled his eyes. "I'm not lording over the doorway."

Caroline was in what was now a fully furnished front room. She sat on the couch with her legs crossed, dressed in a pink blouse, beige pants, and a pair of pink slippers with feathery poofs on top.

"Come on in." She closed her laptop and pushed it aside, a bright smile on her face.

I went inside, avoiding Chief's eyes. That was probably

making me look more guilty, not less, but I'd never been in this position before.

I'd never banged my boss's daughter before.

"You must be awfully tired of those crutches," Caroline said. "How much longer before the cast comes off?"

I took a few more steps in. "Soon. They're supposed to x-ray it again but I'm tempted to just take the cast off myself."

"Gav," Chief said.

"What? I can put weight on it." I demonstrated, resting my casted foot on the floor and taking my weight off my crutches.

"Listen to your doctor," Chief said. "I need you back at work, not in another cast because you didn't let it heal properly."

"Trust me, I'm dying to get back to work."

He patted me on the back. "I know you are."

Okay, maybe he didn't know.

Resting his hands on his hips, he gave Caroline a side-eye glance.

"What?" Her wide-eyed innocent expression looked well practiced.

"I need to go to the hardware store."

"So? Go to the hardware store. I'm certainly not stopping you."

"I'm just wondering if you're going to hide any more of my stuff while I'm out."

She smiled. "I didn't hide anything. I put things away where they should go. It's been an awful long time since you lived with a woman, Norman, and it shows."

"I still can't find my socket wrench."

"It's in your toolbox in the garage."

He crossed his arms. "Why in the hell would it be out there?"

"It's a tool. That's where tools belong."

His eyes narrowed. "I have half a mind to go upstairs and reorganize your closet."

"Careful, there. You might not be ready for what you find."

"What is that supposed to mean?"

"Why don't you go upstairs to my *bedroom* and find out?" She emphasized the word *bedroom* and it was clearly on purpose.

Damn. Caroline was bringing the heat.

He grumbled something incoherent and stalked down the hallway toward the kitchen. Caroline watched him go, her lips turned up in an amused smile.

There was tension in this house all right. Skylar seemed to think they were on the brink of a fight, but I had a feeling they were on the brink of something else entirely.

I was about to ask where Skylar was, or if I should just go upstairs to find her, when Chief came back, his boots stomping on the wood floor.

"I'm going to the hardware store. I'll be back later."

"Wait, I'll come with you." Caroline stood and smoothed out her shirt. "I just need to change my shoes."

"What do you need at the hardware store?" he asked.

"The doorknob on my bedroom door sticks. I want to replace it before I get locked in my room because it won't open."

"You could have just told me. I didn't realize it needed replacing."

"I know. I'm not complaining." She patted his cheek as she walked by. "You can buy me lunch while we're in town."

Chief rolled his eyes. Caroline opened the coat closet, stepped out of her slippers, and into a pair of beige heels.

"Looks like she's made herself at home," I said, keeping my voice low.

"That she has," Chief grumbled.

She cast him a smile over her shoulder. "Ready?"

"I suppose."

She opened the front door and damn it if Chief didn't pause, tilt his head a little, and check out her ass as she walked outside.

Yeah, they weren't on the verge of blowing up in a fight. They were on the verge of fucking each other's brains out.

Which, from Skylar's perspective, still had to be awfully awkward to live with.

"Hey," Skylar said, coming down the stairs. "I didn't realize you were here already."

"That's okay, I was just chatting with your parents."

"Oh boy. I bet that was interesting. Sorry if my mom said something awkward."

"Not really. There was a little innuendo, but that's way less weird for me since they aren't my parents."

"Innuendo? Really?"

"Yeah. And Chief totally checked out your mom's ass when she went outside."

She laughed. "He did not."

"He really did. I wouldn't worry about them fighting. But maybe make a lot of noise when you come downstairs when they've been alone together in case all that tension boils over."

"That's very hard to imagine, but I'll keep it in mind."

"So, writing session?" I jerked my thumb toward the stairs.

"Yes." She tucked her hair behind her ear and turned around to go back upstairs.

I followed her up and into her room. She shut the door

behind me and the sight of her bed sent my thoughts into a tailspin.

Don't do it, Gav. Don't steal another cookie.

I lowered myself onto the edge of the bed and put down my crutches. She sat next to me.

Not at her desk.

Shit.

Damn it, this sucked. She was so fucking pretty, and sweet, and smart, and all kinds of awesome things. Why did she have to be Chief's daughter?

A second later, it was too late. Our lips met and I wasn't sure who'd started it, but I was going to fucking finish it.

I pushed her down onto the bed, caressing her mouth with mine. Now that I was kissing her, I couldn't stop. I braced myself over her, delving my tongue in deep. She'd given me one hell of a blow job last night. Maybe I'd return the favor.

Just the thought of licking her pussy made my dick even harder.

A knock on the door downstairs cut through the quickly building heat. I paused, my lips just an inch from hers.

"Ignore it." She grabbed the back of my neck and pulled me down.

I was happy to do just that, but then her phone buzzed on the bedside table.

She let out a frustrated breath. "Seriously?"

I pushed myself back to sitting and rubbed my hands up and down my thighs while she sat up and grabbed her phone. Now that we'd stopped, I was thinking, and starting to wonder if I should let this happen. Again.

Fuck, this was hard.

"Oh my god." She stared at her still buzzing phone like it was a bloody murder weapon.

"What's wrong?"

She got up and rushed to the window. "What the hell?"

Without another word, she raced out the door. I stood, fumbling for my crutches, as her footsteps flew down the stairs.

My inner alarm blared a warning. Something was wrong.

I followed her down, but paused a few steps from the bottom. She stood with the door open and I could just make out a guy outside. He had slicked back blond hair and wore a wool coat over a button-down shirt and slacks.

I didn't know who he was, but I instantly didn't like him. He had a douchey face and it was a fucking weekend, what was with the fancy-pants outfit?

He handed Skylar a large envelope.

"You could have just FedEx'd this," she said, taking it from him.

"I know, but I was nearby, so I figured I'd drop it off."

"You were nearby?"

"Don't worry about it."

"I am worried about it, Cullen. You live almost four hours away. Why are you here?"

"We rented a cabin for a long weekend. It's a vacation. Maybe you've heard of them."

"Okay, whatever." She held up the envelope. "What signature do you need? Is this the foreign rights contract we were waiting for?"

"No, that's the agency dissolution paperwork."

She let out a long breath. "Right. Fine. I'll sign it. But what happened to the foreign rights deal?"

"They passed on it."

"What do you mean, they passed?"

"They passed. There was a deadline and they didn't have an answer, so they moved on to someone else."

Skylar gaped at him. "You were supposed to take care of that."

"I'm not your agent anymore."

"But you started that deal. I figured you'd at least finish it."

"I've had too many other things going on to worry about one little foreign rights deal for a former client."

"You asshole." She whipped around and stomped into the kitchen, coming back a few seconds later with a pen. She tore the envelope open, smacked the paperwork down on her mom's coffee table, and furiously signed her name. Then she brought it back to the front door and flung it at him. The pieces of paper fluttered to the floor. "There. Happy now?"

"Really, Skylar? Very mature."

"Get out."

I wanted nothing more than to go down there and punch the guy in the face. But before I could make it to the bottom of the stairs, he swiped the contract off the floor and left.

Skylar slammed the door behind him.

I hesitated at the bottom of the stairs while she sniffed hard and swiped her fingers beneath her eyes. I didn't quite understand what had just happened, but clearly it had pissed her off.

"Are you okay?" I asked.

She sniffed again. "Yes. No. I don't know."

"Who was that?"

"Cullen, my agent." She sighed. "Also my ex-boyfriend."

Oh shit.

She went to the couch and sank down, so I crutched my way in and sat beside her.

"Obviously dating my literary agent was not my smartest move."

"That was the guy you were with before you moved here?"

"Yeah. He dumped me for another one of his clients, an author named Pepper Sinclair."

"Are you serious?"

"Unfortunately. That's not even the worst of it, though. By the time he told me, he'd been cheating on me with her for months. And she was married, so she was cheating too."

I clenched my hands into fists. Now I really wanted to fucking punch that guy. "What the fuck?"

"He said I should have seen it coming, but I didn't. I was totally blindsided."

"That's just a shitty way of trying to blame you."

She took a shaky breath and tears ran down her cheeks. "See, I know that, and it makes sense. But I thought... I thought he was it, and we were fine, and maybe we were going to..."

"You thought you were going to marry him."

"I feel so stupid."

"No." I wrapped my arm around her shoulders and drew her close. "You're not stupid. He's the dumb motherfucker who cheated on you."

I held her against me for a long moment, wishing I could do something more to make her feel better.

She sat up and swiped beneath her eyes again. "Sorry. I hate crying in front of people."

"It's okay."

"I'm just so frustrated. I didn't think seeing him again would be that bad. And I was counting on the advance from that foreign rights deal. I can't believe he just blew it off like that."

"I'd really like to hurt him."

She laughed a little. "Me too."

I rubbed her back, not sure what I should do next. It felt like we'd been doused by cold water—and not the jumping in an icy river kind that was actually fun.

"Sorry you had to see all that," she said.

"It's okay. Do you want to..." I trailed off. I couldn't exactly suggest we go upstairs and bang before her parents got home. And the feeling that maybe that interruption had been a good thing kept growing. Not that I wanted her to be upset, but if that shithead hadn't showed up, we'd have been having sex again.

Which, I wanted.

But shouldn't.

Fuck, this was a mess.

"Honestly, I think I just need to be alone for a little while," she said. "I just..."

I knew what she was trying to say. She was thinking the same thing I was. We'd been about to have sex, and if I stayed we probably would. And we probably shouldn't. "It's okay. You don't have to explain."

"Thanks. It's not you, Gavin, I—"

"I know." I leaned close and kissed her temple. "Text me if you need anything."

"I will. Thank you. And I'm sorry."

I gathered up my crutches and stood. "Don't be. I'll see you later."

Walking out her door, it felt like I was leaving a piece of myself behind. It was the weirdest feeling. I hated leaving her, but at the same time, I knew it was the right thing to do.

I couldn't fix this for her. In fact, if I stuck around, I'd probably just make things worse. More confusing.

Because fuck, I was confused. She sure as hell had to be.

I drove home in a haze, barely aware of where I was going. I kept thinking about Skylar. About what it had felt like to kiss her. Be inside her. How she wasn't just some girl. I couldn't chase her and let things play out, for better or worse. Have some fun and not worry about what would happen down the road.

There were consequences down that road. Big ones.

I tried to imagine having that conversation with Chief. That something had gone wrong and whatever had been going on between me and Sky was over. I knew what Chief thought of me. A good firefighter, maybe, but other than that, I was just a crazy kid.

Definitely not good enough for his daughter.

Chief was the closest thing I'd ever had to a father. I didn't want to make him have to say that to my face.

But maybe it wasn't too late to rewind things with her. Sure, we'd made out and things had gotten pretty out of control last night. But we'd been friends first. We could go back to that. It's not like we'd been officially dating or anything. I'd just explain to her that we needed to stay friends. She was just getting out of a relationship anyway.

She'd have to understand.

23

SKYLAR

*G*azing out the window of the Steaming Mug, I wrapped my hands around my coffee cup, enjoying the warmth that seeped into my skin. The sky outside was pale blue, a hue that hinted at the chill in the fall air, and the mountainsides had gone from green to a patchwork of reds, oranges, and golds.

Little pumpkins decorated the tables in the coffee shop. I wondered what Halloween in Tilikum was like. It was my favorite holiday. Something about it being creepy but still safe appealed to me.

Gavin had asked me to meet him here, but I'd come a little early. My head was still a mess after seeing Cullen yesterday. He was such a jerk. How could he have just dropped the ball on that foreign rights contract? The least he could have done was tell me he wasn't going to see it through. And what was with showing up at my dad's house like that, just to get a signature? He'd said *they* had rented a cabin, which of course meant he'd been enjoying a romantic weekend getaway with stupid Pepper Sinclair. Apparently he'd wanted to rub that in my face, the asshole.

I wasn't just upset because I'd been through a breakup, or because he'd tossed me aside like I'd never meant anything to him, personally or professionally. I was upset at myself for ever thinking he could be the one. How had I not seen who he really was? His behavior since he'd dumped me seemed so shockingly horrible, but then again, was it really so surprising?

Looking back, what I'd taken for seriousness and stoicism were mostly him being a jerk. He'd belittled me for being overly sensitive, dismissing my anxiety as an annoying weakness. Even something I was making up. He'd called me dramatic and unreasonable. Told me to just get over it.

I knew I was an anxious, and often hypersensitive person. I did my best to manage the way my anxiety made me feel so it didn't hold me back too much. Was it really so bad if background noises sometimes bothered me, or I got nervous around people I didn't know? Was I really that high maintenance?

Cullen had thought so. He'd thought I was so fragile, he'd cheated on me for months rather than tell me the truth.

I let out a long breath. Like my mom had said, at least I hadn't married him. That would have been a disaster.

It made me wonder if Mom saw her marriage to Dad as a disaster. It was hard to say. I wasn't even sure what had actually happened between them all those years ago.

Last night, I'd escaped into the comfort of one of my favorite books. I'd read it several times over the years, and reading it again was like visiting an old friend. Comfortable and relaxing. Because I knew what would happen, I didn't feel any stress as I read. It had felt good to shut out the world for a little while and live in another one—a world where I knew how the story ended.

I hoped Gavin had understood why I'd needed to be alone. It had seemed like he did. Cullen had showed up like an earthquake, shaking my foundation out of nowhere. I'd needed some time to process. To let all that adrenaline work its way through my system.

Although Cullen hadn't been the only reason I'd been amped up yesterday.

Gavin probably thought I'd invited him over for sex. Despite the way I'd basically attacked him as soon as he'd sat on my bed, I hadn't meant to. I'd honestly asked him to come over so I could write. But once I'd shut my bedroom door, I'd been flooded with lust. A repeat of that potent desire I'd felt for him the other night.

What was I doing?

Sleeping with a guy I wasn't really dating was very out of character for me. But something about Gavin seemed to do that to me. He brought out a side of me I'd never known was there.

And I liked it.

The shop door opened and Gavin came in, dressed in a dark jacket and jeans. His hair was adorably unkempt, his sexiness so effortless. My heart skipped and I nervously tucked my hair behind my ear.

His crutches were gone. He wore a boot on his left leg and he was actually walking.

"Look at you," I said as he came over to my table. "No more crutches."

His lips pressed together in a subdued smile, not quite wide enough to pucker his dimples. "Yeah, I had a follow-up with my doctor this morning. I have to wear this thing for a couple more weeks, but it's better than the cast."

"That's great news."

He sat across from me and a heightened sense of anxiousness pinged through my nervous system. The hiss of milk being steamed suddenly pushed against my ears, like it had weight. I crossed my legs and fiddled with a strand of hair.

"Yep. Pretty soon I'll be good as new."

"Will you go back to work on light duty now?"

He nodded and there was something off about him. He wasn't quite making eye contact.

Or maybe it was all in my head and I was just being overly sensitive.

"Do you want to order coffee or anything?" I asked.

"You know, I'm feeling pretty restless. Would you mind going for a walk?"

"Not at all. I'm sure it's nice to be on both feet again."

"Yeah, exactly."

I gathered up my things and put on my coat. Gavin held the door for me, then stuck his hands in his pockets while we walked side by side. His gait was a bit lopsided, like the boot made walking awkward, and it felt odd not to hear the click of his crutches.

He didn't say anything as we made our way up the sidewalk. A chilly breeze blew through my hair, making a strand stick to my lip gloss. I brushed it off my face, a buzz of worry zinging through me.

Was something wrong?

Or was I just being paranoid?

The silence felt as heavy as the hiss of the milk steamer in the coffee shop, and before I could stop myself, I started babbling. "Did you know a person can survive a stab wound to the gut for up to three days? That's if they don't get medical treatment, of course. It's widely considered one of the worst ways to die."

"Wow, really?"

"Sorry. I was just doing some research this morning and that popped into my head."

"Does someone in your book get stabbed in the gut?"

"Yeah, although it doesn't happen on the page. Their body is found later."

I let out a breath, annoyed with myself. Why was I talking about stab wounds and dead bodies?

Why was I so anxious?

A pair of squirrels darted in front of us. It looked like one of them was carrying a candy wrapper. Or maybe it was an actual candy bar. We paused while they scampered away, running across the street.

I expected Gavin to comment on them. Everyone in town seemed to think the squirrels were little thieves, and that one had been carrying something. He didn't find that amusing?

But he stayed quiet.

We walked across the street and into Lumberjack Park. Leaves littered the ground, crunching beneath our feet. The tension was killing me. Why weren't we talking? I hated being the one to start a conversation—the random morbid fact I'd spewed out a minute ago being a primary reason why—but I couldn't take it anymore.

But before I could say a word, Gavin stopped and turned so he was standing in front of me, his hands still in his coat pockets. "I think maybe we should talk."

A sick feeling spread from the pit of my stomach. It was almost an echo of how Cullen had started the conversation when he'd broken up with me.

"Okay."

"I really like you. But..." He hesitated, glancing down at his feet. "I think maybe things got a little out of control."

I swallowed hard, not sure what to say. I could tell he wasn't done, so I waited for him to continue.

"Hanging out with you is awesome and if you need me to come over while you write, I can totally do that. But the other stuff..." He paused again and he still wasn't looking me in the eyes. "It's not that it wasn't good. It was. I just don't think it's the best idea. You've been through a lot recently, and I'm not really boyfriend material. I'm pretty good at a lot of things, but that isn't one of them."

My legs felt shaky and the sound of a car driving by crawled up my spine and settled there, making my neck knot with tension.

"So you're saying we shouldn't have slept together."

It took him a second to answer. "I'm saying we shouldn't do it again."

I didn't understand the fierce sadness that swept through me. Gavin wasn't breaking up with me. We weren't in a relationship in the first place—not like that. But somehow this felt worse than the moment Cullen had told me it was over.

Tucking my hair behind my ear again, I took a quick breath. I didn't want him to see how much this was crushing me. Because it didn't make sense. We were just friends. Why was this such a big deal?

"I guess if that's how you feel..."

"I don't want to hurt you—"

"No," I said, cutting him off. "You're not."

Wow, was I a liar.

He took a step closer. "Skylar, I know I crossed a line with you, and I'm sorry."

Hearing him call me Skylar made my eyes flood with tears. I looked down so he wouldn't see. "It's fine. I need to worry about the book I'm writing and finding an agent and getting a publisher. The last thing I need is to be rushing into something."

"Yeah," he said, his voice tentative, like he wasn't sure if he believed me.

That made two of us.

Suddenly the rustle of leaves was crackling too loudly in my ears. I felt like I was going to crawl out of my own skin.

"Speaking of all that, I have a lot to do," I said. "I should get home."

"Are you sure? I can walk you back to your car."

"No thanks."

I couldn't stay or I was going to lose it and burst into tears. I couldn't let myself do that. Not out here in the open. I managed to mumble a goodbye as I turned and started to walk away.

"Bye, Skylar."

With tears blurring my vision, I left him standing behind me.

He'd called me Skylar. Not Sky. Twice. And I had no idea why that hurt so much.

24

GAVIN

*A*pparently trying to do the right thing was a great way to feel like shit.

I'd done it twice now, and both times had left me with a hollow ache in my chest. Things were supposed to be better, not worse.

So much for that.

After Skylar had walked away, I'd gone home and sulked with Princess Squeaker for a while. Her only suggestion was to give her kitty treats, which was cute, but didn't help solve my problems.

My brothers were both on duty tonight, and I'd been too restless to sit at home alone. So I'd come back into town, looking for a distraction. Anything to get my mind off Skylar.

A group of cars outside the Knotty Knitter caught my eye. That looked like Grace's car. And Cara's. Gram was there too. What were they all doing there? All shopping for craft shit on a Monday night?

I was curious enough to stop and go inside.

I'd never been in this store. Aisles were jam packed with

craft and sewing supplies. Yarn, fabric, paper, paints, stuff like that. I didn't see anyone, but I heard voices coming from the back of the shop.

I went down an aisle and found a bunch of women sitting on a couch and in upholstered armchairs, all with yarn and big sticks or needles or something. Knitting? Crocheting? I didn't know the difference.

They all stared at me like I'd just walked into the girls' locker room after gym class, not the back of a craft store that was open to the public.

"Evening, ladies."

The corners of Gram's mouth twitched in a hint of a smile and her eyes flicked around the circle, like she was interested to see what the other ladies would decide to do with me.

My great-aunt Tillie Bailey-Linfield was there, along with Violet Luscier—related to me on Gram's side—and my high school math teacher, Lacey Hanson. I'd crushed pretty hard on Ms. Hanson back in high school, but she was married with a couple of kids now.

Fiona waved at me with a cheerful smile. Grace twisted around to look at me, while Cara sat sideways in an armchair, sipping a drink, her legs dangling over one side. She was the only one without any yarn or sticks in her lap.

"Evening, Otter," Gram said.

"Are you lost?" Cara asked with an amused glint in her eyes.

"No, I saw your cars out front. What's going on in here?"

"It's Stitch and Sip," Grace said. "Our knitting and crochet group."

Cara eyed me for a second, then swung her legs to the front of her chair and stood. "Here, you can have my chair."

"Thanks." I lowered myself into the chair, my eyes landing on the woman seated in the corner of the couch.

Wait.

Was that Marlene Haven?

I glanced around, wondering if they could see her or if the Havens had developed invisibility powers. Because how could Marlene Haven be sitting here calmly with Gram and Grace, like it was no big deal? Like there wasn't a feud that went back generations?

"Marlene, can I get you a refill?" Cara asked.

She glanced up, looking over the rims of blue reading glasses. "I'm fine, but thank you."

Well they could obviously see her.

She caught me staring and her mouth twitched in a smile. "Hi, Gavin."

My eyes darted around again. Apparently this was fine. "Hi, Mrs. Haven."

Little knowing smiles passed between the other women. I decided this must be girl stuff that was above my head, so I wouldn't worry about it. I had enough on my mind anyway.

"Here, Otter." Gram tossed me a package of light blue yarn. "Roll that into a ball for me."

She'd given me this job before. Little kid me had sat at her feet while she tipped back and forth in her rocking chair, telling me stories while I rolled yarn.

"So what are we talking about?" I asked.

"I'm trying to plan Grace's baby shower, but she's shooting down all my ideas," Cara said.

"Not all your ideas," Grace said. "Just the male stripper."

Cara rolled her eyes and perched on the arm of Grace's chair. "I thought you'd want your shower to be fun."

"I'm pretty sure we can have fun without a stripper. And

it's a baby shower, not a bachelorette party. How does a stripper go with a baby shower theme?"

"He'd be dressed like a hot doctor. That totally works with a baby shower theme."

Grace tipped her head, like she was acknowledging Cara's point.

"You could have him jump out of a cake," Fiona said. "That would be fun and unexpected."

"Speaking of the cake—"

"No," Grace said, cutting her off.

"You don't even know what I was going to say, my lovely buttercup."

"We're not doing a vagina cake with a doll head coming out of it."

"Are vagina cakes a thing?" I asked. "I think I'd be totally on board with a vagina cake, but I'm not feeling the doll head coming out of one. Seems a little too on the nose."

Cara tapped her phone screen a few times. "Totally a thing. See?"

The picture showed a pink cake with a doll head emerging from an even pinker vagina. There were even little chocolate sprinkles—whoever had been the pussy model apparently hadn't been a waxer.

I shuddered and handed her phone back. "I can't unsee that."

"Why anyone would do that to their lady garden is beyond me," Cara said. "No offense, boo. You're going to do great."

"Women do that to their lady garden because they want a family," Grace said.

"This is why I adopted Fiona," Cara said.

"Grace, you're better off with the doctor stripper," I said. "I'd give her that one so she gives up on the scary vag cake."

"I'm not budging on either," Grace said. "No strippers. No vagina cake."

Cara smiled, tapping her phone screen again. "That's fine because I wasn't going to suggest a vagina cake. I want to get something like this."

She held up her phone again. This cake had baby blue frosting and a big white cartoon sperm on top. He had eyes and a big grin that made him look very proud of himself. The cake read *I did it* in big white letters.

"Aw, look at the cute spermie," Fiona said.

Grace laughed. "Okay, that's adorable."

"See? I've got you, boo."

Tillie clicked her tongue. "Oh, Cara."

"It's the perfect follow up to the penis cake I had made for her bachelorette party. I know how to stay on brand."

"That cake was really good," Grace said.

I shifted, trying to get my leg in a more comfortable position, then kept rolling Gram's yarn. "I didn't get any cake."

"You'd eat a dick cake?" Cara asked.

I shrugged. "It's cake."

"Otter, do you think Skylar would like to come to Stitch and Sip?" Gram asked.

"That's a great idea," Fiona said.

Grace sighed. "I keep meaning to invite her, but I seem to be forgetting everything lately."

"Pregnancy brain," Lacey said. "It's a thing."

Grace laughed.

I hunkered down in the chair. "Yeah, you should invite her."

Cara narrowed her eyes at me.

I ignored her.

"Fiona, how are the wedding plans coming?" Lacey asked.

"Great," Fiona said with a big smile. "We're keeping it really simple, so there's not a lot to do."

"And you're having it at Gram's?" Lacey asked.

Fiona nodded. "We're putting up a tent, so it'll be pretty and also warm."

"I'm still surprised you talked that broody man into a wedding," Cara said. "I thought for sure he'd just whisk you off to Vegas or something."

"We thought about that, actually," Fiona said. "But getting married at Gram's just feels so perfect. Evan's really excited. You just can't tell unless you know what to look for."

Grace swiped a few tears from her cheeks. "I'm so happy for you."

Fiona clasped her hands at her chest and her lower lip trembled. "I'm so happy, too."

Cara eyed the two of them, then abruptly stood. "I love you both so much I could die, but I just started my period and there's way too much emotion in here for me to cope with right now. Come on Gavin, let's go drink."

With the mood I was in, that sounded like an excellent idea.

She slipped on a wool trench coat and blew kisses at Fiona and Grace. "Goodnight, my lovely little sweat peas. Ladies, have a good week."

Everyone said goodbye to Cara. I handed the ball of yarn back to Gram, said a few quick goodbyes, and followed her out to the parking lot.

"Caboose?" she asked.

"Works for me."

"Should we drive?"

I shook my head and stuffed my hands in my coat pockets. The air had a bite to it, but I didn't mind. "No, I can walk."

It was only a few blocks to the Caboose, and streetlights lit the way. Even though the boot was awkward, it was nice to have two legs again.

There were only a handful of cars in the parking lot. Not surprising for a Monday night. I held the door for Cara and we went inside.

She picked a spot at the bar and I eased myself onto a stool.

Hank came over to take our orders. "What can I get you?"

"Two Heinekens and four shots of Jameson. Put it all on my tab." She glanced at me. "I'm buying. Don't argue."

Normally I would have, but she had a glint in her eye that told me to keep my mouth shut. "Thanks. Shots, huh?"

"It's been one of those days."

"Yeah, me too."

"With the way you were pouting at Stitch and Bitch, I figured."

"I wasn't pouting."

She raised her eyebrows.

"I was brooding. Not pouting."

"Fair enough. You are a Bailey. Brooding must be in your genes."

Hank brought over our beers and poured the shots.

Cara slid one over to me and raised her glass. "To brooding."

"To brooding." I lifted the shot to my lips and tossed it back. The whiskey burned going down. "Are you okay?"

"I'm no more dysfunctional than usual. Although my mother did call this afternoon. Hence the whiskey."

"Phone call from your mom and you started your period. Brutal."

"It really is. I can't be expected to function under these conditions."

"Sounds like you need another shot." I slid the other two shot glasses closer.

"It's what I'm here for."

We both swallowed our second shots, the glasses clinking on the bar when we set them down. I blew out a breath while the burn ran through me. I was already feeling lighter, the whiskey hitting me fast.

"So what's wrong with your mom?" I asked. "Or do you not want to talk about it."

"It's complicated. I don't think I want to talk about it."

I took a sip of my beer. "I can respect that."

"What's wrong with you? Or do you not want to talk about it?"

"Nope."

"Fair enough."

We both got quiet, our attention wandering to the TV behind the bar. I drank my beer down fast, adding it to the whiskey in my stomach. Getting drunk sounded great right now. Anything to get rid of this shitty feeling in my chest.

A couple of shots later, or maybe it was a few... or five, I'd lost count, I was well into drunk. I wobbled on my stool. "Cara, are you a lesbian? Be honest."

She laughed. "No, I'm not a lesbian."

"But you're like totally in love with Grace, right?"

"Yes."

"So how does that work if you're not a lesbian?"

"I don't want her sexually. I like my orgasms to come from a man. But Grace is my person."

"Thass pretty cool." Shit, my speech was slurring. I slow blinked. "I think I'm drunk."

"You're definitely drunk." She brushed her hair back from her face and laughed a little. "I am too."

"I have a confession."

"Wait." She put a hand on the bar to steady herself. "Okay, go."

"I stole a cookie from Chief's cookie jar."

"I thought so."

"I didn't mean to. But it was the most delicious cookie in the world."

"Of course it was. Someone said you couldn't have it."

"No, that's not..." I slumped forward and put my forehead on the bar. Groaning, I lifted my head. "That's not why."

"Listen." She put her hand on my shoulder. "You like her, right? And she likes you. So just be happy that you like each other, okay?"

"That's the problem. I like her too much. But she's... and I'm... and now she's mad."

"What's her story? How'd she end up back here anyway?"

"She was dating her agent. Found out he'd been cheating on her."

"What?" Her voice went flat and suddenly she seemed a lot more sober.

"Isn't that bullshit? Who would cheat on Skylar? I don't know what the fuck his problem was."

"Who is he?"

I took another drink of my beer. Not that I needed it. "Cullen something."

"He was her agent?"

"Yeah, you know, publishing deals and shit."

Cara got out her phone and started typing something. "Do you know what he looks like?"

"I think so. Maybe? But I don't know if I can remember right now."

She held up her phone. "This him?"

I squinted to keep the image from going blurry. It didn't help much. Too much fucking whiskey. But I recognized the douchey face. "Thass him."

"Fucker," she muttered, then hiccupped. "He's so going down. Who's the other woman?"

I ran my fingers through my hair, trying to think. "Another writer. Poppy? No. Penelope? No."

"Pepper Sinclair?"

"Yes." I poked her shoulder. "Thass her. How did you know?"

"She's on his client list on the agency website." Her lips turned up in a wicked smile. "I'm going to bury these two."

Something in the back of my mind told me that maybe I should tell Cara not to. That if Grace were around, she probably would. But Grace wasn't around, and I was really drunk. And hell, I wanted Cara to bury that fucker for what he did to Skylar.

So I smiled back. "Get 'em, tiger."

"Don't you worry about a thing." She put away her phone and had to steady herself on the bar again. Apparently she wasn't *that* sober. "I'll make him pay."

I stumbled off my stool. "I should go home. My kitten needs me."

"Let me get you a ride."

"No." I waved my hand and almost knocked myself over. "I'll just walk. Iss not far."

"Gavin—"

I started toward the door. "I'm fine. I'm always fine. I've got this."

25

SKYLAR

*T*he blank screen mocked me with its emptiness. I didn't know why I was sitting at my desk staring at my half-finished manuscript. It wasn't like I was going to be able to write. For one thing, there was no Gavin sitting behind me, somehow lulling my brain into a state of relaxed creativity.

For another thing, no Gavin at all.

I'd been miserable since we'd talked this afternoon. Thankfully, Dad was at work and Mom was out, so I'd come home to an empty house. I'd been able to cry in peace. But even a good, hard cry hadn't completely cleansed me of my misery.

I often used writing to help me cope with my fears, but it wasn't working to help me cope with this, whatever this was.

Because honestly, what was wrong with me? Gavin hadn't broken up with me. There hadn't been a relationship in the first place. Maybe I was subconsciously projecting hurt from Cullen onto this situation. I didn't know why I'd be doing that, but it made a little bit of sense. More than me coming home and ugly crying because a guy I was friends with and had slept with once wanted to back up and stick with being just friends without the sex.

I even understood. I wasn't ready for a relationship, so why couldn't Gavin and I just press rewind and go back to where we were last week? Just friends who liked to hang out. That had been fun. What was wrong with that?

It wasn't what I wanted. That was what was wrong with it.

Only, I wasn't sure what I did want.

Actually, when I thought about it—really thought about it—that wasn't true. I did know. It was just very unlike me to want it.

I wanted to be friends with Gavin. And I wanted him to fuck my brains out occasionally.

Rushing in to a serious relationship was probably not the best idea. But Gavin didn't want a serious relationship either. He'd said he wasn't boyfriend material—which for the record, he was, I had no idea why he thought he wasn't—but I wasn't looking for a boyfriend anyway.

I always played it safe and right now, I didn't want to. I wanted to be a little reckless.

Ginny's words came back to haunt me, as they often did when she was trying to push me out of my comfort zone. *If you don't go after what you want, you probably won't get it.*

She was right.

My phone rang, but I didn't recognize the number. That was odd. I was going to ignore it, but a little spark of curiosity made me pick it up.

"Hello?"

A woman's voice was on the other end. "Skylar?"

"Yes."

"Hi, this is Cara. We met... sometime, I don't know. I got

your phone off Gavin's number. That's not right. I got your number off Gavin's phone."

"Um, okay?"

"He's drunk and trying to walk home from the Caboose." She paused and her voice shifted to a loud whisper. "I'm drunk too."

"Is he okay?"

"Oh yeah, you know how guys are. But he left and I thought maybe you could go find him. Make sure he gets home okay."

I was already on my way downstairs. "Yeah, I can do that. Do you need a ride, too?"

"No, I have a ride coming. This is my fault, so I'll make it up to you. I have a great massage therapist who does in-home appointments. He has magic hands. Do you want a massage?"

"That's okay, you don't have to do that. I'll see if I can find him. Thanks for calling, Cara."

"You're welcome. I'll get your massage later. No, I mean I'll text you later."

"No, you don't—"

But she'd already hung up.

I grabbed my coat and went out to my car, wondering why Cara had called me of all people. Although she'd sounded pretty drunk.

Had he said something to her about me?

There was no way to know, but a sense of resolve shored up my courage. Whatever her reasons for calling, I was going to make the most of the opportunity.

I was going to do what Ginny said and go after what I wanted.

Although maybe I'd do that tomorrow. Having a conversation with a drunk Gavin probably wouldn't work very well.

He wasn't hard to find. I drove to the Caboose and found him lying on the sidewalk right next to where he'd been when I'd hit him with my car. He was on his back with his knees bent, his feet flat on the ground. The dark street was empty, so I just stopped in the road and opened my door.

"Gavin?"

His face turned toward me. "Sky?"

I got out and knelt beside him. "What are you doing on the ground? Are you okay?"

"I'm fine. I'm walking home."

"You're not walking anywhere. You're lying on the sidewalk."

"Am I?" He lifted his head and looked around. "I think I got tired."

"Come on. I'll take you home."

"Thass so nice of you," he said, his voice slurring a little. "Why are you so nice? And so pretty. You're beautiful."

I laughed. "Can you get up?"

"I think so. It's very spinny." He sat up and rubbed his face. "Sky, I have to tell you something."

"Yeah?"

"I drank too much."

"I know. Come on, let's get in the car."

"Iss not my fault."

I helped him to his feet and made sure he was steady. "It's not a big deal."

"Cara wanted to do shots. I don't like her."

"You don't? I thought you were friends."

"We are. But I don't like her *that* way." He laughed, like he'd just thought of something amusing. "Did you think I took her out on a date?"

"I don't know, I didn't really think about it." I ushered him into the passenger seat. "She just called and said you were trying to walk home."

"She called you?"

"Yes. Are you going to fall over?"

Leaning back against the headrest, he closed his eyes. "I don't think so."

I reached across him to fasten his seatbelt, then got in the car. He started singing—it wasn't a song I knew—and waved his arms around like an enthusiastic symphony conductor.

If our conversation earlier hadn't still stung so much, it would have been pretty funny.

We got to his house and it didn't look like his brothers were home. I helped him out of the car and he leaned on me, limping on his booted foot. He kept singing, although it was more mumbling now.

I had to fish his keys out of his pants pocket, which made him giggle like a little kid. We went inside and I shut the front door behind us.

"Princess Squeaker," he called. "Mommy's home!"

His kitten came out and mewed at him. He stumbled forward, leaning over to pick her up.

"I've got her," I said and scooped her into my hands while she squeaked in protest. "Let's just get you to bed."

"This way," he declared and pointed to the hallway.

I followed him to the bathroom and waited outside the door while he went in. Princess Squeaker squirmed, her tiny claws sharp. Gavin started singing drunk opera while he used the bathroom.

"Your mommy's a mess."

He came out, his pants still undone, but I didn't worry about that. Just followed him into what I assumed was his room. He sat on the edge of the bed and pulled off his boot and shoe.

Princess Squeaker thrashed, trying to get to Gavin, so I put her on the bed. "I'll go get you some water."

"You're so great," he said, absently petting the kitten. "You're such a good friend. I really like you."

"Thanks."

I got him a glass of water from the kitchen and when I came back, he'd stripped off his clothes—all of them—and lay face down on the bed.

Was it bad that even though he was passed out drunk that I wanted to bite that adorable ass of his?

Probably.

The bed wasn't made, so I pulled the sheet and comforter out from under him and covered him up to the waist. He shifted and mumbled something.

"What?" I asked.

"Don't go."

I slowly lowered myself onto the edge of the bed and ran my fingers through his hair. I wasn't sure if I should touch him like this, but I couldn't help it. "You want me to stay?"

He didn't open his eyes. "I don't want it to be a dream."

"This isn't a dream. I'm right here."

"Okay. Good."

I hadn't planned on sleeping here tonight—and it probably wasn't the best idea—but there was something about that drunk, sleepy voice of his.

"Stay with me," he said again, his voice muffled by the pillow. "Please?"

That did it. I was sleeping here tonight.

I didn't want to go to bed in my jeans or bra, so I took them off, but left the rest of my clothes on. That seemed like the thing to do, especially because Gavin was naked.

Princess Squeaker cracked her eyes open and watched me warily as I slid into bed next to him. I had a feeling she wasn't sure about sharing her space—or her mommy—with me. But ultimately, she went to sleep curled up next to Gavin.

And so did I.

I WOKE to the feeling of weight on my chest. Was there something on me? I blinked my eyes open and found myself on my back, looking up at the ceiling in Gavin's bedroom. Gavin slept next to me, lying on his side. He shifted a little, a smile on his face.

It was about then that I realized the weight on my chest was his arm, and he was grabbing my boob.

Under my shirt.

His hand twitched, giving me a slight squeeze. I could feel my nipples harden and I turned my face toward him.

He peeked his eyes open and they suddenly widened. He yanked his hand off me and rolled away so fast he fell off the edge of the bed with a grunt.

I sat up. "Are you okay?"

He groaned and held a hand to his forehead. "Where am I? Is this my room?"

"Yeah, you're home."

"Why are you here? Oh shit, why am I naked? Oh my god, did I do it again?"

I smiled. "You drank too much so I brought you home. I don't know why you took all your clothes off. You did that while I was in the other room."

Groaning again, he rubbed his hands up and down his face. "I'll be right back."

I waited while he got up and went to the bathroom, walking gingerly without his boot. He came back and pulled on a pair of boxer briefs, then chugged the glass of water I'd left on the nightstand for him last night.

"Better." He put the glass down and eased himself back onto the bed. "I was grabbing your boob in my sleep, wasn't I?"

"Yeah, you were."

He winced. "Sorry about that."

"It's okay. You were sleeping."

"Are you sure we didn't..."

"Positive. You don't remember last night?"

"I remember some of it. I went to the Caboose with Cara, and there was a lot of whiskey. And I remember walking home and then you picked me up."

"I think you were trying to take a nap on the sidewalk."

He shook his head, laughing softly. "Way too much whiskey. Why did you come get me?"

"Cara called me."

"She did?"

"Yeah, she said she got my number from your phone."

"Man, I don't even remember her taking my phone." He glanced at me, one corner of his mouth hooking in a grin. "Thanks for getting me home."

"You're welcome. You were pretty funny, actually."

"Drunk me is hilarious."

"How is it that you barely seem hungover?"

"I'm a quick healer." He shrugged. "Not that I'm complaining that you're here, but... why did you stay the night?"

"You asked me to."

"I did?"

"Yeah. I'm not surprised you don't remember that part.

I'm not even sure if you were awake. But you asked me to stay, so I did."

The smile he gave me was different than his usual dimpled grin. It was smaller, more subtle, but also somehow more meaningful.

"Thanks."

This is where typical Skylar would have said something awkward and left. Darted away like a scared little mouse.

But I didn't want to run this time. So despite the way my heart started to pound and butterflies fluttered in my stomach, I took a deep breath and drew on what little bravery I could find.

"Can we talk about yesterday? Not the drunk thing, I don't care about that. I mean what you said before. I don't agree."

"You don't agree with what?"

"With going back to being just friends without... you know, without the other stuff."

His brow furrowed.

I kept talking fast, hoping I could get through everything I wanted to say before my courage ran out. "I know you're not interested in a serious relationship, but I'm not either. I'm not asking you to date me or be my boyfriend. But I can't rewind and pretend nothing happened, either. More importantly, I don't want to."

"Then... what do you want?"

"Well..." I nervously twisted a strand of hair. "Why can't we be friends who also sleep together sometimes? Because we're good as friends, aren't we? And let's be honest, the sex was good too."

"It was really good," he said, the timbre of his voice dipping low.

"With where I am in my life right now, I could use a friend and I could use some really good sex."

He rubbed his face and blew out a breath. "The problem is, this is more complicated than that. Because you're you, and I work for your dad. He's not going to want me messing around with his daughter."

"It's none of his business. Even though I'm living with him right now, he doesn't have a say in who I spend time with or what I do behind closed doors. Besides, my dad likes you."

He grunted. "For now."

I laughed and shifted so I was facing him. "We're both adults. We can be friends and have a little fun together. What's so bad about that?"

His lips twitched in a grin. "So your mom was right and you do want to use me to get over your ex."

I playfully pushed his arm. "No, I want to use you for friendship and sex."

Groaning, he leaned his head back. "Friendship and sex are my favorite."

"See? This works for both of us."

"So basically you're telling me you want joint custody of my dick."

I laughed. "That's one way to put it." I took a deep breath. "The truth is, my life kind of sucks right now. I don't know how I'm going to salvage my career, or how long I'm going to stay here, or where I'll go next. But hanging out with you is fun and it makes everything feel a little less awful."

"And orgasms are great."

"Yes, orgasms are... very great. Is that bad?"

"No, it's not bad. It's kind of a dream scenario."

"See? A little fling with the boss's daughter never hurt anyone."

"I don't know, Sky. I could be getting myself into a lot of trouble with you."

"I thought you liked danger."

"I do. I fucking love it." His eyes widened with excitement and he tucked my hair behind my ear. "I feel like I should be resisting harder, but you make a very compelling argument."

"Thank you."

"So, friends with orgasms?" he asked.

"Yes. Friends with orgasms."

The way he smiled and knuckled my chin sent a little tingle through me. But more than that, I felt proud. Maybe this wasn't a new agent or publishing deal, but I'd gone after what I wanted. I'd taken a risk, told him how I felt, and it had paid off.

I hadn't felt this good about myself in a long time.

26

GAVIN

*E*ven though I was stuck on the sidelines of the football field for today's game, I was in an awesome mood. My boot was coming off for good soon, which meant I could go back to full duty at work. And the Baileys were playing the Pines, which meant I wasn't missing the big Bailey-Haven game.

Plus, Skylar had been at my place last night. That probably had a lot to do with the smile on my face.

I totally had a handle on the whole friends with benefits thing with Sky. It kind of felt like we were dating, only we weren't really. I was back on light duty at work—none of the fun stuff, but it was something—so when I had free time, I met her at the coffee shop or at her house so she could write. Or we'd just hang out and talk a lot.

And sometimes we'd wind up back at my place, particularly when my brothers weren't home. There was an element of sneaking around that seemed to make us both hot for each other.

As far as I could tell, Chief didn't know, which was probably for the best. She'd insisted it wasn't any of her dad's business who she slept with, and I could respect that.

Jack stood next to me with his clipboard, squinting in the mid-afternoon sun while our team lined up on defense. Since I couldn't play, I'd appointed myself assistant coach. I was pretty sure Jack appreciated my help.

"They're going to try another pass," I said. The game was almost over and our team was ahead, twenty-one to fourteen. But if they scored, they could tie it up and then go for an on-side kick to get the ball back.

"Evan and Levi see it," Jack said, nodding to them as they adjusted their positions.

The other team's center hiked the ball. Sure enough, it was a pass play, but Levi was there to bat the ball out of the air. Incomplete.

I whistled while Jack tucked the clipboard under his arm so he could clap.

The bleachers behind us were full of people, including Fiona, Cara, and Grace. It kind of made me wish Sky was here. She was doing something with Ginny today. And of course, it didn't really matter. I couldn't play anyway, and it wasn't like Skylar was my girlfriend.

But it would have been fun to have her here.

The bleachers on the other side of the field were full too, with Pines or people related to them.

Plus a few fucking Havens.

Josiah, Zachary, and Theo were over there, probably scouting for when they played us later in the season.

Assholes. I glared at them whenever I caught them looking at me.

The Pines attempted another pass, but Evan had their number. The ball hit him right in the chest and a second later, he was running in the other direction. The crowd cheered behind me, Fiona loudest of them all, as Evan ran it back for a touchdown.

That was it. The game was over.

I slapped Jack on the back. "Nice work, coach."

"Thanks, Gav. Think you'll be ready to play next game?"

"Should be."

"Good. We could use your speed against the Town Team." He shot me a look. "But your doctor has to give the okay."

"I know, I know. Why does everyone keep telling me to listen to my doctor? Doesn't anyone trust me?"

He raised his eyebrows.

"I'm still wearing the damn boot, aren't I?"

"Yeah, you are. I'm just not convinced you feel pain the way the rest of us do."

"I have no idea what you're talking about."

"The first time I met you, you fell off a roof, then got up and walked away like nothing had happened."

I shrugged. "I'm just lucky, I guess."

The rest of the team congregated on the sidelines, exchanging high-fives. Winning was awesome.

I turned around and bounced backward like I'd hit an invisible wall. Chief stood behind me dressed in a TFD jacket. Where the hell had he come from?

"Careful there, Gav," he said.

"Hey, Chief."

He eyed me for a second. Every time he did that, I tensed up, waiting for him to tell me to stay the fuck away from his daughter.

But he didn't. Yet. Just gave me a nod and moved past me to talk to Jack.

I let out a breath.

"Hey, broagie." Logan smacked me on the back. "We should get some filming done today."

We'd started working on the movie we were going to film to hijack the Haven's drive-in—a Bailey remake of *Dirty Dancing*. Since the drive-in would close for the season soon, we'd decided against a full scene-by-scene remake and opted for more of a highlight reel. But we still had a lot of work to do, and not a lot of time to do it.

I glanced up at the clear sky. "Yeah let's do it."

Logan called our other brothers over. "I need you guys for a few hours."

"For what?" Evan asked.

"We have a lot of filming to do."

Evan's expression didn't change, like his face was carved from stone. But he didn't say no, either. That was progress with him.

"Don't punk out on us now," I said. "This will be way fucking funnier if we're all in it."

"Who do I have to play?" Evan asked.

"The grumpy dad," I said. "That'll be easy for you."

"What?"

"Damn it, that's right, you assholes are making me be the mom, aren't you?" Asher asked. "Why don't we get the girls to play the girl parts? Grace and Fiona will help. I bet Cara would too."

"I'm going to pretend you didn't suggest Lunatic Ginger," Logan said. "Besides, it's funnier if it's just us."

"I've got the scene list at home," Levi said. "But we should do the water scene today. We can do it out at the springs so you guys don't get hypothermia."

I shrugged. "Works for me. Although I still think I should be Patrick Swayze."

"Nope," Logan said. "You're the youngest, so you have to be Baby."

"You know this movie surprisingly well," Asher said.

"I did my research," Logan said. "Just get your ass to the springs in an hour."

Asher laughed. "Okay, okay. I need to take Grace home. I'll see you guys out there."

Evan made a noise that was somewhere between an annoyed groan and a menacing growl. But he still didn't say no.

I glanced over my shoulder and waved at Fiona. Evan was a grumpy bastard, but he'd been a lot more cooperative since she came into his life.

I went home to change with Levi and Logan, then we all piled in Levi's SUV. There were several natural hot springs nearby. One had been turned into a spa, and another was on private land and you had to have a reservation. But there was a big one not far from the lake that mostly locals knew about. It was a bit of a hike to get there, but that was good. I needed to build up my stamina anyway.

We hiked out to an old ramshackle cabin near the edge of the pool and put our stuff down. Steam rose from the glassy surface of the water and tall pines towered over us.

This would be a great place to bring Sky. The cabin was kind of creepy, but that was actually a plus. She liked creepy shit.

Asher and Evan came down the trail and Logan passed out costumes while Levi flipped through a spiral notebook.

"Logan and I made a list of the scenes we need to film," Levi said. "It skips the boring shit and the parts where you guys would have to make out."

"Yeah, we have our limits," Logan said. "I added some notes, did you see those?"

"There aren't any tanks in *Dirty Dancing*. Or explosions."

"It would have been a better movie if there had been."

"For fuck's sake, can we just get this over with?" Evan asked.

Levi did a few takes of the grumpy dad scenes with Evan, using the cabin as a backdrop. After a quick wardrobe change, he filmed me dancing down the trail. The original was on stairs or a bridge or something, but it was the best we could do. I hammed it up and even made Evan and Levi both laugh.

They shot a few more things in and around the cabin. Then it was time for the water scene.

Levi elbowed me. "Swim trunks, man."

"Right." I stripped off my clothes and looked down at my legs. "Do my legs look lopsided? I can't tell from up here."

Logan tilted his head and looked me up and down. "Little bit, yeah."

"Damn it."

"Jesus, Gav, put something on," Levi said.

"Just get back in the gym," Asher said. "You'll be fine."

"Are you sure I shouldn't film this naked? You could just block out my junk in editing."

"No," Levi said. "Why would we do that?"

"Because a grown man naked is always funny."

"I'm not lifting you over my head with your junk hanging out," Logan said. "Put on your shorts."

I rolled my eyes, but grabbed my swim trunks and tugged them on. "Fine."

Logan and I got in the pool. The water was pleasantly warm—a nice change after the cold air.

"All right, you guys have seen it," Levi said. "Logan, you have to lift him over your head. Once he's up, just fall backward and Gav, dive in."

I glanced at Logan. "Dude, are you sure you can lift me?"

"Of course I can lift you. Let's do this."

"You guys ready?" Levi asked. "Action."

Logan grabbed me around my ribcage and I jumped up, then back down. We made a few more attempts, but it didn't feel like I was getting very high.

"This is the one," Logan said.

"Don't fucking drop me."

Bending my knees, I pushed off the bottom, mostly with my right leg. Logan hoisted me up and for a second, I was in the air over his head.

"Holy shit, you guys did it!" someone said from the bank, right as Logan's arms started to buckle.

Instead of diving forward, I crashed on top of him, pushing him under. Warm water went up my nose as I belly flopped. Logan's limbs were everywhere, thrashing to get back to the surface.

I did a somersault under water, then my feet found the bottom. I stood and sucked in a lungful of air. Evan and Asher slow-clapped from the bank.

Logan rubbed his eyes. "You fell on me."

"You fucking dropped me."

"Were you recording?" Logan asked. "Because I'm not doing that again."

Levi watched something on his phone. "Oh yeah. I got it all. This is perfect."

We got out and changed back into regular clothes. I was about to ask who wanted to go grab a beer, when Evan did one of the weirdest things I'd ever seen him do.

"If you guys want to come out to my place, I have beer," he said.

We all stared at him. He almost never invited us over willingly. Mostly we just showed up at his house.

"What?" he asked.

"Sounds good," Asher said and patted him on the back.

Logan and Levi exchanged a look that seemed to say, *what the fuck?* I just grinned at him and grabbed my shit. I knew he secretly liked hanging out with us.

We drove to Evan's place. He had a house and a shop on a big chunk of land a couple of miles outside town. Fiona wasn't home, but his big ass guard dog, Sasquatch, was at the door to greet us.

Evan had the coolest dog ever. He looked like he could rip your face off. It was awesome.

Evidence of Fiona was everywhere in the house. She had so many houseplants it looked like a jungle in here. Their pots all had names written on them in white chalk—Myra, Blanche, Rosemary, Frances, Betsy, Joan, Barbara. Fiona's habit of naming her plants was pretty cute, and they made Evan's house a lot more homey.

We grabbed beers out of the fridge and settled in the living room while Evan took Sasquatch outside. When they came back in, his dog eyed us like he wasn't sure he was going to allow us to stay in his den.

Logan shifted uncomfortably. "Is he going to attack?"

Evan's lip twitched in a smile. "Sasquatch, go lie down."

I snickered. He loved scaring Logan with that dog. And it was funny, every single time.

"Where's Fiona?" I asked.

Evan shot me a glare, which I totally deserved. I'd put a lot of energy into flirting with his girl before they got engaged, just to rile him up.

"She's out with Grace and Cara."

Logan shuddered.

I stretched out my booted leg and took a long pull from

my beer. We'd done good work today. "How soon will the movie be done?"

"We'll probably need to do some more filming, and then edit it all together," Levi said. "Shouldn't take too long."

"We should hit them with it on the last Saturday before they close for the winter. It'll be packed."

"Good call," Logan said. "So Gav, who'd you have over last night?"

"Me?" I asked. "Wait, you were home last night?"

His mouth twitched in a grin. "Yep."

Shit.

"You had a girl over last night?" Asher asked. "I thought you were dating Skylar."

Levi coughed on his mouthful of beer. "You're dating Skylar? As in Chief's daughter?"

"No, no, no." I waved that off with my hand. "I'm not dating Skylar."

"Really?" Asher asked.

"Yes, really. I think I'd know if I was dating someone. We're just friends." I took a sip of my beer and eyed him. "Why?"

"I just heard you were dating her."

"I heard that too," Evan said.

"Where the fuck are you guys hearing shit about me?" I asked.

"I heard it too, but I assumed it was just a rumor," Levi said.

"It is just a rumor," I said. "We're not dating."

Logan still had his eyes on me, and that fucking smile hadn't gone anywhere. "So who'd you have over last night?"

"None of your damn business."

"I knew it," Logan said. "I knew you wouldn't be able to

resist. Do you know how much trouble you're going to be in when Chief finds out?"

"Come on, it's not like we're teenagers. She's a grown woman. She can do what she wants."

"Yeah, but Chief's still going to be pissed."

"We really are just friends."

"Yeah, you guys seemed very friendly last night," Logan said.

"Fine, friends with benefits, but that was her idea," I said. "I can't help it if I'm that good. Who can blame her?"

Logan snort-laughed. "Right."

"I was at Cara's the other day. I think you left your TFD jacket there." I was lying my ass off—I hadn't been to her house and I'd never seen a TFD jacket there—but if he was going to pick at me about Skylar, I was going to kick him in the nuts right back.

He glared at me. "Fuck off."

"Oh, it wasn't yours?" I asked. "Maybe it was Levi's."

"Don't bring me into this," Levi said.

I took a casual sip of my beer while Logan kept glaring at me. "I guess it could have been someone else's. I don't know who Cara's fucking these days."

"You didn't see a TFD jacket at Cara's house," Logan said.

"Yeah I did."

"Bullshit."

"If it wasn't yours, why do you care?"

"I don't."

I grinned at him. "Sure you don't."

Asher threw a pillow at me and I blocked it with my elbow.

"Be careful with her," Asher said, shooting me a look with all his oldest brother power behind it.

I picked up the pillow and tossed it back at him. Be careful with her? As if I didn't already know that. I liked Skylar—a lot. She wasn't some toy I was going to toss aside when I got bored. I cared about her. In fact, I felt...

Leaning back against the couch, I took another drink, stopping that train of thought. Because the truth was, I felt a lot of things for her, and I wasn't quite sure what to do about that.

27

SKYLAR

*H*unkering down in my coat, I held my coffee cup, feeling the warmth seep into my hands. The early morning air had a bite to it, and as I looked at the knot of middle-aged men congregating near the river's edge, I couldn't help but wonder if they were all a little crazy.

They were dressed in bathrobes tied around their ample waists. A few wore boots or hats against the cold. Despite the way they rubbed their arms or blew into their hands, they all seemed to be in good spirits. Joking and laughing, their breath misting out in clouds around them.

Ginny stood next to me, her eyes wide with curiosity. She clutched her coffee close, but her attention was entirely on the growing crowd of Tilikum townspeople. Quirky small-town traditions were Ginny's catnip.

We were down here at the crack of dawn for the annual Tilikum Pumpkin Plunge, and all those bathrobe clad men were going to jump into the freezing, glacial fed river.

"I love this take on the polar bear plunge," Ginny said.

"I can't believe they're getting in that water," I said. "I can see jumping in when it's hot out, but it's freezing."

"Obviously that's the point. Did you know it's competitive? The guy who stays in the longest wins."

Involuntarily, I shivered. "They're crazy."

"I know, that's what I love about it. Risking hypothermia for bragging rights. It's adorable."

"You're a little bit strange, you know that?"

"It's part of the fabric of their community. I find it fascinating." She pulled out her phone and took a few pictures.

The crowd continued to grow. Grace and Asher picked their way down the trail. He had an arm around her and her cheeks were flushed from the cold air. Both were bundled up, as were Evan and Fiona, who came down the trail just behind them.

"You're not jumping in?" Ginny asked.

Asher laughed. "Hell no. Those guys are nuts."

"This is so exciting," Fiona said. "I've never been to something like this before."

Evan's eyes swept the river and the group of bathrobe-clad men. "It's just a bunch of old farts making their balls shrink."

Fiona wrapped her arms around his waist and looked up at him. "I think it's adorable."

"You're adorable," Evan said.

"Hey cheesebrogers." Logan approached, dressed in a TFD sweatshirt and jeans. Levi was with him, and neither of them looked like they had any plans of jumping into the river.

"I'm disappointed," Ginny said, looking Logan up and down. "I thought for sure you'd do it."

Logan flashed her a grin. "I don't need to jump in a freezing river to prove my manhood."

"No?"

Cara appeared behind the twins. "He wouldn't want to

engage in that kind of test of manhood in front of an audience. He'd start yelling about shrinkage."

Logan flinched away, like she'd startled him. "What the fuck. Where did she come from?"

Cara cast him a sidelong glance and went to stand in between Grace and Fiona. "I don't know why you're always surprised to see me. It's not like I'm going anywhere."

"A guy can dream."

Cara rolled her eyes.

Gavin came down the trail wearing nothing but sandals and what looked like underwear. He carried a towel draped over one of his broad shoulders. His outfit—or lack thereof —left little to the imagination. He was all lean muscle and olive skin. The sight of him—especially almost naked—sent a flurry of tingles through my body.

Ginny leaned close and lowered her voice. "Wow. I do *not* blame you."

"I know, right?" I said quietly.

"Damn it, Gav," Asher said. "Did you have to wear those?"

"What?" Gavin asked, looking down at himself. He wasn't just wearing underwear. He was wearing underwear with Asher's face right on the crotch. "They're basically a Speedo."

I stifled a laugh.

"You're utterly ridiculous," Cara said. "You know that, right?"

He just grinned at her.

"No more boot?" I asked.

"Nope. I'm officially healed." He lifted his legs one at a time, bending them at the knee, as if to emphasize his point. "Feels good to be back."

"I take it you're jumping in?" I asked.

"Of course I am. I do it every year."

He waved to his fellow river jumpers. They didn't look pleased to see him. A few crossed their arms and they grumbled to each other.

"What's that about?" Ginny asked.

"They're disappointed Gavin showed," Logan said.

"Why?"

"Because he wins every year."

"Aren't you cold?" I asked.

Gavin shrugged. "Yeah."

"And that doesn't bother you?"

"Not really. I'll warm up later." He winked at me, then turned back to his brothers. "Am I really the only one taking the plunge this year? I'm disappointed in you."

"We're happy to let you represent the Baileys," Logan said. "Also, you're nuts and we're not."

"Or I like to have fun and you're all boring."

"How is jumping into ice cold water fun?" Logan asked.

Gavin grinned, his eyes widening. He looked a little crazed. "How is it *not* fun?"

Cara's phone rang and she smiled when she pulled it out of her handbag. "Oh good. I've been waiting for her to call me back." She winked at me—which was kind of odd—and wandered away to take her call.

Quite the crowd had gathered along the riverbank. I caught sight of my dad a little bit downstream. My mom was with him, wearing the cutest knit hat and very impractical shoes. She teetered a little, but Dad caught her before she could fall. Their eyes met and I held my breath. Oh my god, was he going to kiss her?

He didn't, and a second later whatever had been happening over there—if anything—had passed. Dad put his hands in his coat pockets and Mom turned her attention to the river. I'd probably imagined it anyway.

"Is it just me, or are your mom and dad hanging out a lot these days?" Ginny asked.

"Yeah, they are. Mom tends to invite herself along whenever he's going somewhere that isn't work. Although come to think of it, *he* asked if she wanted to come down here this morning."

"Interesting."

The truth was, I didn't know what was going on with my parents. They could go from sharing happy memories of my early childhood to snipping at each other in seconds.

I was also pretty sure I'd caught my mom trying to peek in Dad's bedroom while he was changing the other day.

A man in a dark coat climbed onto a rock near the water's edge and raised a megaphone. "Ladies and gentlemen, the great city of Tilikum would like to welcome you to the forty-fourth annual Pumpkin Plunge."

A cheer went up from the crowd. Gavin hollered and punched his fist in the air.

The announcer held up a crown decorated with pumpkins and orange, yellow, and red leaves. "The winner will be crowned Tilikum's Pumpkin King! Or queen, but I don't think we have any female plungers this year."

"That's because women are too smart!" someone yelled, earning a laugh from the crowd.

"All right, all right. Gentlemen, make your way to the front."

Gavin handed me his towel. "Mind holding that for me?"

"Sure. Be careful."

"I'll be fine." He winked, then made his way down to the river's edge.

The rest of the plungers stripped off their sweatshirts

and bathrobes. Gavin was the lone twenty-something in a sea of middle-aged beer bellies and gray-haired chests. He smiled and shook hands with a few of his fellow daredevils, then started jumping and shaking his limbs out, like he was getting ready to run a race.

Cara came back and stood next to me. "He is a cutie, isn't he?"

"Yeah, he is."

"So I know I haven't gotten back to you about Sven."

"Sven?"

"My massage therapist. I was going to set something up for you, but I actually found a better way to thank you."

"For picking up Gavin? You really don't have to do anything. He's my friend, I didn't mind."

"Be that as it may, I'm working on a little surprise."

"Cara, you really don't—"

"I can't wait," she said, cutting me off. "You're going to love it."

"On the count of three," the man said into the megaphone. "One." The crowd chanted along. "Two. Three!"

It turned out there were three kinds of Tilikum pumpkin plungers. Men who stepped carefully, wincing at the cold, clearly ready for it to be over as soon as their toes hit the water. Men who waded in with more gusto, sucking in quick breaths as each bit of skin submerged beneath the water.

And then there was Gavin.

He let out a whoop and rushed into the river, splashing the men next to him. When he got closer to the center, he dove under, then popped back up and hollered again. He raked his hair out of his face, and his eyes were wide and bright, his smile huge.

The crowd cheered from the riverbank. Gavin's brothers shouted his name, calling out encouragement. Not that he seemed to need it. Two pumpkin plungers turned around and immediately ran out of the water. Another was right on their heels.

"That's it, Gav," Logan shouted.

Gavin jumped up and down a few times in the waist high water. Seconds ticked by, but the longer it went on, the more excited he seemed to get.

Another plunger succumbed to the cold, hurrying out of the water into a waiting towel. Pretty soon it was a mass exodus, more and more men running for the riverbank.

Finally, it was down to Gavin and two other men. One clutched his bony arms around himself while he shivered, his teeth chattering. The other was a burly man with a bald head, thick auburn beard, and the hairiest chest I'd ever seen.

"Earl," a woman called from the bank. "It's not worth it. Get back up here or you'll catch your death."

Earl—the bony one—seemed to agree. He came out of the river, shaking and dripping water from his swim trunks.

"Who's the one left with Gavin?" I asked.

"Gerald McMillan," Cara said. "He thought he could beat Gavin last year, too."

Gavin's eyes met mine and he smiled through chattering teeth. He swung his arms back and forth across his chest, then shook out his hands. Gerald stood still, arms crossed over his barrel chest, like a big hairy tree trunk.

Logan started chanting, "Ga-vin, Ga-vin, Ga-vin," and some of the crowd picked it up. An answering chant for Gerald began down the riverbank.

Gavin jumped, swung his arms, and shook out his hands again, all with that adorable smile of his. Gerald looked miserable, shivers beginning to overtake his big body.

"You've got this, Gavin," Logan yelled.

"Crazy son of a bitch," Levi said, just loud enough that I heard it.

It occurred to me, standing on the riverbank on a chilly fall morning, that maybe I didn't know Gavin as well as I'd thought I did. And maybe that had something to do with the fact that for most of the time I'd known him, he'd been hobbled by a broken leg. Because this Gavin, who seemed to be having the time of his life while he was probably giving himself hypothermia, was kind of insane.

Hypothermia... Another body is found, but on closer inspection, it's discovered that he's still alive, just in a state of deep hypothermia. He's rushed to the hospital and put on life support. If he survives, he might hold the key to finding the identity of the killer—

"Look at him," Ginny said, rousing me from my brief daydream. "It looks like he's having fun out there."

"What? Oh, yeah it does. Did you know a body decomposes four times faster in water than on land?"

She laughed. "Ew."

Gavin flashed Gerald a big grin, then dove back under the water. He came up still smiling and wiped his hair back off his face.

With a full-body shudder, Gerald seemed to decide he'd had enough. He shook his head and hurried to the river's edge.

A cheer rose up from the crowd and Gavin raised his arms in the air. He high stepped out of the water and I opened his towel for him as he raced up the riverbank.

"Holy shit, I'm fucking cold," he said, his voice breathless—with cold, or excitement, it was hard to tell.

I wrapped the towel around his shivering body and he grabbed it, holding it at the top of his chest. River water streamed off him, making little rivulets in the rocky dirt at our feet.

The announcer stepped back on his rock and raised the megaphone. "And the winner is, once again, Gavin Bailey."

He walked over and ceremoniously crowned Gavin. The crowd cheered again while Gavin beamed, his cheeks flushed pink, his smile bright as the morning sun.

I laughed, caught up in the moment, feeling light and free. He turned and met my eyes, that smile warming me from the inside.

"That was fucking awesome," he said. "But I need to get some clothes on."

"Let's meet up at the coffee shop," Grace said. "I've got a salted caramel mocha with your name on it."

"Yes." He held out his hand and fist bumped her.

We followed the crowd back up the trail, people congratulating Gavin as we went. He gave me a smile before veering off toward his truck. I'd driven here with Ginny, and he'd come separately. Which made sense, especially because we were just friends.

But I was aware of that little piece of me that wished I were leaving with him.

Or maybe it was a big piece.

"So, coffee shop?" Ginny asked as we got into her car.

"Yeah, let's do it."

Of course I wanted to go to the coffee shop. Gavin was going to be there.

28

SKYLAR

*P*eople crowded into the Steaming Mug. Ginny and I grabbed a table and put our coats over the backs of our chairs. A few of the other pumpkin plungers—now fully dressed, but still rubbing their arms to warm up—stood in line or waited near the counter sipping hot drinks. Asher and Grace came in, followed by Levi and Logan. Grace kissed Asher before going behind the counter to help the two baristas.

The door flew open and in walked Gavin, dressed now, proudly wearing his ridiculous pumpkin crown. He seemed to be eating up the applause as he strode into the cafe, although as soon as his eyes landed on mine, he beelined for our table.

"Your highness," Ginny said. "We're honored by your presence."

He pulled out a chair and sat, then adjusted the crown. "Greetings, lovely princesses."

"Are you the pumpkin king or the river king?" I asked.

"I'm still cold, is what I am," he said with a smile, then shivered dramatically.

"Your lips are a little blue." I wanted to lean over and kiss them, but I resisted the urge. "I can see why Gram calls you Otter."

"My brothers get to be badass animals like Bear and Wolf. Then I come along and she names me Otter." He shook his head.

"I think it's cute. It fits you."

He smiled at me. "Thanks."

Grace brought Gavin's drink to the table. He wrapped his hands around the warm mug and sighed.

"Nice work today, Gav." She patted him on the back.

"Thanks, Grace. How's baby Bailey?"

She touched her stomach. "So far so good."

"Awesome."

"So Ginny, how do you like our town so far?" he asked.

"This place is amazing. Grace, that reminds me, I found something." She got out her phone and tapped the screen a few times while Grace sat down. "An engagement announcement for John Haven."

"Oh my god," Grace said. "Let me guess, it's not to Eliza Bailey."

"Nope." Ginny handed Grace her phone. "He was engaged to Sarah Montgomery, granddaughter of Ernest Montgomery, one of the town's founders."

Grace gazed at Ginny's phone. "Maybe this means John Haven didn't write those notes to Eliza."

"Or maybe he did," Ginny said. "There's no record of a marriage between John and Sarah. And John disappeared not long after he won that prize money in the race."

"So maybe John was engaged to Sarah, but secretly in love with Eliza," Grace said, handing back Ginny's phone.

"It's very possible. The way this announcement is worded, it sounds like an arranged marriage," Ginny said.

"There are three mentions of the couple inheriting Ernest Montgomery's estate. That got me curious, and here's the interesting thing. Sarah never married or had children. After she died, some of the Montgomery estate was divided up between her extended family. But not all of it."

"What happened to the rest?" I asked.

"That's the big question," Ginny said. "I don't know. I found some mentions of a trust, but I think Ernest Montgomery really did do something with part of his wealth before he died."

"Are you saying you think the Montgomery treasure is real?" Gavin asked.

"That's exactly what I'm saying," Ginny said with a satisfied smile.

Grace looked skeptical, but Gavin's eyes lit up.

"Why do you think it's real?" I asked.

"I'll admit, I don't have a lot of hard evidence. It doesn't help that I can't find a copy of Ernest Montgomery's will. It should be public record, but it might have been destroyed in the big Tilikum fire. But I did find a document that suggests he amended his will years after that engagement notice was in the paper. And based on the records that do still exist, there was a part of his fortune the Montgomery family didn't inherit after he and Sarah both died."

My mind spun with the details, creating a story. This wasn't the type of thing I wrote, but I couldn't help it. It was how my mind worked.

"Maybe John Haven didn't want to marry Sarah Montgomery, he wanted to marry Eliza Bailey," I said. "But their families insisted, so John and Eliza made a plan to run away together. Eliza left first, and John stayed behind to compete in the race, hoping to use the prize money to fund their escape. Only when John went looking for Eliza afterward, she wasn't in their prearranged meeting place. And then John was robbed and murdered."

Everyone stared at me.

"That's good," Gavin said, his tone enthusiastic. "Then maybe Ernest did hide a treasure, only the real treasure wasn't gold, it was his granddaughter's hand in marriage. But no one ever found it."

"Yes," I said, grabbing Gavin's arm in excitement. "And it included a piece of his estate as a dowry for Sarah. But the tragedy is, Ernest died before anyone found it, and Sarah spent the rest of her life alone."

"Wait," Grace said. "The original owners of my house were Montgomerys. I looked up the real estate records to see if I could figure out who might have hidden Eliza's mirror and the love notes, but it didn't occur to me that the Montgomerys would have had anything to do with it. But if there's a connection between John and Eliza, and Sarah Montgomery…"

"Oh my god, this keeps getting better," Ginny said, furiously typing notes in her phone. "There's definitely something going on here."

"Have you been to the Haven House?" Grace asked.

Ginny's eyebrows drew together. "I took the tour, but why?"

"What's the Haven House?" I asked.

"It's like a little museum," Grace said. "They claim it's the oldest surviving house in town, and it's set up with the original furnishings from the early 1900s."

Gavin rolled his eyes. "It's the stupidest thing in Tilikum. They made us take field trips there when we were in elementary school."

"Why is it stupid?" I asked with a laugh.

"Because everyone knows the Havens didn't live there,

but for some dumbass reason, they named it the Haven House."

"I was wondering because some people say Ernest Montgomery built that house," Grace said.

"I looked around, but I didn't notice anything unusual," Ginny said. "But if Ernest built it, that is interesting. Although if there's any truth to local lore, he built half the town."

"True," Grace said. "And I'm pretty sure the house he lived in burned down."

"I bet Harvey will find the treasure," Gavin said. "And then the joke will be on everyone in town who called him crazy."

"I wish I could stay here indefinitely until I figure this out," Ginny said. "It's so fascinating. But I don't think my boss is going to share my enthusiasm for a century-old mystery."

Grace glanced back at the counter. "I should probably go help the girls. Thanks for sharing your findings."

"You bet," Ginny said with a smile.

Grace got up and Logan peeled off from where he'd been standing with Asher. He sauntered to our table and flashed a smile at Ginny.

"Hey. I was thinking about grabbing some breakfast over at Bigfoot. Want to join me?"

"You know what, I'd like that." Ginny turned to me. "Do you mind?"

"Not at all. Go ahead."

"I've got her," Gavin said.

"Thanks." Ginny smiled, then stood and gathered her things.

Logan put a hand on the small of her back and led her outside.

Gavin glanced at me and raised his eyebrows. "Have they been hanging out?"

"A little, I think."

"Huh."

"I don't know how much longer she'll be in town, but I guess we'll see what happens."

The cafe door opened again and my mom walked in, followed by my dad. Mom gave me a little wave and they both headed for our table.

I waved back and Gavin turned to look. He seemed to startle, jumping a little and then straightening his back.

"Hey, Chief," he said quickly.

"Hi, you two," Mom said, her lips curling in a knowing smile.

I tensed, waiting for her to say something awkward. I hadn't admitted to her that I'd been sleeping with Gavin, but I had a feeling she knew. She always seemed to know those kinds of things.

Fortunately for me, she didn't say anything else. Just smiled and glanced over at my dad.

"Congratulations," Dad said with a nod.

Gavin's gaze swung to me, his eyes wide with alarm, then back to Dad. "What?"

Dad gestured to the pumpkin crown. "The Pumpkin Plunge."

He took the crown off and looked at it, like he'd forgotten it was on his head. "Oh, right. Thanks."

"I remember the year your dad won," Dad said. "Although I think Gerald made you hold out longer than anything Charlie had to contend with."

"That's right, I remember that," Mom said, putting her hand on Dad's arm. "He looks so much like Charlie, don't you think?"

Dad looked at Gavin. "You really do. Spitting image of your father."

The levity in Gavin's expression melted away and he glanced down at the table. "Yeah, that's what Gram says."

"We should get in line to order," Mom said, tugging on Dad's arm.

"Bye Mom... and Dad," I said, stumbling over the phrase. Saying it that way felt so odd, like they were actually a couple.

Gavin kept his eyes on the table as my parents walked away.

"Are you okay?" I asked.

He cleared his throat. "Yeah. I'll be fine. Wanna get out of here?"

"Sure."

Gavin said things like *I'll be fine*, or *it'll be fine* all the time, and usually he meant it. But this time, I could tell he didn't.

I followed him out and we got in his truck. He turned on the engine, but didn't drive away.

"I don't remember them," he said finally, his voice unusually quiet.

"Your parents?"

He nodded. "My brothers do, but I was only four. It feels like I never even met them."

"I'm sorry."

"I was an oops baby anyway. They didn't mean to have more kids."

"Really?"

"Yeah. You'd think they'd have figured out how it worked by then, but I guess not." He cracked a smile. "Asher and Evan are only a year apart, and then they had the twins two years later. The last thing they needed was another kid. But along came Gavin."

"I'm sure they wanted you just as much as your brothers."

He shrugged.

I reached over and clasped his hand. It was cold. "You're still freezing."

He met my eyes. "You want to warm me up?"

Just the suggestion sent a pleasant tingle of anticipation through my body. "One way to recover from prolonged exposure to cold is skin contact."

"I love skin contact."

"Me too."

He looked at me for a long moment, a subtle smile on his face. "Thanks, Sky."

"For what?"

"Making me feel better."

"Already? I haven't even taken my clothes off yet."

"You don't even have to. But I want you to anyway, just so we're clear."

I laughed. "Yeah, I know."

That wasn't a problem, because right now nothing sounded better than getting naked with Gavin Bailey.

29

GAVIN

*S*ky was right, I was still cold. The coffee helped, as did my hair finally drying. But I'd been in the water long enough that the chill had gone right to my bones. Usually I'd just take a hot shower after a dip in the frigid river. But getting naked with Skylar was going to be so much more fun.

I was still riding the high of the plunge, the excitement of the challenge pulsing through me. Chief's mention of my dad had pulled me down a little, but now that I was taking Sky back to my place, I was soaring again.

After parking in the driveway—I was happy to see that my brothers still weren't home—we went inside. Princess Squeaker came out yawning and brushed up against my leg.

I picked her up and nuzzled her nose with mine. "Hi, Princess."

"She's grown so much." Skylar reached out to pet her, but Squeaker batted at her hand.

"Hey, now. You don't need to be jealous." I almost added, *Skylar's just a friend*, but there was something about that sentence that I didn't like. Which was weird—because it was true—but I still didn't say it.

I put Squeaker down and grabbed Skylar's hand, tugging her toward my room. The corners of her mouth lifted in a smile as she let me lead her in.

As much as I loved sex—and I really loved it—there was this moment of anticipation before sex that I loved almost as much. Just knowing that in a few minutes I was going to be inside her made my blood run hot.

I shut the door behind us and she took her coat off. Sliding my hands around her waist, I pulled her against me and leaned down to kiss her lips. She wrapped her arms around my neck, pressing herself close.

"Let's get you warmed up." She slipped her hands beneath my shirt, running her palms over my abs, up to my chest.

Our clothes came off between kisses, bit by bit, dropping to the floor. Her skin was warm against mine, and I ran my fingers through her hair, kissing her deeply. She tasted so good, I wanted to devour her.

Maybe I would.

I backed her up to the bed and pushed her onto the mattress. A coil of climbing rope in the corner caught my eye, and suddenly I had an idea.

"Do you want to try something fun?"

A flicker of anxiety crossed her features, but she held my gaze. "Like what?"

"Do you trust me?"

"Yes, but..."

I climbed on top of her and kissed her again—a long, deep kiss. "I won't make you do anything you don't like."

"I know. But if you tell me I need a safe word, that might be a bit much for me."

My mouth hooked in a grin. "No, but I'm planning on eating your pussy so good you'll beg for mercy."

"Oh my god," she breathed. "Okay yes, I trust you."

I got up and grabbed the coil of blue rope. Skylar watched me with flushed cheeks and curiosity in her eyes.

This was a first for me—I'd never tied a girl up before—but I knew how to tie a good knot. The rope was smooth, so I wasn't worried that it would hurt her, as long as I didn't make it too tight.

I knelt beside her and traced the coil of rope between her tits, over her belly button, and slid it between her legs. Her knees tipped open.

"You need me to make you come, don't you?"

"Yes."

"Don't worry, Sky. I'll give you everything you need."

I took one of her wrists and raised it above her head so I could fasten it to the headboard. She watched me work, her arm relaxed in my grip. I finished with one side and slid my finger between the rope and her skin, making sure it wasn't too tight.

"Is that okay?"

She tugged gently. "Yeah."

I repeated the process on the other side, taking my time. The way she was yielding her body to me, giving up control, was such a fucking rush.

"Still good?" I asked.

She nodded.

I moved so I was kneeling in front of her and pushed her legs open. I licked my lips, really glad I always kept rope around. "I'm going to take such good care of you."

"I thought I was supposed to be warming *you* up."

"Fuck, Sky, I'm hot just looking at you." It was true. I wasn't cold at all.

I slid my hand up her thigh and brushed her soft pink skin. She trembled at my touch as I dipped a fingertip into her wetness. I teased her clit a little—I really liked playing with her—before bringing my hand to my mouth so I could suck her taste off my finger.

"So fucking good," I said.

I kissed my way up the insides of her thighs and settled with my face between her legs. I glanced up, and seeing her tied to the bed, stretched out for me, was every bit as hot as the blow job at the drive-in.

Fuck, this girl was amazing.

I licked up her slit, feeling her shudder. Swirled my tongue around her clit. I kept teasing her, little flicks of my tongue while she gasped short breaths. She was already deliciously wet, and I was just getting started.

She tasted so good. Better than any cookie, stolen or otherwise. I went all in, licking and sucking while she writhed, pulling against the ropes. Her moans grew sharper and more frenzied. I slid a finger into her wetness and her silky inner muscles tightened.

I loved doing this to her. Making her feel good. Making her let go.

Her hips moved, her body tensing. I slid another finger inside her and she gasped. I had her now. Pumping my fingers, I relentlessly licked her until she was panting and moaning, her back arching beneath me.

"Oh my god. Yes. Right there. Don't stop."

There was no way I was stopping now. Every moan and jerk of her hips spurred me on. I could feel her heat, the walls of her pussy pulsing around my fingers. My dick ached with the desperate need to be inside her, but she was so close. I could feel it.

"Gavin. Oh god. I can't."

Her words trailed off and she cried out as she started to come. Her pussy clenched, over and over, while she bucked her hips. I didn't let up, moving with her, still licking her clit with the pad of my tongue.

Her body relaxed and I gently slipped my fingers out. Let her take a few breaths.

She opened her eyes and blinked at me. "I don't know what you just did to me, but that was amazing."

I got back on my knees and caressed her thighs. "I'm glad you liked it. Are your arms okay?"

"Yeah." Her eyes flicked to her bound wrists. "I want you to fuck me like this."

I groaned and almost involuntarily, my hand went to my erection. I stroked myself a few times, just taking her in. Enjoying the sight of this beautiful woman tied up in my bed.

"Hell yes, I'll fuck you like this."

I paused to get a condom and roll it on. Fuck, this was going to be good. I positioned myself in front of her and pushed her legs open.

"You want this?"

"Yes," she breathed.

"Fuck, Sky, I'm so hard for you." I held my cock at the base and traced it up and down her very wet slit.

She whimpered.

I thrust in, groaning at the feel of her surrounding me. She was hot and tight. Absolutely perfect. With my hands on her thighs, I slid in and out, my eyes all over her. On her wrists, anchored to the headboard. Her tits, bouncing as I fucked her. The flush in her cheeks and the hard peaks of her nipples.

Our gazes met and something stirred in my chest. She was so beautiful. Her eyes were half-open, her lips parted.

No fear or worry. Just trust and desire.

I leaned down to kiss her mouth, losing myself in her. In her taste and her scent. Thrusting hard, I drove into her, pressure building fast. My tongue lapped against hers and I groaned as I sank myself deep inside.

No one had ever felt this good before. It was like we fit each other perfectly.

She pulled her knees toward her shoulders and I braced myself on the headboard so I could fuck her harder. I couldn't get enough. I was an animal, growling and grunting, my muscles clenched tight.

The bed banged against the wall but I didn't let up. I plunged in and out, burying myself in her, over and over. Her arms strained against the ropes and every noise she made sent jolts of heat through my veins. The tension in my groin built, spreading through my entire body.

"Don't stop," she said.

No chance of that. I fucked her relentlessly, driving in deep. Her pussy tightened around me and I groaned hard.

Still gripping the headboard, I thrust again. My back clenched and the pressure in my groin intensified, white-hot tension overtaking me. She moaned as she started to come again, the pulses of her inner walls rippling through me.

In a rush of pleasure, I came unglued.

I groaned as I came, my eyes rolling back. My climax swept through me, my dick throbbing inside her. I sank my cock in deep, burying myself in her as I rode out the last waves of my orgasm.

Fuck, she felt so good.

Coming back to reality, I opened my eyes. Skylar blinked at me, her cheeks flushed the sexiest shade of pink.

"Don't move." I winked at her and she laughed softly.

"I don't think I could even if I wasn't tied up."

I got up to quickly deal with the condom, then came back and untied her.

She rolled her wrists. I settled in next to her and took one of her hands, bringing it close so I could kiss her reddened skin.

"Are you okay?"

"Yeah, it doesn't hurt."

I kept kissing her, turning her arm so I could press my lips to the soft skin on the inside of her wrist. When I'd thoroughly babied one wrist, I took the other and did the same, kissing her gently.

"Thank you," she said.

"Aren't you glad you trusted me?"

"So glad. Your brothers aren't home, are they?"

"I don't think so."

"Good. I'll be right back."

She got up and went to the bathroom, then came back a couple of minutes later. I reached for her and she crawled back into bed with me.

I drew the covers up over us and took a contented breath as she rested her head on my shoulder. I felt awesome. Sex with Sky was always great, but something about today had been especially fantastic. Maybe it had been the novelty of tying her up. Or maybe I was still high on the rush of the river plunge.

Or maybe it was just her.

Something about that unsettled me. Cut through the post-orgasm glow. There was another feeling worming its way through my chest. Something I didn't recognize. Whatever it was, it made me want to hold her tighter. I rested my cheek on her head, trying to push it aside, and just enjoy the feeling of her in my arms, her warm body pressed against mine.

She lifted herself up, resting her head in her hand. "I should probably get going."

Damn, that was disappointing. "Oh, okay. Do you have something else going on today?"

"No, I just need to get some writing done. The book is coming along, but I hit a snag."

"Is there anything I can do to help?"

She smiled. "You've already done so much. I don't know if I would have written anything without you helping me get started. But I think I just need to push through. It's not so much that I'm blocked, I'm just struggling a bit with how to make this section of the story work. It's like I can't quite picture it."

I touched her face and tucked her hair behind her ear. "All right. I can take you home."

"Thanks."

She got up to get dressed and I tamped down the flare of disappointment. And there was that feeling again. Was I worried about her? I didn't know why I would be. She was writing again, which was great for her. And we were totally cool. We had fun together—fun of various kinds. We'd just had some epic sex. What could possibly be wrong with any of that?

Maybe I was just hungry or something. That didn't really ring true, but I didn't know what else it could be.

I got up and got dressed, thinking about Skylar's writing snag. I'd just had another idea. It wasn't as good as tying her to my headboard—what would be, honestly—but it was pretty fucking awesome.

Two kick ass ideas in one day. It was good to be back.

30

SKYLAR

*T*he house was quiet when I got up. I stretched my arms overhead and took a deep breath. The redness around my wrists had faded quickly, but I was still pleasantly sore between my legs. That was a first for me. I'd never been fucked so hard I could actually feel it the next day. In fact, I'd always thought that was a myth.

Not so when you'd been tied to a bed by Gavin Bailey.

That had also been a first. I didn't want to compare Gavin to Cullen—especially because I wasn't actually *dating* Gavin—but it was hard not to. Cullen had never even suggested something like rope in the bedroom. Not that I would have gone for it—not with him. Which was an eye-opening realization. I never would have trusted Cullen enough to be that vulnerable with him.

With Gavin, it was so easy.

It had been exhilarating and fun. I'd loved the feeling of being in his control. It had been different, and even though *different* often gave me anxiety, it hadn't.

I went down the hall to use the bathroom and my mom's bedroom door caught my eye. It was open. I paused and glanced in. The bed was made already. That was odd. Unlike me, Mom wasn't a morning person. I was usually up before her.

Had she even slept there last night?

She and my dad had both been home yesterday evening. I'd gone up to my room early, and as far as I knew, neither of them had left.

Her empty bedroom was odd. Where was she?

After taking a shower, I got dressed and went down to the kitchen. I flipped on the light and got out the coffee. Apparently Dad wasn't up either.

The scent of coffee filled the air and I took a seat at the kitchen table while it brewed. Mom had left a book she'd been reading sitting out, so I idly thumbed through the pages.

When the coffee had just about finished brewing, Dad came downstairs, whistling.

"Morning, sweetheart," he said with a smile.

"Morning."

He moved around the kitchen and I swear, he had a spring in his step. He seemed lighter, somehow, his spine straight, shoulders back.

"You're in a good mood," I said. "Do you have an unexpected day off or something?"

"No, I have to be at the firehouse at eight." He opened the cupboard and pulled out a travel mug. "Mind if I have a cup of coffee?"

"Help yourself."

He smiled at me. No, he *grinned* at me, there was no other way to describe it. He filled his mug with coffee, then poured a cup for me.

"Thanks. Do you know where Mom went?"

"She's still in bed."

I glanced up from the book. "Really? I thought I saw her door open and her bed was still—"

Oh.

Oh.

Dad froze, and my eyes widened.

Mom had always known the perfect moment to make an entrance, and this morning was no exception. She waltzed in, dressed in her silk floral robe and I did not miss the smile she gave my dad.

Oh my god. Had my divorced parents slept together last night?

"Morning," she said, a cheerful lilt to her voice.

"Good morning." I eyed them both, wondering what the heck was going on.

Neither of them seemed inclined to offer any explanation which, when I thought about it, was probably a good thing. If they'd wound up in bed together last night, I didn't particularly want to know the details.

My phone saved the day. Before the silence could get too awkward, it binged with a text, giving me an excuse to put my attention somewhere other than the looks my parents were giving each other.

Gavin: *Sorry to text so early but I have the best idea.*

That made my lips curl in a smile. I was quickly learning that I liked it when Gavin had ideas.

Me: *What's up?*

Gavin: *It's a surprise. When can I come get you?*

Me: *How about twenty minutes?*

Gavin: *Perfect. See you soon.*

"How's Gavin?" Mom asked, doing nothing to hide the suggestion in her tone.

I lowered my phone. "He's fine."

"What about Gavin?" Dad asked casually.

I avoided meeting his gaze. "Nothing. He just wants to get together this morning."

Dad seemed to be about to say something, but Mom beat him to it.

"I bet it's good to have him back on duty full-time." Her eyes flicked to me and I gave her a grateful smile. I didn't want to get into the nature of my relationship with Gavin right now. Not with Dad.

"Yeah, it makes scheduling easier when we're at full strength." He leaned his hip against the counter and took a drink of coffee. "And Gavin's good for morale. The other guys feed off his energy."

"He certainly seems like a nice young man," she said, and I couldn't tell if that comment was meant for me or Dad. Maybe both of us.

"Somehow he's turning out all right," Dad said with a little grin.

Mom's expression changed, the mirth in her eyes fading into something like surprise. Or maybe curiosity. She tilted her head slightly, gazing at him. "I have a feeling you have a lot to do with that, don't you?"

Dad cleared his throat and looked at his coffee mug. "I don't know about that."

"They were lucky to have you," Mom said, her voice soft.

Dad met her eyes. "Thank you."

I got up and gestured toward the stairs. "Gavin's coming to get me, so I'm going to go blow dry my hair really quick."

"Have a good day, honey," Mom said.

"Thanks."

I went upstairs, idly wondering if I should leave my parents alone together. What was going on with them? Despite not wanting to know the intimate details of anything that might have transpired last night, I was curious. Were they just messing around for old time's sake? Or was there more?

I'd have to talk to my mom about it later. For now, Gavin had a surprise for me, and I couldn't wait to see what it was.

WE DROVE down a bumpy back road. Gavin hadn't told me where we were going and his mischievous smile had me brimming with curiosity. What was he up to?

The road curved, then climbed a small hill before coming to an abrupt end. The trees were thick here, casting a deep shadow over the terrain, and mist hung in the air.

"Okay, you've got me," I said. "I have no idea what we're doing out here."

"I was thinking this might help you finish your book."

I glanced outside, wondering if there was something I was missing. "How?"

"I'll show you."

We got out of the truck and the damp fall air was cool on my cheeks. As soon as my feet hit the forest floor, my senses heightened, my heart beating faster. The gray mist made the view between the trees hazy, and the heavy silence pressed against me.

"It's a little bit creepy out here," I said, stepping slowly to the front of the truck.

"Exactly," Gavin said, his voice quiet but never losing its undercurrent of excitement. "There's a hot spring not far from here and it gets really misty in the morning. Come on."

"Are we going to the hot spring?"

"Not this time. Just follow me."

He took my hand and led me to a narrow trail through the brush. Tall pines towered over us and the mist in the air was eerie. The only sound was our feet crunching on dry debris and the occasional distant call of a bird.

I squeezed Gavin's hand. I wasn't scared, exactly, but this place was unsettling.

After a short walk down the trail, we came within sight of a decrepit old cabin.

"Welcome to the murder cabin," he said, gesturing with his other hand.

"Wait, what?"

"You don't have to be scared for real. There's nothing that can hurt you, and I don't think anyone's actually been murdered here. But I set it up so it's creepy as fuck. I wasn't sure what you were going for in your book, so there's a little of everything. I thought this might give you some ideas."

"You set up a murder cabin for me?"

"Yeah." He shrugged, like it wasn't a big deal. "Shall we?"

It was a big deal, but I wasn't sure how to tell him how amazing this was without making it awkward. We were supposed to be just friends, but things like this—and what we'd done yesterday—were starting to make my heart yearn for more.

And I couldn't go there. It wouldn't be fair to suddenly spring a bunch of messy feelings on him when I was the one who'd talked him into our current... arrangement, for lack of a better word.

But he'd made me a murder cabin.

He'd make such a great boyfriend, if someone could ever convince him she was worth it.

"Don't worry." He squeezed my hand. "I've got you."

I didn't tell him that I wasn't afraid of the cabin. That I was grappling with an unexpected rush of emotion and I wasn't prepared to deal with it. I just smiled and nodded, keeping the rest of it locked up tight inside me.

He slowly led me toward the cabin and I let the atmosphere sink in. The towering trees, the mist, the eerie silence. It made my heart beat harder and a tingle of fear crawl up my spine.

But I actually liked the feeling.

The cabin's wood was gray and weathered with gaps between the boards. The covered porch sagged on one side and the stairs looked like they might break if you stepped on them.

"Go ahead." He dropped my hand and gestured toward the cabin. "Check it out."

"By myself?"

"I'll be right behind you."

I glanced at him, suddenly worried there might be someone waiting to jump out and scare me.

"This isn't a prank," he said, as if he could read my mind. "It's more like... visual inspiration."

"Okay."

With a deep breath, I walked up the porch steps. They creaked beneath my feet. The porch itself seemed to let out a low groan as soon as my weight settled on the old boards. But it held.

I glanced to the side and gasped. A mannequin dressed in an old t-shirt and jeans was sprawled out on the porch, as if he'd fallen there, dead. A long knife stuck out from his chest and something red—it looked a lot like ketchup—was splattered around the wound.

"Maybe your main character is first on the scene and discovers something like that," Gavin said.

I gazed at the fake murder scene. A stabbing victim would be an interesting twist.

She walks up the creaky steps, her weapon drawn. Heart beating fast, the adrenaline flowing through her veins a familiar companion. The interior is dark, apparently abandoned, but her instincts flare to life. She steps onto the porch and catches the metallic scent of blood in the air. Pointing her weapon to her right, she finds the body, the murder weapon still protruding from his chest.

This was giving me ideas already.

"Is there more inside?" I asked.

His mouth turned up in a smile. "Oh yeah."

I pushed the door open and crept in. Tingles raced down my back, but there was something exhilarating about it—about walking straight into fear. I knew it was because this was safe—none of it was real—but it was a heady sensation nonetheless.

Light streamed in through a dingy window and the cracks between the boards, illuminating floating particles of dust. Gavin hadn't been kidding. There was more inside. A lot more.

A sheet of plastic stretched across a section of floor, splattered with fake blood, and a severed arm sat in the middle of it. An ax was stuck in the floorboards nearby. In another corner, a skeletal arm poked out of an old dusty chest. Rusty tools hung from the rafters and a rickety table and chairs were covered with fake spiderwebs. At least, I hoped they were fake.

He'd marked off the shape of a body using tape on the floor and a toy handgun—I could tell it was plastic—lay nearby, like the perpetrator had dropped it there and ran.

Other items in the cabin were more gothic or Halloween-ish. The old mantle had large candle holders and a black raven sat on a shelf.

I crouched next to the tape lines, my vision going hazy. I could see my protagonist doing a slow sweep of the area, investigating every detail. Looking for things that might have been missed. Trying to get inside the killer's head.

Like pieces of a puzzle, the ending to my book clicked into place. I knew what needed to happen.

I got up and whipped around, running right into Gavin. "Oops."

He grabbed my arms to steady me. "Are you okay?"

"Yeah, fine." Maybe I should have stepped back—put a little space between us—but I didn't particularly want to. "Sorry, I didn't realize you were there."

"Just checking to see what you think."

"This is..." I trailed off, having a hard time finding the words. "It's one of the most amazing things anyone has ever done for me."

He smiled, puckering his adorable dimples. "Yeah? I'm glad you like it. Did you get any ideas?"

"Absolutely. You were right, visual inspiration really helped."

"Awes—" Something clinked outside, like the sound of a metal can toppling over, and he broke off before finishing the word. "Did you hear that?"

"Yeah."

We both paused, standing still in the ensuing quiet.

"Hello?" he called, his eyes darting around.

I held my breath, but nothing happened. Was this part of the setup?

"Maybe we should check outside."

I nodded and grabbed his hand. We crept out the half-open door, and the hinges creaked. The sound made the back of my neck tingle and I scrunched my shoulders. He led me past the stabbing victim and down the porch stairs, taking slow, cautious steps.

My heart beat faster and the fun and excitement of the murder cabin started to melt into actual fear.

"You know I don't write horror novels, right?" I whispered as we walked around the side of the building. "I don't need jump scare inspiration."

"I know. I didn't put anything back here."

That wasn't reassuring.

There was a small clearing behind the cabin, the ground strewn with pine needles and twigs. A few pieces of graying wood suggested there had once been a stack of firewood back here, and a couple of rusty old tools peeked out from the debris littered ground.

"Are there bears out here?" I whispered.

"Yeah."

My eyes widened. "Did you just say yes, there are bears?"

"Shh." He put a finger to his lips and peered into the trees. "I don't think it's a bear."

"Then what—"

Something crashed, I gasped, and Gavin dragged me to the ground. He threw himself on top of me, like he was shielding me from... whatever was out there.

For a second, I squeezed my eyes shut, afraid to even look. Was there a real murderer out here? Had that ax inside been left by the cabin's terrifying occupant who was now going to chop us into bits for trespassing?

"What the fuck," he muttered, but he sounded baffled, not afraid.

Of course, this was Gavin. Would a big hulking ax murderer be enough to scare him?

I peeked my eyes open. I was on my back with Gavin braced on top of me, and I slowly turned my head to see what he was looking at.

A rusty tin can with little gray feet scampered across the ground.

"What is that?" I asked.

"I think it's a squirrel stuck in a can."

I felt bad for the little guy, but I couldn't help but laugh. "Oh my god. I thought we were about to be murdered."

He smiled. "I did too for a second there."

"Did something actually scare you?"

"It startled me. Even I can be startled by a weird noise when I'm in a murder cabin."

The squirrel ran around the clearing in a disoriented frenzy.

"Should we try to help it?" I asked.

Before he could answer, a man jumped out from behind a tree. I screamed, and Gavin rolled off me, getting to his feet to stand between me and whoever it was.

"Harvey," Gavin said. "What the hell, man?"

"Wait," Harvey said. He was dressed in a worn leather vest over a flannel shirt, faded jeans, and a pair of brown boots. He had a stick in his hand and he used it to poke at the squirrel.

"Don't hurt it," I said, getting up, relieved that Gavin seemed to know him.

Harvey chased the squirrel a few steps and tried to nudge it with the stick. "I just want my can back."

I quickly took off my coat. "Here, use this."

Gavin took my coat and tossed it on the squirrel. Then he scooped the whole thing up in a bundle in his arms.

Harvey raised the stick over his head and for a second, I thought he was going to hit the squirrel—or Gavin. But he rested it on his shoulder and tilted his head.

"Don't bite me," Gavin said as he gently unfolded my coat, looking for the squirrel. "I'm trying to help, little bro."

He moved a sleeve aside, exposing the top of the can.

"There it is," Harvey shouted.

Gavin jerked the bundle away. "I got it, I got it." He crouched down and lifted the can, then set my coat and the squirrel down on the ground.

The squirrel rubbed its little paws over its face a few times, then scampered off into the woods.

Gavin let out a long breath and handed the can to Harvey. "What was that about?"

"He stole my can." Harvey held it up and pointed an accusatory finger in the direction the squirrel had gone.

"Yeah, they do that," Gavin said with a laugh. "You okay?"

Harvey brushed off his vest. "I'm all right now. Sorry if I scared you, miss..."

"Skylar," I said. "Skylar Stanley."

"Do you need a ride back to town?" Gavin asked.

"No, now that I got my can back, I'm fine." He tipped his old hat to me and gave me a crooked smile. "Nice to meet you, Miss Stanley."

Bewildered, I watched him happily clutch the rusty can to his chest and walk away, into the woods.

"Did that really just happen?" I asked.

"I didn't plan that part, I swear." Gavin grabbed my coat and shook off the dirt. "Are you okay?"

"Yeah, I'm fine."

He held my coat while I slipped it on, then pulled my hair out from the back. The brush of his fingers felt good on my skin.

"You know, Harvey kind of reminds me of one of your characters. The drifter."

"You read that book?"

"Yeah. It's amazing. I totally thought he was going to be the killer. You had me completely fooled."

I stared at him, wondering how many more times he was going to say or do something that tugged on my heart like that. Because if he did, it might start becoming a problem.

Just friends, Skylar. We're just friends.

"I'm glad you liked it."

But he gave me that smile again—the one that was all sweet brown eyes and dimples—and I had a feeling my heart was in trouble.

31

SKYLAR

There were several cars already outside Cara's house when I arrived. She'd invited me to a watch party, although I wasn't sure what we were going to be watching. I'd texted Gavin to see if he was going, and he'd said yes. Knowing he'd be there made me want to go, despite my usual avoidance of parties or other gatherings where I didn't know people very well.

Or even sometimes when I did.

Now that I was here, my anxiety was telling me this was a mistake. What if I started talking about my characters like they were real people? I'd done that at a cocktail party once and it had been mortifying. Or maybe I'd start spewing morbid facts about the rate of corpse decay as it related to determining time of death like I had last Thanksgiving with Cullen's family.

Not good.

But Gavin was here, and it was impossible to resist an opportunity to be with him.

I got out and marched up to the door, knocking before I could turn back into a mouse and dart away.

Cara answered, dressed in a gorgeous black and white off-the-shoulder blouse, black pants, and bright pink heels. Her hair was down and she smiled, her deep red lips parting over perfect white teeth.

"There you are. I'm glad you could make it."

I nervously tucked my hair behind my ear and glanced down at my clothes. Under my coat, I'd worn a t-shirt that said *careful or I'll put you in my novel*, and a pair of jeans. "Thanks. Am I under-dressed?"

She looked me up and down. "Not at all. You're adorable. This is totally casual, so you're fine."

"Okay."

I followed her inside and gazed in awe at her house. It was gorgeous. Big windows showcased a view of the river and the furniture looked both pretty and comfortable. A man in a white coat worked in the kitchen, and there was a bar set up, complete with a bartender mixing drinks.

"I'll take your coat," Cara said, and before I knew what was happening, she was already sliding it off.

"Thank you."

Music played in the background, and I was surprised to realize I knew everyone here. Evan and Fiona, Asher and Grace. Levi stood talking with Grace and Fiona while Logan stood with a beer, looking mildly uncomfortable.

Gavin stood next to the kitchen island, chatting with the chef. As soon as I walked in, his eyes swung to me and his face broke into a smile.

My heart fluttered and my breath caught in my throat. Why did he have to be so gorgeous? It was quite unfair to people trying not to make fools of themselves at a party.

That was me. I was people.

He walked over with a beer in his hand. Thankfully, he

was dressed similarly to me, in a t-shirt and jeans. It made me feel more comfortable. "Hey, Sky."

"Hey. Is that a chef in the kitchen?"

"Yeah. Cara does that. She likes to throw parties, and they're always catered with an open bar. Even on a random Thursday."

"Wow."

"Yeah, they're fun. Even Logan comes, although he always says he isn't going to. This one's kind of small, though. I wonder if she invited anyone else."

"What's going on with Logan and Cara anyway?"

Glancing at his brother, he shrugged. "I don't know how it started, but they either hate each other or…"

I nodded, catching his meaning. "Yeah, seems that way."

That reminded me, I hadn't asked Ginny about her breakfast date with Logan the other day. I wondered if she'd seen him again this week.

"By the way, are you busy tomorrow?" he asked.

"I don't think so."

He grinned. "Awesome."

"Are you going to tell me why?"

"Not yet. But trust me, it'll be fun."

"I have no doubt."

Cara breezed around the room, smiling and chatting. Logan moved whenever she got close to him, as if enforcing a minimum distance requirement. She went to the bar and a moment later, came over with a glass of champagne.

"Here you go."

I took the glass. "Thank you."

"My pleasure. Help yourself to the food. It's just heavy hors d'oeuvres tonight."

Absently, I sipped the champagne, but my mind

wandered. Something about the big windows and the view of the river set my imagination in motion.

Her home, just like her marriage, is picture perfect, her love of the finer things evident in every detail. But her pristine house is hiding terrible secrets, and her life is far from what it seems.

I turned the idea over in my mind. The killers in my books were always men, and the husband could be the primary suspect. But what if the twist was that the wife was the murderer? Would he be covering for her? Or would she have him fooled, too?

"But what's her motive?" I asked out loud.

"Whose motive?" Gavin asked casually, as if I hadn't just blurted out a random question completely out of context.

"Sorry, I didn't mean to say that out loud. I just had an idea for another book, maybe with an unreliable narrator. I've never written something like that before."

"Sounds awesome," he said.

"A book idea popped into your head just now?" Cara asked.

"Not a fully formed idea, but I think I know what I'm going to write next."

When was the last time that had happened? Usually it took weeks of pondering once I'd finished one novel before I knew what the next book would be.

"Oh my god, you just made me even more excited for tonight," Cara said, then turned to Grace. "Grace, how many kids do you want?"

Grace broke off from Asher and walked over to stand next to her. "I'm still working on the first one, so maybe ask me again in a couple of years."

"No, I don't mean with Asher. With me. We have Fiona, but is it too soon for another?" She glanced at me. "She's such a precious little teacup. I like her."

"Oh," Grace said with a smile. "As many as you want."

"Well let's not get ahead of ourselves. You know I hardly like anyone besides you. And our Fiona, but she's such a sparkly ray of tattooed sunshine, how could I not?" She slipped her arm through mine and tugged me close. "But I really like this one. Can we keep her?"

"Definitely."

Cara let out a long sigh. "This makes tonight even more meaningful. Speaking of..."

"Speaking of what?" Grace asked, but Cara had already swept away.

I wasn't quite sure what had just happened, or where Cara was going, but Gavin's arm brushed against mine and suddenly that was all I could think about. He didn't move away and for a second, the little bit of my skin touching his captured every bit of my focus.

The music quieted and Cara held her hands up to get everyone's attention.

"Ladies, gentlemen, and..." She paused for a second, her eyes briefly landing on Logan. "Others. I invited you all here tonight for a very special watch party, dedicated to my newest cupcake, Skylar. With, of course, a special shout out to my boo, who's my one and only true love."

Grace and Cara raised their glasses to each other.

"Tonight's show requires context," she continued. "I recently learned that our Skylar comes to us after the demise of a long-term relationship with a man who was not only her boyfriend, but her literary agent. It also came to my attention that her relationship ended due to the fact that he's a lying, cheating, piece of maggot-infested dog shit who was sleeping with another one of his clients, a married author named Pepper Sinclair."

Gavin slipped an arm around my shoulders and I

wanted to shrink into him. Even better, bury my face in his chest and hide. A few people murmured their surprise and displeasure.

"I'm not bringing this up publicly to make you feel worse about it," Cara said, looking at me. "He's the asshole here, and you have nothing to be ashamed of. I think we can all agree you're much better off right where you are."

Gavin squeezed, pressing me closer to him.

"And he deserves everything that's coming to him." Her tone remained light, but her smile grew cold, and there was something in her eyes that sent a chill down my spine.

"Cara..." Grace said.

She waved us closer. "Have a seat."

Gavin put his hand on the small of my back and led me to one of the couches. The others took seats or stayed standing nearby where they had a view of the large TV. Cara got a remote out of a drawer and turned it on.

"The show aired earlier, but I assume you didn't watch," Cara said, and I wasn't sure who she was talking to. Me? Or maybe everyone. "I recorded it. I haven't watched yet either and I'm absolutely dying."

"Cara, what show?" Grace asked.

She didn't answer. Just pressed a button on the remote and the screen came to life.

It was a national morning show that featured in-depth interviews with celebrities. Sometimes they featured authors if they were big names, and right there on the couch was freaking Pepper Sinclair.

Her hair and makeup were flawless, as usual, and she wore a stylish blouse and slacks. A small table next to her white upholstered seat held a stack of her latest book. She'd made a name for herself writing inspirational women's fiction, but her new release was a memoir.

Barf.

But the perfectly tailored, smiling Pepper wasn't what made my stomach drop. Seated next to her was Cullen.

Double barf.

I could see the foundation and eyeliner they'd used on him to make his face camera ready. His hair was poofier than usual, styled in a slick pompadour, and he wore a light gray suit.

I met Cara's eyes, wondering why she would possibly think I'd want to watch this interview.

The corners of her lips turned up ever so slightly. "Just wait for it."

I leaned into Gavin, not worrying about whether or not it was a friend thing or a girlfriend thing to do. The interview began and after thanking Pepper and Cullen for being on the show, the host started in on questions about her new book.

The book was titled *The Marriage Secret*, and Pepper claimed it was both a story about her journey—whatever that was supposed to mean—and a reflection on how to have a happy and fulfilling marriage. Cullen had been invited to the show to talk about how he'd helped take her career to the next level and the big publishing deal he hoped to secure for the follow-up to this release.

A follow-up? How many books was she going to write about herself?

"Pepper, this book delves into your ingredients for a happy marriage," the host said.

"Wait, I have a question." Fiona held up a hand, like she was in a classroom, and Cara paused the show. "Let me see if I have this straight. He's your ex?"

"Yes," I said. "Unfortunately."

"And he's banging this bitch." She gestured to the screen.

"Yeah, he left me for her."

Was it just me, or did Gavin just growl?

"But she's married to someone else?" Fiona asked.

"She was. I thought she was leaving her husband for Cullen."

"But she wrote a book about how to have a happy marriage?" Fiona asked. "Was she writing about her actual husband, or that guy?"

Cara produced a copy of Pepper's book, seemingly out of thin air. "Oh it's about her husband, all right. It's a bunch of absolute fucking bullshit. She wrote an entire book about how to be a good wife and have a blissful marriage, all while she was being a goddamn home wrecker and sleeping with another woman's man."

"Do you mean she and Cullen didn't go public with their relationship?" I asked.

"No, they most certainly did not," Cara said, tossing the book on the coffee table. "She wrote the most condescending book ever written, all about marriage. It would be a terrible blow to her career if anyone found out the truth."

"Holy shit, Cara," Gavin said.

Cara smiled again and pressed play.

The host continued. "Did you write this book before or after your marriage to your husband ended?"

Pepper's lips parted and she blinked a few times. "Excuse me?"

"You've written a four-hundred-page memoir and instruction manual for achieving a happy marriage, but within the last year, you began an adulterous relationship with your agent, Cullen Bell. Isn't that right?"

A chorus of "whoa," rose around me.

Pepper's mouth dropped open and Cullen shifted

uncomfortably, his eyes darting around as if he were looking for someone to get him out of this situation.

"No, that's... I don't..." Pepper sputtered, tripping over her words, her face flushing. "No, I'm happily married to my husband and—"

"What?" Cullen's face whipped around.

"So are you or are you not having an affair?" the host asked.

Pepper put a hand to her chest, as if she were finding it hard to breathe. "I was not prepared for this line of questioning."

"This isn't what we agreed to," Cullen said, anger in his tone. "You can't spring these questions on us with no warning."

"On the contrary, I think these questions are very relevant, given the content of the book."

"Ouch," Asher said.

"She's not wrong," Grace added.

Pepper fanned herself. "My book speaks for itself and my personal life is just that, personal."

"Except you wrote a memoir offering aspects of your life as examples to live up to. You're putting yourself forward as a model for other women, and yet most of what you wrote here is potentially a lie." The host's voice never wavered. "So I'll ask the question again. Are you two having an affair?"

Cullen glanced at the floor. "Yes. We are."

Pepper shot to her feet. "This is outrageous. How dare you. We talked about this. We agreed."

"We should have made popcorn," Gavin said.

"I told you to change the book." Cullen stood, facing off with her. "If you had listened to me, we wouldn't have had to hide. This never would have happened."

"Why, because you think I'm fucking in love with you?"

The show beeped out her curse word.

Everyone in the room gasped.

"You don't get it, do you?" Pepper asked. "This book wasn't a lie, and I'm not leaving him for you."

"Ms. Sinclair, Mr. Bell, if you'll please take your seats," the host said. "We'll give you both an opportunity to speak, but we need you to remain calm."

"Remain calm?" Pepper asked, her eyes wide and crazed. "How can you expect me to remain calm when you've just ruined me on national television?"

"Pepper, sit down," Cullen said.

"No," she snapped, pointing a manicured finger at him. "This is your fault. You were supposed to get me ten million, but you're as useless at your job as you are in the bedroom. Get this microphone off me."

The camera quickly cut to the host. "We'll be right back."

I gaped at the TV as Cara fast-forwarded. After a commercial break, the host gave a brief summary of what had happened, then moved on to the next segment. Pepper and Cullen were nowhere to be seen.

"Cara, how the fuck did you do that?" Gavin asked, his voice awed.

"What are you talking about, Gav?" Grace asked.

"I told her about what that asshat did to Skylar, and she said she was going to do something about it. Is that what that was? That was you?"

"People really shouldn't mess with my friends," Cara said sweetly, then turned to me. "That went even better than I'd hoped. Oh, and since the show first aired this morning, his agency fired him and dropped her as a client. I also have it from a reliable source that her book is being pulled from all bookstores, and it's no longer available on Amazon."

"*You* told the host about her affair with Cullen?" Grace asked. "How?"

Cara gave her a self-satisfied smile and lifted one shoulder in a shrug. "I have contacts."

"Oh, Cara..." Grace said.

"Don't you worry about a thing, boo. Do you see me getting revenge on anyone from my own past? Believe me, I have a list. But I only use my powers to help others."

"Yeah, you're a real saint," Logan said.

Levi leaned closer to him. "Dude, I wouldn't get on her bad side."

"Besides, I'm not the one who cheated on the beautiful and talented Skylar Stanley. He had it coming. He's lucky all I did is ruin his career from afar."

"Dude, that was amazing," Gavin said. "Cara karma at its finest."

Feeling a bit dazed, I slowly stood. "That was..."

Cara raised her eyebrows.

"That was one of the most amazing things I've ever seen. He made me feel so awful when he broke up with me, and I never thought I'd see him get his due. Did you see his face? That was..." I trailed off again and launched myself at Cara, wrapping her in a tight hug.

She put her arms around me, hugging me back. "I'm so glad you liked it. Wow, doing a good deed really does fill the soul. I should do that more often."

I stepped back and swiped beneath my eyes. Maybe it made me a bad person for being so happy at seeing someone else's life crash and burn. But I wasn't just emotional over Cullen. It was the sudden realization that I had so many people in my life who cared about me. For a shy girl who had a hard time making friends, that was priceless.

32

GAVIN

*E*ver since Ginny had told us she thought the Montgomery treasure was real, the idea that maybe she was right had been swirling around the back of my mind. I'd grown up hearing stories about it. Everyone in town had. But everyone also knew that this town loved its tall tales as much as the squirrels loved stealing our snacks. You couldn't really believe any of them.

But Ginny was an outsider. She had a different perspective. If she thought the treasure might be real, maybe Harvey Johnston wasn't as crazy as everyone thought. Although the tin can episode at the murder cabin didn't exactly support his sanity.

But still. Maybe there was something out there.

What really got me going was the implication that someone—maybe the Montgomerys—had been trying to hide it. I wasn't going to jump to the conclusion that there was a conspiracy that went back generations. But someone had hidden that stuff Grace had found. People didn't randomly put shit beneath the floorboards of a house for no reason. Did that mean there was a reason to hide it? And had a Montgomery done it?

There was just the smallest whiff of intrigue, but it was enough for me. Plus, who wouldn't want to be the guy to find an old town treasure? That sounded awesome.

Although if I was being totally honest, mostly it was just an excuse to do something fun with Skylar.

I picked her up and drove us over to the Haven House. It had a stupid name, but I had an idea.

She looked out the window at the old house. It was a big Victorian home with a pitched roof, a front porch, and a round tower on one side.

"If it was painted black, it would make the perfect haunted house," she said.

"That's what I've always thought. I feel like it's a missed opportunity."

"I don't think it's open today."

"No, it's not."

Her eyes moved to me. "Uh-oh."

"What? It's not our fault they're only open two days a week."

"You're about to tell me we're going to break in, aren't you?"

"Nope," I said with a grin. "We don't have to break in."

"Because you arranged for a private showing?"

I pulled the key out of my pocket. "Because I have this."

"Where did you get that?"

"The fire department has keys to certain buildings around town in case of emergency."

"Don't even tell me whether or not you asked my dad before you took it."

I gave her my best wide-eyed innocent look. "I left a note."

She put her hand on her forehead. "Oh my god."

"We're not going to steal anything. I just want to poke around without someone from the historical society looking over my shoulder. Plus, I'm about ninety percent sure there's a secret basement in there."

"Why?"

"A lot of these old buildings have plans on file with the fire department. It's a safety thing. We have to inspect them once in a while and it helps us in emergency planning. After Ginny mentioned her theories about the Montgomery treasure, I got curious. I checked out the plans for the Haven House—which, for the record, is still a stupid name—and there's a section that doesn't make sense. Unless there's a secret basement. I just want to see if I'm right."

"And you need me for this because?"

"You're my favorite partner in crime."

She laughed, her smile lighting up her eyes. "I don't know how you talk me into these things."

"It's not your fault, I'm really convincing."

"You are very convincing."

"Ready for more adventures of Gav and Sky?"

"I'm as ready as I'll ever be."

We got out and I walked right up to the front door. I didn't look around or make a big deal out of it. Just used the key, acting like I had every right to be here.

Skylar slipped her hand in mine and I led her inside, closing the door behind us.

The air had a musty tinge to it, like a lot of old houses did. The interior had been restored over the years, made to look like it had in the early 1900s. It was a cool house, with thick trim around the windows and doors, and dark beams on the ceilings. Fancy wallpaper decorated the walls and the furniture was ornate. The rooms were roped off so visitors could look but not touch. But I wasn't interested in what the historical society had on display, anyway.

"This is like a Scooby-Doo house," Skylar said, glancing around.

"Who would I be as a Scooby-Doo character?"

She grinned at me. "Shaggy."

"Hey." I reached over and grabbed her ass. "Does that make you my sexy Velma?"

She laughed. "What are we looking for exactly?"

"I'm not sure. Bookcases that open, secret passages, hidden trap doors, that kind of thing."

"Definitely Scooby-Doo." She took slow steps forward. "I guess we should just look around then."

Right off the entryway, there was a living room with upholstered furniture and a piano. Across from it was a big dining room with a large chandelier over the table. It was set with plates, silverware, cloth napkins, and wine glasses, like there was going to be a dinner party.

We walked deeper into the house. There was a study or library with lots of bookshelves, leather furniture, and thick carpets on the floor. We ducked beneath the rope and poked around.

Skylar bent over to look at something on a low shelf. I couldn't help myself, I grabbed her hips and pressed my groin against her.

"Hey." She laughed and stood up.

"What?" I asked, feigning innocence. "You can't just go bending over in front of me with that cute ass of yours."

She playfully smacked my arm, so I grabbed her ass again when she walked by.

"If there really is a secret basement in here, don't you think someone would have found it already?" Skylar asked as we ducked under the rope again and made our way to the kitchen. "Especially if people have been looking for the Montgomery treasure for so long."

"Maybe. Although the stories all say the treasure is buried out in the mountains somewhere. No one's been looking in town. Of course, if none of the stories say it's here, maybe there's a reason."

"Maybe. Most old stories start with at least a kernel of truth. Maybe the kernel in this story is that Ernest Montgomery hid something. Over time it turned into a story of buried treasure."

"Yeah, that's kind of what I was thinking."

"Who runs the historical society?"

I opened a door, but it was just an empty pantry. "I don't know, a few volunteers I guess."

"It isn't the Montgomery family, is it?"

"I don't think so. That would be conveniently suspicious, wouldn't it?"

"Yeah, I was just wondering. Although doesn't it seem like the Montgomerys would want to find the treasure if it exists? If it belongs in their family anyway, why would they hide things that could point to it?"

"That's a good question. I just keep thinking it has something to do with the feud. I don't know what, but that's what my gut tells me."

Skylar went to the pantry door I'd already tried. It was just big enough for a person, although if it had been in use, with shelves and things stacked on them, there wouldn't have been room for someone to go inside.

"What are you doing?" I asked.

She ran her hands along the back. "It's weird that there's nothing in here, not even shelves."

"No one's lived here in decades."

"I know, but it just makes me wonder. If I wrote this

house into a book, I'd put a secret door in here." Her finger-tips traced the sides as she looked around. She glanced down at her feet, then turned a little. "Oh my god, I think there's a seam in the floor."

A little hit of excitement made my heart speed up. "Seriously?"

She moved out of the way so we could see. I pulled out my phone and shined the light on the pantry floor.

Sure enough, there was a square seam.

"Do you think it opens?" she asked.

"Only one way to find out."

I pulled my Swiss army knife out of my pocket and wedged the tip into the crack. I loosened it carefully until one side popped up enough to get my fingers underneath. Then I pried it loose. The whole thing came off in one piece and I set it beside me.

The hole revealed a spiral staircase leading into a dark cellar.

"Oh my god, Gavin," she whispered. "You were right."

"Do you want to come down with me?"

I expected her to at least hesitate—or maybe say no—but she nodded. "Yeah, let's go."

Fucking awesome.

I went first so I could make sure the steps would hold. They creaked, but felt sturdy. I climbed to the bottom and Skylar came down after me.

We found ourselves in a dusty room with dark walls and a wood floor. I shined the light on shapes covered with sheets of fabric, mostly stacked against the walls, like someone had once used this room to store old furniture.

Skylar got out her phone for more light and turned in a slow circle. "I just got like five new story ideas from this room alone. This would be such a great place for a serial killer to hide his victims."

"Right? Creepy basement with a hidden door? It would just need some sound proofing and it's perfect."

"Exactly," she said, excitement in her voice.

We peeked beneath the sheets, but it was just old furniture. Skylar found a dresser, but the drawers were all empty. So was the writing desk.

"Look at this," Skylar said, lifting another sheet. "It's an old chest."

"Is it locked?"

She pushed the sheet back and tried the latch. The chest opened with a puff of dust. "I guess not."

I watched while she opened the lid. This one wasn't empty.

"Holy shit," I said softly.

Inside we found old books and leather portfolios filled with yellowed paper stacked on either side of another, smaller chest.

Sky opened it and we both gasped. It was mostly empty, except for a handful of shiny round coins at the bottom.

"Are those what I think they are?" I asked.

She picked one up and I shined the light on it. There was a fancy M stamped into the metal.

"I think this is a gold coin," she said, her voice slightly breathless. "Do you think this is it?"

"The Montgomery treasure? I don't know, there's not much in there."

She gasped again. "What if it's a decoy?"

"Or a clue, like a scavenger hunt."

"The M has to be for Montgomery, right?"

"Must be. What else is in there?"

She put the coin back and closed the lid, then gently

shuffled through the rest of the contents. She lifted a small book out of the pile.

"This one is monogrammed," she said. "SRM. You don't happen to know Sarah Montgomery's middle name, do you?"

"No, but I bet we could find out."

Using just the tips of her fingers, she opened the book and gingerly turned a few pages. The script handwriting was faded and hard to read, and suddenly I wondered if I should have tried harder to learn cursive.

"Oh my god, Gavin, this is amazing. They're letters, and they're all signed by Sarah."

"Letters in a journal?"

"Sometimes people used to write two copies of their letters, one to send and another in a journal so they could keep them. These first ones are addressed to an Aunt Ruth."

"What do they say?"

"This one just talks about having tea with another aunt named Pollyann, and she sends her regards, and stuff about learning to play piano." She turned the page and I waited while she skimmed the next one. "This one is kind of the same, although she does talk about having a row with cousin Betsy."

"A row?"

"It means an argument."

"Oh. Drama."

She laughed softly. "Yeah. I wonder if these get better later." She carefully opened to one of the last pages and gasped.

"What?"

"She wrote to Eliza."

I crouched down closer. "Seriously?"

Even I could read the words *Dear Eliza* at the top of the page.

"Dear Eliza," Sky read aloud. "It has been months since I last saw you, my dear friend. I am all too aware that penning this letter is a waste of time and energy. And yet I cannot seem to stop myself from writing to you, as if someday I'll discover the truth of your whereabouts and I will have means to deliver these letters. Or perhaps it is my way of convincing myself that you are still alive, when no one else seems to believe that could be true."

"Holy shit," I muttered.

"My dearest Eliza, I hope that things are not as they seem. I hope you did not meet your end in tragedy, although my heart fears the worst. And deep down, I think soon I will have to face the truth of your demise. Yours truly, Sarah."

I opened my mouth to say something, but whatever it was died in my throat. Something above us creaked.

"Is someone up there?" Sky whispered.

Another creak. It sounded like the floorboards.

"Maybe. We should go."

She nodded.

For a second, I thought about grabbing the journal. This was fascinating stuff, and I knew Grace and Ginny would die to get their hands on it. But borrowing the key to come in here and snoop around was one thing. Stealing historical artifacts was another.

Besides, if Gram found out, she'd kill me.

I went to the stairs and peeked up while Sky covered the chest. It didn't look like anyone was up there, but it was hard to see much of anything. We'd just have to take our chances and if someone was in the house, hope that I could bullshit my way out of trouble.

I was pretty sure I could.

With Sky right behind me, I crept up the spiral staircase. I didn't see anyone in the kitchen, so I crawled out and helped Skylar. We quickly replaced the floor and pressed it down, hoping no one would be able to tell we'd been in here. Although the seam did look more pronounced. But there wasn't anything we could do about that now.

I quietly shut the pantry door and took Sky's hand. We tiptoed our way to the front of the house, peeking into the rooms off the hallway before darting by. We didn't see anyone, and there weren't any more creaks. Maybe it had just been the house settling.

We made it outside and I locked the front door.

"See? No problem."

She tugged on my hand. "Still. Let's get out of here."

I ran with her to my truck, feeling a buzz of excitement. But it wasn't just from sneaking into the Haven House and getting away with it. Sure, that was fun, and finding actual gold coins hidden in a secret basement was pretty badass.

But it would have felt awesome to lay on her bed while she sat at her desk writing. Or to hang out with her on my couch watching a movie. Basically doing anything with Sky was great, whether or not we were doing something mildly dangerous. Or taking our clothes off.

And I found myself wishing, not for the first time, that I could actually date her.

33

SKYLAR

*I*t was my second time sneaking into the Haven's drive-in movie theater and my body vibrated with nervousness—or excitement. Or maybe both. We'd gotten away with it once, but what were the chances we'd do it again? Gavin had said about seventy-five percent, which didn't seem so great to me. But he and Logan had been confident, and it was the drive-in's last night of the season, which meant it was now or never.

So here I was, hiding near the fence with a view of the back of the concession building, and a walkie talkie in my hand.

Although after breaking into the Haven House the other day, this didn't seem like such a big deal. I was getting good at this stuff.

The truth was, I kind of loved it.

We'd told Ginny and Grace about what we found in the basement of the Haven House. I wished I'd been able to at least get some photos, but they were just glad nothing bad had happened to us. Grace was going to work on getting permission from the historical society to go down there. I was excited to see what else we could find in that chest. And I really wanted to go through the rest of that journal.

There were answers down there. I could feel it.

I stared at the back of the concession building, willing Gavin and Logan to come out. I wasn't quite sure how they were going to pull this off. They somehow had to get into the projection room—which, to be fair, wasn't terribly difficult, as Gavin and I had discovered—put in the hard drive with their movie, and get out again without getting caught.

They'd posted me as a lookout, but I wondered if they should have given this job to someone less jumpy. Every time anyone got within twenty feet of the building, I had the urge to call and warn them.

From where I was standing, I could just see the big screen. The regularly scheduled movie had already started and it was still playing. So far no one had come out of the building, Baileys or otherwise. My mind conjured up all sorts of things that might be happening in there. Most of them were probably wildly unrealistic. I doubted they'd discovered a serial killer victim or stopped a murder from happening. I imagined them bursting in on the psychopathic drive-in movie operator. The ensuing scuffle would rage on while the innocent movie-goers were none the wiser.

I wondered if I could work that into a book somehow.

Asher, Evan, and Levi, along with Grace, Cara, Fiona, and Ginny waited on a little hill just outside the theater where they could see the screen. Gavin, Logan, and I would meet them there once the hard drive was in place.

I took a deep breath to help slow my racing heart. It was dark and I was in the shadows of the trees. The likelihood of anyone seeing me was very low.

In fact, if I was being honest, I felt more exhilaration than anxiety.

This was fun.

A couple of months ago, I wouldn't have imagined myself doing something like this. Then again, since meeting Gavin, I'd done a lot of things I wouldn't have imagined before.

I really liked this version of me. I'd never be a daredevil, but maybe I had a little more courage than I'd once thought.

The back door of the concession building opened and Logan, then Gavin walked out. They both tugged on the brims of their baseball caps, then stuffed their hands in their pockets and walked toward me. I marveled at their ability to act so casual. My feet tingled with the desire to turn around and run, and I wasn't the one out in the open.

Excitement flared as they got closer. "Did you do it?" I whispered.

Gavin flashed me a wide smile. "Oh yeah. It was touch and go there for a minute, but I think we did everything right."

"Of course we did everything right," Logan said. "Let's get to the viewing spot."

We ducked through a hole in the fence and crept back to Gavin's truck. The viewing spot was around the other side of the drive-in, up a small hill. Everyone waited for us in camping chairs, bundled up against the chilly fall air.

"Are we good?" Levi asked.

"All systems are go," Gavin said.

We took our seats. Asher and Grace passed around binoculars. Logan produced a pair of opera glasses, which struck me as rather random, but no one else commented on it.

Levi and Logan had put something in the hard drive that would allow them to start the movie remotely.

"Do it, rice-a-broni," Logan said.

Levi nodded and tapped his phone screen a few times.

Holding my breath, I lifted the binoculars to my eyes. The screen went blank and we were just close enough to hear the faint sound of people shouting to turn it back on.

For a few seconds, nothing. Just a blank screen.

It lit up again and a cheer rose up from the movie goers. A second later, the opening credits started rolling, and the cheering died.

I stifled a giggle at the credits. A Bailey Brothers Production. Bailey Dancing—they'd even used a font that looked like the original movie poster. Starring Logan Bailey, Gavin Bailey, Asher Bailey, and Evan Bailey. Produced and Directed by Levi Bailey.

A chorus of boos rang up from the movie-goers below.

Gavin and his brothers flew to their feet, fists in the air. They whooped and hollered and high-fived each other.

"Is it still going?" Logan asked, lifting his opera glasses to his eyes. "We jammed the door shut, but I don't know how long it'll take them to get in and turn it off."

"It's playing," Grace said. "Did you guys do the whole movie?"

"Nah, it's only about ten minutes long. More like a high-light reel."

"Oh my god, Gavin, did you play Baby?" Fiona asked.

"Yep. No one puts me in a corner either," he said.

I watched through the binoculars, laughing so hard it was difficult to stay focused on the screen. They'd filmed a series of scenes that roughly told the story of Dirty Dancing, with Gavin and his brothers playing all the characters. Logan sauntered around in a leather jacket, his hair slicked back, doing an exaggerated impression of Patrick Swayze as Johnny Castle. Gavin absolutely nailed the dancing on the stairs scene. He'd even worn a peach tank top and jean shorts.

Some of it had been filmed where Gavin had set up the murder cabin. Evan, playing Baby's father, glared a lot. Asher, playing Baby's mother—complete with a bouffant wig—made me laugh so hard I almost fell out of my chair.

It got to the scene where Johnny and Baby practice the lift in the water. Logan made a few attempts to lift Gavin. He finally got him up, and for a second, he held Gavin overhead —until his arms buckled and Gavin crashed down on top of him. They both came up sputtering and spitting out water.

"I can't believe it's still going," Levi said.

"We jammed the door pretty good," Gavin said.

"I can't believe the people down there are staying," Grace said. "I thought for sure the cars would all start leaving."

"We dumped a bunch of hay bales to block the entrance before we came up here," Evan said, his tone nonchalant.

"Nice," Gavin said, and reached over to fist bump his brother.

"Here it is," Logan said. "The big finale."

Everyone aimed their binoculars at the screen.

Gavin sat at a table with Evan and Asher. Logan approached and pointed dramatically.

"No one puts Gavin in a corner," we all shouted in unison.

They started the dance, and although they were pretty terrible, it was so funny the lack of choreographic accuracy didn't matter in the least. The boos from below were louder now. I aimed my binoculars at the cars. Some people had gotten out and stood yelling at the projection booth. Others tossed popcorn toward the screen. There was a jam of people trying to leave, the cars backing up around the turn-around. It was mayhem down there.

The movie cut off, the screen going blank. We all surged to our feet again, laughing and cheering.

Gavin grabbed me, lifting me off my feet, and spun me around. I threw my arms around his neck and suddenly he was kissing me. Right here, in front of everyone.

And in that moment, I had a terrible realization. I was madly in love with Gavin Bailey.

34

GAVIN

The day of Evan and Fiona's wedding brought out a rare sight. My brother smiling.

Evan didn't just smile. He smiled more than he scowled, and that was saying something. He'd been a lot happier since Fiona, but today he'd achieved a new happiness level. One I hadn't seen on him since we were kids.

It was pretty fucking awesome.

They'd set up a tent in Gram's backyard, decorated with twinkle lights and outfitted with heaters against the cold. Despite the fact that Evan and Fiona had both insisted they'd have a small wedding, Fiona's habit of making friends with everyone was evident. There was a great turnout.

I stood up front with my brothers and my eyes kept straying to Skylar, sitting with her parents and Ginny. She looked so pretty in her dark blue dress with her hair pulled back. Our gazes caught and I gave her a quick wink. The way it made her smile at me did weird things to my insides.

In fact, this whole wedding was doing weird things to my insides. I didn't know what that was about. Every time I looked at Skylar I felt a fullness in my chest. It was freaking me out a little bit because I didn't think I was supposed to be feeling like this toward her. Yeah, I liked her a lot, and the sex was off the charts fantastic. That was great and everything, but we were just friends.

You weren't supposed to feel like this about someone who was just a friend. Were you?

Fuck if I knew.

The ceremony was short and to the point. Cara and Grace cried through the whole thing, and even I got a little choked up when they said their vows.

And just like that, I had another sister.

When the ceremony was over, my brothers and I helped move chairs to make room for the food. The whole thing was pretty low key, which was what Evan and Fiona wanted. Family, friends, good food and drinks. A big ass cake that Cara had insisted on buying for them. Someone turned on music, and everyone started eating, drinking, and mingling.

I found Skylar standing with her parents. Caroline was wearing the hell out of a form fitting red dress, and Chief was clearly enjoying it. His eyes traced her curves when she wasn't looking and he grinned a little. Holy shit, he was totally hitting that tonight. I wondered if that was why he'd been in such a good mood lately.

Go Chief.

"Hey, Sky." I nodded to her parents. "Caroline. Chief."

Sky's shy smile was the fucking cutest. "Hey."

"It was a beautiful wedding, don't you think?" Caroline asked. "They look so happy together."

"I had a feeling she'd be the one for Evan," Chief said.

"Did you?" Caroline asked. "How did you know?"

"She seemed to be able to put up with him."

"An important quality in a wife," Caroline said.

Gram came over to stand next to me. She was wearing a

light peach floor-length dress and Fiona had put flowers in her braid.

"Congratulations," Chief said and gave her a hug.

"Thank you," she said. "It's nice to see another one of my cubs happily married."

"You did an amazing job with them," Caroline said. "You should be proud."

"They give me a lot to be proud of." She glanced at Skylar. "Hi there, Sparrow. How's the book coming?"

Sparrow?

Wait.

Had Gram just nicknamed her?

Except it seemed like she'd called her that before. She had, at Asher's birthday. I'd hardly noticed at the time, but holy shit, Gram gave her an animal name.

Uh-oh.

"It's coming along really well," Skylar said. "I'll probably finish in the next week or so."

"That's wonderful."

"Thanks. It's been a struggle, so it feels great to be so close to finishing. Then I just have to decide what I'm going to do with it when it's done."

"You know what I think," Caroline said. "You don't need another agent and you can be your own publisher."

"I know, Mom. That's just such a different way of doing things."

"You can be your own publisher?" I asked.

Skylar nodded. "Yeah, these days you can. There are definitely some advantages."

"But it makes you nervous."

"It does. But you know me, everything makes me nervous." She shrugged.

I stepped closer to her and gently took her hand. "I totally believe in you."

"Thank you."

She gazed up at me and for a second, I forgot that Gram and Skylar's parents were standing right here. I was about to lean down and kiss her when Chief moved slightly, catching my attention from the corner of my eye.

Dropping her hand, I moved back.

Gram glanced at me with raised eyebrows as if to say, *I saw that.* "You do what you think is best, Sparrow."

"Thanks, Gram. I will."

Gram gave my arm a squeeze, then made her way to the next group of guests to chat.

Caroline slipped her arm through Chief's. "How sweet of you to ask me to dance."

"I don't recall that I did."

She smiled. "I'm sure you were just about to."

The corners of his mouth turned up and he shook his head, then led her to where people had started dancing.

"What's going on there?" I asked, gesturing toward Chief and Caroline.

"I'm not sure, but I think my mom's been sleeping in his room."

"Nice," I said.

She laughed. "I guess. They must know I know, but they haven't said anything."

"Maybe they're still feeling things out. Seeing where it's going to go."

"Yeah, probably."

"Wouldn't it be crazy if they actually got back together?"

She gazed at them for a moment. "It would. I used to think they mostly just drove each other nuts, but lately... Just look at them."

Chief had one arm around Caroline's waist, his other hand clutched hers near his chest, and they smiled at each other as they danced.

"They look awesome together."

"They really do."

Evan had his bride in his arms, and Grace and Asher danced together next to Chief and Caroline. Logan swept up with Ginny and they joined the other couples on the dance floor.

I was just about to ask Skylar to dance, but she spoke first.

"Um, Gavin?"

"Yeah?"

She sidled up closer and slipped her hand in mine, then tilted her face up toward my ear. "You know how sometimes I get overstimulated and then..."

"And then?"

She looked up at me with those big brown eyes and bit her lip, desire written all over her face.

Oh shit.

"Now?"

She nodded. "I told you it happens at the worst times."

I glanced around the tent. It wasn't exactly ideal, but it wasn't the *worst* time. Turning, I looked behind us, toward the house. No one was inside, except the caterers coming in and out of the kitchen.

But upstairs...

My brain was already buzzing at the prospect of sneaking Skylar up to my old room.

I slipped her hand in mine. "Let's go."

I casually led her toward the entrance to the tent, acting like I wasn't in any hurry. Like my dick wasn't already so hard I could barely stand it. I'd done a lot of crazy things when I was younger—hell, I'd done a lot of crazy things my entire life—but one thing I'd never done was sneak a girl into my room when I lived here. Not once.

I was making up for that shit right here and now.

We slipped into the kitchen and the caterer didn't even notice us. I led Sky to the stairs and put a finger to my lips.

"Step lightly. The stairs creak."

She nodded.

We tiptoed up the stairs without making a sound, and I led her to the tiny room that had been mine for most of my childhood.

I'd been the only one of my brothers to have his own room, but that was because it was basically a closet. My old twin bed was still in here, and there wasn't space for much else. As a kid, I hadn't cared. I'd liked being outside, regardless of the weather, so I'd mostly used my bedroom for sleeping. I hadn't needed more space than I had in here.

Ushering her inside, I quietly shut the door.

"Was this your room?" she asked.

"Yeah."

"Are you sure we won't get caught?"

I thought about it for a second. "Pretty sure. I'd give us an eighty percent chance of getting away with it."

Her eyes smoldering, she stepped closer and ran her hands up my chest. "Good enough for me."

Leaning down, I met her lips with mine. She pushed against me, rubbing up against my erection. Fuck that felt good.

Until I realized we had a problem. I hadn't exactly anticipated sneaking Skylar up to my old room in the middle of my brother's wedding. I didn't have a condom.

"Um, Sky?" I asked between kisses.

"Yeah?"

"I don't have a condom on me." I kissed her again, darting my tongue into her mouth. "But don't worry. You're not leaving this room until you've had an orgasm."

She laughed softly. "Or we can not use one. I'm still on birth control and I got tested for literally everything after Cullen. So if you're safe…"

I stared at her for a second. "I've never had sex without a condom before."

"Really?"

"Never. I didn't think I had so many firsts left, but you've been checking them off like crazy."

"What firsts?"

I stuck out one finger. "First blow job in a projector room at a drive-in theater."

"Does that really count? Because most people never do that."

"It was still a first for me." I held out another finger. "First time tying a girl up."

Her lips parted. "You'd never done that before?"

"No. Weird, right?"

She laughed again. "Yeah, you were very good at it. So what do you think about this first?"

"I think you should take your fucking panties off."

She hiked her dress up and slid her panties down her legs while I unzipped my pants and pulled out my cock.

"We should probably hurry," she whispered.

I sank down on the edge of the bed and grabbed her by the waist. "Don't want to get caught."

She reached down to grip my shaft and stroked it a few times. The danger of someone possibly walking in on us only made me harder. I slipped my hand between her legs and traced two fingers along her slit.

"That's my girl," I murmured, stroking her gently. "So wet for me already. Get over here."

She climbed onto my lap and I held the base of my erection while she lined herself up. The tip slid against her wet skin and I almost lost my mind.

"Holy fuck, Sky."

I let go and grabbed her ass cheeks while she slowly slid down on me. My eyes rolled back and I knew I needed to keep quiet, but I couldn't contain the groan that escaped my throat. She felt so fucking good wrapped around me like this. So hot and wet. I could feel every bit of her. Every pulse and shudder. I was either going to come harder than I ever had in my life or I was going to die like this and honestly, I didn't really care which it was.

With her arms draped around my shoulders, she squeezed her thighs to slide up and down my length. Her head tilted back and she breathed out a sigh.

"Is that what you needed?"

"Oh my god, yes," she said.

"Take what you need, Sky."

She could take it all.

Her breath came in short gasps as she rode me faster. I kissed her neck, sucking on her soft skin, my heart thundering in my chest. The feel of her surrounding me and the adrenaline pumping through my system were a potent combination.

She moaned and as much as I loved hearing her make that sound—and as hot as the danger of getting caught made me—I didn't want anyone to actually walk in. I clamped my hand over her mouth and her eyes snapped to mine.

With our eyes locked, she kept riding me, the heat in her

gaze like a dare—a dare to hold out and let her do this for as long as she wanted without coming unglued.

I'd take that dare all day long. Skylar could fuck me for as long as she wanted.

She whimpered against my hand, grinding against me as she rode up and down. The pressure in my groin intensified as I held her gaze, watching her eyelashes flutter and her cheeks flush. I could feel her heat rising, her walls tightening around me.

Without warning, she stopped, my cock buried inside her. I let my hand drop and she brought her mouth to mine, kissing me deeply. My hands went back to her ass and I guided her up and down while our tongues tangled.

She moved faster and I slammed my cock into her every time she dropped down on me. The first pulses of her orgasm squeezed my cock and I groaned into her mouth. She tilted her hips to rub herself against me as she came, still kissing me.

The feel of her coming with no barrier between us set me off like a rocket. Grabbing her hips, I pounded into her, my cock throbbing. It felt so fucking good, I couldn't think. I could barely breathe.

After what felt like the longest orgasm of my life, I stopped, breathing hard. She wrapped her arms around my shoulders and slumped against me, spent.

"Better?" I asked, my voice quiet.

"So much better."

Feeling rather pleased with myself, I helped her get back to her feet and pointed out the nearest bathroom. I fixed my pants and she darted down the hallway to clean up and put her panties back on.

When she came out, there was still no sign of anyone up here. We'd totally gotten away with it.

Awesome.

Although it was probably pretty obvious. If I looked anything like she did, the fact that we'd just had mind-blowing sex was written all over our faces.

Oh well.

She paused at the top of the stairs and smiled at me. And there was that feeling in my chest again. It made me want to grab her and hold her close. To whisper things in her ear I wasn't supposed to say. Not the dirty things I whispered to her when we were alone. The words on my lips were more dangerous than that.

But she started down the stairs, heading back to the wedding reception. So I left them unsaid.

35

GAVIN

*L*uckily for Evan and Fiona, the storm that blew in waited until the week after their wedding. One day it was blue skies and crisp fall air, and the next, the wind kicked up and rain drenched the town. It wasn't cold enough to snow yet, but on a day like today, we had to worry about landslides and falling tree limbs. By early afternoon, I was surprised anyone in Tilikum still had power.

Levi and I had gone on duty this morning. Logan was off today, so he and Asher went over to Gram's to make sure everything was storm ready. There was only one tree close enough to the house to fall and do damage, but one was all it would take. Asher texted that everything looked fine and bragged about the fresh muffins Gram had fed them.

Dick.

Things were surprisingly quiet at the firehouse, but I knew that wouldn't last. I could feel something buzzing in the air, like electricity. Storms were unpredictable.

We ran a call at the Nelson's house because Mike Nelson was having chest pains. Turned out, he'd eaten two heaping plates of Mrs. Nelson's leftover baked spaghetti and the red sauce had given him crazy ass heartburn. He was getting checked out at the hospital just in case, but as soon as he'd admitted to what he'd had for breakfast, Mrs. Nelson had smacked him with a rolled-up magazine. I had a feeling he was going to be fine.

Shortly after we got back, I went upstairs to get some lunch. Levi was already at a table in the kitchen, so I grabbed my food and sat down with him.

Levi didn't say much—just met my eyes with a quick chin tip and kept eating.

"You okay, man?" I asked.

"Yeah. Why?"

"You just seem like you have some shit on your mind or something."

He shook his head. "Not really."

"Are you sure? Because if you do, maybe you should talk to someone about it. Just because you're a guy doesn't mean you can't share your feelings."

That comment earned me a solid big brother eye roll. I got those a lot. "I'm fine, Gav. Eat your lunch."

Levi wasn't fine. I'd lived with him long enough to know that. But he kept everything locked up so tight, I wondered if even he knew what the fuck was wrong anymore. I was used to Evan being grouchy, but Levi was angry about something. I could feel it. Especially in moments like this, when everything was quiet. He gave off mad vibes like a smoking coal.

If it had been Logan, I'd have brought up Cara, or basically anything I knew would rile him up. But my instincts flared suddenly, telling me to leave it.

So I did.

"Crazy that Evan's married, huh?" I said.

"Yeah it is. Fiona's great, though."

"Yeah dude, she's the best. She must be some kind of unicorn to be able to handle Evan's grumpy ass."

Levi chuckled a little. "No shit."

"They got married fast."

"So?"

I shrugged. "Just an observation."

He was quiet for a moment, poking at his food. "That's Evan, though. Once he makes a decision, he's all in. And I guess when you know, you know."

"So why wait?"

"Yeah. If there's nothing getting in your way, why wait?"

I nodded slowly.

The buzzer sounded, alerting us to a call. Levi and I were instantly on our feet and heading for the stairs. A moment later, we were in our turnouts and boots, climbing into the engine.

Christian, the engineer, got in after us. "We've got a tree down on the Freight Street bridge. It struck a vehicle, trapping two passengers, and the structural integrity of the bridge is questionable."

Oh shit. That bridge was old, and a big enough tree could do some serious damage.

The engine bay door was already open and we headed out, lights flashing. The ambulance followed behind us.

Freight Street crossed the river on the south end of town. There was a running joke that the bridge was ready to collapse, but no one actually thought it would. People drove across it every single day.

But this storm was something else, and I had a feeling this could be bad.

The wind whipped through the trees and rain fell in sheets. We stopped on the east side of the bridge and one glance at the car stuck out there sent a shot of adrenaline through my system. It was Caroline.

Her little red car had almost made it across, but a downed tree with a thick trunk had smashed the front. From this angle, I couldn't tell how bad the damage was.

I got out, focusing on protocol. On my job. In a small town, it wasn't unusual to know the people involved when you ran a call. This was no different.

Except there were two passengers.

Was Skylar stuck out there? Or was it Chief?

If we were running a call with Chief Stanley involved, they would have told us.

Fuck.

The sudden deluge of rain had already swelled the river, turning it into a churning mass of debris-filled water. The huge tree had fallen near the far side, smashing through the guardrail and into the lower supports. It had probably bent the frame of Caroline's car, preventing them from being able to open the doors to get out. And her car was fucking tiny to begin with. No back seat, no back doors, nowhere to go.

Christian barked orders and I took a few steps closer to the bridge entrance.

It was going to fall.

I didn't know how I knew, but I was positive.

"Levi," I shouted, whirling around to find him. "The bridge is going to go. It's not going to hold."

As if it wanted to make my point for me, the bridge supports groaned.

For a sickening second, I could see it happen. The supports failing. The car plunging into the icy cold water with Caroline and Skylar trapped inside.

Because there was no doubt in my mind it was Skylar out there.

Levi had already pulled out the jaws of life and the compressor to run the hydraulics. "Let's go."

I grabbed the case with the spreader and hydraulic hoses while Levi and Christian followed with the compressor. Rain pelted us, the wind driving it sideways. The bridge felt solid, but I knew it wasn't. Between its age, the damage from the tree, the debris in the river, and the gusts of wind, it was anyone's guess how long it had left.

When we got to the car, I forced myself to focus on the task at hand, not the condition of the vehicle or who was inside. Christian ran to the driver's side door—there was better access there—and I could hear him speaking to Caroline, asking questions and reassuring her, while Levi and I deployed the jaws of life.

I'd done this a million times in training, and even in the field more than once. I went through the motions, connecting the hydraulic hoses to the compressor. A few more seconds, and we were ready.

My heart pounded a mad rhythm in my chest as I went to the driver's side. The front of the car was smashed, the metal frame folding in on itself. It looked like the tree had fallen right in front of them and they'd hit it head-on.

I paused long enough to look at the passengers. Caroline's eyes were wide, but she was calm. No sign of major injuries so far. And sure enough, Skylar was in the passenger seat. The car was partially caved in on her side, and she'd scooted closer to her mom.

"Don't worry," I said. "We've got you."

I wedged the spreader into the crack between the door and the frame while rain pelted my face. The bridge supports groaned again and my eyes flew to Skylar. My heart raced and an overwhelming sense of urgency filled me.

The compressor roared behind me. I held the spreader while it opened, loosening the driver's side door from the bent metal frame of the car. Christian pulled on the door, helping free it.

"Can you get your legs out?" he asked Caroline.

She nodded. "Yes."

A few more seconds and the door broke free. Christian and I lifted it off and set it next to the car. The bridge groaned again, and this time I felt it shudder. I glanced at Levi and he nodded. He'd felt it too.

Fuck.

I took Caroline's hands and helped her out of the vehicle. Levi took over and I went back for Skylar.

She'd already climbed across to the driver's side. I helped her out of the car and without a word, picked her up, one arm around her back, the other supporting her legs.

"I can walk."

I didn't reply. I knew she could walk, but I also knew I was going to lose my mind if I didn't get her off this fucking bridge. Now.

Carrying her in my arms, I raced to the bridge entrance. The engine was on the opposite side, but we'd get someone over here to pick us up. There was no way I was hauling my ass back over that bridge, especially not with Skylar.

Levi was on his radio updating the crew and Christian rushed off the bridge just behind me. I set Skylar down next to her mom, and Caroline threw her arms around her.

"Are you okay?" I asked, feeling strangely frantic. "Are you injured?"

"No," Skylar said, her voice breathless. "I don't think so."

A huge gust of wind roared through the trees, followed by an ear-splitting crunch. The bridge lurched to one side as the broken supports failed. Caroline's car slid sideways down the bridge deck, getting tangled in the huge tree's branches.

Like an inevitable chain reaction, more supports failed and the bridge deck cracked. With a crash, the end broke free and crumbled into the churning water below. Caroline's car plunged into the river with the tree practically on top of it.

Skylar launched herself into my arms, one hand covering her mouth. "Oh my god. Oh my god, we were just... We could have been in there."

Wrapping my arms around her, I held her tight against me.

Holy fuck. If we hadn't gotten there in time...

I couldn't even think it.

Chief pulled up out of nowhere, skidding to a stop, and flew out of his truck. His eyes were wild as he ran to his daughter and his ex-wife.

Reluctantly, I let go of Skylar so her dad could hug her. I felt dazed, like I couldn't focus. My usual calmness under pressure seemed to have shattered, and now I couldn't remember what I was supposed to be doing. All I could see was the image of Caroline's car plunging into the freezing river.

If we'd gotten here minutes later, they would have been in there. They would have gone under.

Somehow we wrapped things up at the bridge and our crew was sent back to the station. I climbed out of the engine, not quite sure how I'd gotten here. I knew Chief had taken Caroline and Skylar with him after the paramedics had cleared them. And I knew that emergency crews had already blocked off the broken bridge from both sides. As for the rest, it was mostly a blur.

I went through the motions of taking off my gear and

getting it ready for the next call. It was automatic, drilled into me so deeply that I didn't have to think about what I was doing.

I didn't know what the fuck was wrong with me. I'd been on scarier calls than that. Once I'd literally walked into a burning building minutes away from collapse to get someone out. I'd pulled people out of wrecked cars, stopped a guy from bleeding out, performed CPR. Yeah, today had been a close call, but that was part of the job. It had never bothered me before. I'd always come back feeling energized. Like I'd triumphed. I'd won.

Now, I had no idea what I was feeling. But it wasn't triumph. It was something else. Something that made my chest feel like I had a hundred-pound weight sitting on top of it. Like my lungs were filled with icy cold river water and I was about to drown.

Somehow I made it through the rest of the day. I held it together and did my job. I was on duty until morning, but instead of hanging out with the guys and playing cards, I hit the bunks early.

My head was still swimming, my heart beating too hard.

What if I'd lost her today?

That thought was so awful, so soul-crushing, I almost couldn't think it.

But I did, and then I started thinking about all the ways I could lose her. All the terrible things that could happen. She could get in another accident, or get sick, and there'd be nothing I could do.

I tossed and turned, trying to go to sleep. Trying to get this shit out of my head. But I couldn't.

It wasn't just the thought of Skylar dying that had my palms sweating and my shoulders clenched tight. There were other ways to lose someone.

Skylar wasn't my girlfriend. We didn't have a real commitment to each other. When whatever we were doing ran its course, she'd move on. She'd date someone else—someone who'd probably marry her. Because who wouldn't? Her douchebag ex aside, what guy with a brain would date Skylar and not lock it down as soon as they could? She was smart and beautiful and talented and fun. She was quirky and shy and adorable. Sexy and so fucking incredible.

Wait.

I sat up in bed, almost hitting my forehead on the bunk above me.

Sparrow. Gram had called her Sparrow.

She knew.

Holy fuck, Gram knew before I did. But of course she did, Gram knew everything. That should have tipped me off, but like an idiot, I'd totally missed it.

Everything made sense now. And I knew exactly what I had to do.

36

SKYLAR

*T*he morning after the bridge, I woke up sore. I didn't have any major injuries, but my body felt the effects of almost being crushed by a tree and nearly drowning in a river. My back ached and my neck was painfully tight.

Dad did his best to keep me in bed all morning, bringing me coffee and breakfast, reading material, and my laptop. Anything to encourage me to lie down and rest. The accident had shaken him pretty badly.

It had shaken me too. But surprisingly, it hadn't sent me into a tailspin of uncontrolled anxiety. I was sore and tired, but mentally calm. I even wrote the ending to a chapter because the perfect idea hit me.

I was about to get up and go downstairs—I didn't really need to stay in bed *all* day—when Ginny called.

"Hey, Gin."

"Were you really trapped in your mom's car, and plunged into the river, and Gavin had to dive in and break the windshield with a rock to get you out before you drowned? Because when you texted me last night, you did not tell me any of those details."

"What? No. That's not what happened at all."

She let out a relieved sigh. "Oh my god. Someone said the bridge broke right as you were driving over it and your mom's car submerged in the river with you in it."

"Haven't you figured out that you can't listen to people in this town? It hasn't even been a day and they're already exaggerating. No, I told you, a tree fell on the bridge and we hit it, or it hit us, I'm not entirely sure. We were trapped in Mom's car, but the firefighters got us out. We were safely on land when the bridge collapsed. By the way, did you know that one out of every nine bridges in the US is structurally deficient?"

"You researched bridge collapses, didn't you?"

"First thing this morning."

She laughed. "Naturally. Well, I'm glad you're okay. Was Gavin on the scene?"

"Yeah, he was. He helped get us out of Mom's car."

"Wow. That must have been intense for him."

"Yeah, he seemed kind of out of it afterward. Normally it's like nothing ruffles him, but if I didn't know better, I'd say he was scared."

"Of course he was. He had to rescue the girl he hasn't admitted to being in love with yet."

"Ginny, stop. He's not in love with me."

"Wanna bet?"

"No."

"That's because you know I'm right. Has he been over to see you?"

"No, he was on duty overnight. He texted me last night and once this morning, but that doesn't mean he's in love with me. It means he's worried about a friend."

"Yeah, well, I still say he has feelings for you. I bet he comes over today and tells you that your accident yesterday made him realize he wants to be more than friends."

I sighed. "I don't think so."

She paused. "Do you want him to?"

I wasn't sure if I was ready to admit how big my feelings for Gavin were, even to Ginny. It felt like saying it out loud was too dangerous. "I don't know. Maybe?"

"You know what I think. If you want him, you need to be up front."

"I know, but that's not really fair to him. He tried to keep us from crossing the *just friends* line and I'm the one who said we can be friends who have sex sometimes and it won't be a big deal."

"Yeah, I know. Friends with benefits can get messy."

"Well, it's not messy now, and I'm certainly not going to let it get messy today. Gavin and I are fine. What about you and Logan? Are you guys actually dating, or..."

"Nice subject change. No, we're not really dating. He's a lot of fun, and he's hot as sin, but I'm not in town much longer."

"I'm going to miss you when you're gone. It's been nice having you so close."

"It's been a lot of fun. I'd love to find more excuses to stay, but I have to move on to the next thing."

"I know."

"You rest up today and let me know if you need anything, okay?"

"I will. Thanks, Ginny."

"Talk to you soon."

I hung up and got out of bed. I was still in a t-shirt and pajama pants, but it seemed like a pajama pants sort of day. Mom's door was closed—which was odd. Had she slept there last night? Maybe she'd needed space after yesterday. I didn't see Dad, so I crept downstairs to get a snack.

After I grabbed a few things out of the fridge, there was a knock at the front door. I answered it, and Gavin barreled his way inside.

"Hey, Sky. How are you feeling? Are you okay?"

I shut the door, eying him. His hair was disheveled and his eyes were a little crazed.

"I'm fine. Just a bit sore."

He stood in front of me and gently grabbed my shoulders. "Are you sure?"

"Yes. Thanks to you."

For a second, he held my gaze, then let out a breath. "Is this a good time? Can we talk?"

"Okay, but—"

Before I could finish, he let go and headed for the kitchen.

"Are *you* okay?" I asked, following him.

He walked a circle around the kitchen, as if he couldn't keep still. "I was up all night thinking."

"All night? Thinking about what?"

He stopped and met my eyes. "About us."

Oh my god, was Ginny right? Had yesterday made Gavin realize he wanted to be more than friends?

"What about us?"

"I think we should get married."

I stared at him, dumbstruck. "Wait, what?"

"Hear me out." He started pacing around the kitchen again. "We're really good together, and I don't just mean the sex. I mean all of it."

"Okay, but—"

"Yesterday I realized how awful it would be to lose you. I looked at the bridge and I knew you were out there and I could see it happen. The bridge collapsing and the car sinking into the river. I've never felt so fucking helpless in my life. And then last night I started thinking about how you dying in an icy cold river after a bridge collapses isn't the only way I could lose you. You could be struck by lightning or hit by a semi-truck or fall off a ladder and break your neck."

"I don't think any of those are likely causes of death."

"Still. The bridge made me realize I don't want to lose you. Ever."

I tried to keep the tremor out of my voice, but I felt so shaky. "But Gavin, marrying me won't keep me from dying."

"I know it won't. But if I don't marry you, someone else is going to, and then I lose you that way."

"We're not..." I took a breath, trying to find my bearings. "This is really sudden. We're not even dating and you want to jump to marriage because yesterday scared you?"

"No, I'm not scared."

"Yes, you are."

He shook his head. "It's not fear, it's clarity. I'm finally seeing things clearly."

I stared at him for a long moment. That wasn't clarity in his eyes. He looked irrational and frantic, not clear.

"Are you? You don't seem clear to me. You seem afraid and exhausted."

"It's fine, I'll sleep later. And I don't get scared. You know this about me."

"You don't think you get scared, but maybe you just don't recognize it as fear. It's okay if yesterday scared you. It scared all of us."

"Sky, I get it, this is out of the blue. But I can't..." He trailed off, running his fingers through his hair. "I can't lose you. I didn't buy a ring yet, but—"

"Wait." I held up a hand. "Slow down. I thought maybe you'd tell me you want to be more than friends and give us a real shot, but marriage?"

"Gram called you Sparrow."

"What?"

"She calls you Sparrow. I should have realized, but I didn't until last night. She doesn't give everyone a nickname. It used to just be me and my brothers and Grace. But that's the thing, she's a fucking psychic or something. She knew Asher would marry Grace, even when they were kids. That's why she always called her Gracie Bear. And the first time she met Fiona she called her Cricket. Look what happened, Evan married her."

"But that doesn't mean that you and I—"

"Sure it does."

"Gavin, we can't just rush in like this."

"Why not? If you're sure, why wait?"

"Because I don't think you're sure at all. I think you're afraid and you don't know how to handle it. You're not asking me to marry you because you know you want to marry me. You're asking me because you're scared, and for some crazy reason, you think a ring on my finger is going to make the feeling go away. It won't. That fear is still going to live inside you, and until you face it and put it in its place, it's going to keep eating away at you. Trust me, I know all about fear. I'm scared of everything."

He crossed his arms and his expression darkened. "Then maybe I'm not the one who's scared, here. Did your piece of shit ex freak you out so much, you're afraid to try again?"

"This doesn't have anything to do with him."

"No? Could have fooled me. You have a shitty breakup and the next guy has to pay for it."

"The next guy?" I put my hands on my hips. "Since when are you the next guy? I think you skipped a step or five."

"You know what, forget it. I'm sorry I had the wrong idea. I thought maybe I was more to you than a warm body with a dick, but apparently I was wrong."

"Are you kidding me right now? Of course you mean more to me than that."

He shook his head and stomped down the hallway toward the front door.

"Gavin." I followed him, my heart racing. "This isn't fair. You can't marry someone for the wrong reasons. It won't work. You're supposed to be in love, not just afraid they're going to die or marry someone else someday."

He yanked the door open, but paused and looked back at me over his shoulder. "I am in love with you."

Those words stunned me into silence, and before I could take a breath to answer, he walked out and slammed the door behind him.

37

GAVIN

*T*he first rule of bridge jumping was don't look down. Same went for bungee jumping or skydiving, or any time you were about to throw yourself off a stable surface into the air. Instructors would tell you to look at the scenery, keep your eyes on the horizon, look up at the sky. Anywhere but down.

I climbed over the bridge railing and kept my eyes forward. I knew what the water looked like below me. It was deep and wide—too deep to make out much at the bottom of the dark water. This was going to be cold as fuck, but I was a strong swimmer. I'd get back to the bank.

And I'd worn a helmet. I was crazy, but I wasn't stupid.

My brothers had asked me a thousand times why I had a death wish. I told them, every single time, that I didn't want to die. Quite the opposite, actually. I wanted to *live*.

And I'd spent the last twenty-four hours fucking living.

No, I wasn't out here hoping I might not make it out alive. I was out here to show this fucking bridge who was boss.

It wasn't the bridge that had almost taken Skylar. I

couldn't jump from that one, even if it hadn't been smashed by a giant tree. This was a bridge I'd been wanting to tackle for a long time. Not many guys had jumped it, even my friends who were into this shit.

I sucked in a couple of breaths and hit my chest a few times. Then I said fuck it all, and looked down.

The wave of disorientation hit me hard, but I was ready for it. I held on to the railing behind me and waited until my brain got its bearings. My heart beat furiously, but that was why I was here.

Once again, I was the shark. I had to keep moving.

After leaving Skylar's house yesterday, I'd been too amped up—crawling out of my own skin. I'd gone straight for Evan's place to take my dirt bike out on the trails. After a hard ride, I'd been physically tired, but mentally I hadn't been able to stop. I'd wound up at the Mountain Goat Tavern playing blackjack with a bunch of guys from the sheriff's department.

They'd cleaned me out, so I'd gone home to crash for a few hours. Sleep hadn't helped. I'd woken up with a bunch of energy, and the feeling of my chest being crushed hadn't gone anywhere.

So I'd gone rock climbing. And when that didn't help, I'd decided I needed to tackle this fucking bridge.

It was symbolic. I hadn't been myself since Skylar and Caroline's accident. If I came out here and jumped off this bridge—alone, in the cold—it had to make me feel better. I was going to fucking conquer this, right here and now.

The water flowed below me, little eddies and whirls on the surface. Everything seemed to get quiet and still, and for a second, my heartbeat slowed.

I loosened my grip on the railing.

"Gavin!" Logan's panicked voice rang out from my right.

He ran toward the bridge with Levi right next to him. They were followed by Evan and Asher.

Damn it.

"Gavin, don't fucking jump!"

Gritting my teeth, I almost let go. It wasn't like I was trying to kill myself. I'd be fine.

Physically, at least. I wasn't fine, and I knew it. But I had no idea what to do about that.

But something in Logan's voice made me hesitate. And I didn't jump.

And something about *that* made me mad.

Anger was a feeling I could understand. So I grabbed onto it.

They hit the bridge deck and I swung one leg over the railing and hoisted myself over. Logan reached me first. He grabbed my shirt and jerked me away from the edge.

"What the fuck?" I yelled, shoving him off me.

My brothers circled around me, like they were worried I'd make a run for it and throw myself off the edge. Asher crossed his arms and Evan locked me in a dangerous stare.

"What the hell are you doing?" Logan asked.

Levi ran his hands through his hair. "Jesus, Gav, you scared the shit out of us."

"You guys are right on time. I didn't need an audience, but why the fuck not?"

"Are you insane?" Logan asked.

"I can make the jump," I said. "The water's deep enough."

"It's like forty fucking degrees out here," Asher said.

I scoffed. "Whatever. I'd make it to the bank."

"Like hell you would," Levi said. "You'd fucking drown out there."

"You can't bridge jump alone, especially this time of year," Asher said.

"You guys realize I'm an adult, right? I don't need your asses babysitting me all the time."

"We just chased you down when you were on the brink of throwing yourself off a goddamn bridge," Levi said. "And this is after you almost wrecked your bike, lost who the fuck knows how much money playing blackjack, and went rock climbing alone on a day when it might have rained. And that's just the stuff we know about."

"It didn't rain." I shrugged like it wasn't a big deal.

Levi lunged at me, but Evan stepped in and put a hand on his chest.

"Not here," Evan said, his low voice rumbling. "We take him to the Arena."

My whole body lit up at the suggestion. The Arena was where my brothers and I settled our differences, Bailey brothers style. It had started when we were kids. Gram had given us boxing gloves and made us duke it out when we had a problem. When we'd gotten older, we'd taken it up a notch, and created the Arena. Sure, it was a little barbaric— a sort of gladiatorial test of will between brothers. But it worked.

And right now, getting a chance at one of my brothers in the Arena sounded fucking great.

"You coming, or do we have to hog tie you first?" Levi asked.

I undid the latch on my helmet and took it off. "No, I'm in. Let's fucking do this."

~

LOGAN SHOVED me in his truck instead of letting me drive my own, but I'd deal with that little grievance later. If he wouldn't get in the ring with me, I'd find a way to get in a shot at him.

I was buzzing on adrenaline, ready to take them all on at once. They'd interrupted my bridge jump for no good reason, but I wanted to fight even more than I wanted to jump.

What we called the Arena was a clearing down a dirt road near Lake Tilikum. Stakes marked off the four corners of the ring and grass and weeds provided the only padding. The ground could do as much damage as an opponent out here.

We parked and I flew out of the truck, my hands clenched into fists. I stalked over to the ring and paced back and forth, waiting for them.

I didn't want to think about the last time I'd been in the Arena. I'd gone up against Asher when he'd been in the middle of his post-prison meltdown. I'd been amped that day too, but it had been different. I'd been in control. Today I wasn't, and I knew it.

But I didn't fucking care.

Levi tossed me a pair of padded gloves. I would have bare-knuckled it, but gloves were always one of the rules. Gloves, no nut shots, and no knockouts. Even when we were out here because we were pissed as fuck, we weren't trying to injure each other.

I'd always viewed the Arena like an ancient system of justice—trial by combat. The guy who was in the right would win. A voice in the back of my head tried to tell me that probably meant I was about to lose, but I brushed it off. What the fuck did it know, anyway.

I shoved on my gloves while my brothers stood along the

side of the makeshift ring. I gave them a quick sweep, wondering who was getting in here with me. I expected Asher—he was the oldest. Seemed like an Asher thing to do. And maybe he wanted a rematch, since I'd beat him last time.

But Evan was putting a pair of gloves on his big hands.

Well, fuck.

Asher was dangerous as hell. He was a coach now, and still actively trained. But so did Evan. He didn't compete, but he'd never stopped going to the gym. And I knew from experience how strong he was.

Fuck it. I'd taken him on before. I'd beat his ass now.

Evan stepped into the ring. "You need to calm the fuck down."

That was all the warning I got. He lunged for me, going for a takedown, but I side-stepped just enough. Immediately going on the offensive, I surged in and locked up with him. He pulled down on the back of my neck, but I wasn't giving him anything that easily. We pushed and pulled, testing each other's strength and balance.

Moving fast, I dipped low and shot in, wrapping my arms around his waist. We hit the dirt with a thud. That was going to hurt later, but for now, all I felt was the adrenaline flowing through my veins. He grunted and spun, almost getting the reversal on me, but I managed to maintain control.

I hooked his arm and leg for a submission hold, but he was too fast. And my technique was shitty, but I wasn't going to admit it. Normally, I rode the line between crazed and clear. Amped and calm. I could see things clearly, predict what I needed to do next.

Today I was just fucking flailing. I couldn't focus.

My heart beat too fast. Evan flipped me onto my back

and the air rushed from my lungs. I fought as hard as I could, but I was out of control. Any semblance of skill went right out the window. Two moves later, he had me twisted like a goddamn pretzel and I couldn't breathe.

I held on, refusing to give up. Refusing to tap out. My chest burned from the lack of air and my vision started to go dark.

Fuck.

Growling in pain, I hit the ground with my free hand, tapping out.

Evan got off me, and I laid on my back with bent knees, staring up at the cloudy sky. Took a few shaky breaths. My brothers didn't say anything. Evan didn't gloat. He didn't trash-talk or rub my face in the loss. He just waited, giving me a second to get my shit together.

After all, that was why they'd brought me out here in the first place.

I didn't know what it was about getting my ass beat by my brother, but it did calm me down. My heart rate slowed and the frenzied storm in my head finally broke. It left me feeling hollow—my chest oddly empty. But I could finally slow down.

Evan reached out a hand. I took it and he helped me to my feet. Then he wrapped me in a hug.

I hugged him back, feeling a deep surge of emotion tighten my chest. I wasn't going to cry, but I was pretty fucking close.

Evan stepped back and ruffled my hair like I was a little kid again. "Are you ready to tell us what's really going on?"

I ripped the Velcro off one of my gloves. "I asked Skylar to marry me."

Logan laughed and I shot him a glare. "Wait, you're not kidding?"

"No, I'm not kidding."

Levi eyed me. "You said you aren't dating her."

"I wasn't dating her."

"Then why did you propose?"

I took the other glove off and let them drop to the ground. "I pulled her out of that car and it made me realize I don't want to lose her. Ever. I felt something right here." I put my hand on my chest. "I don't know what it was, but I had to make it stop. And the only thing I could think to do is make sure I can keep her."

"Brosaster, you can't just randomly propose to your fuck buddy."

A flare of anger shot through me. "She's not my—" I stopped, because he was right. "Okay, fine, she was basically my fuck buddy, but don't talk about her like that."

Logan put up his hands. "No disrespect."

"I'm fucking in love with her, you guys. And she turned me down."

"Holy shit," Asher said, shaking his head slightly.

"What?"

"Something actually scared Gavin Bailey."

"What? No it didn't."

"Of course it did," Evan said. "Skylar's accident scared the shit out of you."

"No wonder you've been acting like a psycho," Levi said.

I took a few steps backward. Deep down, I knew they were right. I was scared as hell. I'd never been scared of anything in my life, but the thought of losing her forever scared the fuck out of me.

"Gav, it's normal to be scared," Asher said. "But maybe proposing to her wasn't the best way to cope with your fear."

"Maybe I screwed this up a little bit." I raked my hands

through my hair. "I sort of forgot to lead with the fact that I'm in love with her."

Logan winced. "So you just said hey, I think we should get married?"

"Basically."

He whistled. "Not your finest performance, my brother."

"She fucking called it, too," I said. "She told me I was scared. And then like a fucking idiot, I threw it back in her face. I turned this into a flaming pile of burning garbage."

"Yeah, you did," Logan said.

I scowled at him. "Thanks."

"Doesn't mean you can't fix it."

Asher's phone rang and he pulled it out of his pocket to answer. "Hi, Gram."

She was calling about me. She had to be.

"Yep. No, he's fine... I will... Okay, love you too." He ended the call and met my eyes. "She wants you to come over."

"Now?"

He nodded.

Rubbing the back of my neck, I groaned. I felt like I'd been caught doing something wrong and I had to face a scolding. "Fine. Can someone give me a ride back to my truck?"

"Only if you promise you're not going to do anything stupid," Logan said.

One corner of my mouth hooked in a grin. "How long are we talking? Like for the rest of the day, or..."

He punched me in the arm.

I followed him to his truck, feeling calm, but still shitty. I didn't know what I was going to do about Skylar. Had I fucked things up forever?

Or worse, did she not want me at all?

Maybe I'd been nothing but a diversion. Great for the orgasms, but not for anything serious. And the truth was, I couldn't even blame her for that. It wasn't like I'd ever given her a reason to get serious with me. I'd never given her a chance.

I'd never given us a chance. And maybe that had been my biggest mistake of all.

38

SKYLAR

I stared miserably into my mug, only dimly aware that it was empty. It had been a long twenty-four hours. Ever since Gavin had walked out yesterday, I'd been in a daze.

What the hell had happened?

Had he really come in here and randomly suggested we get married because the accident on the bridge had made him realize he didn't want to lose me?

And had he seriously waited until he was walking out the door to mention being in love with me?

What the fuck was that about?

My words to Ginny came back to haunt me. *It's not messy now, and I'm certainly not going to let it get messy today. Gavin and I are fine.*

So much for that. I didn't know how it could get any messier.

Cupping my chin in my hand, I leaned my elbow on the table. I'd spent most of the last day in my room, trying to wrap my head around what had happened. Was it my fault that it had gone so badly? What else could I have done? We couldn't get married. He was crazy.

Wasn't he?

"Hi there, sweetheart." Mom lacked her usual breeziness when she came into the kitchen. "How are you feeling?"

"A little sore, but I'm okay. How are you?"

The airbag had deployed, but fortunately it hadn't hurt her too badly. She just had a little bruising on her chin.

"Still sore, but better than yesterday." She poured herself some hot water and dunked a tea bag in her mug, then came over to the table to sit with me. "Are you sure you're feeling okay?"

I sighed. "Not really, but it's not because of the bridge. Gavin came over yesterday and..."

"What happened?"

"He said we should get married."

Mom's lips parted and she hesitated for a second before replying. "He proposed?"

"He didn't propose so much as say he thought we should get married because the accident made him realize he doesn't want to lose me."

"Wow. I didn't know you two were so serious."

"No, that's the thing, we aren't. We're friends, but that's all."

She blew on her tea. "Well, that's not *all*, honey."

I hesitated for a moment. "There was... another dimension to our relationship."

With a smile, she tucked my hair behind my ear. "We're both adults, you don't have to beat around the bush with me."

"Fine, we've been sleeping together. But we were supposed to just be friends. And now he's mad at me because I didn't die of happiness at his non-proposal?"

"If he's mad, it's because you wounded his pride and he wasn't ready for it."

"I didn't mean to hurt him. But what was I supposed to say? It's totally understandable that the accident freaked him out, and if he'd come in here and said it made him realize he wants more with me, I would have been ecstatic. I want more with him, too."

Tears pricked my eyes. Oh my god, it was true. I really did want more with Gavin. And I might have ruined it.

She put her hand on my arm. "Give him a little time. He'll calm down and you two can figure out where you ought to be."

"Thanks, Mom. By the way, where's Dad?"

"I don't know." She glanced away.

"You slept in your own bed last night, didn't you?"

She nodded. "I did, and I probably should have been all along."

It was my turn to put a comforting hand on her arm. "Mom, what happened?"

"The accident didn't exactly bring out the best in either of us. I should have known better. We've been down this road before and it didn't end well."

I hesitated, not sure if I should ask. But it had been one of the defining moments of my childhood, and I didn't know the answer. "Why did you and Dad split up?"

She stared into her tea for a long moment before answering. "I could say it was your dad's job and how often he was away. How I felt like he prioritized his career over his family and how much I hated the fire department for being more important than me. And those things were true—or at least, they felt true at the time. But if I'm being honest, that wasn't what broke us. We could have worked through the growing pains of a young marriage and a young career. We were working through them."

"Then what broke you?"

"When Charles and Helena Bailey died."

"Gavin's parents?"

Mom nodded slowly. "I didn't see it at the time, but in hindsight, yes. Charlie and Lena were our best friends. Your dad and Charlie grew up together, of course. When I met your dad, Charlie and Lena were dating, and the four of us became best friends. Inseparable, really. We double dated, went camping, took road trips. We were in each other's weddings. I threw all of Lena's baby showers and she threw mine when I was expecting you. They were family.

"When they died, it was so shocking. Traumatic, even. Your dad and I lost the people we were closest to, besides each other. Everyone grieves in their own way, but looking back, I think we grieved our way apart. We stopped doing so many of the things we loved because it hurt too much without Charlie and Lena. Your dad turned to work and his crew to get through the pain. I coped by throwing myself into work and motherhood. We were grieving the same thing, but we didn't grieve together.

"Eventually, we weren't communicating at all, except to argue. Little frustrations grew into big resentments. And none of it felt like things we could work through. But how can you work through anything when you aren't really talking? When every time things get hard, you both retreat into your own world, instead of finding common ground? Pretty soon there is no common ground. It's just a battlefield."

"So you left."

"I did. At first we said it was just a separation, but time went on and it didn't seem like anything was going to change. I filed for divorce, but that was after we'd agreed to it."

"When you moved back here, did you think something would happen with Dad?"

She took a slow, deep breath. "I probably wouldn't have admitted it the day I blew in here with a moving truck. But yes, I did. Or maybe I just hoped."

"You still love him, don't you?"

She opened her mouth to answer, but the front door flew open and Dad came in. "Caroline?"

"We're in here," she called.

Dad strode into the kitchen with purpose, his eyes on Mom. "Can you come outside? I have something to show you."

She glanced down at her clothes—a silky long-sleeved shirt and floral lounge pants. Even in comfies, Mom was fashionable. "Sure, why not."

"Skylar?" he asked.

"Okay."

We followed Dad out the front door.

Parked in the driveway was a beautifully restored Cadillac convertible. It was bright cherry red with red and white interior, whitewall tires, and big fins on the back.

"Oh my god," Mom said. "Is that a '59 Cadillac?"

"Nineteen fifty-nine Cadillac series 62 convertible," Dad said, pride in his voice. "Just like—"

"Just like the one we had when we got married." She wandered closer to the car and lightly touched the fender with her fingertips. "Is this yours?"

"Sure is. I hired Evan Bailey to restore it for me. He texted this morning to say it was finished."

"It's beautiful."

A flood of memories filled my mind. I remembered this

car—or the one Dad used to have. We'd gone for drives on sunny days with the top down. Stopped for ice cream in town or driven the winding mountain highway between here and Echo Creek. I remembered the wind blowing in my face. My parents smiling at each other in the front seat.

Those were good memories. Happy memories.

Dad stood in front of my mom, his hand resting on the driver's side door. "When I bought it, I said I wanted it so I could take Skylar out again. Maybe reconnect with her a little. But then you came home and I thought..."

"You thought what?" Mom asked.

"We had a lot of good memories in that old Caddy. I thought maybe we could make some more."

"Norman—"

He stepped closer and took her hand. "Caroline, I know we went wrong all those years ago. And I figure we still have some things we need to work through. But you are the love of my life. Not were. *Are*."

My eyes filled with tears and I put a hand to my mouth. I couldn't believe this was happening.

"What are you saying?" she asked, her voice barely above a whisper.

"You're home, where you've always belonged, and I want you to stay. We'll do the hard work and we'll figure this out. But I'm tired of living without you. Having you home reminded me how much I love you, even when you're driving me crazy. Maybe especially when you're driving me crazy."

She laughed. "I love you too."

Dad pulled her in close and her arms went around his neck as he kissed her.

Oh my god. I'd just witnessed my parents getting back together.

As happy as I was for them, I felt like I'd suffered emotional whiplash. I had so much going through my mind, I hardly knew what to do with all of it. Gavin saying that we should get married. The way he'd left, hurt and upset. And now my dad declaring his love for my mom and asking her to stay. It was so much, I thought I might burst.

Dad stopped kissing her and glanced at me with a bit of guilt. "Sorry, Skylar."

"No, don't be. This is amazing."

"Should we take her out?" Dad asked. "Go for a nice drive? It's chilly, but we can bundle up. Or I can put the top up if you want."

"Leave it down," Mom said, a giddy smile on her face. "I have warm clothes."

"Why don't you two go," I said.

"Are you sure?" Dad asked.

Mom gave me an understanding smile and put a hand on Dad's arm. "We'll go for a family drive soon."

I walked over and hugged them both together. My heart was so full and so broken at the same time. I couldn't have been happier for my parents. With everything they'd been through, they'd always loved each other. I could see that now.

As for me, it was like I didn't know up from down anymore. I'd thought I had a good handle on my relationship with Gavin—such as it was. Boy, had I been wrong.

And now I didn't know what I was going to do.

39

GAVIN

I walked into Gram's house with my shoulders slumped. I'd been a dumbass, and with the way stories got around in this town, she probably knew all about it. Why else would she have called Asher?

Facing the music was never fun. If I was lucky, maybe there would be cookies at the end of it.

Kinda felt like I deserved a little bit of luck today.

"In here, Otter," she called from the kitchen.

I found her sitting at the big table with a book and a mug of tea. She smiled at me and gestured to the chair across from her.

I pulled it out and dropped into it.

"Is it really so bad?" she asked.

"Yes."

She didn't laugh at my misery. Just reached across the table to squeeze one of my hands. "You have grass in your hair."

I reached up to brush my hands over my head a few times. I didn't particularly want to explain why. Gram didn't know about the Arena. Actually, she probably did, because she basically knew everything. But if she did, she pretended she didn't.

"What happened out there on that bridge?" she asked.

"A tree fell in the storm. Hit the bridge while Caroline and Skylar were trying to drive across. They were stuck, but we got them out before the supports failed."

"I know about that part. What happened to you?"

I looked down at the table for a long moment. "I guess I got scared."

"Good."

"Why is that good?"

"Fear is normal. Healthy, even, when it's directed at the right thing. But it also takes practice to manage. And you can't practice if you don't recognize what you're dealing with."

"I'm not lying when I say things usually don't scare me. I can stand on the edge of a cliff or run into a burning building and I'm not afraid."

"I believe you. You've had a lot of practice at managing that kind of fear. You know how to do more than manage it. You know how to use it to drive you. But injury or death aren't the only things to fear. Your dad had to learn that lesson the hard way, too."

I kept my eyes on the table.

"He liked danger. It didn't seem like anything scared him. He wasn't afraid of heights or spiders or storms or flying. He wasn't even afraid of pretty girls."

That made me crack a smile. "What finally scared him?"

"I think he had little doses of fear when he and your mom were dating. They were young and learning how to build a relationship. That's bound to be rocky. But even marriage didn't truly scare Charlie. Just like your grandad, once he set his mind to something, he was relentless until he got what he wanted. And what he wanted was your mom."

"Do you think they just knew?"

She nodded slowly. "I think they did. They knew what they had was special, even before they were ready to make it official."

"If marriage didn't scare Dad, what did?"

"Fatherhood," she said with a smile.

"He was afraid to have kids?"

"Oh, no. He was excited to have a baby. The whole time Lena was pregnant with Asher, he was the happiest, proudest father-to-be you'd ever seen." She paused, smiling again. Her eyes were unfocused, like she was reaching back in time and seeing things as they'd once been. "It wasn't until Asher was born that Charlie really learned about fear."

"How?"

"There's something about holding a newborn baby in your arms that brings it all home. Charlie was so jumpy with Asher, he drove your mom crazy. Always afraid someone was going to drop him or he'd get too hot or too cold. Worried about every little peep he made. Although when it came down to it, those things weren't what really bothered him. Having a child brought his biggest fear to the surface. The fear of losing the people he loved."

"And you think that's my biggest fear too?"

"It's up there. And a close call can certainly bring that demon out of hiding. But I think there's something else you're afraid of almost as much. A fear you carry in your heart every day."

Reluctantly, I met her eyes. I wasn't sure I wanted to hear what she had to say.

"You have lost people you love, and anyone would fear

living through that pain again. But I think underneath that, you're afraid that you don't matter."

"Do we have to talk about this now? I've had a rough couple of days."

"I know you have, but yes, we do."

I scrubbed my hands up and down my face, letting her words sink in. She was right. I was afraid I didn't matter. That my life was irrelevant.

"I don't remember them," I said, not quite sure where I was going with this. Only that I needed to finally say it out loud, here in this house. "I don't have a single memory of Mom and Dad. They lived, and did things, and got married, and had a bunch of kids, and I've got nothing of that."

"You were so young."

"I know. And I know it's not their fault that they died. They didn't want to leave us."

"No, they didn't."

My throat felt thick and tears threatened to prick at my eyes. "I don't even know if I miss them, or just the idea of them. How can you miss someone you don't even remember?"

"You can, Otter. Because your spirit knew them, and your spirit remembers. Even when our minds don't hold onto our memories, our spirits do." She pointed to my chest. "In there. That's where they still live. They're a part of you, and they always will be. You weren't old enough to keep the memories they left you, but they made you out of themselves. Out of their love."

"Yeah, well, except they didn't mean to have me."

"What makes you think that?"

"I know I was an accident. They didn't plan to get pregnant again."

She smiled, deepening the lines around her eyes. "When

you put your hand on a stone, or the side of a mountain, what does it say to you? It says I am immovable. I am as permanent as the earth itself. But we know that isn't so. Water flows relentlessly past the stone, grinding it away to sand. Gavin, you have the spirit of water in you. Relentlessly flowing from the mountain to the sea. You were a surprise, but you were also inevitable. There was nothing that was going to stop your spirit from entering this world."

"Even if they didn't want me?"

Gram got quiet for a second. I couldn't quite meet her eyes, but I knew she was watching me.

"Wait here," she said, finally.

She got up and a few seconds later, I heard the stairs creaking with her soft steps. I waited, the weight on my chest still painfully heavy. I was calm, and okay, I could admit the bridge jumping stunt had probably been reckless and stupid. And maybe it was good that my brothers had stopped me.

But I still felt awful.

Gram came back with a stack of light blue books in her arms. She set them on the table in front of me. They were all the same size, about as big as one of my old school binders. All the same faded blue. The top one said *Baby Book* on the cover.

"What are these?"

"These are the baby books your mom made for each of you." She took the top one and pushed the rest to the side, then laid it in front of me. "This one was for Asher."

I flipped through the pages. She'd filled out a lot of it, writing in milestones. Weights, firsts, notable moments in his first year of life. She'd tucked a plastic bag with a lock of hair from his first haircut, photos of his first steps, and more from his birthday party when he turned one.

"Evan's is a little more sparse," Gram said, shifting Asher's book out of the way. "That tends to happen with the second child." She turned a few pages to show me, then moved it so she could set the next two side by side. "The twins, well, I think she had her hands full simply surviving by that point. She wrote a few things down, but understandably, there's not much here."

"Mine must blank, then."

Without replying, she moved Levi and Logan's baby books to the side and pushed mine in front of me. "Why don't you have a look and see?"

I flipped to the first page and Mom had written my full name—Gavin Matthew Bailey—and my date of birth. I was totally expecting the rest of it to be blank, but when I turned the page, there was more. In fact, I kept flipping, and mine was filled out every bit as much as Asher's.

There were photos and little handwritten notes. Milestones and the dates. She'd used stickers and different colored pens—red, blue, purple, yellow. Everything, from my first bath to my first steps to me with cake all over my face on my first birthday, was included.

"You were a surprise," Gram said as I gazed at the pages. "They didn't think they'd have any more babies after the twins. And I won't lie and tell you they weren't worried. They were. They had their hands full with four, and they had moments where they wondered if they could handle five. And then you were born and your parents could not have been more in love with you."

I looked away again because now she really was going to make me cry.

"A baby book doesn't measure her love for her children. She didn't neglect the twins' books because she loved them any less than you or Asher. But don't you doubt for one second that they wanted you. You fit into their family—into *our* family—like you were always meant to be. Because you were. They loved you with everything they had, and they wouldn't have given you up for anything."

I turned to the last page, and tucked inside was a loose photo of me and my parents—just the three of us. I was in Dad's arms, wearing nothing but a diaper, and Mom was standing next to him, holding one of my hands. There were balloons in the background and I had chocolate cake on my face, so it was probably my first birthday.

A few tears broke free and I let them fall without shame. Because damn it, it wasn't fair. It wasn't fair that they'd died and left us behind. That we'd had to grow up without them. That they'd missed it.

But as I looked at this picture, I realized something else. Gram was right. They'd loved me. You could see it in their faces. They didn't look like a couple who were frazzled, at the end of their rope trying to survive their youngest child's babyhood. They looked like young parents enjoying their baby's first birthday. And something about that meant more to me than I knew how to express.

And I also realized I loved them right back.

They did still live inside me. Even though I couldn't remember them, they were right here. And they had been all along.

Nodding slowly, I set the photo down. "Thanks, Gram."

"Now you need to decide what you're going to do with your fear."

I hesitated for a long moment, thinking about that. About what I was really afraid of. I was scared of losing Skylar, and that fear had made me irrational.

Except...

"I really do want to marry her," I said aloud, without really meaning to.

Gram didn't reply, just raised her eyebrows with a little smile.

"I don't want to marry her just because I'm afraid. I want to marry her because I'm in love with her. She's it for me. I literally can't imagine my life without her."

She nodded along as I babbled.

"Help me out here, Gram, what would Dad have done? I know I want to be with her, but she isn't ready, and that's okay, I'll wait. I'll give her as long as she needs. But I screwed this up pretty badly and I don't know how to fix it."

"Out of the five of you, you're the most like your father. So I think whatever your instincts tell you to do is probably exactly what he would have done."

I grinned at her, feeling better than I had in days. "Awesome."

"Before you go, don't forget your cookie."

"I didn't think you made any."

She got up and retrieved her cookie jar from the counter, then brought it to the table and opened the lid.

"Sneaky." I reached in to grab one. "I couldn't even smell them."

"I had to make you sweat it a little bit."

I stood and gave her a gentle hug. "Well played."

"No more reckless stunts for at least a day or so, you hear me?"

"I hear you."

"Good." She patted my arm. "Then go get your Sparrow."

"Thanks." I turned to go but glanced back over my shoulder. "Gram, what was Dad's spirit animal?"

"You don't know?" she asked, sounding genuinely surprised.

"No."

"He was Otter, too. Playful, mischievous, and a bit of a trickster. And he loved water every bit as much as you do."

I smiled and suddenly, I was glad she'd never listened to me and changed my nickname. Otter was perfect.

"What about Mom?"

"She was Blue Jay—a beautiful songbird known for its high intelligence and tight family bonds."

"Air and water."

"A good combination," she said with a nod.

"How do you always know?"

She smiled and held out the cookie jar. "Why don't you take another for the road."

Since she obviously wasn't going to answer my question, I took another cookie and said my goodbyes.

It was getting late, and I had to go on duty first thing tomorrow morning. For once in my life, I wanted to take my time and think things through. So as much as I wanted to go see Skylar right this second—make sure that I didn't screw things up with her forever—I decided to wait. Flying by the seat of my pants hadn't worked very well, and I wasn't a total dumbass, I could learn from my mistakes. I'd use my shift tomorrow to make a plan. One that was foolproof.

40

SKYLAR

I stared at my laptop screen with a mix of disbelief and satisfaction. I'd actually done it. I'd finished the book.

It still needed revisions, and an editor would help me polish it. But it was all there, beginning, middle, and end. An entire story from start to finish.

I let out a long, relieved breath. A part of me had been afraid I'd lost it. That I'd never finish a book again.

But here it was, in all its messy, unedited glory.

I'd thought a lot about why I'd gotten blocked in the first place. What had happened to me all those months ago? I'd written twelve novels and then suddenly I could hardly write a word.

Looking back, I didn't think it was one single incident. It was a hundred little fears always swirling beneath the surface that had finally broken through. The fear of failure after success. The fear that it had been a fluke and my career would be over. That this would be the book that exposed all my weaknesses. That I wasn't really a good writer, I'd just somehow gotten lucky. The fear that I'd already used up every good idea I'd ever have. That I'd be exposed and everyone would learn the truth. That I had no idea what I was doing.

Somehow, Gavin had soothed those fears. He calmed my mind. Made all those worries disappear. When I was with him, I felt my focus and confidence return.

I hadn't written the entire book with him sitting on my bed behind me. But those writing sessions had gotten me started. They'd allowed me to break through my block.

There was something ironic about Gavin Bailey calming my fears. Because *he* scared me. Or at least, he had at first.

Now? I wasn't afraid. He'd pushed me out of my comfort zone in so many ways. He hadn't set out to show me I was brave, but he had. Because that was the thing, when I was with him, I did feel brave. It was like he sucked all the fear out of the room and made it disappear.

I missed him so much.

For the millionth time, I thought about texting him. Or even calling. Why was I hesitating? Because I didn't know what I wanted to say?

Or was it because I *did* know what I wanted to say?

I was so confused.

Confused or not, I decided to celebrate my little victory with some coffee at the Steaming Mug, so I saved and backed up my manuscript—again, just to be safe. I brushed out my hair, dabbed on a little makeup, and changed into a burgundy sweater and jeans. I slipped my feet into a cute pair of leopard print flats—because why not—and went downstairs.

Dad was on duty today, and Mom was out. A sense of peace had settled over the house since Dad had asked her to stay. I glanced around at the furniture—at Mom's things from her old house that had somehow fit perfectly in the empty spaces here.

It was very poetic. They filled the empty places in each other's lives.

They'd decided to see a couple's therapist to help them navigate this new phase in their relationship. There were still old wounds from the past that needed healing. And for two people who'd been single for twenty years, learning to share their lives again was going to take some work. But I'd never seen either of them as happy as they were now.

I slipped on my coat, grabbed my purse, and opened the front door. I jumped backward with a shriek, startling at the sight of the man on the step.

Cullen's hand slowly lowered—it looked like he'd been about to knock. "Sorry, Skylar. It's just me."

I gaped at him. "What are you doing here?"

"I need to talk to you."

"Why? Because your life imploded on national television?"

He blinked in surprise. "You saw that?"

"Yeah, I saw it." I decided not to mention that my friend Cara had somehow tipped off the interviewer about his affair with Pepper.

"Okay, well, can I come in?"

I crossed my arms. "No."

"Really? Come on, Skylar, I just want to talk."

"I can't even fathom what you think you have to say to me."

He took a deep breath, as if coming to terms with the fact that I wasn't going to invite him in. "Have you been writing?"

My lips twitched in a smile. I didn't have to tell him this —or anything—but I was feeling pretty great about it, so why not? "Not that it's any of your business, but yes. I finished my next novel."

"That's great. Have you found someone to represent you?"

"Why, are you here to try to win me back?"

"Yes."

I stared at him in disbelief. He could not be serious. "Wait, what? I thought you got fired."

"I did, but I'll find another agency."

"Especially if you bring a client with you," I said wryly.

"No, that's not why I'm here. It's not about my job. I care about your career because I care about you. I want you back, Skylar."

I laughed, because honestly, what else could I do? "It's too late for that, Cullen. Way too late. If you cared about me, you shouldn't have cheated on me."

"I know I made a huge mistake. I regret it all, Skylar. I'm so sorry."

I hesitated, my eyes flicking up and down. He looked awful. His clothes were disheveled, his normally well-groomed hair needed a trim, and his skin was pale.

Cara karma indeed.

"Thank you for saying sorry. I forgive you."

His eyes lit up, but I raised a hand before he could reply.

"I'm not finished," I said. "I'm not forgiving you for you, I'm forgiving you for me. What you did to me was awful. It was a total deal breaker. Even if you were the only hope I had of resurrecting my career, I still wouldn't sign with you again. And as for anything else, you burned that bridge. Thoroughly."

"Skylar, please."

I shook my head. "I told you that one day you were going

to realize what you lost. I'm sure that feeling sucks, but you have to live with what you did."

He opened his mouth to say something, but I was finished with this conversation. I stepped out, then shut and locked the door.

"I was just leaving. Goodbye, Cullen."

"Skylar—"

I didn't answer. Didn't even look at him again. Just walked to my car. I was done with him.

THE LAST TIME Cullen had shown up on my doorstep unexpectedly, I'd been left feeling miserable. This time, I felt free. If there had been any doubt in my mind that I was over him—that I'd totally moved on—there certainly wasn't any now.

I walked into the Steaming Mug, once again filled with a conflicting mix of emotions. I was proud of myself for how I'd handled Cullen's surprise visit. But everything with Gavin felt so wrong, and I still wasn't sure what I was going to do about that.

Cara waved to me from a table near the back. "Hi sweet sunflower."

I went to her table and took a seat, so glad she was here. "You're not going to believe what just happened."

"Sounds juicy. Tell me everything."

"Cullen just showed up at my house. He actually thought I might take him back."

"What?" she asked, her voice flat. "Is he still there? Do you need me to take care of him for you?"

"No, I'm sure he's gone by now."

"Are you sure? It would just take a few calls."

I laughed, although I wasn't quite sure what she meant by *take care of him*. Maybe I didn't want to know. "Really, it's fine. I'm glad it happened. It gave me a chance to reject him to his face. That was so satisfying."

She grabbed my hand and squeezed. "Look at my baby, standing up for herself like the badass she is. I'm so proud of you."

"Thanks, Cara. Thanks for everything."

She brushed her hair back from her shoulder. "It's my pleasure."

Grace came over to the table with a mug of tea and sat down.

"There you are, boo," Cara said. "How are you feeling?"

"I'm feeling great. Really energized today."

"You look amazing," I said, and she really did. Grace was the epitome of the glowing pregnant woman.

"Thank you," she said with a smile. "Have you heard from Gavin today?"

Just hearing his name made my breath catch. "No. Why?"

"I think something was going on. Asher left yesterday and said there was a brother emergency. He was gone for a while. When he came home, he said everything was fine, but he wouldn't tell me any details."

"Such a guy," Cara said.

"Right? I was just wondering if something happened to Gavin, since everyone's been talking about him."

"Who's been talking about him?" I asked.

"I'm sure it's exaggerated, but people were saying he was having some kind of meltdown."

"Poor Gav," Cara said.

"Oh no," I said. "If he's having a meltdown, it's my fault."

"What happened?" Grace asked.

"The day after the accident on the bridge, he came over and kind of said we should get married."

Cara laughed. "Oh god, that's such a Gavin thing to do."

Grace nudged Cara with her elbow. "Be nice."

"I'm not wrong."

"It just caught me completely off guard," I said. "I thought he'd say he wanted to date me, not get married."

"And he's so adorably clueless, he thought you'd be ready to run off to Vegas with him right then and there," Cara said.

"Something like that. He got mad and left and I haven't talked to him since."

"Don't worry," Grace said. "He's not the only Bailey who can be ridiculous when it comes to love. It probably runs in the family."

Cara nodded. "Isn't that the truth."

"That's the thing, I didn't even know he loved me. He left that part out until the end when he was upset."

"Oh, Gavin," Cara said, shaking her head.

"Tell me this," Grace said. "Do you love him?"

"Yes," I said, the admission coming easily. "I do."

"Then I'm sure you two will figure it out," she said.

"Why don't you just marry him?" Cara asked.

Grace laughed, as if Cara must be joking. "That's kind of abrupt, don't you think?"

"Why?"

"You know, for being anti-marriage, you're very happy to get the people around you engaged."

Cara scoffed, like she was offended. "I'm not anti-marriage."

"Yes, you are."

"No, I'm just realistic. I know I'm not wife material, but that has nothing to do with other people. Besides, don't we always want the best for our children? I want Skylar to be happy."

"And marrying Gavin will make her happy?" Grace asked. "Okay, I see your point. Gavin is amazing."

He really was. He was so amazing. "But he couldn't have been serious."

"I think he was," Cara said. "He wouldn't have said it otherwise."

"Gavin loves to joke around, but if he said he wants to marry you, he meant it," Grace said. "Trust me, I know him. I know he's crazy sometimes, but the Baileys are the most loyal men you'll ever meet. They're men of their word, every single one of them."

Cara rolled her eyes, but didn't argue with her.

"Wait a second," I said. "You two are basically normal, rational women."

"She is," Cara said, gesturing to Grace.

"And you're both telling me that not only was Gavin serious when he said he wanted to marry me, but it wouldn't be insane if I admitted that maybe I kind of want to marry him too?"

"Of course it's insane," Cara said. "But that doesn't mean it's wrong."

Grace laughed. "It's not insane. I knew I was going to marry Asher before our first date."

"There's no rule book that says a relationship has to start at step one and proceed to steps two, three, and four," Cara said. "And if there is, fuck the rule book. Be true to yourself, kitten whiskers. If you aren't ready, tell him to slow the fuck down and date you like a good boy. But if Gavin's ring on your finger feels like the right thing for you, then don't be afraid to take the plunge."

I stood suddenly. "I'm sorry but I have to go."

"Just promise me I can plan your bridal shower," Cara called as I rushed out the door.

Suddenly, the need to see Gavin was overwhelming. It felt like every second that ticked by pulled us further apart. I had to see him, and tell him in person how I felt.

I had to go for what I wanted.

I drove to his house and didn't see his truck out front. But I stopped anyway, just to be sure. Levi was in the front window building some sort of structure—it looked like a big cat tree. He saw me coming and opened the door.

Logan blinked sleepy eyes at me from his spot on the couch. He had Princess Squeaker curled up on his chest. "Hey, Skylar."

"Is Gavin home?" I asked, not even bothering to hide the desperation in my voice.

"He's on duty until tomorrow," Levi said.

"You can go see him at the—"

I was already running back to my car.

A crazy sense of urgency filled me, like if I didn't talk to Gavin right now, I might never get the chance.

41

GAVIN

I didn't exactly have a plan yet, but to be fair, my shift had been busy. Only one call out, but the engine needed washing, gear needed to be checked, and a preschool class came in for a tour. I drew field trip duty, but I didn't mind. Hanging out with a bunch of four-year-olds for an hour was awesome.

That probably said something about my maturity level, but I decided not to worry about it.

After the kids left with their red plastic fire hats, I had a little time to think, and I realized what was really holding me back. I needed to talk to Chief.

It wasn't because I needed his permission to be with Skylar. She was a grown woman and could make her own decisions. But Chief was family—hers, of course, but mine in a way too. I needed to make things right with him before I could move forward with Skylar.

Assuming she wanted to move forward with me. I hated the cloud of doubt that hung over me, but the truth was, I didn't know for sure what she wanted. And if she didn't want me, I was going to have to figure out how to live with that.

For now, I was going to stick with blind optimism and talk to her dad.

I went to his office and took a fortifying breath as I knocked on the open door. "Hey, Chief. Can I have a minute?"

"Sure, Gav," he said without looking up. "Come on in."

There was that feeling again. Like something was crawling through my stomach and leaving tiny footprints behind. Was this fear?

I didn't like it, but maybe I just needed more practice managing it.

It made me think about Skylar. She felt like this all the time, and she did shit anyway? Holy fuck, she was amazing. I loved her so much.

Chief raised his eyes. He looked good—younger, some-how. He sat up straight and his hair was neatly trimmed. "What's up?"

Uh-oh. I hadn't really thought this through, but before I could think better of it, I started talking. "I stole a cookie from your cookie jar. More than once. I know I said I wouldn't and you could trust me not to. I think I even said I know how to bake my own cookies, and I did that too, but it wasn't the same. No, that's not what I'm trying to say."

Fuck. This wasn't going well. Chief looked at me with a mildly bewildered—or maybe it was horrified—expression on his face.

"Let me try this again." I pressed my lips together for a second and took a deep breath. "I'm in love with your daughter."

Now he really looked surprised. "What?"

"I'm in love with Skylar. She's the most amazing woman I've ever met. She's smart, and talented, and beautiful, and sweet, and I could keep going, but you already know her.

I've never been in love before, and maybe you're wondering how I know I'm in love with her if it's my first time, but trust me, I know. I'm crazy about her, Chief. I'm done, I surrender."

He gazed at me for a long moment, like he didn't know what to say. "Does she know all this?"

I winced. "Kind of? Not really. I tried to tell her the other day, but I was still freaked out by the accident and I did a supremely shitty job of it."

He nodded slowly. "I see."

"Look, I haven't done things right when it comes to her, and I know that. And there's a good chance she's going to shoot me down anyway and none of this will matter. But before I go any further, I need to clear the air with you. You've been the closest thing I've ever had to a father and I meant no disrespect. And I'm probably not the kind of guy you'd want her to be with, but if I can fix things with her, I swear to you, I'll be good to her. I'll be good *for* her. You have my word."

His brow creased. "What makes you think I wouldn't want you to be with her?"

I glanced away. Damn, what was it with me and hard conversations lately? "You probably want her to be with someone more stable and mature. It's okay, I understand."

"Gav, I want her to be with someone who makes her happy. Someone who challenges her, cares for her, and protects her like she's the most important thing in his world."

I met his eyes. "I can do that, Chief."

The corners of his mouth turned up. "I know you can."

A rush of emotion hit me so hard it almost knocked the breath from my lungs. I rubbed the back of my neck, waiting for it to pass. "So you're saying you'd be cool with me dating your daughter? Assuming she wants to date me, and I know that's debatable right now."

"If it's what you both want, of course I'm okay with it."

"Since we're having this conversation, what if I want to do more than date her? Because I'm just going to be up front with you, Chief, I plan on marrying her. If I can convince her to marry me. But I think I can do it, I can be really convincing."

His eyebrows lifted, and he stared at me for a few seconds. "You want to marry my daughter?"

"Oh yeah. I'd marry her tomorrow if she'd let me."

He stood, and for a split second, I thought he might hit me. In that same split second, I knew I'd take it if he did.

But he didn't. Instead, he walked around his desk and hugged me.

He clapped me on the back, then stepped away and gave me a short nod.

I had no idea what to say.

Apparently he didn't either because he went back to his seat without saying anything.

"Thanks, Chief," I said, knowing it wasn't nearly enough. But I also knew that Chief understood. I turned to leave, but paused and glanced back at him. "My parents would have thought this was pretty cool, wouldn't they? Their kid falling for your kid."

"They would have been ecstatic." He scratched his chin. "Actually, I'm realizing that I just lost a twenty-some-odd year-old bet."

I grinned at him. "You should have known not to bet against me."

"Isn't that the truth. Your dad would be proud of you, son. You're every bit the man he would have wanted you to be."

I had to glance away again, but not because I didn't want to hear it. For the first time, the mention of my parents wasn't too painful to take. It was bittersweet—the familiar hurt still there—but it wasn't all bad. There was a little bit of happiness too. "Thanks. That means a lot to me."

He opened his mouth to say something else—probably to tell me to get back to work—when tones rang out. We had a call.

I sprang into action, heading straight downstairs to gear up. Before I had everything on, the engine bay door was already open. I glanced outside as I stepped onto the engine and my heart squeezed. Skylar was out there, standing next to her car, like she'd just parked and gotten out.

Our eyes met as the engine exited the station, and the weirdest thought ran through my head. *What if that's the last time I ever see her?*

That was fucking morbid.

She watched me go and my chest felt like it might cave in. Why was she here? Looking for her dad? Was it too much to hope for that she'd come to see me?

Fuck.

I took my seat as the engine rumbled out onto the street, lights flashing. Hard as it was, I had to put Sky out of my mind for now. I had a job to do.

We got the rundown on the situation as we drove through town. Structure fire at the Haven House. First call-in was a neighbor reporting smoke coming from the building. Second call came in a few minutes later. It was closed today, but there was a volunteer from the historical society trapped inside.

The Haven House. That was so weird. Sky and I had just been there.

Adrenaline hit me, making my senses sharp, my body

ready. I felt every bounce of the tires as we rushed across town. By the time we got on the scene, smoke was pouring from vents near the roof. Dispatch had the volunteer on the line—a woman named Sally Oliver. She was trapped in an upstairs bathroom.

We poured out of the engine and the hose crew got to work. Chief flew out of his truck and started giving orders.

"Get the pipe over on the alpha side," Chief said, pointing. "We've got an electrical box arcing on bravo, don't get fucking zapped. Interior attack, I want two in, two out. Christian and Jacob, you're in first. Steve and Mason out. Gavin and Matt, primary search. Get her out of there for me."

"Got it, Chief," I said. Matt and I gave each other a quick nod and headed for the building while Chief kept barking orders.

A quick visual sweep of the outside made it hard to determine where the fire was burning. There was a lot of smoke everywhere. A voice in my radio reported that Sally was still in the upstairs bathroom and she had smoke leaking in the top of the door. We didn't have a lot of time.

Christian and Jacob went in ahead of us, stretching the line inside so they could start attacking the fire head-on with water. Matt and I masked up and followed.

The smoke and heat were intense inside. I didn't know where the fire had started, but it had obviously burned unchecked for a while before anyone had seen it. We should have been here ten minutes ago.

Visibility was low, but I could see wallpaper curling at the seams and waves of smoke rolling across the ceiling. The heat beat at me even through my gear.

The stairs were near the center of the house, so I waved

Matt on. I had a bad feeling about this. We needed to get up there. Now.

I took another step and something felt off. The floor was too soft. My hand shot out to stop Matt from going forward.

"There's a basement down there. If it's burning, the floor's gonna go."

Matt pressed on the floor in front of him with his boot. "Shit."

I could see the stairs from here. It was the most direct route to the second floor, and to Sally Oliver.

Any other day, I wouldn't have hesitated. I would have made a run for it. I could make it.

But if I didn't make it, I'd probably die. And I'd never see Skylar again.

"Chief, we need to get to Sally from the outside. Floor in here's gonna go."

"Copy that. Get out of there, Gav."

A beam cracked nearby and a shower of sparks and debris flew toward us.

"Working on it."

I whipped around and pushed Matt ahead of me. I couldn't see a damn thing and the heat hitting my face shield was getting bad. Another ear-splitting crack filled the air and I glanced back as the floor in front of the stairs started to collapse.

Holy shit.

Over the roar, I could just make out voices through my radio. "Conditions worse... ladder access to upper window... report in..."

The floor beneath my feet felt wrong. Like stepping on foam, not wood. Heat beat at me from every direction, and something crashed behind me, but I didn't look back.

I didn't see any light from outside, and as we got closer

to the front of the house, I realized why. Something had collapsed, blocking the front door.

Fuck.

The heat was starting to hurt, even through my turnouts. I had air, but the temperature was getting too high. I hoped someone had gotten Sally out, but there wasn't anything I could do about that right now. I switched focus. Matt. He had a wife and kids. I wasn't going to let him die in here.

We veered toward the windows in one of the front rooms. Matt quickly broke the glass with his ax. He gestured to me to go first, but I shoved him toward the window.

"Get the fuck out of here."

He climbed through and turned around, reaching to help me get out.

Another loud crash rang out and the whole building shook. I looked back and it was like a gaping hole to hell opened up behind me. The floor collapsed inward, exposing a raging inferno underneath the building. The walls tilted and a sickening feeling hit me.

I was never going to see Sky again.

42

SKYLAR

*W*ith a racing heart, I pulled up across the street from the Haven House and got out of my car. Smoke filled the air and emergency vehicles lined the street. There was a flurry of activity, the controlled chaos of firefighters running hoses and cops directing traffic and keeping bystanders away from the blaze.

I knew I couldn't get close, and there wasn't anything I could do. I'd waited at the station after watching the engine pull away with Gavin on it. But the sense of urgency had only grown. I couldn't just sit there and wait. When I'd noticed the plume of smoke rising from the middle of town, I'd gotten in my car and driven straight here.

Dad was in front, issuing orders, talking on his radio. It occurred to me that I'd never seen him on a call before. His reserved demeanor was gone. The man I saw out there was completely in charge, shouting over the noise. He was in control, but there was worry in his face.

Something was wrong.

I ran across the street to see if I could get a better view without getting in the way. A firefighter carried a woman in his arms. She looked scared, but definitely alive and breathing. He took her to one of the waiting ambulances and the paramedics took over.

The house rumbled, a low groaning sound. Fallen debris blocked the front door and smoke billowed out of the windows and rose from what was probably a hole in the roof. It groaned again and the sound reached right inside my chest and wrapped around my heart.

Where was Gavin?

Several firefighters aimed streams of water at the building, but none of them were Gavin. Dad paced around, talking on his radio, gesturing with his arms.

Glass flew out a front window, as if it had been broken from the inside. A second later, a firefighter climbed out.

Was it him? I couldn't tell from here.

He turned back to the window and reached inside.

Gavin was in there. I didn't know how I knew, but I was certain of it.

A crash reverberated through the ground, the vibration traveling through my feet and up my legs. My stomach clenched as the whole house shook. It looked like it was about to collapse.

Oh my god, Gavin, get out. Get out. Please, get out.

"Get him out of there," Dad bellowed.

Two more firefighters rushed to the window. Smoke poured out, pooling against the porch roof above it. The building shuddered and something crashed inside.

I held my breath, wondering if my heart would explode.

The smoke obscured everything. I couldn't see what was happening. The building shook again, the noise of old beams failing more horrifying than the collapsing bridge.

Two firefighters backed away from the window. Then a third, the one who'd been inside.

He had another one, his arm around his shoulders.

They rushed him onto the lawn and pulled off his helmet and mask.

It was Gavin.

He took heaving breaths and the other three worked to pull his gear off. A paramedic raced toward him, but Dad reached him first.

I couldn't see anything with all the people surrounding him. Tears ran down my cheeks and my shoulders clenched tight. He was alive. I'd seen him breathing. He was alive.

With another ear-splitting groan, the building caved in. Beams split and cracked, the walls fell inward, and the roof seemed to disappear. I turned and shielded my face with my arms from the blast of smoke and debris. When I looked back, the Haven House was a pile of burning rubble.

I waited for what seemed like an eternity while they loaded Gavin on a gurney. Dad got up and went back to work. His eyes caught mine and with a quick nod, he pointed to the ambulance.

That was all the invitation I needed.

I rushed to the ambulance, still parked in front of the engine. The back doors were open and Gavin was sitting up, talking to the paramedic.

He smiled at me, a big grin that puckered his dimples. "Hey, Sky."

"I believe some thirty percent of firefighter deaths are due to internal trauma from being crushed by falling debris," I blurted out. "Did anything hit you?"

The paramedic got up and smiled at me. "He's okay, Miss Stanley. Go ahead." He climbed down and gestured for me to get in.

I took the hand he offered and got inside the back of the ambulance. Gavin watched me with an amused twitch of his lips. I sat on a seat next to the gurney, wishing I could throw myself on top of him instead.

But only if they'd already checked him for internal injuries.

"Nothing fell on me." He held up a lightly bandaged arm. "Just some minor burns. It got too hot in there, even for my PPE. What are you doing here?"

"I saw the smoke."

"Are you okay?"

"Of course I'm okay. I wasn't almost trapped in a burning building. Are you okay?"

His eyes held mine and he nodded. "Mostly."

"Do the burns hurt?"

"No."

"Then why mostly? What's wrong?"

"I'm really sorry about the other day."

"We don't have to talk about that now."

"I know, this totally isn't the time. But I don't care. Sky, I'm in love with you."

I sucked in a quick breath and touched my fingers to my lips.

"I realize we were supposed to just be friends. I broke the rules, but I've never been much of a rule follower. And I'm so sorry for acting like a lunatic. You were right, the bridge scared the shit out of me. But that's because I'm crazy fucking in love with you."

Staring at him, a sense of elation poured through me. Gavin loved me. It was crazy love, but how else would Gavin Bailey love someone? That was who he was.

"Gavin, I'm so in love with you."

His mouth turned up in a wide smile. "You are?"

"Crazy in love."

He reached out to touch my face. "Wow, you made that

so easy. I thought I was going to have to work a lot harder to convince you."

I laughed. "Hardly. I've been in love with you for a while. I was just afraid to admit it."

"Me too."

Careful of his arms, I leaned in and pressed my lips to his. He slid his hand in my hair and his mouth was soft but insistent.

Someone cleared their throat.

Oops. It was my dad.

He stood at the back of the ambulance. "You okay, Gav?"

"Yeah, Chief. Nothing serious. Did you get Sally out?"

"We did. She'll be fine."

Gavin let out a breath. "Good."

Dad's eyes flicked to me, then back to Gavin. "Don't leave until they release you. And unless the entire town catches fire, you're off for the rest of the night. You hear me?"

"Loud and clear, Chief."

He hesitated, like there might be more he wanted to say, but he just nodded and walked away. My dad had always been a man of few words.

"I talked to him about you earlier," Gavin said.

"You did?"

He nodded. "Not because either of us need his permission to be together. I just wanted to be up front. Tell him how I feel about his daughter."

"What did you say?"

"That I'm in love with you." He paused, his dimples puckering. "And I'm going to marry you someday."

Little flutters of happiness pulsed through my body. I stared into his soft brown eyes and I knew. He was right. He *was* going to marry me someday.

"Ask me again."

His eyebrows lifted. "Now?"

I nodded. We were sitting in the back of an ambulance at the scene of a fire that could have killed him, and none of this was textbook. None of it was normal. We hadn't really dated, we hadn't even known each other that long, and it didn't matter at all. This was right. Every single bit of it.

I felt it, deep in my soul.

His face grew serious, his brow furrowing, and he reached over to take my hands in his. "Skylar Stanley, will you marry me?"

"Yes," I said, my voice more confident than it had ever been. No shy Skylar here. "Yes, I will marry you."

"Holy shit, this is the best day of my life." He grabbed my face and kissed me hard. "I love you so much."

I laughed through his kisses. "I love you too."

"You need a ring," he said, glancing around. He grabbed a roll of medical tape and ripped off a small piece, then took my hand and wrapped the little strip around my ring finger. "That'll do for now. I'll get you a real one when I can."

I held up my hand and admired the white tape circling my finger. "I love it. It's perfect."

He took my hand and brought it to his lips. "It is perfect, isn't it?"

"It's all perfect. Crazy, but completely perfect."

One corner of his mouth hooked in a grin, puckering his dimples. "Crazy is kinda my thing."

Smiling, I leaned in to kiss him again. "It's one of my favorite things about you."

"I love you, Sky."

"I love you too."

And I did. I loved him so much. I never wanted to be without him, and now I'd never have to.

43

GAVIN

*I*cy rain pelted the football field, soaking through my clothes. Not that I cared. This was football weather in the mountains. And tonight was the big Bailey-Haven game.

It was fucking on.

Technically, I wasn't supposed to play tonight. But as far as I was concerned, some minor burns weren't enough to sideline me. If we'd been playing anyone but the Havens, Jack probably would have made me sit the bench. But we were playing the Havens, which meant all bets were off. And a mildly injured Gavin was definitely taking the field.

The Bailey team had played a great season, both with and without me. We hadn't lost a single game, not even to the Montgomerys, who'd beaten us last year.

Of course, the fucking Havens were also undefeated.

For now. We were going to kick their asses tonight.

I stood on the sidelines with my brothers, waiting for the fourth quarter to start. It was a tie game, and they had the ball, but I was confident we were going to walk out of here with the win.

We had to. Bailey pride demanded it.

Glancing into the bleachers, I waved at my girl. Sky was bundled up in a thick coat and wore a light blue knit hat someone at Stitch and Bitch had made her. Gram had started teaching her to crochet, which was so fucking cute. Asher and Evan hadn't told me how awesome it was to see your girl bonding with Gram.

She waved back from beneath the big umbrella that covered both her and Cara. Grace and Fiona shared another one next to them. They were troopers, coming out here on a stormy night to cheer on their team.

Bunch of cute little badasses is what they were. I loved those girls.

Especially Sky.

No one had been all that surprised when we'd told everyone we were engaged. I'd expected a bunch of lectures from my brothers about not rushing in. But they'd just congratulated me with slaps on the back and Bailey bear hugs. Like they trusted me to make this big decision about my life and not fuck it up.

Maybe they just realized that I knew. Sky was it for me. It was as simple as that.

Grace was so excited, she'd brought me a t-shirt that said, *Soon-To-Be Trophy Husband*. She'd gotten it from her brother Cooper.

I was wearing it under my sweatshirt.

"How you feeling, Gav?" Jack asked. "If you're hurting—"

"I'm good."

He nodded. "I want you all over Zachary Haven. Rush that damn pass."

"With pleasure, Coach."

Logan nudged me with his elbow and nodded across the field. "Look at those dicks."

Theo and Garrett were glaring at us from the other side of the field.

"They're still pissed about the drive-in," I said with a chuckle. "Is it weird that I can't wait to see what they do to try to get us back?"

Logan laughed. "Yeah, you are weird, Gav. By the way, I bought Princess Squeaker a pink cat bed I saw in the window at Happy Paws. It's totally her new favorite place to sleep."

"Where is it? I didn't even see it."

"It's in my room."

I shoved him. "Stop trying to steal my cat."

"I'm not. It's not my fault she likes me better than you."

"Whatever. She'll always love her mommy best."

The Havens took the field so I popped my mouth guard back in and tossed a wink over my shoulder at Sky. I was cold and tired, but it felt great. My leg was getting stronger, and I was about to get all up in Zachary Haven's face.

Levi and Logan were playing both sides of the ball with me. Asher and Evan were on offense, waiting on the sidelines for us to get the ball back for them.

Adrenaline lit me up from the inside as I stared Zachary down. Even though I was obligated to hate him, I had to admit, Zachary was a great quarterback. He was quick and had a good arm. Our eyes met and his narrowed, so I grinned at him.

We took our places and I vibrated with excitement, waiting for the snap. My fingers twitched and I ground my teeth into my mouth guard.

They hiked the ball and I took off like a rocket, heading straight for Zachary. He pulled back for a pass, but I didn't give him time. I squeezed through two defenders and forced him to throw it away.

Hell yes.

Levi gave me a high five on my way back to the line of scrimmage.

Second down. My feet kicked up mud as I flew forward. Theo knocked into my shoulder, trying to keep me away from Zachary. I spun, letting my momentum carry me around, and two seconds later I was rushing Zachary again. He got off a pass but it was incomplete.

"Dude, did you hear I'm getting married?" I asked Zachary. I pointed out Skylar. "That's my girl, right there."

His brow creased, like he was confused. "So?"

"So, she's one more girl you'll never have."

"Fuck off, Gavin."

I laughed and went back to the line.

The crowd cheered as the Havens set up for third down. If we held them here, they'd have to punt, and we'd get the ball back. Then Asher could go to work.

I locked Zachary in my sights. We had this game. I could feel it.

They hiked the ball and my legs ate up the distance between me and Zachary. He side-stepped, then planted his feet, setting up for a pass. Not on my watch. He released the ball, but I jumped, reaching for it. My fingers caught the bottom, tipping it away. Another incomplete.

"Fuck," Zachary bellowed.

I did a little celebration dance and waved at Sky again. She was on her feet cheering for me while Cara held the big umbrella out of her way.

The Havens had no choice but to punt, even though they were clearly pissed about it. We got the ball back and the energy of the game was definitely on our side. Three first downs in a row thanks to a pass to Evan, a pass to Logan, and a great run by Levi, and we were in scoring range. Two plays later, touchdown Baileys.

Unfortunately for us, the Havens came back strong on their next possession. They were ready for me, doubling up coverage on the line. Zachary completed a few good passes. Then they surprised us with a reversal to Josiah, and he ran it in. Touchdown Havens.

Fuck.

Tie game again and the clock was running down.

They kicked off to us and Levi ran it back to about the fifty-yard line. Great field position, but we had to take advantage of it. First down, Asher handed off to Levi. Not a bad run—about five yards. We ran the same play again, and this time I blocked for him. Six yards and a first down.

Next play, Asher faked to Levi, then stepped back for a pass. Evan was wide open in the end zone. Asher threw a perfect spiral right into Evan's chest. He caught it and the crowd went wild.

Touchdown Baileys. After kicking the extra point, we were up by seven.

But there was still time, and now the Havens would have the ball.

We kicked off and Theo ran it back to the forty. If they could get a couple of first downs, they had plenty of time to score. We had to hold them here.

I clenched my teeth around my mouth guard as we took our positions on defense. Excitement warmed me from the inside. Zachary's eyes narrowed and I grinned at him.

I'm coming for you, asshole.

They hiked the ball and I launched for him, my feet digging into the muddy field. Incomplete. Second down he faked to Theo, but I wasn't fooled. I went right for him and he had to throw it away. Another incomplete. Third down.

This time, he did hand it off to Theo, rather than attempt another pass. Logan was on it, pulling Theo's flag before he made it even five yards. Fourth down, but obviously they'd go for it. The game was almost over. It was their last chance.

My fingers twitched as I took my position. Zachary called out the play. They hiked the ball and I had one objective. Pull Zachary's flag before he could lose the ball.

A defender tried to get in my way, but I darted around him. My legs burned with the effort of my sprint—especially my left—but I kept pushing. Zachary planted his feet and drew his arm back, ready to throw.

I dove for him, reaching for his flag. My hand wrapped around something and a second later, I hit the ground with a thud. Mud splattered in my face and dirt shoved up my nose.

And in my hand was Zachary Haven's flag.

I held it up and Zachary tossed the ball on the ground.

That was it. We won.

The Bailey crowd cheered and my brothers ran over and hauled me to my feet. I was soaked, dirty, and freezing, and I fucking loved it. We'd beat those asshole Havens.

We ran to the sidelines to exchange hugs and high-fives. Someone tossed me a towel, so I wiped the mud off my face.

I turned, and there was Skylar.

Her smile lit up the rainy football field. "That was amazing. Congratulations."

"Thanks, baby." I grabbed her and pulled her in for a kiss.

"You must be freezing." Her eyes met mine. "Should we go warm you up?"

I fake-shivered. "I'm so cold. I'll need *lots* of warming up tonight."

She laughed. "Good."

Chief walked over and patted me on the back. "Nice job out there."

"Thanks, Chief."

"Listen, I don't mean to take away from your victory, but I wanted to be the one to tell you. We suspect the fire at the Haven House was arson."

"No shit?"

He nodded. "It's not definitive yet. We're going to need to do a full investigation. But there's enough to make us suspect that somebody set that fire on purpose."

"Why would someone burn down the Haven House?" Skylar asked.

"That's what we're going to find out. Whoever did this almost killed several people, including you. I do not take that lightly." There was a hint of menace in his voice.

"Let me know how I can help," I said.

"I will. Now go celebrate your win."

I opened my mouth to say, *hell yeah, I'm going to go celebrate naked*. But I was getting naked with his daughter and that just wasn't the kind of thing you said to your boss. Even if he was cool with you marrying her.

So I just said, "Thanks Chief," and left it at that.

But I really was going to go celebrate naked. And it was going to be the best thing I did all night. Even better than beating the Havens at flag football.

Because there was simply nothing better than being with my girl.

44

SKYLAR

*C*ara really did know how to throw a great party.

She'd gone all out for this one, with a caterer, full bar, balloons, and a big sign that read, *Congratulations Skylar*.

I'd told her she didn't need to throw me a book launch party. But I'd discovered that trying to get Cara to stop doing something once she'd set her mind to it was pretty much impossible.

Besides, this book deserved to be celebrated. It represented a turning point in my career. I'd written it after the worst bout of writer's block I'd ever had. After losing my publisher, and my agent, and my then-boyfriend.

I'd started it with Gavin nearby, his calming influence shoring up my confidence. I'd continued, and finished, with his encouragement, and his love.

And that was the true magic. The real reason I'd been able to write at all. The essence of creative energy was love, and Gavin had unlocked a deeper love than I'd ever known.

Even when we were both trying to convince ourselves we were just friends.

I'd dedicated the book to him.

So many of my family and friends were here. Dad and Mom held hands over near the bar while they chatted with Gram. She'd read an early copy of the book and said it had kept her up so late, she'd overslept the next morning and her peckers hadn't been pleased.

Evan and Fiona had brought me a cute little succulent as a gift. Fiona said its name was Beatrice, but I was welcome to change it if I wanted. I just hoped I'd be able to keep it alive. Cara breezed around the room, chatting and drinking, always circling back to Grace. Grace's baby belly was just starting to show, and Asher kept absently rubbing it.

They were so adorable.

Logan seemed to have planted himself near the bar. He stood with a glass of whiskey in his hand, talking to Levi and Ginny.

I was going to miss Ginny. She was checking out of her rental house tomorrow and heading back to Denver, where she was based. I'd read a draft of her piece on Tilikum and it was amazing. She'd woven the feud and unanswered questions from the past into a lively description of life in our quirky little mountain town. She'd really done it justice.

Gavin brought me another glass of champagne.

"I should probably slow down," I said. "I think this is my third glass."

He tucked my hair behind my ear. "It's your party. Have as much as you want. I'll stay sober and make sure you get home okay."

Logan laughed loudly from across the room.

"You might have to make sure your brother gets home okay."

"Yeah, I think he's using whiskey to cope with his proximity to Cara tonight."

I laughed and took a sip of my champagne.

Gavin took my left hand and brought it to his lips for a kiss. We'd chosen my engagement ring together—a silver band with a deep blue sapphire. I'd tried on a few rings with a diamond, but we'd both been drawn to this one. And as soon as I'd tried it on, we'd agreed it was the one.

A little non-traditional, maybe. But it was perfect.

"Have I mentioned how proud I am of you?" Gavin asked and kissed my hand again.

"Thank you. I couldn't have done it without you."

"I think you could have, but it wouldn't have been nearly as fun."

"Definitely not as fun."

I'd decided to take the leap and publish my book independently, rather than going through the process of finding a new agent and shopping the book around to the big publishers. It had been a daunting prospect, but Gavin had helped. We'd learned a lot together. The book had gone live yesterday, and so far, the reception had been amazing.

And doing everything myself was so empowering. I wasn't at the mercy of a big company. The fate of this book, and all my future books, was in my hands.

"Time for a toast," Gavin said and winked at me. He stepped forward and raised his glass. "Hey, everyone. Let's all lift our glasses to our resident literary genius, and my future wife, Skylar Stanley. She's not only a talented author, she's a beautiful person inside and out. And she has great taste in husbands, since she picked me. Congratulations, Sky. I'm so proud of you, and I can't wait to see what the future holds for us. Cheers!"

A chorus of, "Cheers," went around the room. I raised my glass in thanks to everyone here and took a sip.

Gavin hooked an arm around my waist and pulled me close for a kiss.

The caterer served more food and the bartender was a hit. Sven, Cara's massage therapist, showed up to give shoulder, neck, and foot massages. He looked like a huge Viking, with broad shoulders, a thick beard, and a blond man-bun. Cara said his hands were magic, and she wasn't wrong.

After Sven's massage and more champagne, I was relaxed and more than a little bit tipsy. Gram and my parents went home, leaving Gavin and Grace as the only sober people at the party. Everyone else made multiple trips to the bar. The noise level rose, but for once I didn't mind. Gavin and I laughed, and danced, and celebrated, and laughed some more.

It was the best book launch party I'd ever had.

Of course, it was the only book launch party I'd ever had. But that didn't diminish its importance to me. In fact, that made it even more special.

The night wore on and some of the guys started a poker game. There were mini cheesecakes and fancy chocolates, and more drinks. Cara gave me a cupcake she'd made herself. It was light and fluffy with delicious buttercream frosting on top. Gavin congratulated her on no longer sucking at baking. She laughed like that was the funniest thing she'd ever heard. Of course, by that point, she was pretty drunk.

Eventually, I started to get sleepy. I didn't even have to ask Gavin if he minded leaving. He knew without me saying a word. He said goodbye to the guys at the poker table and grabbed my coat for me.

I'd lost track of who was still here and who'd left already. I didn't see Ginny, but she'd probably gone home to finish packing. I was meeting her for brunch tomorrow, so we could say our goodbyes then.

I thanked everyone for coming and waved goodbye. Gavin put his hand on the small of my back and led me toward the door.

"Oh, wait. I wanted to thank Cara again." I glanced over the people left, but didn't see her. "I don't know where she went."

"I don't know, either," Gavin said. "She probably went upstairs to pass out."

Still feeling tipsy myself, I leaned against him and giggled. "Probably. That's okay, I'll see her soon."

Gavin led me out to his truck and helped me in. It had been the best night. I was pleasantly buzzed, enjoying the success of my book, and the company of friends and family. I was engaged to the most wonderful man I'd ever known. It was hard to imagine being any happier.

As bad as my life had been when I'd moved to Tilikum, now it was that much better, and more.

We left Cara's but Gavin didn't head back to his place. Instead, he drove toward Gram's.

"Where are we going?"

He glanced at me with a little grin. "I have a surprise for you."

We drove down the long private drive toward Gram's house, but didn't stop there. Instead, he parked outside the house next door, where Grace's mom and stepdad, Jack and Naomi Cordero lived.

"I've been talking to Jack," Gavin said. "He and Naomi are building their dream home. It's actually not far from Cara's. I went out there yesterday, it's amazing. Great view. Anyway, they're going to sell this place and I kind of thought maybe we could buy it."

My eyes widened. "Are you serious?"

"Yeah, they'll give us a really good deal on it. It would give us a great place to start our life together. I grew up out here, it's an awesome place for kids."

"Kids?"

"Yeah. We'll have our own Bailey cubs in a few years, don't you think?"

I laughed, but not because it was funny. Because this was real. This was my life. I was marrying Gavin Bailey and we were going to have babies and raise them here in Tilikum, and I couldn't imagine anything better.

"Yes, we definitely will." My eyes filled with tears. "This is the best surprise."

"Yeah? You like it? We can go inside and look around when it's not the middle of the night. But I just thought this would be perfect for us."

"It's so perfect. Everything is so perfect."

I laughed again and Gavin looked at me with raised eyebrows.

"Sorry, I was just thinking about the first time I saw you."

"When you hit me with your car?"

"Yeah. You were lying in the road and I was freaking out, and I had no idea I'd just hit the man I was going to marry."

He reached over and ran his fingers down my cheek. "It does make a great story. And that was just the beginning of the adventures of Gav and Sky."

It was just the beginning. Knowing Gavin, we had a lot of adventures ahead of us. And I couldn't wait. Because he made me brave. He made me better. And we were going to spend the rest of our lives loving each other.

Loving like crazy.

EPILOGUE

LOGAN

My head swam and the walls spun in a dizzying circle. I was so fucking drunk I could barely stand. But I really didn't care. All that mattered was getting my fucking pants off.

Why was that so hard?

Too much alcohol. That was why.

She grabbed my shirt and yanked me toward her. Our mouths crashed together, tongues darting out. She tasted like bourbon. So fucking delicious.

I kept fumbling with my pants and finally got the button open. Zipper down. Good. Get them off. Gotta get naked. Was she naked? Didn't know. Couldn't see. Probably because my eyes were closed.

Her hand wrapped around my dick and I grunted hard. Apparently my pants were down around my ankles. Had I blacked out for a second? Maybe.

Fuck it. I didn't care. Felt too good.

We stumbled a few steps and tipped over. I couldn't quite remember where I was, but I was sure glad there was a bed here to catch me. I rolled over, pinning her on her back, and crawled on top of her.

I thrust between her legs, but my erection hit fabric. Damn it, what was in my way? I needed to fuck her, and I needed to do it now.

Bracing myself with one arm, I reached down between us. Panties. I hooked my finger beneath them and groaned. Silky wetness waited for me in there. I slid my finger up and down a few times.

She ripped them down her legs and kicked them off, then grabbed my shirt and hauled me closer. Suddenly her tongue was in my mouth and her pussy was hot and ready for me.

I shifted my weight, trying to line up my cock with her opening, but I lost my balance and toppled over. Damn it. I couldn't be too drunk to fuck her. I was hard as steel. If the room would just stop spinning for a fucking second, I could get this done.

She whimpered something that sounded like *fuck me now*. I sat up and manhandled her, rolling her onto her stomach. Then I grabbed her hips and lifted her ass in the air. Kneeling behind her, I drove my cock in.

The rush of sensation almost knocked me over again. She was so hot. So wet. So tight around me. I held her hips and thrust into her, slamming my cock into her pussy.

So fucking good.

She arched her back and I reached up to grab a handful of her hair. Oh yeah. Now I had her right where I wanted her.

I plunged into her, yanking on her hair, my dick sliding through her wetness. She cried out a steady stream of yeses while I fucked her as hard as I could. I was an animal—grunting, muscles flexing. I couldn't remember where I was or how I'd gotten here. I just knew that this was fucking awesome.

Her pussy clenched around my cock and I grunted again. She arched harder, moaning, and her inner muscles pulsed. I slowed down, thrusting with her rhythm while she came all over my dick.

Hell yes. Not too drunk to make her come.

The room tilted, and I closed my eyes to keep from falling over. The tension in my groin skyrocketed, heat and pressure building. My back stiffened and I drove into her again, sinking my cock in deep.

I exploded inside her, coming so hard my consciousness faded. I just kept thrusting, plunging in and out of her while my cock throbbed. The hot pulses of my orgasm kicked the breath from my lungs and by the time it was over, I wasn't sure if I could take any more.

Fuck.

I slid out of her and she slumped onto the bed, like she couldn't hold herself up anymore. I certainly couldn't. My sense of balance was gone, and I fell onto the mattress next to her, my vision going black.

I WOKE up in a dark room. Where the fuck was I?

Still too drunk. Couldn't think.

Shirt was on. No pants. Where were my pants? Groaning at the way my head swam, I rolled over. Somehow got to my feet. My pants were on the floor, so I grabbed them and tugged them on. Took a few tries.

Too fucking drunk.

Wait, had I fucked someone tonight?

Blinking, I looked around. The room was empty. Bed

made, although the covers were rumpled. No one was in here, so I probably hadn't.

Confused, I grabbed my dick through my pants. It really felt like I'd fucked someone. And why had my pants been off?

But maybe it had been a dream.

A really good dream. But still a dream.

And I took my pants off all the time. That wasn't weird.

I was too drunk to know for sure, or to figure out why I was in someone's bedroom in the first place. I had a vague memory of Levi telling me I should go lie down. Maybe I had.

Whatever. I needed to find my phone.

It was hard to keep my eyes open as I stumbled out of the room. Where was my phone?

I just needed to call Levi for a ride.

DEAR READER

Dear reader,

Gavin, Gavin, Gavin.

Did you expect his story would be next? Not everyone did. I've had a few readers tell me they thought he should be last, because he's the youngest.

But, to the surprise of no one, Gavin wouldn't wait his turn.

One of the biggest challenges in writing this book was dealing with a hobbled Gavin. He breaks his leg and suddenly he can't be fully himself. The injury forces him to slow down. To look. To really see things, instead of charging in full speed ahead.

He wasn't exactly happy about that. Which made it harder on me.

Don't these Bailey boys realize I have their best interests at heart? No, they don't, and he was just as stubborn and difficult as his brothers. But it's easy to forgive him with that smile.

I hesitated a little when it came to making Skylar a writer. Being a writer myself and creating a character who does what I do feels... weird. Or maybe like taking a short-cut. But it really fit her personality, both in her love of quiet and solitude, and her interest in serial killers. Maybe I wasn't sure about making her a writer, but she WAS one, so I just had to roll with it.

Sometimes these heroines are just as stubborn as their heroes.

I loved exploring a female lead who has to cope with anxiety. I know so many people who suffer from the same problem and it impacts their lives in many different ways. I did my best to be true to her and the ways she experiences anxiety, both mentally and physically.

And pairing a shy girl with crazy Gavin? I mean, obviously.

Overall, these two were a joy to write. The way they circle around each other for a while, denying their feelings, made it so satisfying when things finally broke open between them. Easy-going, fun-loving Gavin had a lot more going on deep inside than it seemed. And Skylar was perfect for him, the calm to his storm.

I hope you enjoyed their story!

CK

ACKNOWLEDGMENTS

This book was released in November 2020, and 2020 hit it hard. But with the help of some awesome people, disaster was averted.

Thank you to Talia for jumping in to help finalize the cover and working with the existing series design.

Thank you to Eliza for swooping in and doing a last-minute edit. We were down to the wire and you saved the day!

The beautiful cover photo was definitely not a disaster, thanks to the talent of Wander Aguiar and his team. And thanks to model Lucas Loyola for your gorgeous smile.

A big thank you to David Woody, retired firefighter, for fact-checking the technical details and helping me with accuracy. And thank you for everything you do for fire-fighters and their families.

Thank you to my beta readers, Nikki and Alex, for sticking with me on this one and helping me sort through the mess. And for reading it approximately 327 times. And to my proofreaders, Erma and Alison, for helping catch those last pesky typos that always try to sneak through.

And to all my readers who have come with me on this journey, thank you. Without you, the Bailey Brothers wouldn't exist, except as some voices in my head. Thank you for loving them with me.

ALSO BY CLAIRE KINGSLEY

For a full and up-to-date listing of Claire Kingsley books visit
www.clairekingsleybooks.com/books/

For comprehensive reading order, visit www.
clairekingsleybooks.com/reading-order/

The Bailey Brothers

Steamy, small-town family series. Five unruly brothers. Epic
pranks. A quirky, feuding town. Big HEAs. (Best read in order)

Protecting You (Asher and Grace part 1)

Fighting for Us (Asher and Grace part 2)

Unraveling Him (Evan and Fiona)

Rushing In (Gavin and Skylar)

Chasing Her Fire (Logan and Cara)

Rewriting the Stars (Levi and Annika)

The Miles Family

Sexy, sweet, funny, and heartfelt family series. Messy family. Epic
bromance. Super romantic. (Best read in order)

Broken Miles (Roland and Zoe)

Forbidden Miles (Brynn and Chase)

Reckless Miles (Cooper and Amelia)

Hidden Miles (Leo and Hannah)

Gaining Miles: A Miles Family Novella (Ben and Shannon)

Dirty Martini Running Club

Sexy, fun stand-alone romantic comedies with huge... hearts.

Everly Dalton's Dating Disasters (Everly, Hazel, and Nora)

Faking Ms. Right (Everly and Shepherd)

Falling for My Enemy (Hazel and Corban)

Marrying Mr. Wrong (Sophie and Cox)

(Nora's book coming soon)

Bluewater Billionaires

Hot, stand-alone romantic comedies. Lady billionaire BFFs and the badass heroes who love them.

The Mogul and the Muscle (Cameron and Jude)

The Price of Scandal, Wild Open Hearts, and Crazy for Loving You

More Bluewater Billionaire shared-world stand-alone romantic comedies by Lucy Score, Kathryn Nolan, and Pippa Grant

Bootleg Springs
by Claire Kingsley and Lucy Score

Hot and hilarious small-town romcom series with a dash of mystery and suspense. (Best read in order)

Whiskey Chaser (Scarlett and Devlin)

Sidecar Crush (Jameson and Leah Mae)

Moonshine Kiss (Bowie and Cassidy)

Bourbon Bliss (June and George)

Gin Fling (Jonah and Shelby)

Highball Rush (Gibson and I can't tell you)

Book Boyfriends

Hot, stand-alone romcoms that will make you laugh and make you swoon.

Book Boyfriend (Alex and Mia)

Cocky Roommate (Weston and Kendra)

Hot Single Dad (Caleb and Linnea)

Finding Ivy (William and Ivy)

A unique contemporary romance with a hint of mystery.

His Heart (Sebastian and Brooke)

A poignant and emotionally intense story about grief, loss, and the transcendent power of love.

The Always Series

Smoking hot, dirty talking bad boys with some angsty intensity.

Always Have (Braxton and Kylie)

Always Will (Selene and Ronan)

Always Ever After (Braxton and Kylie)

~

The Jetty Beach Series

Sexy small-town romance series with swoony heroes, romantic HEAs, and lots of big feels.

Behind His Eyes (Ryan and Nicole)

One Crazy Week (Melissa and Jackson)

Messy Perfect Love (Cody and Clover)

Operation Get Her Back (Hunter and Emma)

Weekend Fling (Finn and Juliet)

Good Girl Next Door (Lucas and Becca)

The Path to You (Gabriel and Sadie)

ABOUT THE AUTHOR

Claire Kingsley is a #1 Amazon bestselling author of sexy, heartfelt contemporary romance and romantic comedies. She writes sassy, quirky heroines, swoony heroes who love their women hard, panty-melting sexytimes, romantic happily ever afters, and all the big feels.

She can't imagine life without coffee, her Kindle, and the sexy heroes who inhabit her imagination. She's living out her own happily ever after in the Pacific Northwest with her husband and three kids.

www.clairekingsleybooks.com

Printed in Great Britain
by Amazon